Link

a novel by

John Beiswenger

Copyright © 2003 by John L. Beiswenger

ISBN 978-0-7414-1348-2

Printed in the United States of America

Published December 2012

INFINITY PUBLISHING
1094 New DeHaven Street, Suite 100
West Conshohocken, PA 19428-2713
Toll-free (877) BUY BOOK
Local Phone (610) 941-9999
Fax (610) 941-9959
Info@buybooksontheweb.com
www.buybooksontheweb.com

Acknowledgements

"Thank you, my beautiful and loving wife Kim and my amazing son Daniel, for the time."

Foreword

The story principally takes place in the facilities of Search International, Inc., a product research firm near Madison, Wisconsin. The work they do is called product research because all of the research done by its engineers, medical professionals and scientific staff is specifically focused on the development of new products for client-manufacturers. Commercialization was the company's only objective until an unusual accident occurred, an accident that led its management and its biotechnology research staff--known as the BioChip team--into a discovery beyond their imaginations, a discovery which could well be considered the most important to mankind of all time.

Please note: You are going to be present right alongside scientists as they uncover some of the secrets of Creation. You may not always understand their terminology, but the key concepts developed by them will become clear as the story unfolds.

It all begins in the year 2010.

Chapter 1

Virtual Outdoors

The roar alone was frightening, but to be in a one-man craft on this river and blind, for all practical purposes, caused chills up Mike Young's spine and tightened his chest like a bass drum. The sweat was beginning to trickle down his back, and he knew the whitewater was yet ahead.

He could hear the first coach on the shore shouting encouragement, but even this caused him to double his grip on the paddle, since the movement of her voice was clearly accelerating away from him to his back as his boat moved faster toward the experience.

"Be ready," the second coach barely had time to shout, and he to comprehend, when the front of the boat dipped sharply.

"*I'm in the chute*," he thought, when immediately a rock slammed into the bow, jolting him into the realization that this wasn't going to go well unless he took control.

But taking control wasn't going to happen, and he remembered thinking that he had confidently selected this run because he had felt it matched his skills. His confidence was gone now, and more fear went through him as he could sense the boat was turning sideways in the raging flow. He pulled on the paddle with all his strength and pumped hard to move the craft into alignment with the stream, none too

1

soon, either, because the stern glanced off another rock. Had he hit that rock going full bore sideways, it would have been all over.

Down again the bow went, and the craft landed in a whirlpool which spun him around twice before he even had a chance to drop a paddle into the stream. And when he did, the paddle slammed forward, almost ripping out of his hands from the force of the moving water.

"Get a better grip on the paddle," another coach shouted. "Steer in the direction of the whirlpool, and it will send you downstream." He did and it did, bouncing him from side to side.

"*This isn't fun,*" Mike thought. "*I've got to go with an easier run.* Stop," he shouted, and as the sound of the torrent dropped to a gentle trickle, the last coach said, "Try an easier run. Work up to this level of exercise."

Mike removed the surround-sound mask, looked around his family room, stood, staggered, and stepped out of the simulator. Embarrassed, he told his wife Jill that he couldn't handle it.

The next day, Mike Young spoke with Gary Richardson while the two were taking a break at a lunch table in the cafeteria of Search International's facilities. Gary, a senior professional engineer and a long-time employee of Search, patiently listened to Mike's tale of his experience on a company-designed outdoor action simulator that he had borrowed from the company's archive and taken home.

"Do you own one?" Mike asked Gary.

"Listen," Gary answered, "I liked being one of the designers, but I don't feel the need to be one of the users. I'd rather just sit behind the yoke of my Cessna and fly into the sunset. That's my exercise."

"Tell me, virtual reality video has been around for a long time. Why didn't you use it on the Outdoor Action Exerciser?"

"Well," Gary began, rather bored by the common question, "first of all our purpose was to provide exercise, not a grand visual tour of the great outdoors. Second, VR would have added about 200 bucks to the price tag and, third, our research clearly showed that even the best VR doesn't come within a mile of the human imagination for realism. VR just looks too perfect and too cartoonish to combine it with the rest of the simulator's great effects. Take the surround-sound earphones. The first comment you made about the experience was, 'The roar alone was frightening,' and you could tell where the coaches were standing, not like ordinary stereo phones. Next, the simulator's platform; you felt everything very realistically. Now what if we had added cartoon-like images to what was going on? It would have taken away from the effect."

"Let me tell you something else," Gary went on. "Based on your description of the run, I'll bet you a Coke from that machine over there that you have personally canoed down rapids before, right?"

Mike started for the vending machine as he answered. "Yeah, and it's always been something I wanted to try again...without the risk, of course. I'm not a very good swimmer."

"I thought that would be the case," Gary said. "Your memory made it all real for you. You knew what each threatening rock looked like, yet you didn't see any of them, except in your mind. You saw the water, the rocks, the shore and probably the coaches, all in your mind, because the memories were there, even though you weren't aware of them. And you were concentrating on a specific activity you had experienced before. We know that serious concentration releases related memories that otherwise wouldn't surface, and what happened was that you were re-experiencing a portion of them."

"Concentration released memories, and I re-experienced them? Where did this come from?"

Gary was silent.

"Gary? Were you talkin' out of school?"

"I guess. But that's all you're going to get."

"Link?"

"Yup."

Mike Young nodded. He knew that it had all begun with something he had done.

Chapter 2

Link - The Product Research Project

One of Search's research teams was working on a product line of human/machine interface devices to simplify the use of a new generation of computers that would soon be available to the general public. The ICs (integrated circuits or "chips") in the new machines were so small that the entire motherboard, except for the add-ons, could fit on a thumbnail, making them incredibly fast. The computers, in fact, were so fast and so powerful that they could almost keep up with the average human mind, completing complex tasks before the user could move his or her hand to enter the next command.

Just a few years ago, 5 gigahertz machines were still a disappointment to serious graphics users and design engineers because at times they had to wait several seconds for operations to be completed. Reliable voice recognition had finally arrived and was in heavy use where silence was not a requirement; however, it wasn't well-liked because many complained that they could think faster than they could talk. Also, designers and engineers said they didn't verbalize their thoughts as they worked, and the need to go back and forth between verbalization and visualization slowed the creative process.

The new machines would not be rated in terms of clock speed but in CEPS (command entries per second), because the execution time would be insignificant. The first machines would be rated at 2.2 CEPS, well above current human command entry speeds using present human/machine interfaces, especially voice recognition. Designers and engineers wanted to think their way through the process. They wanted to picture the geometry in their minds and have it appear on their monitors instantly. Thus the challenge and the reason for the project.

The new interface that was to receive most of the attention looked very much like an ordinary mouse still in use at the turn of the century. This mouse, however, promised to be very, very different. The user would be able to merely grip the "Link," as it was called, and look at the display.

Yes. The company intended to design a system to transfer information directly from the brain, through the nervous system, to the hand and fingers and therefore to the Link. The Link was electrically connected to the computer's power supply, but its sensors were optically coupled directly to the computer's central processing unit.

Small successes had already been achieved, before the "accident" occurred. Test subjects could mentally control a fish, on a type of screen saver, causing it to swim slower or faster and backwards. A magenta-colored screen could be changed to dark green; a square on the screen had even once been reformed, by an operator, into a poorly concentric circle; and some ASCII text could be consistently generated by an experienced user. The consensus was that within another year the concept work would be completed and a design begun. They felt that the research team was on the way to a successful project and an exciting new product. But now the Link project was dead.

Actually, the Link itself was just a very sophisticated set of sensors in a mouse-like housing, plus hardware and software onboard the computer to translate the signals from the Link into computer commands. That was all there was to it. The design team never considered it to be anything more. But after what happened, and after the "phenomenon" was repeated, Search management had to find out how such an incredibly strange experience was possible. The project was dead, but the research was very much alive.

Chapter 3

The Accident

On a normal Friday in the lab, experiments and tests were going on; but because of the lateness of the day, the staff was generally winding down for the weekend. Some were in the process of cleanup work and others were taking equipment to the security cage.

Mike Young, assisting with the cleanup, pushed a computer cart past the Link research workstation. There were power cords and coaxial cables coming from every direction and going to the station, some taped to the floor. One of the wheels on the cart caught on a cord and tipped the cart, but Mike moved quickly to stop the computer from falling. However, as he did so, his body slammed into the back of the Link workstation, knocking over one of three oscilloscopes being used to monitor the experiment. The scope crashed down on the hand of the engineer who was gripping the Link, but his hand was not injured because a can of soft drink, sitting next to his hand, absorbed most of the force. Soft drink spewed all over the engineer and the work surface.

Other factors figured in, the engineers discovered later, that contributed to the accident, such as the mild acidity of the soft drink, the chance arrangement of the printed circuit traces in the Link that carried plus 5 volts DC near the engineer's thumb and minus 5 volts near his small finger, and, of course, the engineer's left wrist had a standard grounding strap attached to it to reduce static noise. But what happened as a result, in connection with the experimental work he was doing, was beyond comprehension and expectation.

Scott Dennison, the project engineer, "saw" something, the other engineers surmised, on the display for a millisecond or so that they later learned related to his thoughts at that moment. He was terrified, hysterical, and shortly afterward went into a sort of stupor, unable to concentrate on what others around him were saying to him, including the emergency room physicians at the hospital where he was taken. His condition lasted into the night.

When he returned to the research facility Monday morning, he asked for his paycheck, collected his personal things, and would not discuss the incident further. The company's management was left in a quandary.

Others had been watching the engineer's progress when the "accident" occurred, and it was, by policy, also recorded on videodisk. No one had seen anything on the display, because of the ruckus caused by the falling scope and spraying soft drink, but the videodisk did show a color-mixed display sweep--single pixels moving across the display a line at a time. Some said that when the scan was accelerated, one could see a vague image of someone's hand holding a watch. Scott, the engineers thought at the time, probably saw the image because he was deeply concentrating on what was appearing on the display, generated by him. After his hysterical shout, Scott became silent when he recognized what the image really was. It was clear when he left on Monday that he wanted nothing more to do with the Link, or the program, or the Company, for that matter.

The research team believed they could probably reproduce the events quite accurately, but not exactly. They also knew that sooner or later it would become necessary.

No one wanted to be the owner of the hand on the Link during the first test. "Did you see his face?" those asked to volunteer would say. "Did you hear what the guy screamed?" they would ask.

The videodisk had also recorded his words, "My uncle, he was taking it! I saw him! Just like my dad said! My dad! Oh my God, it was my dad!" after which he said no more.

All of the company's top people were called in to explain the "image." How was it generated? How did it happen? Where did it come from? The display sweep was in color with pure resolution, limited only by the monitor and CD recorder. The engineering staff had no immediate explanation, even though they analyzed every video signal being generated or received by the research facility at the moment the accident occurred. Nothing even remotely close in description was found.

"Could it have come from the mind of the engineer?" was a question that was not even discussed. Not till it happened again. Not till they reproduced the accident with a volunteer.

Chapter 4

The BioChip Assignment

It was not by chance that Search had been commissioned for the study. A wealthy entrepreneur hired Search to learn how it might be possible for the human cell to contain the amount of information it has been known to contain for decades. The failure of the Gnome project (which was going to "write the book of life") and every subsequent study was due, the entrepreneur believed, to the fact that scientists had arrogantly and erroneously avoided the concept that there was a "design" involved. ("Never mind that this also meant there was a Designer," he would say.)

The entrepreneur wanted to be the first to identify the human cell memory system as a "design," patent the concept of using a live cell in a memory chip, and develop the concept as a new technology. He wanted Search to build the first silicon/organic memory device. He believed that such a device could literally contain all written and graphic information presently available in all computers on earth and deliver it almost instantly. Search management believed the project had merit (though it did not share his vision), and the company accepted the challenge.

Project team members had already written many articles on the subject, not providing answers, but asking the forbidden questions such as: "If all of the DNA in a cell amounts to less than a gigabyte of data, and we know the cell must contain much more, where is the rest of the data stored?" and "If the neurons of the brain at top speed are only functioning at something less than 1,000 Hz., how is it possible to recall memories from childhood in great detail within what seems an instant?" Their willingness to ask these kinds of questions of their peers actually got Search the assignment.

It was a tall order, to say the least, but Gary Richardson already had a concept for the silicon component that would be necessary to interface with the cell. He called it JL-1, for Jacob's Ladder, which eerily figured into the research to come. He had heard that Jacob's Ladder in the Bible reached between earth and heaven or, as Gary applied the term, between the organic and inorganic components, since he didn't really believe in a heaven.

The staff on the project, code named "BioChip," was not exactly what one might have imagined. There was Gary Richardson, a seasoned microprocessor design specialist; Joan Kenny, a mathematician; LaShauna Jackson, a biophysicist specializing in the human brain; Clyde Hart, a research physician who had spent his whole career, to that point, studying the functions of the human cell; and Christopher Brown, a former Jesuit and human bioethics specialist on the faculty at the University of Wisconsin. Search's chairman George Evans had brought "Father" Christopher (as everyone called him) into the project because of the obvious human-bioethical questions involved in live-cell research. Neither the ex-priest nor any of the management team could have guessed what he would come away with.

Shortly before the accident the BioChip assignment team met for the first time in the company's large conference room.

"Well, I know what Carl Sagan used to think about it," LaShauna began.

"Sagan?" Gary asked.

"My mentor has had a letter from Sagan on his wall for many years," she continued. "He wrote to Sagan to say that he knew that Sagan knew no scientist understood just what we've been commissioned to discover, that is, how so much information could possibly be stored in the human cell."

"He answered your friend?" Joan asked.

"After several letters that weren't very complimentary to Sagan."

"Well, what did he say?" Gary prompted.

"He said, 'Natural selection is precisely a process which can extract an enormous amount of information from chaos-- including the amount of information in the gene. This works, of course, only if life has been around for a few billion years.'"

"I'd hate to see his closets," said Joan, straightening the books, notes and pens in front of her.

"What?" Gary asked her, sounding irritated. He didn't see the connection.

"Nothing," Joan answered. She smiled. She liked Gary. He had her kind of mind, but not her kind of heart, as she told others.

LaShauna's story had not really broken the ice on this new team's relationships. It seemed they all had little in common. Father Christopher, though articulate and outspoken in his writing, was a small, quiet individual who didn't look like a priest at all. Gary was clearly an agnostic. He was somewhat disdainful of the others, living in his own technology twenty-four hours a day. He had little time for other professions or those in them, even those that employed the product of his work. The mathematician, Joan Kenny, believed in God because she could "see Him in the numbers," but carried her faith little further. The research physician, Clyde Hart, a nominal Catholic, was a classic research type--glasses, simple haircut, unassuming, and the

13

sort of scientist that wonders exactly what temperature his soft drink is and how that compares to the biophysicist's coffee, with which he was distracted at the moment.

"Who cares?" Gary said coldly. Clyde did a double take. "Who cares," Gary went on, "what Sagan used to think? Have you read his article about how we're just a bunch of moths banging into a porch light?" Clyde relaxed, realizing Gary's attack was not directed toward him.

"Well, I just thought it might be a starting point for this discussion," LaShauna said.

"Belay all that. What I need to know from you," Gary said, pointing a finger at LaShauna, "is what kind of signal voltage will I have to work with when the brain cell receives data?"

LaShauna was clearly the friendliest, warmest individual in the room. She seemed to show great respect for everyone, yet was very confident in her role. On the other hand, she also seemed to know best what she and her associates did not know, keeping a balance on things.

"I understand," she said, "and I know you're going to be pleased with the answer, but let's not get ahead of ourselves . . . yet. We need to start with a better understanding of the human neuron. Let's get state-of-the-art as quickly as possible on that subject first. I understand, Clyde," she said, turning to him with the smile which always seemed to be there, "that you have a presentation for us which includes some basics, but gets us into the doubtful areas quickly."

"Yes. Would you like me to begin?" Clyde asked humbly.

LaShauna nodded. Gary slumped back in his chair.

"I think a good starting point would be an excerpt from an article in the September 1992 issue of *Scientific American* entitled, 'How Neurons Communicate,' by Gerald D. Fischbach."

Clyde began to read:

14

"'A neuron which has been excited conveys information to other neurons by generating impulses known as action potentials. These signals propagate like waves down the length of the cell's single, tentacle-like axon and are converted to chemical signals at synapses, the contact points between neurons . . .'

(That is, contact points on dendrites leading to other neurons)," Clyde added, lifting his head, which he did each time he added his parenthetical remarks.

"'When a neuron is at rest, its external membrane maintains an electrical potential of about minus 70 millivolts' . . . (The inner surface is negative relative to the outer surface.)"

Gary looked up. Clyde continued.

"'At rest, the membrane is more permeable to potassium ions than to sodium ions. When the (neuron) is stimulated, the permeability to sodium increases, leading to an inrush of positive charges. This inrush triggers an impulse--a momentary reversal of the membrane potential (an action potential). The impulse is initiated at the junction of the cell body and axon, and is conducted away from the cell body.

When the impulse reaches the axon terminals (synapses) it induces the release of neurotransmitters. Neurotransmitters diffuse across a narrow cleft (in the synapse) and bind to receptors in the postsynaptic membrane. Such binding leads to the opening of ion channels and often, in turn, to the generation of action potentials in the postsynaptic neuron. (Action potentials) have also been traced by fine-tipped micro-electrodes positioned close enough to a (neuron) or an axon to detect the small currents generated as an action potential passes by.'" Clyde finished.

"Seventy millivolts is plenty to work with," Gary said, "and we won't have to worry about the slow electrochemical connections of the synapses, which must slow down the process in organisms, since I will be connecting directly to the dendrite and axon leading to and from the neuron. But at 1,000 Hertz tops, how are we going to use a neuron to store and search for data at the speeds we must?"

"And how is memory stored in a single cell?" Clyde asked. "Isn't that contrary to the beliefs of all neurologists?"

LaShauna responded forcefully. "We took the project because we suspect that today's scientists are wrong about where and how memory is stored, but that doesn't mean we have all the answers yet. Let's continue."

Joan held up a book. "We have some support from a Ph.D. by the name of Paul Pearsall. He's the author of *The Heart's Code.*"

"I've read it," said Father Christopher. "He believes in cellular memories, even ancestral cellular memories, but he attributes the ability primarily to the cells of the heart."

"He's a psychoneuroimmunologist," Joan expanded, "a licensed psychologist who studies the relationship between the brain, immune system, and external factors. He has documented dozens of cases in which heart transplant recipients have also received some of the memories of the donors."

"Cut it out!" said Gary in disbelief.

"A little girl who received the heart of a murdered child was reported to have 'recalled' the child's killer so well that she described him, and he was eventually convicted," Joan continued.

16

"If that's true, why didn't the story hit the national news?" Gary asked.

Joan frowned at Gary and continued. "As a scientist, Pearsall says, his brain doubts that we will be able to show with scientific certainty that all body cells can really remember in the sense most people think about memory."

"That sounds exactly like what we have been asked to do!" said Clyde.

"If he believes that a few heart cells can carry and ultimately transfer a recallable image of a murderer, how can he doubt as he does?" Gary asked.

"Because nowhere in his book does he even discuss how these memories can be stored in single cells." Joan answered.

"Oh, great!" Gary threw up his hands. "Just another . . . "

LaShauna raised her arms level with her chest. The discussion stopped. "If we are going to make any progress," she said, "we are going to have to accept certain information as true and proceed to see where it leads us."

"You're calling for a hypothesis," Clyde said.

"Yes. Thank you, Clyde. We already agree that--," LaShauna paused as she moved to the whiteboard, "Number one--There is way too much information stored in the zygote to be explained by DNA coding."

Over the squeaking of the dry marker someone asked, "Zygote?"

"The single cell after conception," LaShauna answered without looking away from the board.

"Number two--The speed of the brain is far too slow to explain the apparent instant recall of memories," Gary contributed.

"Good," said LaShauna, like a schoolteacher.

"Number three--We should accept the fact that complete, recallable memories can be stored in a single cell," contributed Clyde.

"Okay," she said, writing furiously.

"Number four--That the memories are recallable from the single cell," Father Christopher suggested.

"This is going well," LaShauna said as she continued to write while the team members searched their minds to add points.

"Number four should say that the memories are both accessible and recallable," Gary corrected.

"Okay." LaShauna made the correction.

"Maybe we had better define what a memory is," said Joan.

"Right," LaShauna responded and paused. "How's this?" she asked. "A percept is an instantaneous collection of sensed data. Let's define a memory as an indefinite series of percepts."

"So we can assume this data is encoded in some fashion as it relates to the senses?" Gary asked.

"Where and how is this data stored?" Joan asked.

"Let me ask you, Gary," LaShauna said. "Accepting our four hypothetical statements thus far and our definition of memory, what kind of a data storage component are we looking for? Can you give us some parameters?"

"For instantaneous recall of memories?" Gary asked.

"Do you really mean instantaneous or just very, very fast, like so many nanoseconds?" Clyde questioned.

"Faster," LaShauna responded. "Let's consider instantaneous recall for the moment." Turning back to Gary, she said, "Well?"

"Nanoseconds? Microscopic," he answered, looking at Clyde. "Instantaneous?" he said turning toward LaShauna. "Zero mass," he said emphatically.

"Zero mass!" Joan exclaimed. She looked at LaShauna. "And you said this was going well?"

Chapter 5

The Volunteer

"It has to be one of us," she said, referring to the company's management team standing around the Link workstation. "Perhaps it should be a physician." With that simple statement, Anna Pierson, Search's lead research physician, confirmed that she would be the first test subject. It didn't surprise anyone.

Anna had just received her Ph.D. in medical research, and her enthusiasm for her work had never been greater. She was the sort of person who walks into a room and immediately charges the atmosphere, but without calling attention to herself. Her light brown hair was always clean and neat, but simply fixed. Her eyes were exceptionally penetrating. Even the engineers had remarked, "When you look into Anna's green eyes you're looking into her soul," so impressed were they with Anna. She was always confident of her training and abilities, yet was also always willing to listen to the ideas of others.

With her boyish voice, Anna asked, "Okay, where are we?"

The group immediately gathered closer together and settled into the work at hand. "Here's what we've got so far," they told her. "Scott may have received a mild shock, with the current flowing between his thumb and small finger, but also between the thumb on his right hand and his left wrist. The connection to his left wrist was direct; a wire leading from ground was attached to a conductive strap on his lower arm. The connections to his thumb and small finger on his right hand, however, were completed by the soft drink."

"The soft drink?" Anna asked.

The company's white-haired chairman, George Evans, had personally participated in the test involving Scott Dennison, something he was prone to do. George was the founder of Search and was always vitally interested in breakthrough test events.

"The soft drink was mildly acidic," he said in answer to Anna's question. "It contained a bit of sodium. So it conducted electricity."

"What kind of voltage?" she asked.

"Across his hand, 10 volts DC. Across his chest, 5 volts DC," answered Allen Nolte, head Search engineer.

"Dangerous?" she asked.

"This is no time to tell this story," said Allen, "but I read in an old text that some scientists wanted to know how much voltage a human could stand. They got this volunteer," he continued, pointing to Anna, "from a prison, connected a wire to a strap on his leg, and put him in a swimming pool up to his neck. A second wire was connected to a probe placed in the water with him. They told him they would start at a very low voltage and then gradually increase it until he felt he could stand no more, then they promised to turn it off, and turn him loose. They set the voltage at 6 volts DC, threw the switch, and killed him!"

"Is this true?" Anna said raising her brown eyebrows.

"Doctor, you won't even feel 10 volts," Allen said.

"Did the prisoner feel six?" she asked.

"Why did you tell her that story?" George scowled.

"Doctor," he said respectfully, "Scott didn't complain about getting a shock, he--"

"No, he went into shock, became hysterical," Anna snapped with feigned concern. "What kind of current are we talking about?" she said more seriously.

"A couple of milliamps, tops," George answered, smiling. "Let's demonstrate. You, Allen, you told the story," he said looking at the engineer. "Demonstrate."

Allen Nolte was a good, hard-working engineer, but he frequently put his foot in his mouth, because he had the habit of saying whatever came to his mind. This probably came from being raised with four older brothers.

Allen began, "We've got digital and analog microammeters in series with the grounding strap we are going to connect to your left wrist."

"This is a demonstration! Connect it to **your** left wrist," Anna and George said almost simultaneously.

"All right, like so," Allen said as he strapped the lead wire to his wrist. "Any current passing through your body will also pass through the microammeters. Now, I'll grip the Link, and George will pour the same soft drink over it and my hand. So . . . there, you saw that the meters are displaying a tiny current, but I feel absolutely nothing."

"See any frightening scenes?" someone asked.

A few laughed.

Again and again the team tried the experiment. Anna was asked to concentrate on the display screen and attempt to get the system to display the word "NO," as others had done. She succeeded, but as technicians poured the soft drink over her hand and the Link, nothing out of the ordinary happened. As evening approached, they called it a day.

George Evans got a call at 10:30 that night from Ed Lukin. Ed headed up the chemistry lab and had been a tremendously creative resource to the company over the past ten years. Up until that day he had not been involved in the Link project, but George had asked him to observe the tests with Anna. George had great respect for Ed's mind, and the feeling was mutual.

"What's up, Ed?"

"I think I know one way the accident differed from your experiment today," he said.

"You still at the office?" George asked. Ed frequently solved problems by working into the night.

"Yeah, I'm all right. Hear me out."

"Shoot," George responded.

"When the oscilloscope fell on Scott's hand he was not injured . . . ." he began.

". . . because the can of soda broke its fall," George said, completing Ed's sentence.

"Yes, but how did it break the scope's fall?"

"By crushing the can and squirting the soft drink out at a limited rate, literally lowering the scope to his hand--almost gently."

"Right," Ed said, "but what happened to the pressure in the can during this process?"

"It shot up dramatically."

"Exactly," Ed continued. "Now let me give you some new information. The soft drink fluid didn't exit entirely from the pop-tab opening while the can was being crushed. The side of the scope cabinet landed squarely on the top of the can, blocking its natural exit. I examined the can and found a very narrow split in its side wall."

"I wouldn't be surprised," George responded, "but what does that have to do with anything?"

"The split would have been at the exact height and position as the wrist of Scott's hand which was holding the Link . . . ." Ed began to explain.

22

"And some of the soda, exiting the can at very high pressure, may have been pressure-injected into the blood vessels of his wrist!" George concluded.

"You're quick, George. You got it, and I think that's the difference."

"Nice job, Ed. I don't know what I'd do without you."

"All in a day's work."

"I've relied on you for a lot of years, Ed."

"And I on you for the opportunities of my career. Before I joined Search, I was stuck in the mud. You and your open mind taught me creativity."

"It's nice of you to say that, Ed. It has been fun, hasn't it?"

"I love going to work."

"So do I. See you in the morning."

"Right. I'll have things set up by the time you come in."

"Get some sleep. Oh, Ed, I'm going to assign the BioChip team to the Link project investigation."

"What are you going to tell the client?" Ed asked.

"We'll tell him a conflict of interest has developed --it has--and we have to clear it up before continuing his project. We've got to get to the bottom of this accident, and I believe the BioChip team's study of the human cell may point the way."

"So do I. It's a good move."

"We'll have a two-pronged approach going," George said. "You, Anna and Allen Nolte will be handling the empirical side, while the BioChip team will be concentrating on the theoretical."

"Sounds good."

"Goodnight, Ed."

"Goodnight, George."

The next morning Dr. Pierson was ready for another series of experiments. She didn't like the idea of having some soft drink injected into her wrist, but wasn't all that concerned. Ed had, by morning, calculated what the dynamic pressure of the fluid exiting the can might have been at the time of the accident. He jerryrigged an airless paint sprayer to duplicate the condition, aiming the nozzle at the same location on her wrist, which was probably exposed on Scott's arm. They asked her to concentrate as before, then they activated Link's circuitry, poured the soda, and when George nodded to Ed, he pulled the trigger on the sprayer.

"Something!" Anna shouted. "Something. I saw something or felt something, I don't know which."

"Could it have been what Scott experienced?" George asked.

"I doubt it," She said. "He described a very clear image. I did not see or experience anything that was very definitive. It felt more like having a dream, one I can't remember."

"What do you think, Ed?" asked George.

"We're closer, but not there yet," Allen interjected. "Let's think about it some more. We've reproduced the electrical aspects quite accurately. Injecting the soft drink brought us closer."

"What about the chemicals already in Scott's blood stream?" Ed asked.

"Boy, that's a can of worms. I mean, how can we know?" said Anna.

"Allen, you went to lunch with Scott, didn't you?" George asked.

"Yeah, we planned the afternoon's work over some Chinese food."

"Glutamic acid," Ed said.

"Ed?" George asked, turning his head towards him with a snap.

"Glutamic acid is found in some Chinese food. What's more, it improves learning in normal mice."

"Mice? The animal type?" Anna asked. "How do you know this?"

"I ran across it after we got the BioChip project. Glutamic acid can run from less than 20 parts per million to 89% of some spices."

"You're amazing, Ed," she said. George nodded.

"Allen, can you tell us what Scott ordered?" he asked.

"No, but I'll bet our waitress can."

"Call the restaurant," George said pointing to the phone on the wall. "What else, Ed?"

"Scott was a smoker," Ed said.

Allen overheard and shouted back as he walked toward the phone to call the restaurant. "He would have had a cigarette after lunch that day."

"And what significance would that have, Ed?" Anna asked, knowing Ed would have the answer.

"Nicotine can improve learning and memory and has been linked to rapid information processing, working memory and long-term memory."

"Same explanation as to why you know this?" George questioned.

"Yup."

"Any other brainstorms, Ed?" he asked.

"We've already got three of the other pharmacological memory-improvement ingredients."

"Where?" Anna asked.

"In the soft drink. There's caffeine, citric acid and glucose, all mentioned in the research I found. They're all named as having a positive affect on memory--usually in the aged."

"I feel much older just listening to all of this," Anna sighed, "and, as you know, I don't smoke."

"We can apply a nicotine patch hours before the next test," George suggested.

Ed nodded.

Allen Nolte left the room while they were talking and quickly returned. "I've got a faxed copy of our check from the day of the accident. We can order exactly the same thing for Anna."

Anna looked at George. "On the plus side, I like Chinese food," she said, summing up the preparation she was willing to go through. "Ed," she said turning to him, "if you know what's in the soft drink that we're interested in, can you at least get rid of the rest before we try this again."

"I already did, Anna," Ed said. "That wasn't really soft drink I shot you with. I just called it that. I'm sorry if I concerned you."

"You could have told me too, Ed," George added. "Okay, then, let's try again tomorrow after lunch."

"Let's make it 4:30, just like the time of the accident," Anna said. "Now that we know about the food aspect, let's give my digestive system time to convert the glutamic acid."

By 4:30 the next day everyone of the management team was as nervous as Anna. As the test setup was being finalized one could hear other engineers, scientists and technicians winding up their work for the weekend. Mike Young walked by, glanced at Anna, and kept walking. In another area the security cage gate slammed shut. They were ready to begin.

Blood pressure and heart rate monitors were attached to Anna as she sat in the very chair that Scott had sat in. The nicotine patch had been in place for four hours, and Anna was still suffering from the spicy Chinese food she said she had enjoyed.

"Power on," Allen announced.

"Begin to concentrate, Anna," George instructed, "and on the same subject you were concentrating on last time, so that we can judge any direct improvement."

"Okay," Anna said. She paused a full minute, and then said, "I'm ready, Ed."

The soft drink was poured on her hand, and Ed pulled the trigger on the sprayer, injecting the chemicals into her wrist."

"Ohhhh," Anna groaned suddenly, with a strange, heavy tremble in her voice. "I saw him beat her," she said loudly. Her heart rate shot up. They all turned to look at her face. She was staring at the display, but unreceptive to their calls.

They waited, silent at first, but later called out encouragement to her. "It's going to be okay." "We're here. We're your friends." "Take your time." "We're praying for you," Ed added. "You'll be all right."

After almost an hour she finally spoke and asked for a drink and something to eat. George got her a cup of flavored coffee and three pecan sandies, which he knew she liked. She ate a cookie slowly, washed it down with coffee, and said in a calm, but halting, yet almost scientific manner,

"I saw for an instant . . .

an image . . .

relating to what I was thinking . . .

at that moment . . ."

She paused longer.

"But, I saw it . . .

through the eyes . . .

of my grandmother.

I'm upset . . . a little light-headed,

but, I'm all right.

I want to go home now.

Please call my husband."

With that, she got up, shaking, her pulse still very high, and she promptly collapsed. Dr. Clyde Hart, who had offered to stand by these last two days, looked after her, and her husband Michael was called. When he arrived, Anna was feeling better, and George explained to Michael what had happened. Michael took her home.

Anna's words kept going through George's mind all evening and night. He didn't sleep at all. She had said, "I saw for an instant an image (of) what I was thinking at that moment." What did it mean? How could that be possible?

It was almost morning when a dark thought hit him. News of this could not leak out of the research center, and already two people had left the building having had the "Experience," and a dozen had gone home with the knowledge of it.

George called Carlos Martinez, who was the company's facilities manager and also George's son-in-law. He could always count on Carlos when something out of the ordinary happened and unusual actions had to be taken, especially when they related to secrecy or security. Carlos had already talked to 11 of the 12 and had heard them assure him that no breach had occurred. Charlie Schuster, the company controller, the twelfth member, was unavailable, but never one to talk about a research project as secret as Link.

The following morning was sunny, and spirits were high.

"It's good to see a smile on your face, Anna," George said as she walked toward him down the hall.

"Forgive my reaction yesterday," she said. "I have never experienced anything even remotely similar, nor have I ever heard anyone describe an experience so haunting which would compare, except perhaps for an out-of-body experience I once heard a patient relate. What happened to me caused me to feel that I had violated a privacy. It was like owning a box which contained secrets belonging to someone close to me, then opening it in breach of the promise I had made never to learn the contents."

Anna went on. "It was so very real, not like a dream which always has that fuzzy background, but for an instant, I was there. I smelled the room, felt the tension, heard the sounds, and worst of all, I saw what was happening through the eyes of my grandmother. I felt her horror and pain. My grandfather had just hit her! I'm just glad my experience ended so quickly."

"You got all of this from a single frame-scan on the display?" George asked.

"I don't know what you mean?"

"The display you were watching, you saw the image which we recorded, and you felt all these things?"

"I saw nothing on the display!" Anna said. "It all happened . . . in my mind."

Chapter 6

Carlos Martinez

Carlos Martinez grew up as the son of a hotel maintenance worker in Guadalajara, Mexico. When he graduated from high school he joined his father's small staff at the hotel.

"You're too smart for this work," his father would often tell him. "You should be responsible for all of the maintenance of the hotel," he would say. "Get to know some of the American businessmen. They can help you get a good job in California." Carlos watched for the opportunity.

Early one hot summer evening, Carlos had just finished changing a fuse in a room air conditioner when the guest staying in the room asked him how to get an outside line to use for his laptop computer. Carlos had never operated a computer, but he had helped his father set up for a computer manufacturers' convention at the hotel, and he stayed around to talk with one exhibitor who was generously willing to answer Carlos' questions.

"You want a data-line connection for a modem?" Carlos asked the guest.

"Why, yes. That's exactly what I need," the guest answered, somewhat surprised.

"Behind the desk in all of the rooms on this floor is a direct, outside-line jack," Carlos said. "But you will have to use an 800 number or a credit card to call the United States."

"My business computer line in California is on an 800 number," the guest responded. "Thank you . . . and your name is?"

"Carlos, Carlos Martinez."

"I'm Darrell Johnson, Carlos, and I'm pleased to meet you."

Carlos smiled and decided to learn more about the stranger.

"What kind of business do you have in California?" he asked.

"I'm involved in bio-engineering, and I design and build electronic prostheses," Darrell answered.

"Do you have a large building in need of a maintenance staff?" asked Carlos with a smile.

"Oh, no," answered Darrell. "I have a small office and lab on a university campus. But, I'm curious. Why do you ask?"

"I am looking for work in California," answered Carlos, "so that I can go to school and get a degree."

"In what field?"

"I don't know exactly," answered Carlos, "but I like the work of maintaining large complexes like this hotel."

"Perhaps you'd enjoy industrial engineering," said Darrell. "That's a degree you can get at the university where my office and lab are located."

"This is very interesting to me," said Carlos showing his excitement.

There was something about Carlos that attracted Darrell. The young man was bright, articulate, polite, and ambitious. Darrell decided to take a chance on his intuition.

"Carlos, would you be interested in part-time work in my lab while you attend school on the campus?"

Carlos' eyes opened wide.

"Would I? Yes, sir, I would."

"Are you married, Carlos?"

"No, sir, not till I graduate will I think about that."

"Good," said Darrell. "Then when can you start?"

Carlos began to think. "*I don't even know this man,*" he said to himself.

"May I give you my answer tomorrow?" asked Carlos.

"Certainly," answered Darrell.

"Tell me, sir," said Carlos, "are you here for the medical convention?"

"Yes," answered Darrell. "I'm an exhibitor."

"Ah," responded Carlos. "May I see your booth?"

"Right now, if you like," answered Darrell, "but I'm sure the show doors are closed."

"I can get us in," said Carlos.

The two left Darrell's room and took the elevator to the mezzanine floor where the medical product exhibits were located. The hall was lighted dimly, making the chrome and painted metal of the products stand out and the displays look all the more technical.

"My booth is over here," Darrell pointed.

Carlos saw a booth filled with artificial knees, elbows, wrists and hands. In the corner of the booth was a mannequin within a complete, power-driven exoskeleton. In a chair, on a pedestal in the center of the booth, sat a lower torso, legs, feet and all. Carlos was astonished.

"All electronic?" he asked.

"All computer-driven," answered Darrell.

"Mr. Johnson," said Carlos, "I don't have to wait until tomorrow to give you my answer. If you can help me with the immigration authorities, I can start after I give my employer two weeks' notice."

"What about your family?" Darrell asked.

"My father will be very pleased for me," Carlos answered, "and my mother and sister will miss me."

Two weeks later Carlos joined Darrell's small company, and he enrolled at Pepperdine University in Malibu, California. His classes were a short walk from his work. The two became good friends, developing a great respect for each other over the years he was there. Just prior to Carlos' graduation, Darrell took him to lunch to celebrate and to give Carlos some news.

"You've done very well, Carlos. Top of your class. I'm very impressed."

"I owe it to you," Carlos said.

"No, that's not so. You had the talent, and you had the ambition."

"I'm very grateful for the opportunities you gave me," said Carlos.

"I know you are, Carlos, and here's another one," said Darrell.

"Another . . .?"

"Another opportunity," answered Darrell. "I just came back from a meeting I had with some engineers at a company called Search International in Madison, Wisconsin. That's where I was during your finals. Search engineers helped me with a biofeedback circuit I was having trouble with. I also met with an old associate of mine, George Evans. He owns the company. I spoke to him about you. Search just acquired a professional engineering firm and its new, large, high-tech facility. George needs a facilities manager, and I told him you're the man."

33

Carlos was stunned. "But I can't leave you," he said, thinking of all he owed Darrell.

"Oh, yes, you can, and you should. I can't fully utilize your training like George can."

"Why would Search International hire me? I am just graduating and still have not been naturalized."

"George will hire you because I told him he should. That's how well we know each other," said Darrell.

"What about my Mexican background?" Carlos asked, dealing for a moment with reality.

"George will never mention it and won't give you an inch because of it."

Carlos thought for a moment. He could not turn this opportunity down. "I have forgotten," he said. "Where is Wisconsin?"

"Between Minnesota and Lake Michigan," answered Darrell. "You'll find out when you land in Milwaukee. It's right on the lake," he finished, handing Carlos a flight ticket jacket.

"My ticket?" asked Carlos.

"Your ticket," confirmed Darrell.

"This has already been a great adventure, Darrell. I'll forever be grateful and forever loyal to you."

"It's been an adventure for me, too, Carlos. You can be sure I'll stay in touch with you."

Carlos' first days at Search were very stressful. The pace set by George was felt throughout the company. He would suggest a nearly impossible schedule for himself and his staff, then he would meet his goals and wonder why others had fallen behind. He was kind but firm, friendly but disciplined. He gave his people the responsibility and authority they asked for. The opportunities at Search were enormous.

"Carlos," George called to him one day, pointing him toward his office.

Carlos did not know what to expect, even though it was a year now since he had joined the firm.

"Sit down," said George, "and get that look off your face."

Carlos sat in the same seat in which he had once heard George say, "You're hired, but I suppose Darrell already told you so."

"I trust you," said George. "Darrell trusted you. You've done well here this last year. I want you to be responsible for security at Search, and I'm going to give you the authority you'll need. I am making you a vice president."

"But, George . . ." began Carlos.

"You are now responsible both for facilities and security, unless you don't want the job."

"I want it," said Carlos, "but I will need additional training."

"Go get it," said George.

The two stood, smiled, and shook hands. Carlos began to leave.

"Carlos," George called. "I would like you to join me, my wife Rachel, and my daughter Jennifer for dinner tomorrow night at my house."

Carlos spun around with another surprised look on his face. It turned into a smile.

"Yes, of course. Thank you."

"Seven," said George. "We'll barbecue some steaks together."

A year later Carlos married Jennifer. George was delighted, and he told Carlos' father, who attended the wedding with Carlos' sister and mother, everything a father would like to hear about his son. Most important to Carlos' father were the words, "I trust him," spoken by George.

Chapter 7

Search International, Inc.

"George, this is Dave Kasten. He's science editor for the *Madison Journal.* Dave, this is George Evans, our chairman," said Carlos.

The two men met outside the door to George's office. Carlos had arranged the meeting after intercepting a call from Kasten to the company. Kasten was known, nationally, as an investigative reporter with a focus on leading-edge science stories.

"What can we do for you, sir?" George asked.

"I'll be candid, Mr. Evans. I overheard a conversation at Shanagan's Bar which intrigued me and, being a journalist, I just had to follow up."

"Why don't you come into my office, and please call me George. Can we get you something to drink?"

"A Diet Coke would be great."

"A science editor that drinks aspartame?" George asked, raising his gray eyebrows.

"Okay, a regular Coke will do," Kasten responded with a grin, "but I love the taste of Diet."

"Carlos, can you do the honors?"

"Sure. You want me to sit in?" he asked, knowing the answer.

"Yes, sir," George answered.

"I'll tell the receptionist we're both tied up. Be right back."

"Get me a Coke, too, Carlos?"

"Right."

"Mr. Kasten, please have a seat."

"Fascinating office you have here, Mr. . . . or rather, George."

"It's just a collection of memorabilia. Models and things from projects I've been involved in. When you get to be my age you have lots of memories and experiences no one wants to hear, especially the young people."

"That would be a good starting place. What is it you do here?"

"Search does product research. We start with a blank piece of paper--today a blank computer screen--and create new products for client-manufacturers."

"R and D."

"I never liked that description. First of all, we don't do research for the sake of research. We start with an identified user need, create an idea which would satisfy that need, and then we develop a product concept based on the idea. The product concept is tested for feasibility, it's costed, and then we confirm the product's marketability. At that point we usually hand off the project to the client's engineering or marketing staff."

"Sound's complicated."

"Not really. It's usually fun."

"Why Search International?"

"We've had an associate firm in the orient since 1970," George answered.

37

"Let me tell you what I overheard," Kasten seemed anxious to say.

George gestured to Kasten to proceed. Carlos came back in the room with the drinks, handed them to Kasten and George, then sat alongside George's desk.

"I was sitting at a small table with a friend, and there were two guys at the bar talking. The one fellow said he had just quit his job. When the other guy asked, 'Where did you work?' he said, 'Search.'" Kasten paused.

"There must have been more," George said, taking a drink of Coke.

"Yes, I didn't catch it all, but the guy said he was working on a spooky project here and wanted nothing more to do with it."

"Scott," George said to Carlos, trying to sound free with information.

"He said you tapped his brain, and he hasn't been back to work since. Was he on some sort of military project?" asked Kasten.

"No, we don't do military projects. Most of the products we create are for the consumer market. All involve high-volume."

"High-volume?" asked Kasten sipping his drink.

"High-volume production. From 50,000 units per year and up," answered Carlos.

"Can you tell me what project this Scott was on?"

George answered, buying some time to think. "Sometimes we can tell you what the product is, but not who the project is for. Other times we can tell you who we are working for, but not what the project's about.

"And in this case?" pressed Kasten.

"Scott was on an internal project," said George, "which means we were funding the research and planned to license the product concept at a later date."

"And, what was the project?" asked Kasten, not letting go of his question.

"He was part of a team which was developing a new mouse," George answered.

"A mouse?"

"A computer mouse," Carlos answered.

"Aren't there enough . . . mice on the market?"

"This one had a new twist," George said with a grin.

Carlos jumped in again, hoping to stop George from going too far. "I think I can tell you what Scott was talking about, but we still don't know exactly what happened. He was sitting at a design station and received a very low-voltage shock. It could have passed through his body, but certainly not his brain. Anyhow, he became hysterical, claimed he saw something, and wouldn't tell us anything more. That was it. We still haven't figured it out."

"Was he wired up to get the shock?"

"Oh, no, that was just an accident. He had a ground strap on one wrist and the mouse in his other hand. A soft drink spilled, and he got a 5-volt shock. That's all," Carlos concluded.

"What's a Link?"

George and Carlos paused, perhaps a little too long. They hadn't known that Kasten had heard Scott use the code word for the project.

"It's what we called the new mouse," George said.

"You said the new mouse, the Link, had a new twist. What did you mean 'had?'" Kasten asked.

"We dropped the project," said Carlos.

"As a result of the accident?"

"We have the design team on a more important assignment," said George.

Kasten blinked, paused, and said, "That's it?" He sounded disappointed. He heard the ring of truth from the two men which he always looked for in those he interviewed, but it still seemed like there was more to the story.

"Afraid so," said George.

Again a pause as Kasten tried to put a positive spin on the meeting in his mind.

"I'd like to do an article on Search International some time. When you complete a project and put it into production, I'd like to write about the steps it takes through the product research phase. For human interest, I'd like to interview you, Mr. Evans--George--to report how you got into this business in the first place."

"Ok! You name the date, but my schedule might not clear for a few months."

"That's fine, that's fine, I'll give you a call. Thanks for your time." He paused and added apologetically, "You understand, I had to follow up on what I heard."

"I would have, if I were you," George said, rising. "Carlos will show you out." George walked with him to his office door. "See you again, and thanks for coming by."

Kasten waved and walked toward the reception area ahead of Carlos. All three knew it wasn't going to end there.

Chapter 8

Bordering On?

The BioChip assignment team arrived at the conference room early to set up and prepare the computer-slide projector. It was to be their first report to management regarding the Link Project. LaShauna stepped into the darkened room and turned on the lights. As she did, she saw Gary Richardson sitting at the far right corner of the conference table.

"Gary!" LaShauna exclaimed. "Are you all right?"

"Yeah, I'm all right," he answered.

"But you were sitting in the dark," Joan said, clearly concerned for Gary. She walked over to him and put her hand on his shoulder. He pretended not to notice.

"I got here early," Gary explained.

"Are you sure you're all right? I heard about the accident at the airport," said LaShauna.

Fr. Christopher entered the room, saw something was going on, and slowly closed the door. He wanted to hear what the others were saying, hoping the presentation was being postponed. "Father" Christopher Braun had never had a stomach for controversy. His approach to bioethics was quite liberal. Most of his university colleagues held strong liberal leanings, and he found less resistance to his findings when he simply followed the liberal line.

Fr. Christopher had remained unmarried, after leaving the priesthood, and lived with his mother near Milwaukee. "Everyone is entitled to his own opinion," she often told him.

"It wasn't an accident," Gary belted out. "I just overshot the runway a bit, and put a furrow in the farmer's field. I didn't even bend anything on my plane."

"But you've landed at that airport hundreds of times," said Joan. "What distracted you?"

Gary paused. "Scott Dennison. Ok? Scott distracted me," Gary admitted, staring at his hands folded on the conference table.

"Was he flying with you?" Joan asked.

Gary and Scott were both licensed private pilots. They flew together now and then, but had no relationship outside of flying.

"No. He hasn't flown with or talked to me since the Link accident. I saw him standing by the Cessna building with some guy in a suit as I came over the beginning of the runway, or at least I thought I did. This whole damn project passed through my head, and I overshot. That's it."

"You know," said Clyde, watching LaShauna, who had begun to load the video disk into the projector, "I can't believe we are about to put on such a presentation before the guy who signs our paychecks. I get the feeling that this project is a life-changing assignment, and I just don't know where it's going to lead."

LaShauna took charge. "Listen, team," she said with a confidence-building smile. "This is just a first-phase report. No one expects us to have all the answers, especially George Evans, who understands the research process better than all of us. Let's just do our job. It'll go ok."

42

The first slide appeared, looked clear, and everything was ready. Minutes later George, Anna Pierson, Allen Nolte and Carlos began to file in. Some of the attendees dropped their hybrid notebook-computers onto the conference table. Ed Lukin was at home taking care of his wife, who was unusually ill with the flu.

A very different atmosphere existed in the room which was noticed by all. This was the first time the cause behind the strange new "phenomenon" was to be discussed in-group, and the BioChip team was about to drop its first multiheaded clusterbomb. Everyone took a seat, and LaShauna began.

"In a sense, we have nothing to report. We can't explain what has been happening with known scientific theory. But," she added as she called the group's attention to the first slide, "we are developing a hypothesis which seems to have real merit."

LaShauna paused and began again.

"You all know that the BioChip team was working on research to determine, first, how the single human cell at conception, the zygote, could possibly store as much data as it does; second, how the neural networks of the brain can store as much information as they must, in terms of memory; and third, how some vastly larger data or memory storage repository must be at work within the neuron or brain cell."

"That was not exactly my understanding of the questions directing the BioChip project," George said, "but I imagine you advanced the questions as you uncovered answers. Proceed."

"Thanks, George," said LaShauna. "We want you all to assume for the purposes of our discussion that there is, in fact, a huge, heretofore unknown, repository of data within the human cell--other than the DNA coding of the genes. Let's just refer to it as the repository for now. We will also assume it is at the functional center of the nucleus of the neuron."

"Big assumption for such a large storage device that is so small no one even knows it's there," said Allen.

Charlie Schuster poked his head in the door and asked George, "Can I sit in on this?" Though corporate controller, and 62 years old, Charlie had a fascination for leading-edge technology. He had no technical background, just a personal interest. He lunched with the engineers every day. His favorite part of the *Wall Street Journal*, which he read at his desk for more than an hour each morning, was the "New Technology" section. Search was very profitable, in part, because of his interest. He always seemed to know when to question the economics of a project, and George Evans usually listened.

"You're always welcome, Charlie," said George. "Come on in. The items on the slide are the three questions which were driving the BioChip team's work. Continue, LaShauna. Allen, just go along with it for now," he added.

"What's 'it'?" asked Charlie with an apologetic grin.

LaShauna called for the next slide, which displayed hypothetical statement "A," that there is a data repository at the functional center of the nucleus of the neuron or brain cell.

"Oh," said Charlie, with another big grin.

"They're presenting a hypothesis. Let's listen," said George.

"Now," LaShauna said, continuing the presentation, "the neurons of the cortex, the primary control center of the brain, receive data from every sensor neuron, or nerve cell, in the body, and neurons in other parts of the brain, in a pulsed-analog-parallel fashion. We propose that when the corresponding cortical neuron receives such a signal it fires and the data is thereby transferred to the repository-- hypothetical statement 'B.'"

Half of the participants leaned forward as if to improve their grasp of what was being said. LaShauna called for the next slide, which added statement "B."

"For the purposes of this hypothesis, we will define parallatum, a new word, to mean one bit, to use a computer term, of the parallel collection of all sensed data sent to the repository at any given instant."

The next slide added the definition of parallatum (parallata, plural).

"But, let me step back a microsecond," said LaShauna. "The data arriving at the base of the brain is averaged for approximately .5 to 1.0 ms, probably controlled by the locus ceruleus, after which it is sent on to the cortex where it is stored for 10 to 20 ms, perhaps longer under some circumstances or in some individuals. The locus ceruleus is a region in the brain stem in which the neurons can have an enormous number of synapses, often extending over a large region of the cerebral cortex."

"Wait a minute," called out George. "You promised that we 'uneducated' participants would not be intimidated by your neurobiology. I'm intimidated."

"I doubt that, George, but bear with us. We don't intend to spend much time on this. Some of what we've learned came from *The Biology Coloring Book*, written by Robert D. Griffon, and we didn't even color the pictures. Some came from several medical encyclopedias, and much from Francis Crick's book, *The Astonishing Hypothesis*. We didn't have time to get into the biology of the brain too deeply. Believe me, this is 101 stuff."

"Okay, sorry," said George. "Let me paraphrase what I got so far--and what I think I need. Pulsed-analog data from the millions or billions of sensors in the body, including, I suppose, data coming from the optic nerve, arrive in parallel at a special part of the brain--the cortex. There the brain cells transfer the data, which you're calling parallata, to the repository, after a delay of 10 to 20 milliseconds. Why the delay?"

Gary responded. "It's not really a delay. The data received by the neurons of the cortex is not in sync. The sensor neurons fire when they fire, and the data arrives at the transferring neuron when it arrives."

"What a mess!" Nolte said. "Just a jumble of analog signals."

"Right," Gary continued. "Asynchronous, pulsed-analog, parallel data is not going to be comprehensible. But, somehow, we believe, the parallata is transferred to the repository at a fixed frequency."

Joan stepped into the presentation. "So the data is held by the neuron until it is transferred at a fixed frequency--synchronizing the data for storage in the repository."

"Yes," said LaShauna, "and here is a word we have redefined for the purposes of this hypothesis. A percept is, hereinafter, a full set of parallata transferred at a given time. We think a series of these percepts are stored by the repository as memories, and they're instantly reflected back to the neuron-set which transferred the percepts. This would allow the brain to experience comprehensible data from millions or billions of sensor neurons which are actually firing at random."

LaShauna called for the next slide, which added the new definition of percept.

"And the final slide," she said, "defines hypothetical statement 'C'--that percepts are instantly reflected back to the neuron-set which transferred the data, producing comprehensible data."

"Fascinating," said George. "Sounds like something those studying consciousness would like to hear--or maybe not. Now how does your growing hypothesis apply to the phenomenon?"

46

The room was quiet. Anna looked at George, then to LaShauna, over to Ed, and back to LaShauna. Clyde nervously shuffled his index-card notes. Gary frowned and shook his head in disbelief that he was a part of such a conclusion, which LaShauna was about to deliver.

"Here it comes," LaShauna said with perceptible dramatics. "We think that what Scott and Anna experienced were single percepts called up from their repositories."

"Man!" Allen blurted out, "You've left so many dangling questions. How can you expect us to take your hypothesis seriously? I took notes." He was on a roll. "One, there's a huge data-storage repository--one that no one knows about--at the functional center of an already microscopic brain cell. Two, there's some undiscovered mechanism or carrier to transfer and thereby synchronize data being transferred to the repository by the neurons of the cortex. And, three, these 'percepts,' as you have redefined them, comprised of comprehensible data, understandable by the mind, are transferred back to the brain instantly, so that the brain can--what--experience them for the first time?"

"You've got it right," LaShauna responded. "Gary's present assignment is to determine the nature of the 'mechanism or carrier' which transfers the data from the neurons to the repository."

"I've got it right?" laughed Allen. "I don't even know what I'm talking about," mimicking his favorite comedy team.

"You really are right, Allen," adds Joan, "except, although the parallatum is reflected instantly, it probably takes a small amount of time to transfer the data back to the neurons. They are, after all, physical, temporal components."

LaShauna took charge again. "Let's discuss item number one on Allen's list, our hypothetical Statement A. Gary says that for such a repository to exist--to store every percept for a lifetime, and to be able to recall it in detail, as

47

the mind apparently does, in little more than an instant, it would have to be so small as to have no mass and yet it must have a nearly infinite capacity for data."

"I thought Gary was an agnostic," Allen blurted, which struck everyone as a statement very out of character for him, except for his propensity to say whatever came to his mind. Allen made the statement because of where he saw the discussion going--an area very uncomfortable for him.

At first, no one spoke. Gary got up and left the room. Then, LaShauna continued as if the question was strictly technical, and as if Gary's departure was planned.

"Well, he is," she said, "but he says, if secular astronomers can talk about a perfectly symmetrical, atemporal sphere of no volume with infinite mass as the singularity of the creation of the cosmos, he, Gary, can specify his ideal memory chip as an atemporal, zero-mass particle with infinite capacity."

"Why again must the repository have infinite capacity?" asked George.

"Because it must be capable of storing every last sensory-instant of every second of life," Joan answered. "If you live to 100 and a sensory-instant is defined as .10 milliseconds, then the repository must record 3 to the 13th power times--what?--10 billion sensory neurons?"

"You guys are serious!" Charlie belched.

"Gary may or may not be," Joan said, referencing indirectly Gary's walkout, "but the rest of us are. The repository, my friends, must be an atemporal particle, a component of the brain cell existing outside of time."

"Wait a minute," Allen said, recovering from his earlier statement about Gary. "Each repository or atemporal 'particle,' if you must, would only receive serial information from its related neuron. To form a comprehensible percept, you will have to synchronize every particle or connect them all together."

LaShauna paused, but only to prepare her listeners. "There is only one particle involved."

"You mean in each cell?" Allen said.

"No, it's the same particle at the functional center of every nucleus in every cortical neuron. An atemporal particle has no dimension and only a functional location."

Allen's mouth dropped open. He wasn't saying anything. No one was saying anything. Some had began to rub their arms.

Finally, George spoke. "Being atemporal, the particle, containing the repository, has no dimension, no shape, no volume, and no physical location. One and the same particle is at the functional center of every neuron in the cortex of the brain--and I have goose bumps on my arms the size of golf balls. Father Christopher, what is your take on all of this?"

"I . . . haven't even considered the ethical side of . . ." and he stopped.

More silence. Then George spoke again, and LaShauna began to nod.

"We may be bordering on the discovery of the human soul!"

Silence again.

Quietly George asked, "Is that the end of your report?"

"For now," LaShauna said.

"Very well," George responded. "Keep going, but keep one foot on the ground--and ladies and gentlemen, I mean it. I want Ed Lukin to hear this when he returns on Monday, but in more detail."

"Yes, sir," several BioChip members responded.

Everyone except the remaining team members got up and left the conference room.

Clyde finally spoke. "What have we gotten ourselves into?"

Joan went quickly to search for Gary.

In the hallway, Allen walked along with George Evans. "Allen," George said, "keep your hat on. If this leads nowhere, I'll kill it quickly."

Chapter 9

Women's Right to Choose League

"Mr. and Mrs. Kasten! How nice of you to join us. Senator Margaret Sneed is here, and she has asked to talk to you."

Dave Kasten and his wife Dorothy had been invited to the Washington, D.C., party to kickoff yet another television advertising program intended to deliver the Women's Right to Choose League's message of tolerance to the homes of millions of Americans. Kasten wasn't entirely sure why he and Dorothy had been invited, but he assumed he would find out sometime during the evening. The gracious welcomer directed them into the spacious hotel ballroom. Literally hundreds of guests and League members milled around with refreshments in their hands. A buffet table along the wall displayed at least forty feet of delightfully presented hors d'oeuvres. Kasten scanned the ballroom, and his eyes stopped on a tall woman in a white blouse with a red blazer and skirt. Her eyes had caught his, and she headed his way.

"Mr. Kasten, I'm so pleased you could make it," she said. "I've been asking about you all evening. And Mrs. Kasten, I presume. How do you do? I'm Senator Margaret Sneed."

Her toothy smile was so large her mouth seemed to occupy a full third of her face.

"Senator," said Kasten, "This is my wife, Dorothy."

"I'm so pleased to meet you, Dorothy," the Senator said. "Your husband is almost the guest of honor here tonight."

"How's that?" Kasten asked.

"Oh, you don't know? Our new advertising campaign is designed to take away the guilt-pressure faced by the poor dears that find abortion is the only answer to their problem. We'd all like to see the number of surgical abortions drop, and they are now that methotrexate (RU-486) is in wide use, but some just don't want to take the risks associated with the drug--you know, liver damage, kidney failure, viral infections. That sort of thing--so they turn to surgical abortion. Thank God it's a safe procedure, and available, but it too has its side effects."

"Side effects?" asked Kasten.

"The largely underground anti-choice forces still get their propaganda to those that are already suffering tragically. They just don't seem to care about the rights of these--often children--to decide their own futures. Instead they expose them to their blood-and-guts barrage, calling the children and their caregivers murderers. The side effects are the emotional damage that results."

"And how do I figure into all of this?" asked Kasten.

"Oh, Dave," said the Senator, smiling widely again. "Your science articles on how the human products-of-conception look very much like those of many animals--just so much prehistoric-looking tissue--are the heart of our new campaign. We're going to do a computer animation--very realistic--of one species of animal in each ad, showing it from its full growth stage back to nothing but products-of-conception beginning with a single cell. Concurrently we'll show a human the same age of the animal and trace it back, too. The startling results are, of course, that animals and humans both look the same when reduced to nothing but a tissue growth in the mother; certainly nothing that could be called human. Something more like a useless appendix or a tumor."

"And the purpose of the ads?" asked Kasten.

"Well, of course, to show that there should be no guilt connected with the removal of the unwanted tissue, any more than the removal of an infected appendix or a malignant tumor."

"I see," said Kasten, "and you're going to use my articles to develop this line of advertising?"

"Well, not directly, Dave. Copyrights, you know, but your work will be at the foundation of this humane campaign. What we hoped you'd do is support our program with a timely article that revisits the revelations you have published."

Kasten did not know how to respond. An uncomfortable moment passed.

"You will consider doing another article, won't you, Dave?" the Senator asked with a sorrowful frown.

"I'm really more into investigative reporting these days, you know, what's happening in the scientific world that the scientists and engineers would rather we didn't know."

"Oh, I understand, Dave," she said, "It seems that scientifically-based companies are so greedy these days. Altruism is dead. Developing new drugs and products to help mankind has gone by the wayside. It's all profit, profit, profit. Mankind be damned."

"This new activity occupies most of my time," Kasten said, trying to build on her statement to get himself off the hook.

"Perhaps you could just re-issue some of what you've written along the lines I described. Perhaps we could even arrange to do it for you?" she suggested.

"I'll have to think about it," said Dave.

"Oh, yes, by all means. I don't want to push you into it tonight, but I can tell you, it'll be a big help to have your articles hit the news again as we launch our program. Now, just forget about it this evening. Enjoy yourselves. I'll be in touch."

The senator, still grinning broadly, pointed the couple in the direction of the crowds and buffet table. She turned away and immediately began talking with another couple. Dave Kasten and Dorothy moved into the crowd. When a reasonable distance separated them from the senator, Dorothy, a quiet, thoughtful woman, said to her husband, "I'm not comfortable here."

"I understand, dear," he answered. "Let's move across the ballroom to those other doors over there."

They left for Wisconsin early the next morning. Kasten did not return the senator's many phone calls.

Chapter 10

The Fabric of the Soul

A discussion was already in progress when Ed Lukin walked into the conference room at Search. The BioChip team had assembled, including Gary Richardson. George Evans and Allen Nolte had just asked about the role of the cortex, the main control center of the brain.

"Well, keep in mind," LaShauna was saying, "that data is received by cortical neurons about every half millisecond, and it fades after 20-some milliseconds, so the data stored in the cerebral cortex is constantly being 'refreshed,' as the video guys would say, every half millisecond, while you're awake, that is."

"And when you're asleep?" George asked.

Clyde finally took the floor. "The locus ceruleus is basically inactive when you're asleep, even during REM sleep," he continued. "That's one of the reasons we think that region of the brain is responsible for the transmission of the data to the cortical neurons where it becomes parallata. The exact function of the locus ceruleus is not known . . ." and he added just loudly enough to be heard, "until now that is."

"Such confidence," Ed laughed. "Say, I thought I was early, but here you guys are fully involved."

"How's the wife, Ed?" George asked.

"She's fine, George. Thanks."

Anna and Carlos entered the room. "How you all doin'?" Carlos said. George smiled and began to explain the purpose of the meeting to Ed Lukin.

"Ed, the BioChip team is going to recap in more detail what we heard on Friday. They have developed a hypothesis which is rather interesting."

The last slide from the previous meeting, which had been revised, was on the screen.

"Gary," George said, "why don't you review for Ed the two statements and definitions you have on the screen."

Gary looked stunned that George would call on him. He immediately understood it was George's way of saying, "Forget about walking out at the last meeting." George always left extra room for his technical personnel.

"Okay, George," he began, without looking at the slide. "A. At the functional center of every cortical neuron is an atemporal particle of zero mass. A biological singularity. It is, or it contains, a repository of data. The repository has infinite capacity for data, and the data can be recalled instantly."

Ed's eyes widened. "*This kind of thinking coming from Gary's mouth!*" he thought. George grinned at Ed's facial response. Gary continued.

"B. When the cortical neuron receives data from the sensor neurons or other neurons of the brain, it fires and transfers the data to the repository." He continued, still without looking at the screen. "We're calling each bit of data transferred to the particle a parallata, and a full set of all parallatum transferred at one instant a percept. Further, we have now defined a memory as being an indefinite series of percepts."

He paused for Ed to take it all in. Then he continued.

"Percepts received by the particle are instantly reflected back to the neuron-set which transferred the data, allowing the brain to experience comprehensible data from millions or billions of sensor neurons which are actually firing at random."

"Consciousness!" George said.

Ed responded and said slowly, "I knew when I walked in here, by the expressions on your faces, that you had come up with a remarkable theory."

"It's just a hypothesis, Ed," LaShauna said, obviously pleased with Gary's presentation. "It only suggests, it doesn't prove. There's more."

"Fasten your seat belt," said George.

Ed turned to George and back to Gary and LaShauna. With that last cue from George, LaShauna knew where to go next.

"The same particle," she delivered, "is at the functional center of every cortical neuron."

Ed stared at George. He saw George's face flush as his head dropped down. George raised his head and turned toward his dear friend and said, "They're talking about the fabric of the soul."

Ed thought he saw moisture in the corners of George's eyes.

It was Father Christopher's turn. "Yes!" he said, "We may have started down a path leading to the scientific discovery of the human soul! Proof of its existence."

"Praise God," Ed said softly, shaking his head.

"Then the eyes," added Allen with a smile, "are truly the windows to the soul." He looked over at Anna.

LaShauna continued, noticing the ongoing nonverbal exchange between George and Ed. "We think we can demonstrate that other scientists have been wearing cultural blinders since Darwin gave them his no-longer-plausible escape route from recognizing the unthinkable fact that we are not studying an evolutionary creation but a design! Most scientists are hiding in their Darwinian caves, hoping the rocks fall down on their heads, rather than face God."

Gary wrote down what LaShauna said, and added, "Is the atemporal really so hard to imagine in light of Einstein's General Theory of Relativity, which changed our concept of space and time? Many scientists now believe that 10 to 20 billion years ago the entire universe was contained in a . . . perfectly symetrical mass . . . of infinite density . . . with a volume of zero . . . existing only for an instant . . . before time began!" He paused between each characteristic for emphasis.

"Why this impassioned defense of the Big Bang theory?" Ed asked.

"We're not defending the theory," LaShauna interjected. "We just want you, Anna and Allen, who are involved in the empirical side of the Link project, to consider our hypothesis to see if it leads us all to a better understanding of the phenomenon. We are just saying that other scientists are already considering the existence of the atemporal state. We want you to."

Anna stood up, and the room became very quiet. "What has been going through my mind," she began, "during both of these presentations, is that I am the only one on this staff whose particle has been tapped. Up until now I have been thinking it was just a physiological phenomenon. Now that I have heard your hypothesis twice, I can, in fact, relate what you say to the experience, and I believe there is substance to your hypothesis. But I must also add that I believe our lives will not be the same from this point on. If we are, in fact, experimenting with the soul, nothing will be the same again."

Chapter 11

Anna

George Evans felt he had to speak with Anna, but not at Search. He felt responsible for what she had been through, even though she'd been a willing volunteer. He had permitted the tests, and it was his vision which had led the company to this place in time.

"Anna," he said as the two left the conference area. "I'd like to talk with you. This evening, if possible."

"Sure, George. What time?" It was the kind of answer George had come to expect.

"Well, I don't want to take you from your family. Let me bring dinner--a bucket of chicken or . . ."

"Some Chinese food?"

"Anna, you're making me feel worse."

"No, I'm serious. My family and I really do love Chinese food--but anything will be fine. We usually eat at six, and you and I can talk afterward, while the kids watch a video. Michael will probably want to sit in."

"Oh fine, fine." George said. "Six o'clock then."

Anna smiled and left George standing at the door of his office. "Six," she confirmed as she walked away.

George called his wife Rachel to tell her his plans.

The Piersons were always pleased to have George visit. Usually, he came with Rachel, but not tonight. The children always had some project of theirs to show him, and his sincere interest was enjoyed. Dinner was a time for kidding and laughter. The jokes and teasing were usually at George's expense, but Anna and Michael could see how he set his own traps, and then would walk into them at the right moment, to the delight of all three children. They were all very bright, and it was a challenge to keep the "pretend" from surfacing.

After dinner Anna placed a video disk in the system's drive and set the volume. The children took their favorite places while George, Anna and Michael slipped into the sun room, softly lighted for nighttime use. They sat on cushioned wicker furniture around a large glass coffee table. There was already a pitcher of iced tea surrounded by simple tumblers on the table. Anna always planned everything she did.

"Very nice," said George. "May I pour?"

"Please," she said.

As he did so he began the discussion which had been on his mind since Anna spoke at the BioChip team's presentation earlier in the day.

"Anna," he said, "just before you and I left the conference room today you made a statement which I'm sure is on the mind of everyone that was in the meeting. You said--"

"--that our lives will not be the same from this point on, and perhaps nothing will." Anna finished the sentence for George, glancing at Michael as if to acknowledge that she had already discussed the subject with him.

"George," she continued, "I wasn't speaking for myself. I felt compelled to say what I did. Over the weekend Michael and I prayed for guidance from the Holy Spirit. I came away knowing that what I would hear today, in our meeting, would confirm that God was in the process of revealing a truth through the Search family which has been ignored by mankind for thousands of years. It seems to the two of us, Michael and me, that God has trained me--perhaps all of those on the two Link research teams--to play a role."

"And what is this truth you speak of?" George asked.

"First let me say that I, that is, we, the research teams, don't have all of the revelation yet. It's still coming, a piece at a time. But I can tell you that what we are learning will cause all of us and maybe a large part of the Christian world to think in far more real terms about who we are."

Not for an instant did George's eyes leave hers.

"And the simple truth we're learning," Anna continued, "is that we are truly body-soul beings; that our souls are fully involved in every thought, action, memory and decision. We are a unity of the spiritual and the physical."

George did not respond immediately. Anna's statements were strangely similar to the thoughts he too had been having. Then he asked, "Have you expressed these things to anyone on the BioChip team? With Ed?" he added.

"No," said Anna. "To no one except you and Michael, and I think we should not until our work is completed."

"You've included me in that last statement?"

"Yes, I have."

"Then you think the work should continue?"

"Yes, most definitely," she answered.

"And you?"

"I will continue to be the test subject for now," she said, anticipating the rest of his question.

"And you, Michael?" George asked.

"George," her husband responded, "I am concerned, but I stand behind her decision and agree with her entirely."

"Do you and Ed have additional tests planned?" George asked Anna.

"Yes, two," she said.

Chapter 12

Concentration

"Anna," said Ed Lukin, while helping her to prepare for the next series of tests, "I've reduced the soft drink formula further. It now contains only the ingredients which probably precipitate the results we're looking for. I've eliminated those chemicals which most likely have nothing to do with the phenomenon. You'll notice I also eliminated the high-pressure paint sprayer. We will be using a conventional inoculation gun."

Anna was sitting in an executive office chair which faced a large video monitor. All of the electronic equipment, to which she was being attached, was now located behind her, permitting her to focus strictly on the display. Her arms were resting on the arms of the chair. One chair arm had been replaced with a Formica board, making it look like a particularly comfortable seat taken from a hospital blood lab.

"That all makes me feel a little better," said Anna, "but not much."

"Anna, it's entirely up to you if we proceed with this test," said George, who had just come into the new test room configured for the Link research project.

"I'm okay, George, just a little nervous again. What we need, I've been thinking, is a sedative which allows me to stay alert and concentrate, but one which makes the extreme emotional trauma of the experience more manageable."

"Are you looking for one, Anna?" he asked.

"I think I've got one, and I plan to try it now."

"Good," said George, and Anna proceeded to drink from a small plastic cup containing a milky solution.

"I don't like this at all," said Ed, looking at George. "The purpose of these tests is to see if the test subject--you, Anna," he said turning to Anna and back to George, "will experience a memory without concentrating on some aspect of it. As you know, during the first test Anna will purposely be distracted--Allen will take care of that--while during the second test she will be permitted to concentrate. We wanted to change only that one aspect of the test. It was risky enough to also change the injected formula, not knowing exactly how the reduced solution will affect the results. But now Anna proposes to--and has--introduced a new chemical into her system at the same time. This is not scientific."

George agreed. "I don't like the idea of proceeding with any test before we have a good handle on the biochemistry."

Anna spoke up. "Gentlemen. We can always go back to the original combination of elements. By cleaning up the formula, and introducing my special sedative, we are reducing," she emphasized, "those risks I'm sure we all see as potentially dangerous. Let's proceed."

The men paused, then nodded. Ed went back to work. The continuous blood pressure and heart rate monitors were attached to Anna, just as before. She had gulped down a glutamic acid cocktail four hours ago at the same time the nicotine patch was put in place. "Are you ready, Anna?" George asked when the monitoring equipment was operating.

"I'm ready, George," she said quietly, starting to feel the effects of the sedative she had given herself.

"Power on," Allen announced. "Starting the video disk recorder. Anna, you're going to see a series of brain-busters on the screen to keep you from concentrating on the memory you've chosen to recall.

"Brain-busters?" Anna laughed.

"Couldn't you have called the displayed problems something else?" asked Ed, smiling.

George shook his head, but said nothing. He was already trying to solve the first problem on the computer screen in front of Anna, and now so was Anna. The second problem flashed, then the third, and fourth. A click and a hiss was all she heard. The milliameters recorded a tiny current passing through her.

"Anna?" queried George.

"Nothing," said Anna calmly. "A funny feeling maybe, but nothing more."

They repeated the sequence twice.

"Let's move on to the second test," said Ed. "Okay, Anna?"

"Yes," she said. "Test 2."

"Anna, start concentrating deeply on the memory you've chosen," said George. "Quiet, everyone."

After a few minutes Anna nodded her head, signaling to Ed that she had achieved the level of concentration she felt was necessary. A click and a hiss was heard again. The milliameters jumped, and Anna sat up abruptly.

"Oh my," she said softly, and tears gradually filled her eyes.

"Anna," George asked after a tense moment for everyone. "Are you all right?"

"Oh, yes," she said sweetly. "I always cry at weddings."

"At weddings?" Allen repeated.

"My grandmother's. She was married in 1941. Thirty-four years before I was born, and yet I just saw my grandfather waiting for me . . . that is, for my grandmother as she walked down the aisle. It was a grand scene. The first thing which caught my eye was the narrow white carpet that stretched in front of me past the rows of pews and guests to my soon-to-be husband and his best man, standing on the right side of the aisle beyond the pews. My . . . grandfather was dressed in a black cut-away tuxedo coat with pin-striped pants and white spats. He wore a white, double-breasted vest with a wide, fluffed, red tie around one of those white wing collars. There was a white corsage in his lapel above a neatly folded pocket handkerchief. His hair was slicked back with a plainly visible part on the left side. The best man was dressed similarly, but wore a black vest with a conventional white shirt and narrow rose-colored tie. They were both smiling broadly at me, and my eyes were focused on them."

"Aw, cut it out," said Allen, disbelieving the degree of detail Anna was reporting.

Anna looked directly at Allen as she continued. "In my broader peripheral vision, extending out from my line-of-sight, I saw the dark oak pews with little doors on each, and I saw wrought iron candle stands fixed to the pews every fourth row. They were all lit, except for one midway on the left. I didn't know any of the faces which were behind the pew doors and candle stands, but I felt my grandmother knew every one. There were fancy hats on both sides of the aisle. My grandmother's bridesmaids stood in a row to the left, on the first step of the altar. All I could see was the bodices of their light green dresses and their heads, of course, topped with short, dark green hats.

"Anna!" Allen said, "Get real!"

"Further in my peripheral vision," she continued, "I saw large marble pillars supporting multiple arches down the side aisles. Behind them were marble walls and glowing window coves which were matched above the arches with more windows that illuminated the high, decorated stone trusses with warm, reddish sunlight. Yes, it was a beautiful scene. I wonder what her dress was like?" she finished.

"All that in an instant? A blip on the oscilloscope? Impossible," said Allen, and to George he asked, "How do we know all this wasn't just Anna's imagination?"

"I can tell the difference between being there and imagining it all," said Anna.

"But we're scientists. We must be certain," he responded.

"Allen," George said, his eyebrows lifting with an idea. "Run the video disk back to the imaging lab."

"All we'll have is a single display sweep," said Allen; "color pixels running across the display a line at a time."

"I know," George responded. "Let's assemble the image pixel-by-pixel. You have the equipment. Bring us a printout when you're done."

"Okay, but . . ." Allen was hesitant. He was in favor of the assignment, but didn't want to miss anything.

Sensing his concern, George assured him. "We'll fill you in. Get started." And Allen left quickly.

Anna continued with her description of what she had experienced. "This time I believe I heard music."

"Not possible," said Ed. "According to the BioChip team you received only one percept. One instantaneous group of parallata." He laughed at the complex thought.

"Well, it wasn't music, of course, but I am sure I heard a beautiful chord, just for an instant."

"Maybe it'll show up on the disk," said George. He had his mind on something else.

"Anna?" George called.

"Yes, George," Anna replied, sounding still calm and sweet.

"Would you consider a third test . . . right now?"

"George, I'm not sure we have a full dose left," said Ed.

"Check," said George. Ed stepped to the lab table against the wall.

Anna lifted her head toward George. "I'm quite all right, George. If you have another test in mind and Ed's prepared, I don't see why not."

"You said you wondered what your grandmother's dress was like. Would you like to find out?" he asked.

Anna thought for a minute, and then said, "I know what you're thinking. All I would have to do is concentrate on a scenario which probably occurred. My grandmother certainly looked into a full-length mirror before the wedding after donning her gown."

"Did you ever see a picture of your grandmother looking in the mirror at her wedding dress?" asked Ed from across the room.

"Not that I can remember--there's that word again--and the existence of such a photo would be very unlikely, since the photographer was certainly a man back then, and he would not have been invited into the dressing room with me . . . that is, with my grandmother."

"Anna, that's about the fourth time you said 'me' when you meant your grandmother."

"I'm not having an identity problem, Ed. Wait till you try this. It's like taking on the role of the person whose senses you're re-experiencing."

"Does the dress still exist, Anna?" George asked, getting back to his idea.

"My mother tells me that my grandmother's wedding dress is in a labeled box, tied with a wedding ribbon on the day it was put away by my grandmother. It's in my mother's attic, and it has never been opened."

"I have enough chemical," said Ed, suddenly sounding very anxious to proceed. "Okay, Anna? Everything is set. Start to concentrate, and give me a nod when you're ready."

Anna made an obvious effort to concentrate very deeply on her thoughts of how her grandmother must have appeared in the mirror, minutes before her wedding, 69 years ago. After a long pause, she nodded to Ed. Her eyes were closed. Ed pulled the trigger on the pressure inoculation gun.

Anna squealed. "Gorgeous," she said, "Beautiful." and then, "Oh, George, Ed" and the tears returned, but flowed freely this time."

"That beautiful?" Ed asked.

"Is there something else, Anna?" George asked.

"Yes. Oh yes," she said. "Next to me, on my left, my mother was looking over my shoulder, crying with happiness for me, her daughter."

"Anna?" Ed said.

"Yes, Ed, I know. It was my great-grandmother standing next to my grandmother. You just won't understand till you experience it for yourself. It was so unexpected to see her standing there."

"You recognized her from photographs?" asked George.

"Yes, my mother has many photographs of her, of both of them."

"The dress, Anna. Try to describe the dress in great detail," said Ed.

"Well, looking in the mirror, I couldn't see all of the train, but it was long, I am sure. The white brocade-satin dress was form-fitted--very nice--with a square neckline ending in a heart-shaped 'V' which was filled with grape-cluster lace. She wore a beautiful string of small white pearls. Her hair was parted also on the left, entirely off her forehead, and her head was covered with a billowy lace attached to a shoulder-length veil sewn over a floor length veil lying over the train attached to her shoulders. The sleeves were billowy at the top and form-fitted from the elbow down. At the wrist the satin was interrupted by an inch of veil material and the sleeve ended in a point on the back of her hand."

"Fascinating," said Ed.

Allen had come back in the room, eyes wide, as Anna was finishing her description.

"That's it," he said excitedly. "She has been describing this dress." And he held up an 8 1/2 by 11-inch computer rendering of the view from the back of the church which her grandmother had seen. Her grandmother's eyes must have been clearly focused on her husband-to-be, since there was a barely perceptible out-of-focus condition encompassing all other details. But, in the peripheral limit of her grandmother's vision, and in the lower right-hand corner of the image, was her grandmother's hand and forearm, resting on the arm of a man in a formal coat. The sleeve of her dress was easily visible. It matched Anna's description exactly.

"This is too weird!" Allen exclaimed.

"We have another image for you, Allen," said George. "You're going to be even more impressed with this one. Did you, by chance, check the audio track on the last disk?"

"Sure," Allen answered. "But it contained only a single complex wave."

"And did you break it down into its components?" asked Anna.

"Yeah, but I don't know what you're after," said Allen.

"Would the complex wave contain the notes A, middle C and E?" asked Anna.

"Well, let me see. A, 440, C . . . Yeah, that's it! How did you know?"

"I heard it, Allen! I heard it!" Anna answered.

Allen's mouth dropped open.

"Anna's a classical guitarist," said George. "She knows her chords. Anna," he continued. "Do you think your mother would allow us to untie that ribbon?"

"The image Allen is going to produce will convince her," Anna said with confidence.

As Anna was being disconnected from the myriad of electronic gear, Ed said, "Well, Anna, that confirms it. The act of concentration plays a role in the process of recalling memories."

"And a first grade teacher could have told us that," Anna quipped.

A few days later, Anna's mother arrived at Search with the box, which contained the wedding dress of Anna's grandmother. Anna had described the dress with extreme accuracy from a percept stored in her grandmother's particle 69 years ago. But how did it come to be in Anna's memory? That would take longer to discover. In the box with the wedding dress Anna also found a diary placed there by her grandmother.

Chapter 13

LaShauna

"You're always so nice, LaShauna," said Ed, "Something must get your goat."

Ed and his wife Betty regularly invited LaShauna to their Skyline Drive home for dinner. LaShauna had no family nearby. Her folks lived in a small town in Indiana, and the Lukin children were in their late teens with many activities of their own. Besides, LaShauna and the Lukins were members of the same Presbyterian church. Anna and Michael Pierson lived down the street from Ed and Betty, and occasionally they would all go out together. Now and then LaShauna would watch the Piersons' children for them when Anna and Michael were away. She would inevitably walk them over to the Lukins' if the weather was nice.

"Sure," LaShauna answered. "Some things get my goat."

"Like what?" Ed pressed.

"Never mind," laughed LaShauna.

"No, really," said Ed.

"Well, for one, I hate it when people call me an African-American."

Ed gulped and looked into her eyes.

"If this subject is too sensitive for you . . ." she began.

"No, I just didn't expect you to say that," said Ed.

"It's really no big deal, but I'm not an African-American. I'm an American, and my ancestors are not African. Mine are from the West Indies. I don't know that they ever saw Africa. Also," LaShauna continued, "I don't like to be expected to support African-American causes. Most are just divisive anyway, and divisiveness is not what we need in America."

"I certainly agree," said Ed.

"My mother always taught me to look forward, not backward. It never occurred to me that I might not be able to become a biophysicist because of my ancestral background."

"When did you know you wanted to become a scientist?" asked Ed.

"Probably when I was ten."

"Ten!"

"I was in fifth grade," said LaShauna, "and our teacher really had a problem trying to get us to understand simple scientific stuff. Then one day this guy in his sixties--I can't remember his name--came to our classroom and actually demonstrated the simple principles that we couldn't seem to get. He made it all appear so simple and fun. He asked, 'Who wants to grow up to be a scientist?' He was such a nice man; I raised my hand. I wanted to be a scientist from that day on. Besides, I won a one-pound bag of M&Ms from him."

"How'd you do that?" Ed asked.

"Well, at the beginning of his demonstration, the man said, 'I want someone to tell me what's scientifically wrong with the statement, M&Ms melt in your mouth but not in your hand.'"

"You knew the answer?"

"Yup."

"I don't," said Ed.

"Then I'll tell you," laughed LaShauna. "M&Ms are candy-coated chocolate. They don't melt in your mouth. They dissolve."

"You're right," said Ed.

"And you know what, Ed?"

"What?"

"George Evans looks just like that man who came to our fifth grade class."

"Really?"

"And now I'm going to tell you a secret."

"Okay."

"When I was interviewed at Search I already had two other good offers. Before George interviewed me, I had made up my mind to join one of them."

"George changed your mind?"

"Not really. I was so stunned by how much George looked like the man who visited my fifth grade class that I didn't hear a thing he said about salary and benefits, and," LaShauna continued, "when he asked me if I wanted to be a scientist at Search, do you know what I did?"

Ed shook his head.

"No joke, Ed, I raised my hand."

Chapter 14

Jacob's Ladder

The BioChip team began its third report to George Evans and the empirical team in the large Search conference room.

"Last time," LaShauna began, "we told you about a special component, the particle, we believe to be at the functional center of the nucleus of cortical neurons--neurons of the cortex of the brain. Keep in mind, the term particle is a bit misleading; it's not made up of atomic components, but is . . ."

"Yes," interrupted Allen Nolte, "it's made of heretofore undisclosed stuff, it's atemporal, it has no mass, and the same particle can be found in every neuron at the same time. This hypothesis is really hard to deal with," he admitted.

"We've diagrammed it for you on your handout," said LaShauna, "so you'll be able to see . . ."

George stepped into the conversation. "As an enlightened scientist, one who believes when studying nature, especially organic life, that one is studying a design, one may very well also believe that the Designer is a Being unaffected by time, existing outside of our space-time continuum. This belief may be based solely on the observation of creation, that is, what the Designer has accomplished which appears to have taken an unimaginably long period of time."

"Not six days?" asks Allen.

Charlie Shuster slipped into the room unnoticed.

"Oh no you don't," LaShauna said, "The Bible tells us He took six days, so He took six days. Listen now to where the development of the hypothesis is leading us regarding time." She turned to face the entire group and continued. "The experience of time in everyday life conceals its true nature. Time is not a constant. It's dependent upon the relative motion of the observer. Energy, mass, motion and time are all directly related. The mass of an object increases with its velocity, that is, 'm' is directly proportional to D/t," she wrote on the whiteboard, "and energy is equal to the mass of an object times the speed of light squared, $E=mc^2$ or $E=m\ (D/t)^2$," she adds to the board with the dry marker. "Notice how time, 't,'" she circled, "figures into each statement. Since these things are known about the nature of time, it should not be difficult to consider the concept of a timeless or atemporal existence in which events happen in sequence, but with no time between events."

"I read," added George, "that C. S. Lewis once wrote something like this, 'We are so little reconciled to time that we are astonished by the passage of it. We are like a fish which is constantly surprised by the wetness of water, as if it was destined to become a land animal.' What he meant, of course, was that we are surrounded by time like the fish is with water and preoccupied with it because we are, in fact, destined to become atemporal beings."

Joan Kenny nodded and asked LaShauna, "Can I give them the practical example I came up with?"

"This would be a good time," laughed LaShauna. Joan stood up and faced Allen.

"Okay. Now, let's imagine two space vehicles leave earth for outer space."

"Oh, good," said Charlie. "Space stuff."

Allen looked around the room and back to Joan.

"You're in the first one, and Clyde is in the second."

Clyde lifted his head as if to ask, "Why me?"

"The liftoff of Clyde's ship is delayed so that you're exactly 186,000 miles apart when you run the first experiment, and Clyde is exactly 185,717 miles from earth when the second experiment is begun, 283 miles short of 186,000."

Ed silently volunteered to write the numbers on the whiteboard. Joan continued. "On earth there's a megawatt spotlight which can produce a highly-collimated beam, and there's another such light mounted on Clyde's ship. On Clyde's ship there's also a huge, silicon-array photo cell, shaped like a flat donut, meaning that there's a hole in the center through which light can pass. On your ship, there's a similar silicon array without a hole. Do you have it so far?"

Some nodded, and Allen said, "I got it . . . so far."

"Me, too," said Charlie.

"Now," Joan continued, "Let's deal with the alignment of the beams, which haven't been turned on yet, mind you, and the silicone arrays. The light on earth is aimed at Clyde's ship very precisely, and the two ships are aligned so well that the beam of light from earth will strike Clyde's array, generating a signal on board his ship. But some of the beam will pass through the hole in his array and will continue on to strike your array, generating a signal on your ship. Any questions so far?"

"None," Allen said for all of the meeting participants.

"Speak for yourself," said Charlie.

Joan continued again. "The light onboard Clyde's ship can be positioned directly behind his silicon array, and the beam from his light, when so positioned, will both strike his array and yours, just as the beam from earth. Okay, now both ships are moving away from the earth at 17,000 miles per hour, or roughly 283 miles per second. That means the relative speed of the two ships is zero."

"Yes," Allen said.

"They're not moving at all, relative to one another, that is," Charlie said like a scientist.

"All right, here comes the experiment. Both of you have extremely accurate clocks on board, synchronized to perfection, and you're prepared to record the exact time your respective arrays produce a signal from the light beams. When signals are generated by the arrays on the ships, a radio signal is sent to a base station on earth, where there is also an extremely accurate clock, synchronized with yours, to record the time the signals are received."

Joan inhaled and exhaled with deliberation. "You're doing fine," encouraged Gary.

"Experiment number one," she continued. "Clyde positions his spotlight and turns it on. He records the time his array generates a signal from the light, and you record the time your array receives the light and generates a signal. What will be the difference in the times recorded?"

"One second," said Allen smiling. "The ships are 186,000 miles apart, both moving at the same speed, and light travels at 186,000 miles per second."

"Sounds right, of course," Joan said. "Now for experiment number two. The beam on earth is turned on, and Clyde records the time his array generates a signal, and you record the time your array generates a signal. What will be the difference in the times recorded?"

"One second," said Allen, who isn't smiling this time.

"But, Allen," said Joan, "although the two arrays are 186,000 miles apart, your array has moved 283 miles further from where you were when the light passed through Clyde's array, because you were moving at 17,000 miles per hour away from the earth. That means that the light coming from

78

earth traveled 186,283 miles between the two arrays . . . in one second, doesn't it?"

"Well, the speed of light is a constant." Allen said. "It's 186,000 miles per second."

"Then the light beam coming from the earth took longer to travel between the ships than the beam generated aboard Clyde's ship?"

"I don't know," said Allen. "I've lost it."

"Me too," said Charlie.

"Both beams traveled between the ships in one second," Joan explained, "and to you and Clyde, that second was a normal second."

"Here it comes," said Anna.

"But the signals coming back from the space ships to the earth base-station tell a different story. The personnel on earth, of course, compensate correctly for the time the radio signals take to arrive from each ship. They record that it took one second for the light beam from earth to reach Clyde's ship. He was, therefore, at that point, 186,000 miles away. It took 2.0015 seconds for the beam from earth to reach your ship, Allen, since when it struck your array you were 372,283 miles away. That means it took 1.0015 seconds to go from Clyde's array to your array."

"What's wrong with this picture?" Anna quipped.

"For you, Allen and Clyde," she said, addressing them as though they had really made the trip, "the time between events had slowed, relative to the passage of time on earth. What the observers on earth say took 1.0015 seconds took only one second as far as you were concerned. And by the way, when Clyde used his light, they recorded 1.0015 seconds between events also. Travel faster, and the difference will increase. Time is relative." Joan was finished, and she sat down.

"Nice job, Joan," said Gary with a smile.

79

"Very nice presentation, Joan," said George. "Now, LaShauna, how does this lesson on the physics of the space-time continuum apply to what you've been proposing--that there are two states of existence: temporal, in which there is time between events, and sequential, in which events happen sequentially but with no time between them?"

"It's still hard to make a complete connection. We're not even sure the sequential state is part of the space-time continuum, but we believe it is. The mathematics we have fails when one removes time from the equations, as the Big Bang theorists will tell you. But believing that the sequential state is just part of God's creation causes us to think a new mathematics may take over at the . . . line," she emphasized, "between the two states, which is a cue for Gary."

Gary stood and got right to the point. "The neuron is in the temporal state. The particle with which it must communicate is in the sequential state. To enable communications between a temporal component (which expects time between events) and a sequential component (which processes data with no time between events), a third component, if you will, is necessary; one which effectively subtracts or adds time between the data, or events, so to speak. And so we have the need for Jacob's ladder!" he said with excitement uncommon for him, confusing everyone except Anna.

"Jacob's ladder?" she said. "I know Jacob's ladder. Genesis chapter 28, verse 12. 'Then (Jacob) had a dream: a ladder rested on the ground with its top reaching to heaven, and God's messengers were going up and down on it.'"

"Now a Bible lesson!" laughed Charlie. "You guys are amazing."

"Actually," said Gary, "I prefer to call the component an extremely high frequency field. The line LaShauna referred to between the temporal state and sequential state is, in fact, no line at all. There's a field between the two states. Parallata from the cortical neurons pass through the field and

80

are stacked with no time between events in the particle. And vice versa, parallata from the particle are sliced off, a percept at a time, and delivered to the neurons of the cortex, with time re-inserted between events."

"Comprehensible data, making consciousness . . ." George began.

". . . and vision," Anna interjected.

". . . possible," George concluded. "Now connect your hypothesis with the Link phenomenon."

Gary responded. "The hypothesis suggests that during your empirical studies you're causing a percept to be transferred from the test subject's particle, through the field to a cortical neuron-set in the test subject's brain where it is re-experienced."

"Simple as that," Charlie laughed. "Twilight Zone," he added.

"You said, 're-experienced?'" George confirmed.

"Well," responded Gary, "It may have been a first for Anna, but not for the percept."

"I think I'll keep quiet now," said Charlie with an exaggerated grin.

"LaShauna, does your growing hypothesis suggest why the recalled percepts we've recorded so far are from the memories of ancestors? And how did Anna's grandmother's memory of her wedding get into Anna's particle?" George asked.

"Let's take a lunch break now," said LaShauna. "After lunch Dr. Clyde Hart," pointing to Clyde with her open hand, "and Father Christopher," she added, nodding to him, "will address that very question." Her formalized announcement added much mystery to the upcoming session.

Gary didn't go with the others to their favorite local restaurant, even though George volunteered to buy. Instead he headed for his usual Coke and a bag of chips in the company's lunch room. Mike Young was there, eating the lunch his young wife had prepared for him. Gary greeted him warmly, which somewhat surprised Mike, who thought of himself as an irritant to Gary.

"Was that a Link meeting you came from?" Mike asked sheepishly.

"Yup," answered Gary.

Mike nodded with downcast eyes.

"You know," Gary said, "sometimes I think that you think you caused the Link research project. You may one day find out that there are some of us who are glad you bumped into that work station."

"Really?" asked Mike.

"Really," answered Gary. "Me included."

"Can you tell me a little about what's happening?" asked Mike, hoping to hear more about the Link project.

"Nope," Gary said with a smile, returning to his Coke and chips.

"Say, Mike," Gary said to change the subject, but not really.

"Yeah?"

"If you were sitting there in front of me, but only for a microsecond, would I know you're there?"

"You're joking."

"No, not really. If you were in this room and directly in front of me for just a microsecond, would I know you were there?"

"I doubt it," answered Mike.

"If the reason you were only in front of me for a microsecond--and I couldn't see you--was because you were moving so fast, relative to me, what could you do to help me see you?" Gary asked.

"Slow down," answered Mike.

"And what could I do to help see you better, if you didn't slow down?" Gary asked.

"Speed up?" said Mike, wondering if he got it right.

"Interesting, isn't it?" Gary smiled and rose from his seat.

Mike shook his head as Gary left the lunchroom. Not only had Gary suddenly become friendlier to him, he had "*gone weird,*" Mike thought.

Gary waited for the others to return to the conference room. This time the lights were on when LaShauna came in. Gary smiled at her when she saw him and hesitated. On the whiteboard he had carefully and completely summarized the current "Link Hypothesis."

1.   There are two states of existence, the temporal state and the sequential state. In the temporal state events are spaced by time. In the sequential state events are sequential, but not [necessarily--Gary Richardson] spaced by time.

2.   At the functional center of cortical neurons is an atemporal particle of zero mass existing in the sequential state (defining "particle"--a biological singularity).

3.   The same particle is a component of every cortical neuron (the "fabric of the soul"--George Evans).

4.   A state-bridging field ("field") enables communications between the sequential-state particle and the temporal-state (physical) component of the cortical neuron ("Jacob's ladder"--Gary Richardson).

5.   Data from the cortical neurons passes through the field to the particle where it is are stored sequentially and then reflected back through the field to the same neuron-set where it is then received as comprehensible data (enabling

"consciousness"--George Evans, and "vision"--Anna Pierson).

6. The data storage capacity of the particle is infinite, and the particle is able to return "search results" instantly to the cortical neuro-network where the "memory" (a series of percepts) is re-experienced.

The rest of the BioChip team and other attendees filed in and took their seats. The pressure was on Clyde and Father Christopher this time. LaShauna sat with the Empirical team, suggesting that she expected to be a spectator. She thanked Gary for the hypothesis summary, and asked Clyde and Father Christopher to begin. Then she noticed that Gary had added "necessarily" to hypothetical statement number 1, identifying himself as the contributor. She raised her hand to stop Clyde from getting up.

"Gary, what do you mean by the word 'necessarily' in Item 1?"

Gary shrugged his shoulders.

"You're not going to tell us?" asked Anna.

"Not now," answered Gary.

Allen saw his chance. "LaShauna," he said, looking down at his notes on the conference table, "this sequential state. You're going somewhere with this I don't want to go."

"Stay with us, Allen," she responded. "Let me try to make it more comfortable for you. Although time is not involved in the sequential state--or not necessarily involved," she added, looking over at Gary, "an observer still experiences each event in sequence, just as we do in the temporal state. The sequential state, therefore, is not totally different from the temporal state."

Allen cocked his head to one side and looked at LaShauna.

"The experience," LaShauna explained, "of being in the sequential state would not be unlike dreaming. We have all awakened from lengthy, detailed dreams which appeared to

84

have gone on for hours, only to find that according to the clock just a few minutes have elapsed. It was our subconscious mind which was controlling the sequential spacing."

"I've experienced that," Allen offered, feeling a little better about it all.

"In fact," LaShauna continued, "if any one of us were solely sequential state beings, we would appear to have amazing powers. We could move mountains and do it with a tablespoon. Although we would do it one spoon at a time, it would take no time at all to accomplish the task."

"Now you're making me feel worse!" said Allen.

"Then God must be a sequential-state being," said Anna, "and if we were also, wouldn't we be like God?"

"No," Father Christopher answered. "Being in the sequential state would make us unbelievably powerful, but we still could not create from nothing or destroy into nothingness."

"This is fascinating," said Ed, "but tell us again why we need to know about the sequential state?"

"Because by including the concept of the sequential state in the hypothesis, we can explain (1) how one particle can be at the functional center of the nucleus of every . . . cortical neuron," she said with a slight hesitation; "(2) how the particle can have an infinite capacity for data storage; and (3) how the particle can permit the brain to recall a memory almost instantly."

"LaShauna, I think we had better let Father Christopher and Doctor Hart begin their talk," George suggested. "We find the sequential-state aspect of the hypothesis very intriguing, but perhaps you could schedule a discussion meeting for those who are interested, focused on the questions and answers the subject raises."

"I agree, George," said LaShauna. "We could spend all day on this, but what we would really like to do is address the questions you raised just before our break. Gentlemen?"

Clyde got up, followed by Father Christopher. Both appeared to be nervous. Clyde spoke first. "It was LaShauna who really precipitated our development of these next hypothetical statements. She called the two of us aside a few days ago and asked, 'If the particle has infinite capacity for data, transferred to it by the physical brain, what other information might it contain?' She has constantly posed this sort of searching question to the BioChip team during our work, 'What other information might (the particle) contain,' indeed." Clyde looked at Father Christopher, cueing him to continue.

"I've long been bothered," Father Christopher began, "by a related question which has kept me seeking every opportunity to work alongside research people like we have on the BioChip team. The question which has troubled me is: 'How can the single human cell at conception--the zygote--possibly contain all of the information necessary to cause it to develop into a unique, living, thinking human being?' Scientists today still typically respond to the question with an absurdly incomplete answer, that is, 'DNA coding.'"

"The answer to LaShauna's question," continued Clyde, "and the next hypothetical statement we would like to add to the hypothesis, is . . ." he paused and looked at Father Christopher, then back to the group. "The particle," he began again, "contains the source of all necessary information relating to the human cell, including an encoded, perfect likeness (defines hereinafter the word 'likeness' as used in the hypothesis) of the physical body to which the cell belongs. Now, don't confuse the encoded likeness with the imaginary 'homunculus' some scientists like to poke fun of when they hear Christians talking about the soul."

"I won't," said Charlie. Most everyone turned to look at him, and Charlie slid down in his chair.

Clyde, on the other hand, continued without missing a beat. "Biochemists today suggest that the genome is the encoded 'blueprint' of the human being. Hypothetical statement number 7, which I just presented, is only suggesting that it takes much, much more than DNA to encode a human being."

"'What then,' I asked Clyde during our discussions," said Father Christopher, "'is the function of DNA?' He answered without so much as a hesitation that (and this is our hypothetical statement number 8) 'Information from the particle regarding the likeness is filtered, figuratively, through the hereditary traits encoded by the structure of DNA in the nucleus of the cell.'"

"My response," said Clyde, "was not as remarkable as Father Christopher makes out, since the logic was obvious. If the particle contains the likeness, as we say, and DNA encodes the hereditary traits, as most all scientists agree, then the true likeness stored by the particle must be modified by these traits as the likeness information is passed through the nucleus of the cell wherein resides most of the DNA. Temporal factors," Clyde continued, "such as the physical health of the cell and other environmental factors, can affect the communications between the particle and the temporal component."

Gary continued his note-taking.

"Perhaps you can see where we're going?" asked Father Christopher of the participants.

"Nope," said Charlie.

"Ditto," said Allen.

"Conception," said Anna.

"Yes, Anna," said Father Christopher. "Hypothetical statement number 9: 'At the true moment of conception, the particles of both male and female unite, creating a new, unique particle incorporating a perfect likeness of a new and unique body."

Clyde jumped in. "Hypothetical statement number 10: 'Concurrently at conception, the building blocks of DNA from both male and female fuse into the chromosomes of a new and unique cell (the zygote) as controlled by the new particle.'"

"Oh . . . my . . . God," said George slowly.

"Praise Him," Ed Lukin whispered.

"I see you have your answer, George," said LaShauna.

"Memories stored in the particle are passed on from generation to generation at conception," George said, "through the uniting of the parent particles."

Tears began to appear in Anna's eyes. "From generation to generation," she repeated.

LaShauna stood up and faced the group. "Normally," she said, "these ancestral memories cannot be recalled with any clarity, because the exact neuron-set does not exist in the subject with which to re-experience the percepts. You, George, Anna, Ed and Allen, have found a way--partly through the 'accident'--to bring memories to the surface which otherwise could not have been recalled."

"Yes!" Anna said with conviction and tissue in hand, "And because I have no doubt inherited a similar brain structure from my grandmother, I am able, through concentration, chemical enhancements and the neuron-triggering low-voltage pulse from the apparatus, to recall from my particle--from my soul, mind you--the memories I inherited from my grandmother."

"Oh my," Charlie sighed. He understood what Anna had said, and it frightened him. It frightened everyone.

"We have one more bombshell to deliver," said Clyde. LaShauna nodded. "You may have picked up on it already, but someone surely would have spoken up if they had appreciated it fully."

"I can't wait," said Charlie.

"Gary," said Clyde, "would you do the honors?"

Gary moved back to the whiteboard and began changing the phrase "cortical neuron" to "cell" in statements 1 through 4 as others watched. When they saw what he was doing they turned back to Clyde. He continued, speaking slowly and deliberately.

"The particle is at the functional center of <u>every</u> cell, not just neurons, and <u>every</u> neuron is capable of two-way communication with the particle, not just cortical neurons."

Clyde let the concept sink in for a few minutes. He expected questions, and after a few minutes he got what he was waiting for.

"If every neuron in the body communicates with the particle," began George, "and it is the particle which is the repository of all memory, then what is the purpose of the brain?"

Clyde was ready. "It's not the purpose of the brain to remember anything! The brain is the temporal component of the control process. One of its highest-level roles is to facilitate focus, allowing humans to concentrate on the most important parallata returned by the particle."

Gary finished the changes on the whiteboard, sat down and went back to his note-taking.

"Too much to absorb in one meeting," said George, not to anyone in particular. "Let's call it a day."

Chapter 15

George Evans

Dave Kasten, science editor of the *Madison Journal*, returned to interview George Evans.

"Mr. Kasten," George said warmly, greeting him in the reception area. "Good to see you."

"Please, call me Dave," he responded. "Good to see you, too."

"Of course. How are you?"

"Fine, George. Thanks for taking the time."

They continued to talk as they walked down the long corridor to George's office.

"Well, I can't say we aren't too busy, but, frankly, I need a break from the high-tech world once in a while . . . ."

"To talk with a low-tech reporter?"

"Now, that's not what I was going to say," laughed George. "Did you know I'm a flight simulator addict."

"You've lost me."

"It's my hobby. I get away from this high-tech stuff some nights by sitting down at my flight simulator at home," George explained.

"I would think someone in your position would just take the yoke of your corporate jet," Kasten said. "Do you have a license?"

"The answer to both is, 'I'd love to, but my wife won't let me.'"

"Why not?" Kasten asked. "Is she afraid of flying?"

"No, she just knows me too well. I can't concentrate on routine activities. I have trouble mailing a letter. She doesn't want me to fly into the sunset as my mind wanders."

"You're not serious!"

"Oh, yes. And she's right. She can't send me to the store without a lengthy note on what to get and how to pay for it. Besides, I seem to get lost as soon as someone changes a familiar sign on a corner at which I've been turning for years. Zoom, I go right by."

"George, how do you do what you do if you can't concentrate?"

"What I do, Dave, is never routine."

"There must be some things in your day-to-day business management activities which are just plain routine," Kasten suggested.

"Nope. My people have found every last one and have given each task to someone else, or I'd mess it up."

George ushered Kasten into his office with the sweep of his hand. The room was spacious, with a conventional desk for conducting business and a not-so-conventional work surface in the center of the room.

"Well, your ability to run this company with the problem you say you have is certainly a good lead-in to my first question," said Kasten. "What is it you do here?"

"As I said last time we met," George said as he moved around to his desk chair, "we start with a blank piece of paper and create new products for the high-volume consumer-product markets."

"Yes," Kasten said, as he took his seat in front of George's desk. "but I'm here to interview you. I want to know what it is that you personally do here."

George thought a moment. "Dave, I've concluded that my only real contribution these days is getting our creative people to work together . . . doing things they never thought they could do . . . and doing them in a period of time they thought impossible. Now and then, I toss in an idea or a concept. It's fun."

"So, you manage the creative process at Search."

"That's it."

"How did this all start?" Kasten asked.

"Now you've asked a question I can't answer with one sentence and without some technical help," George laughed.

George rose and walked over to the octagon work surface which was the focal point of his office, and he motioned for Dave Kasten to sit at one of the chairs facing three of the open sides. His main work surface was a five-sided affair which wrapped around a circular table. George sat down on his chair, turning toward Kasten as he did so. Gripping one of the arms he caused the chair to rotate about the center of the table. George stopped it when he was still a sociable distance from his guest.

"Neat," said Kasten.

"I offered to have one made for each of our top managers. No takers."

George's fingers gripped the opposite arm, and the room's soft florescent lighting dimmed and a shaded lamp in a ceiling fixture came down to table height, making the room appear much friendlier, but the center table now reminded Kasten of a casino's black jack table.

"Care for a hand of poker?" George laughed, knowing what most people thought at this point.

"That's exactly what the lighting change made me think of!" remarked Kasten.

"I like to do things with lighting to set a mood, change an attitude, warm things up a bit, or sharpen them up, if necessary," George said.

"Impressive. Back to my question." Kasten flipped open his laptop to take notes.

"Rachel and I started this business in Chicago in '82." The press of another button brought down a video monitor, and slides relating to the early years started flashing by. George seemed to ignore the slides and kept talking out of sync with what was being presented. "I'm a manufacturer at heart. I've always liked to see product which I helped design coming down the production lines. I liked to see it in the stores, and I liked the thrill of realizing hundreds of thousands of people thought enough of the design to put their money, plastic or green, down on the barrel head."

"Rachel?" queried Kasten.

"I thought you met her last time you were here. Rachel's my wife." George said.

"Do you have any children, George?" Kasten asked.

"Two. One by a former marriage. He's a professor at Milwaukee School of Engineering. Rachel and I have a girl, Jennifer, who's married to Carlos. You met Carlos last time. He's my son-in-law."

"Well, that's interesting. He seemed very protective of you," said Kasten.

"That's part of his job," George responded. "What about you?" he asked.

"Me?" asked Kasten, taken aback.

"Wife, kids, family?"

"Oh, yes, well, my wife Dorothy and I have been married forever, and we have a daughter who's married and just gave us our first grandchild."

"Boy?"

"Girl. You were saying you're a manufacturer at heart," said Kasten, trying to get back to his interview.

"Yes, well, Rachel and I long since concluded that the best way to benefit from getting the right product with the right features at the right price at the right time to market was to create the concept, and then to license the technology to client-manufacturers, rather than developing it ourselves, making it and marketing it. Too risky, you know," said George.

"Give me some history of what happened next," Kasten said, with his fingers clicking away at his laptop.

"We grew, and here we are." George grinned. Kasten stared at the slides. "In six years we had five businesses. Search International, Inc., which does product research, Northtech Corp., a product engineering group, Technology Marketing, Inc., which markets the product concepts Search develops."

"The intellectual properties?" Kasten confirmed.

"That's right," George said, "and then there's Touch-Control, Inc., which manufactures small, low-cost touch screens for consumer products, while HealthMed, Inc., manufactures a line of bedside health monitoring devices which connect patients with their physicians."

"You guys make HealthMed products?"

"Not here, but yes, we make them. Do you own a color LCD digital alarm clock which lets you touch the numerals to set the time?"

"Yeah. One of yours, too?" asked Kasten.

George nodded. "I'd guess you have a half dozen or so of the products we either make or have licensed others to make. How about exercise equipment? Do you have an Outdoor Action Simulator?"

"No, but my colleague does," answered Kasten.

"Well, we designed that three years ago."

"And licensed it?"

"And licensed it. Do you use a Telcom or an ordinary telephone?"

"Got you there. I use a Telsis, connected to my computer," said Kasten.

"Same thing, except for the software. We did both."

"I'm impressed! I probably owe you guys for my granddaughter," said Kasten.

"Now you're talking about HealthMed. Did your daughter have problems?"

"Yes, not only in trying to get pregnant, but in keeping the pregnancy."

"God seems to use us now and then to answer someone's prayers," said George.

"Is that how you look at it?"

"Most definitely. You don't have to be a Christian to work here, but most of us are."

"To what do you attribute this?" Kasten asked.

"Faith comes from God. No one else. Humans can't truly believe in the atemporal without God's grace, but let me tell you this. What we've learned here together has made it so illogical not to believe in a divine Creator, an omniscient, atemporal being, the Designer of all things, that our people just have to consider God a reality. When that happens, and the individual gives serious thought and time to learning more about God, God does the rest."

"And how does the belief in God translate to a belief in Christ?" Kasten asked, with some growing discomfort.

"Because sending Christ to join us and teach us about the Father is exactly what our God would do," George answered, pointing his finger toward the ceiling.

"George, I'm uneasy talking about religion," Kasten admitted. "I've gone to church all my life, but I don't really think about God much. Can you tell me what it is your people have learned for you to talk so convincingly about a Designer?"

"Take the Health Data Recorder project which your daughter's family benefited from. That's when we started to hire research physicians. I told them, in no uncertain terms, that I wanted them to face each problem with the firm conviction that the human body really does represent a design, contrary to what they had learned in school; that I never wanted to hear the word 'evolution,' unless they were speaking about 'within a species,' because the concept of species to species evolution is so absurd that I would be forced to consider their logic questionable."

"Can you do that? Aren't you opening yourself up to lawsuits?"

"I told them they didn't have to confess a belief in God, just in a Designer. The whole success of HealthMed is based on this--I'm sorry to say, unique--approach. Those who worked on the HealthMed projects saw it all for themselves. There's not an atheist in the bunch."

Kasten's face flushed. George knew he had touched a few soft spots. He was surprised. He hadn't been preaching, just talking about his approach to research. "Maybe we can talk more about God sometime over a beer at the Black Eagle Hotel? How about Friday at 5:00?"

"A beer at the Black Eagle!!!?" Those were Kasten's words, but what he meant was, "Talk about God over a beer at the Black Eagle, where people might hear us!!!?"

"A beer a day is good for you," George said with a smile. "My top research physician Anna Pierson said I should have one every day."

"What has happened here?" Kasten thought. *"What happened to my interview? I'm trying to get inside this guy, and he's getting me to meet with him to talk about God?"*

"Okay, you're on," Kasten heard himself say aloud. "Now, tell me more about your background. What's your degree in? I presume you have a doctorate in . . ."

"No doctorate, Dave. No degree either. Oh, I've taken courses in physics, but nothing really deep."

"Boggles my mind," muttered Kasten, entering this into his laptop.

"Well, if it makes you feel any better, every professional here does have a degree. It just doesn't take one to get people to be creative, and that's what I do."

"So you developed all these businesses in Chicago, then bought the Northland Engineering building, and moved here to Madison?"

"We bought Northland, not just the building."

"Why Madison?"

"Good research people don't want to work and live in Chicago. It's not logical."

Kasten wasn't listening. He had something else on his mind about which he wasn't too comfortable.

"George," he said, "I heard that Scott Dennison joined a medical equipment manufacturer. Are they likely to be a competitor of Search?"

"Not really," answered George. "Most medical equipment manufacturers are primarily interested in high-tech diagnostic equipment. I wish Scott the best."

"Anything more on the Link project?" Kasten asked, trying to catch George offguard.

"Nothing more I can tell you," George said as his face straightened.

"Nothing more you can or will tell me?"

"Dave, I admit to you that the spin-off from the Link project we told you about, and which brought you here to begin with, has generated some very exciting discoveries, but I promise you, when there is more to tell you, I will."

97

"I'm going to hold you to that," Kasten said, rising. "See you Friday night then. A beer might get you to open up."

"Who knows?" George teased. "Thanks for coming in."

"One last question," Kasten added. "You still own the other companies?"

"A small share. They're owned by our employees, but Search is still mine. No one wants the risk," he laughed. "If they ever shoot all of the product liability attorneys, maybe our employees will be interested."

Kasten frowned, grinned, nodded and waved.

"*He's a patient man,*" George thought. "*When this thing breaks, I really hope he's the one who gets the scoop.*"

Carlos lurched into George's office as Kasten walked down the hall. He had expected to sit in on at least the last half of the meeting with Kasten, but had been occupied elsewhere. He looked upset.

"Relax," George said to him. "Everything's cool. I trust the guy. I'm going to have a beer with him Friday."

Carlos said nothing, but began to feel in his gut that the Link research represented a real danger to him and to others he loved, including George and Rachel. It was an irrational fear, but he knew the danger was connected in some way to the news reports which would inevitably disclose the remarkable discoveries which his father-in-law and the Search staff were uncovering. For this reason, Dave Kasten seemed to him to be playing an unwitting role in the dangers which lay ahead. His presence, therefore, aroused Carlos' concern.

Chapter 16

Status Report

Anna Pierson, Ed Lukin and Allen Nolte had made substantial progress in stabilizing the Link test process. George had asked them to provide a status report to him and the BioChip team. The meeting was held in the Link test lab so that the new equipment in use could be seen by all. LaShauna, Clyde, Joan and Father Christopher were mulling around the room chatting with Anna and Allen. Gary stood by the doorway, his notebook supported at his waist by both of his hands. George Evans walked in and ended the tour.

"All right, where are we? Anna, what's your analysis of our empirical progress?"

"Well, George," she began, "Ed, Allen and I have compared notes, and here is how we see the process at the moment. We're now able to reproduce the experience without causing emotional distress. Only one percept is recalled each time, but we can repeat the process only seconds later and obtain additional percepts. The percepts always relate quite exactly to what I'm trying to recall, although there have been some surprises. After I experience a percept, it's hard to concentrate on a subsequent memory. Sometimes I end up recalling a percept of an event which I didn't know was on my mind. I've been intentionally concentrating on memories of events I feel sure would have been experienced by my grandparents. Sometimes I'm wrong, of course. Always--you BioChip members will be thrilled to learn--the percepts recalled are from events which occurred before the conception of the next in line. For example, even though I know the details of certain events in my grandparents' lives which took place after my parents were conceived (I've been reading my grandmother's diary), I cannot recall them with the Link process. On the other hand, if they occurred before my parents' conception, I can usually recall them at will."

"Fascinating, eh, LaShauna?" asked George.

"Fascinating, George," she answered.

"Before I detail the current process for you, Allen is going to tell you about the latest Link hardware we're using." Anna looked over at Allen to cue him.

"The Link is no longer a hand-gripped device." Allen picked up an assembly from the small table behind the revised dentist chair now used during the Link experiments. The video monitor was now on gimbals, hanging from the ceiling so that it could be comfortably positioned in front of the test subject and yet viewed easily by those monitoring the test. The wall behind the monitor and the ceiling above was painted a stark white, leaving nothing to distract the subject.

"We place this device around Anna's biceps, just above the joint. As you can see, it looks very much like a blood-pressure cuff, except that facing the meaty part of her arm . . ."

"My arms are meaty?" laughed Anna.

". . . is this one-inch diameter, donut-shaped ring," Allen continued, responding to Anna's feigned objection with only a smile. "In the ring we have incorporated all of the sensors we had in the hand-gripped Link." Allen picked up a bundled cable, with an overall diameter of about three-fourths of an inch, including a high-pressure hose, two twisted pairs of wires and a thin, white, coaxial cable. "At

100

the center of the ring," he said, "we attach this special terminator, which is a gold-plated high pressure nozzle. The metal nozzle is held by the cuff tightly against the arm, making a good electrical and hydraulic connection."

"Hydraulic?" asked Charlie Schuster, who had just entered through the door.

"Hi, Charlie," called George.

Charlie smiled, and Allen continued. "Through the high-pressure hose and nozzle, we inject the juice, Charlie."

"Oh," he responded.

"Attached to Anna's other arm, at the wrist, is still a standard grounding strap. The ten-volt pulse is applied between the grounding strap and the nozzle. Power to the Link circuit is supplied by one twisted pair, and the data received from Anna's particle--it still really feels strange to say that--is carried by the coax to the recording equipment over there," he finished, pointing to an impressive array at a test station against the wall directly behind the chair, adjacent to the door.

"And the second twisted pair?" asked Gary.

"Oh, yes," responded Allen, "I forgot to tell you about how we monitor Anna's vital signs. On the opposite side of the cuff, facing Anna's inner arm, we continuously pick up her blood pressure and heart rate. That information is carried by the second twisted pair to the recording equipment."

"You can get rid of both twisted pairs and do it all with the coax," said Gary.

"Uh, maybe you can help us with that," Allen answered.

"Thanks, Gary. By all means," said George. "Now, Anna, tell us about the process."

"Okay. A little alcohol is applied to the surface of my 'meaty' arm which will interface with the nozzle. Next the cuff is attached to that arm and the grounding strap to the wrist of my other arm. It's now a very simple procedure to attach the Link to a subject, and the test process is also quite comfortable. We're soon going to ask you, George, for permission to start using other test subjects."

George said nothing.

Anna continued. "Next I begin to concentrate on the memory I want to recall. When I'm ready I nod my head, as before. I don't hear or feel a thing from the Link apparatus. The next thing that happens is that I experience a percept which is extremely vivid--as though I were there--for less than a tenth of a second. It is so vivid, however, I can remember it in detail from that moment on as though it really happened to me."

"It did," Gary interjected.

"Well, yes, it did," Anna confirmed. "The re-experience is that much like a first experience."

"What happens to your blood pressure and heart rate during the re-experience?" Clyde asked.

"It, too, seems to relate to the memory. If I've recalled a difficult situation, my blood pressure and pulse respond to it. If the situation I experience is not tense, my blood pressure and heart rate rise only slightly."

Ed added information that Anna didn't cover. "We no longer use a nicotine patch, but Anna drinks a laced milk shake about an hour before the test. It includes Anna's special sedative, which is working very well. The formula," Ed emphasized, "of the shake and high-pressure inoculation are quite complex and refined now. Its purpose in the test remains the same--to enhance the ability of the test subject to concentrate and recall memories, that is, to enhance the brain's ability to communicate faster and more completely with the particle."

"I assume you've taken all of the precautions necessary to secure the formula and any quantities of the concoctions you keep on hand?" asked George.

"Carlos has been all over the security procedures in place, and he's satisfied."

"Continue, Ed," said George, comfortable with Ed's answer because of his trust in Carlos.

"As you know," Ed said, "the hypothesis suggests that the particle, the repository of all memories, including ancestral memories, is at the functional center of every cell. We believe our tests confirm this."

"Explain," said Gary.

"We're now recording percepts with the Link apparatus attached to Anna's arm. I can assure you, the formula that we administer does not pass the blood brain barrier fast enough for us to obtain the instant results we get."

"Can the process be advanced further?" George asked.

A chill went through everyone, including George. Where was this leading them? The question went unanswered except for a smile from Anna.

Charlie and Carlos left the meeting together. Charlie spoke to Carlos quietly. "I like technological breakthroughs, love being there--and with this company I've been to a few. But this work leaves me feeling uneasy and elated at the same time."

Carlos nodded. To himself he thought, "*I know what you mean, Charlie.*"

Chapter 17

Med-Diagnostics, Inc.

Scott Dennison did not want to move from the area, and there were not many product research and development companies in or near Madison, Wisconsin. He had gotten married just a month before he left Search, and he did his best to find work as a test engineer within a reasonable drive from his home. He had received good electronics training at DeVry, but Scott never pursued an electrical engineering degree. His job at Search had been a blessing. Search had offered variety and he had been given the responsibility of testing the product of a major project, Link. But Scott had a temper and was quick to blame others for things that happened to him, even accidental things. He could not return to Search, because management--that is, George Evans--was, in Scott's mind, responsible for the traumatic experience he had had.

Med-Diagnostics was a manufacturer of portable electrocardiograph and ultrasonic equipment. Their Delavan, Wisconsin, research lab was only a thirty-minute drive from Fort Atkinson, where Scott lived. He planned to leverage his quasi-medical-design experience at Search to acquire a job at Med-Diagnostics. He was pleased to learn that they wanted to interview him a second time.

When Scott arrived at Med-Diagnostics, he was ushered into a small conference room just off the main lobby. Two managers were waiting for him. One was from the company's corporate headquarters in Sweden, the other was an American.

"Thank you for coming in today, Mr. Dennison," they told him almost in unison.

"No problem," Scott answered.

"We are obviously interested in you," said the American.

"Thanks."

"We believe that your recent experience at Search International may be very valuable here."

"How's that?" asked Scott.

"We understand you were involved in the testing of a piece of diagnostic equipment."

"Yea, you could call it that," Scott responded.

"You may not know that Med-Diagnostics is very interested in developing diagnostic equipment to test for early signs of Alzheimer's disease."

"No, I didn't," said Scott.

"It's a growing market, and we intend to capture a large portion of it," said the Swede.

Scott nodded.

"We heard from our source," said the American, "that Search's ongoing Link project deals with memory recall, and as you know the Alzheimer's patient suffers, during the early stages of the disease, from subtle changes in the ability to recall memories."

Scott nodded again.

"Detecting small changes in memory recall," said the Swede, "is very difficult to do. The fact that scientists are not even sure how memories are stored in the brain hasn't made our job of developing a diagnostic tool any easier. If Search has stumbled onto such a device, we'd like to know more about it."

"I signed an employment agreement . . ." began Scott.

". . . with a secrecy clause, I'm sure," the Swede interrupted. "We've assumed that, and we are willing to execute an agreement with you that holds you harmless in the event that Search brings suit against you."

"You indicated on your résumé," continued the American, "that you were the lead test engineer on the Link project."

Scott nodded.

"Why did you leave the company?" the American asked.

"They were careless, and it nearly killed me," answered Scott.

"What happened?"

"I was hooked up to the Link, a scope fell on my hand, and an image shot through my brain," Scott answered.

Both men sat up and looked at each other.

"Are you happy with the salary and benefits package we've proposed?" asked the American.

"Sure," Scott answered.

"Then you'll join us?" asked the Swede.

"When can I start?" asked Scott.

"You already have," answered the American.

Chapter 18

Donors

"Can the process be further advanced?" George asked Anna and Ed, repeating his closing question of the day before. "Can we go back further in one's ancestral memory?"

The two were seated with George in his office at his large work surface. They were prepared to answer his questions.

"Ed believes he knows a way," Anna volunteered.

"Ed?" George cued.

"Are you familiar with functional MRI, George?" Ed asked.

"Magnetic resonance imaging? Yes. Functional MRI? No."

"MRI is primarily interested in a static image of the brain structure. Images are viewed in 2D or 3D renderings. Functional MRI, or fMRI, can deliver both anatomical detail and physiological information, creating a structural and functional model of the brain."

"I see," said George, grasping enough of what Ed had said to wait for the rest.

"It's been known for many, many years that there is a close relationship between cortical neuron activity and bloodflow in the brain. Since this is true, fMRI can show which part of the brain is active when a specific activity is taking place in some part of the nervous system."

"I've seen reports on this process," George murmured.

"The process is actually quite simple," continued Ed. "They inject an isotope to improve the image obtained and take a picture of the brain when the body is at rest. That's the control image. Then they ask the patient to move, say, the fingers of the right hand. They take a second picture of the brain, and through imaging techniques, subtract the control image. What they have left is a picture of the area or areas of the brain involved in the movement of the fingers of the right hand."

"Fascinating, as always, Ed. Fascinating that you know these things, that is," said George.

"Oh, I had some time to kill when you sent me to that medical products exposition in Atlanta, and I sat in on an fMRI seminar."

"Unbelievable," George said, looking at Anna.

"I told my wife that God Himself prepared me for the Link research project," Ed added.

"I believe He did. Anna has said almost the same thing to me about herself."

She nodded.

Ed continued. "In the brain at rest, there is a close relationship between bloodflow and regional cerebral metabolic rates for glucose . . ."

"There's that word again," George interjected.

". . . and oxygen. When the brain is active, regional bloodflow may increase as much as 50 percent, far in excess of the brain's demand for oxygen--which I believe means there is a greater capacity for neural activity possible."

"It would seem so," agreed George.

"The mechanisms controlling this increase in bloodflow are not fully understood," Ed continued, "although they know it involves various brain-produced chemicals, including neurotransmitters such as serotonin, acetylcholine, neuroactive peptides and nitric oxide."

"Okay," said George, accepting the information, but not assimilating it.

"The brain is most active," said Ed, "when a person is under extreme stress. Bloodflow peaks, and some individuals can actually think better. That means their ability to recall information improves. Many top salesmen cannot give a convincing presentation, I am told, unless they are under stress. One guy at the seminar told me he gave presentations to an audience of executives each week about mental healthcare. He became so accustomed to the question-and-answer portion--because he had heard most of the questions before--that his mind was not ready to respond to some unexpected question. So before the meetings began he would try to think of all the things that could go wrong until he had himself sufficiently stressed to be his sharpest."

"You talk to just about anyone when you travel, don't you?" asked George.

"Sure. I learn a lot that way."

"So do I," said Anna. "Continue, Ed."

"I believe that there is yet another neurotransmitter, produced by cortical neurons, which is only present when an individual is under extreme stress. I believe that this neurotransmitter so improves the data rate of the synapse that the brain's metabolization of oxygen, and perhaps glucose, is maximized, fully utilizing the increase in bloodflow."

"--to fully utilize the capacity of the brain," Anna added.

"And how are we going to find this undiscovered neurotransmitter?" asked George.

"Let me ask you, George, at what moment in a person's life do you think his ability to recall memories exceeds all others?"

"For me," answered George, "it was when my grade school teacher asked me a question while I was looking out the window at the robins which had just returned in spring. I felt my face flush, and I gave her such a good answer--when she expected none--that her mouth dropped open."

"Better than that, George," prompted Anna.

"I can't imagine," he said.

"When your life flashes before your eyes!" Ed said with excitement.

George's gray eyebrows raised. "In fear of imminent death?" he asked.

"In fear of imminent death," Anna responded.

Ed added, "People who experience a near-death episode often say they recalled, in great detail, their entire life in just an instant."

"Involuntarily," Anna added.

The three of them paused, searching each other's eyes for individual reaction to what they had been discussing.

"I ask you again, how are we going to find this new neurotransmitter?"

Ed responded slowly. "In the cortex of an individual who died a violent death, knowing that death . . . "

". . . was imminent," George concluded. After another pause he asked, "And where can we find such a cadaver?"

Anna answered. "My husband is the head of neurosurgical research at the University," she said quietly. "He can help us with the search, and he can acquire such a cadaver. Unfortunately, it's not uncommon for individuals to die violently today."

George nodded his head. After a moment of silence he said, "You're authorized to proceed."

Chapter 19

Friday Night

It was George's custom to leave work at 4:30 on Friday afternoons and to stop at the Black Eagle Hotel tavern where many of the local businessmen gathered. He would stand at "his" end of the bar, say hello to friends and acquaintances who would drop by, listen to the chatter of the attorneys who gathered at the far end of the bar, have his two beers, and head home to Rachel and a special Friday night dinner-- usually something barbecued on the gas grill his company had designed for a client. Tonight would be different, as he told Rachel, because Dave Kasten had promised to meet him there at 5:00.

Ed Lukin arrived shortly after George. Ed drank no alcohol, but he liked to sample the selection of non-alcoholic beers, and he was usually ready for some fellowship on Fridays; so he would often stop in at the Black Eagle on the way home to get the local news.

"Hi, Ed," George called to him as he came through the lounge doors.

"TGIF," Ed responded.

"I'm glad you stopped today, Ed," said George as Ed took a stool next to him.

"I can't stay long tonight, but what's on your mind?" asked Ed. "As if I didn't know."

George laughed and nodded. "A simple question has been going through my mind about the Link project."

"A simple question without a simple answer?"

"Right on the head as usual," said George. "Here it is. Should we be doin' what we're doin'?"

"Anna and LaShauna--both good people--think we should," Ed responded immediately.

"Have you asked them that?"

"No. I've known Anna for two years--she lives right down the block from me--and I've known LaShauna for three--she's been over to our house a dozen times. I've worked closely with both. Never have I seen them wrapped up in a research assignment like this one, and neither of them would be, if they didn't approve."

"I understand, Ed. I don't know LaShauna too well, but Anna is already like a daughter to me. At the same time, you and I've been around long enough to know that young people don't always see the whole picture."

"I think these two do," said Ed.

"You think these ladies in their thirties have a grasp on the international ramifications our work may one day have?"

"International ramifications? I thought you were concerned about the ethics involved."

"We've got Padre Chris--excuse me--Father Christopher worried enough about that. No, I'm beginning to think the Link technology we've developed could also be used for evil, great evil."

"What do you have in mind?" asked Ed.

"Intrigue."

"Spy stuff?"

"If, as you and Anna said earlier today, memories of an entire lifetime can be recalled from the particle in just an instant--involuntarily--think of how the technology could be used to get information from some poor soul hooked up to a broadband recorder, just before they killed him."

"That never crossed my mind," said Ed.

"We'd better drop the subject for now," said George, looking over at Black Eagle's front window. "Here comes my date."

"Date!"

"I asked Dave Kasten from the *Madison Journal* to meet me here at 5:00."

"I know about him," said Ed. "Carlos filled us all in."

"Hi, Dave," George called out as Kasten entered the doors.

A little late, he rushed over to where George and Ed were standing.

"Hello, George. How are you?"

"Fine. Dave, this is Ed Lukin. He's the chief chemist at Search."

The two men greeted each other cordially.

"Have you been with the company long?" Kasten asked Ed.

"Twelve years," George answered, trying to cut off Dave's inquiry.

"George," said Ed, "I've really got to get going. Nice meeting you, Dave."

"Yes," responded Kasten, "see you again."

"Have a good evening," Ed said to both, waving as he headed for the lounge doors.

Both men watched Ed pass the window, walking toward Black Eagle's parking lot.

"What's new?" asked George.

"Such a question for a news reporter," laughed Kasten. "Actually not that much. I could use a scoop, like what's happening at Search."

"Link, again?"

"You know me."

"No story yet, Dave, just a lot of meetings, reports and experiments to find out what happened to Scott Dennison."

"No story yet?"

"I think there will be a story for you, sooner or later."

"Promising."

"That wasn't a promise."

"Encouraging, then."

"Okay, encouraging. If a story does develop, I'd like to see you get it first. I think you might present it honestly, without a lot of hoopla and hype."

"Thanks. What will I need to do and when?"

"You'll need to think more often about God."

"'Preachin' already?"

"No, I'm not. The Link research has a spiritual aspect. We have a bioethetist involved," said George.

"I can't make the connection. An accident involving Dennison leads to a bioethetist being called in, and to report on it I need to think more about God?"

"You need to think more about God regardless, Dave."

"Now you _are_ preaching."

"There's a sign in the company's lunch room," George continued. "It says,

'The cosmos did not come from nothing.

Life did not begin by accident.

Oh my God, there is a God!

How then shall we live?"

Kasten smiled.

"Seriously think about that sign, and it'll change your life," said George.

"Some scientists do think that the cosmos came from nothing and life began by accident," Kasten said.

"Can any thinking, logical being really believe that?" George asked.

"I don't," said Kasten.

"Well?"

"Okay, I'll think about it. Now, what's the 'spiritual aspect' of the Link project?"

"You have a daughter, don't you?"

"Yes."

"Does she take after you in any way?"

"Sure, but she looks a lot like her mother."

"Wasn't talking about looks. Do you find that she has an appreciation for some of the same things that you do?" asked George.

"Yeah. We've always been close, and I enjoy showing her things I like."

"Think hard now, Dave. Were you surprised at any time that she had an appreciation for things you like but couldn't remember telling her about?"

"Yes, that's a fact. She came home one day with some jazz music she had just heard and purchased. It was my absolute favorite when I was her age, but there was no way for her to know that. My wife hates jazz, so we've never played it in our home."

"There you go."

"There I go where?"

"How did she inherit her taste for jazz?"

"I don't know."

"We think we do."

"Really? Is it in her genes?"

"Do you seriously believe that a dog wags its tail because of some genetic code? Because if you do, you have the faith to move mountains."

"Okay, I'll bite. Why does a dog wag its tail?"

"It's not in the genes. Another example. Do you remember kindergarten?"

"Here we go again," Kasten said.

"Do you remember the classroom, the teacher or some other feature?"

"Yes, as a matter of fact. I remember all of us kids laying on little mats for a nap. I never slept."

"What color was yours?"

"My what?"

"Your nappie mat."

"Blue on one side and red on the other. The red side was like velour, and the blue side was vinyl. The red side was too itchy and the blue side too sticky. My mother made it. I can still see her sewing it together. She was so disappointed that I didn't like it."

"You remember all of that, and it was how many years ago?"

"Well, I'm 52 . . . so it was 46 years."

"And where has that memory been all this time?"

"You're talking to a science editor. It was stored in my neuro-networks."

"Do you seriously believe that?"

"No."

"Then why did you answer that way?"

"Scientists believe it."

"Scientists may say it, but not many really believe it. Let me tell you what I read some years ago. One group of scientists determined quite accurately that it takes 6 hours for the brain to 'wire' a neuro-network for a skill. Now a skill is something you do over and over, not a one-time event. Who was with me when you came in?

"Ed Lukin, of course."

"He left only ten minutes ago. How could your brain remember it, if it takes 6 hours to wire up a neuro-network?"

"Short-term memories are stored in the cortex," Kasten said.

"How?"

"I don't know."

"We do," George said. "When I asked you about your nappie mat, how long did it take you to recall all those details?"

"Just an instant," Kasten said.

"If all those details were stored on your computer, along with everything else on your hard drive, how long would it take you to find it with a keyword search."

"Probably about five or ten seconds."

"How fast is your computer?" George asked.

"Several gigahertz."

"But your mind was able to bring it up in an instant?"

"It's faster."

"Au contraire. There is no evidence that the brain can operate faster than one kilohertz."

"Well, I don't know how it does it."

"We do. Next question. Who created the human brain?"

"God, of course, the Creator of all of us."

"And is God a physical being?"

117

"No, spiritual," answered Kasten, getting that uncomfortable look on his face again.

"You're a science editor, and you believe that?"

"Yes."

"Well, if God understands the spiritual and can create such a complex organ as the brain, then would He have been limited to the use of the physical when He gave us a mind?"

Kasten just stared at George. *"Was this genius really saying this?"* he asked himself.

"No, Dave, I'm not crazy. Did I whet your appetite?"

"Are you purposely trying to scare me off?"

"Remember the sign in our lunchroom. Once a scientist truly believes in God, it opens up many doors in scientific research which would otherwise be closed to the unbeliever."

The bartender came over to them and asked, "Are you guys going to talk all night or have a drink?"

"Two beers," said Kasten, "and I think my friend will have one, too."

Chapter 20

Noise

After months of work, successes and failures, Anna's husband Michael Pierson and Ed Lukin acquired brain tissue from dozens of 'donors.' Half died violently and half peacefully. Several of the individuals had faced their killers. Two had been executed by drug lords. In the frontal cortex of the brains of those who had died violently an as-yet-unidentified protein was indeed present. Was it the neurotransmitter Ed was looking for? Michael named it "Promaxonin." In the lab dish, it definitely improved the data transfer rate of frog synapses.

"You want me to test Promaxonin? Now?" asked Anna Pierson. "You haven't gone through proper laboratory protocol for testing with humans yet."

Anna and Ed were alone in the Link test lab.

"It's up to you, Anna," said Ed. "We know how many parts per million we found in the donors' brains. We can start with a solution 10 to the minus 4 in concentration, and we can give it to you topically."

"No injection?"

"No. In fact, I've developed a topical paste to take the place of injecting the juice as well. There won't be <u>any</u> injection."

"How is a topical application on my arm going to reach my cortex?"

"It isn't," Ed answered.

"No?"

"I would like to direct this test toward the concept of hypothetical statement 2: 'At the functional center of <u>every</u> <u>cell</u> is an atemporal particle of zero mass existing in the sequential state.' It'll be safer to start there."

Anna paused, but began to nod her head. "I agree," she said. "When?"

"I can have my part ready tomorrow afternoon," said Ed.

"Have you talked to George and Allen?"

"Yes," answered Ed, "They wanted me to talk with you alone first. No peer pressure from the other team members," he explained.

"Tell Allen he can get the test ready," said Anna.

When George Evans entered the test lab the next afternoon, he remarked how different the setup looked without the high-pressure hose extending from the blood pressure cuff. The cuff now looked quite ordinary, except for a single coaxial cable leading to the test panel behind the comfortable dentist chair in which Anna was seated. Gary had helped Allen to accomplish this change.

The topical paste was applied to the donut-shaped Link, and the cuff was attached to Anna's arm. As Allen was connecting the grounding strap to Anna's left wrist, she let out a scream.

"Allen, get it off!"

"Did I pinch you?" Allen asked.

"No, the cuff, get it off!" she screamed again, tearing at the cuff's Velcro with her free left hand. Her right arm was jerking uncontrollably, making that difficult.

The cuff was removed, but Anna was still clearly agitated. "Get me a wet cloth. You've got to get that paste off my arm," and she leaped from the chair to do it herself, crashing into Ed, who was on his way to her with a moist towelette. She grabbed it from his hand and wiped aggressively at the spot where the chemical had been applied. When she was satisfied that all of the paste was removed or diluted, she leaned back against the arm of the chair and held her head in her hands, shaking her head slowly from side to side. Ed's face was white. George and Allen stood silently in shock. *"What had gone wrong before the test even began?"* they all wondered.

"Oh, brother," Anna finally said. "It was terrible. As the paste was absorbed into my skin I began to hear a deafening, painful noise, a steady rushing sound on top of a full range of horribly loud tones, like every key on a church organ played at the same time with every stop pulled out. At the same time I saw a brilliant and continuous array of flashing colors. I've never experienced anything like it, nor was I ever so scared I would lose my mind at any moment."

The test was aborted as a failure, but the experiment was a success. The paste containing Promaxonin had caused all of the sensor neurons just under the epithelial cells of her skin to achieve a hyper-efficient data transfer rate to the particle, bypassing the modulating effect of the brain.

Chapter 21

Carlos and Family

It was that time of the summer when families got together for backyard picnics. This summer was no different, and Jennifer Martinez had invited her parents to join her and Carlos for an outdoor-cooked meal, always a favorite of George and Rachel. It was the perfect sunny afternoon, with not a cloud in the sky.

"Couldn't ask for better weather," said George to Carlos as he stepped out of his "travel vehicle," as he called it. George liked to move about in a 23-foot converted GMC motor home, built 40 years earlier, but rebuilt by George from its aluminum "airframe" up. It had every means of communications equipment on board to keep him in touch with Search personnel. People worked at Search 24 hours a day, almost every day of the year. In recent years, George had begun to keep more reasonable hours for himself and Rachel. Family activities always came first.

"Beautiful," Carlos answered as he extended his hand to Rachel as she too stepped down.

"Was that a compliment?" she joked.

"Well, ah . . . of course, Rachel. You always look good. Too good for that old guy," he said, pointing toward George, who was headed up to the house where Jennifer was standing.

"Hi, honey," George said, smiling at Jennifer.

"Hi, Daddy," she answered, and opened her arms for a big hug. "Why don't we go right out back," she suggested.

"Great," George answered.

Their new country-style home was large, but on a treeless lot in a new development. They had recently built an arbor for their patio, and flower baskets hung all around it. The electric grill--yes, developed by Search--was already roasting a large chicken, and it was apparent that either Carlos or Jennifer had been sitting alongside shucking corn.

"Corn!" George exclaimed. "Terrific."

"Dad, we have the same food for this picnic every year--but you're surprised?"

"Do we?" asked George.

Carlos and Rachel arrived, coming around the corner of the house. Rachel was carrying flowers that Carlos had picked for her on the way. They were a very close family, and today was going to cement the relationships as never before.

"Grandpa, Grandma, Grandpa," the children called, as they came through the back patio door.

"Hey, kids," George responded. "How're you doin'?"

Hugs went all around.

After the meal the children went to play toward the back of the lot where Carlos had constructed a most unusual sandbox-slide-swing-rocketship-clubhouse, in and on which the children seemed to spend every hour of daylight and a few later than that. The two adult couples sat on cushioned wooden chairs around a circular picnic table. Fresh iced tea had just been poured.

"Relaxing, very relaxing," George said.

"And you needed it," said Rachel.

"Things tough at work, Daddy?" Jennifer asked.

"Not tough," George answered, "just . . ." He didn't know how to phrase the thoughts which began to go through his mind. It started with images of his people--Anna, Ed, LaShauna, Joan, Clyde, Gary. Never before did he feel so responsible, and for what? He couldn't describe the risk he had undertaken, exposing them to pressures and experiences he didn't even understand.

"Daddy?" Jennifer called, seeing him drift off.

"Yeah, tough," he agreed.

"Why," she asked, "what's going on?"

George looked at Carlos, hoping to see his usual reassuring expression. Carlos' eyebrows were up in anticipation of George's response.

"What has Carlos told you?" he asked, trying to avoid the possibility that Carlos had not been filling his daughter in on the details of the Link project.

"Oh, I know about Link," she answered, as usual reading her father's mind. "Is it that disturbing for you?"

"Yes, it is," answered Rachel.

George always told Rachel everything that had happened that day over dinner in a ritual which began by his describing in detail who he had met as he walked in the door of the reception area. Rachel had worked with George every day from the beginning until they built their special home ten years ago.

"I'll stay home and work on making this ultramodern castle into a real home," she had said to him one day, and she had never returned to work. To keep abreast, she wanted George to tell her everything that had happened each day, which now was more of a ritual that helped George relax, since Rachel was no longer that interested in the business.

"When you've seen a hundred inventions," she would tell friends, "you've seen them all." George held over 100 patents, and she just couldn't muster the excitement of a new one anymore, not like she had felt when they first began. The Link project, however, had her concerned and interested.

"We may be on the brink of discovering scientific evidence that humans, in fact, have a soul," he had told her not long ago, which began and ended his report for that day.

"Daddy?" Jennifer called again.

"I'm sorry, honey," George looked puzzled. Had he missed something?

"What is it about the Link project that's so disturbing?"

"What isn't?"

"Tell me."

"This project is so difficult, so deep, so exciting, so earth-shaking, mind-blowing, that I look on it as the biggest, best and last project of my career," George answered. "At the same time, I am not at all sure we should be doing it."

Never had Jennifer heard her father talk like this about his work. Consumer product research had never been "earth-shaking" or "mind-blowing." Her father had developed common things like hair dryers, fax machines, cooking appliances--nothing that would change the world.

"Why shouldn't you be doing the Link project? A new computer mouse? What's so deep about that?" Jennifer asked.

"You know that it links the brain directly with a computer?" George asked, searching for how much Jennifer really knew.

"Sure, but you told us that you saw something like it, after you began the project, demonstrated by an Israeli engineer at a medical show," she answered.

"That's right, I did, but we've gone a lot farther then the Israelis did."

"How much farther?"

"Jennifer," George answered, "we believe we've discovered the true repository of one's memory."

"The brain?" Jennifer joked. "You've discovered the brain?"

"No, honey. The repository is stored in an atemporal particle of no mass and infinite capacity at the functional center of every cell." He just blurted it out.

"English," Jennifer said.

"*Is she ready for this?*" George thought. This was his little girl.

"Well?" Jennifer pressed.

"Memory is stored in the soul, and we can tap it!"

"Soul? Tap it?"

"At first by accident, and now after months of intense research, we can obtain a single percept from a cell, if the test subject concentrates."

"Obtain? Percept?" Jennifer was growing impatient now.

"We can literally record the instantaneous image of a memory on a video disk."

"That's fantastic!" Jennifer said. Rachel was not smiling, and Jennifer noticed.

"Now think about where I told you memories are stored," George added.

"You're joking now." No one was smiling except Jennifer.

"No, Jennifer, we can record what is stored--one percept at a time--in a human's soul."

Jennifer's eyes were wide, but she wanted information.

"Percept?" she asked.

"Just a single instant of a memory--an image, a scent, a musical note, a sad feeling, fear, pain."

"All recorded on a video disk?"

"No, all re-experienced by the offspring of an ancestor."

"Oh, you lost me now." Jennifer was becoming very uncomfortable, not just more and more curious.

"The memories we've recorded thus far, which were re-experienced in full detail by Anna Pierson, our test subject, came from her ancestors. She saw, heard, smelled and felt everything through the senses of her grandmother."

"Oh, Dad, this is too weird." She glared momentarily at Carlos for not telling her before.

"It's all true, and our research is going even further."

"What?" she demanded.

"Honey," said Carlos, "I was going to explain everything as soon as I understood it myself. I still don't. So what could I say? Your dad isn't even sure we know what we're doing at Search. Anna Pierson is probably unsure herself after today. I wonder how her husband feels about the tests now?"

"What happened today?" Jennifer had always been a persistent questioner.

"We know what happened. She's ok," said George.

"What?" Jennifer demanded again.

"From a single cell she saw a blinding flash and heard a thunderous roar," Carlos said.

"From a cell in her eye? Her ear?"

"From a cell on her arm," George said.

Jennifer paused, and then she said, "Nothing in my education has prepared me to understand what it is you're telling me."

"Nor in mine," said George. It flashed through everyone's mind that George's education had principally been the very process of doing what had never been done before. He had learned to be comfortable with the role of being asked to do what others had failed to do. But now he was clearly uncomfortable with the work of this project, so uncomfortable that he had considered it the last project of his career.

"I no longer support the project," Rachel told Jennifer, looking also at Carlos and George. "Is tapping the memories of our ancestors stored in our soul something God wants us to be doing?"

"Anna and LaShauna said this in response to that very question from me," answered George. "You haven't heard this, Rachel. They said that, 'Man will finally realize, from our work, that the soul truly exists and can be understood as part of the body-soul unity we all are. Secular scientists, many of whom profess to be atheists, will for the first time have to deal with the spiritual aspect of man. Our work must continue.' Ed Lukin told me that both women said pretty much the same thing to him."

"You run the company, George. What do you think?" asked Rachel.

Jennifer looked at her father, who had his eyes down, staring at the iced tea in his hands.

"I'm but a bystander on this project. Perhaps that's why it should be my last."

"There is something thrilling about our work," said Carlos, "and something dangerous as well."

"In what ways?" asked Rachel.

"I'm not talking about what Anna experienced today. I feel confident Ed and Anna know what they're doing and are taking every precaution. That's why she wasn't injured."

"Then what are you saying, Carlos?" asked Jennifer.

"George, tell her," said Carlos.

George knew what Carlos was referring to. Since Carlos was responsible for every aspect of security at Search, George and Ed both told him what George had said to Ed at the Black Eagle. He certainly wasn't going to repeat it in detail now.

"The military, foreign and domestic, the FBI, CIA, and all those involved in intrigue, could abuse the technology we're developing." He stopped there.

"I'm against it, too," said Jennifer, siding with her mother. "Destroy everything and swear your people to secrecy."

"And what about the good Anna and LaShauna believe it will do?" asked George.

"It's just too risky for today. Maybe when people stop killing each other over money, power and control, such research will benefit mankind," said Jennifer.

"That's how I feel also," said Rachel. "That project is going to change lives, but not for the better."

The children out back began to argue, and Jennifer got up to settle them. The sky had darkened early because a storm front was on the horizon.

Chapter 22

American History

"I've called you all together," George began, "because the Link research project needs a new volunteer to further test the process. We must draw from members of the theoretical team and empirical team for our next volunteer, because no one outside of you people know what is involved."

There was no immediate response. Some flashed back to Scott Dennison's experience. Others considered that they would need the bravery of Anna to volunteer. George stood at the head of the conference table in Search's large conference room.

He continued, "Now you know how Anna and Ed have constantly improved the process. They tell me, and I have no reason to doubt their word, that the experience has become very benign. You may even enjoy it."

"I'd be happy to try it," volunteered Joan.

Gary looked over at Joan and shook his head to say "no," almost imperceptibly.

"Hang on a minute, Joan," said George. "We have some specifications for the next volunteer. You may qualify, but listen to what Anna and Ed have to say about the ideal candidate."

"We are hoping to find someone," began Ed, "who has a family tree they can document leading back at least ten generations."

"200 years?" someone asked.

"200 or more years," responded Anna.

"I'm more interested in thinking in terms of ten generations," said Ed. "If that's 200 years or 250 years, it doesn't matter. The ten generations would start with your parents, not with you."

"If you have long-term American history in your family's background, " said Anna, " that could mean we will need your family tree to go back to the time of the Stamp Act."

"Well, that leaves me out," said Father Christopher. "My Braun surname is German, and my family has been in America only since 1916, just before World War I."

"I think I'm your candidate after all," said Joan. "I assume it's ok if the ten generations are on my mother's side?"

"Yes, of course," said Ed.

"Well, Mom's maiden name was Otis, and after she told me we were related to James Otis, I took an interest--I love history anyway--and I researched our family tree right down to my mother."

"Sounds good, Joan," said Anna.

"Who's James Otis?" asked Allen.

"An American statesman and orator. He was killed by lightning," answered Joan.

"Something he said?" asked Allen. Everyone laughed, including Joan.

"He was elected to the Massachusetts Assembly in 1761, as a matter of fact, at the age of 35. His son Jacob was born the year after. I can go right down the list for you."

"Please do," said Anna.

"Well, next came Joshua in 1780."

"All names starting with J--James, Jacob, Joshua?" Gary asked, smiling at Joan.

"No, that ended with Elisha Graves Otis, born in 1811."

"Hey, I know him," said Allen. "He invented the elevator."

"Not exactly, but his didn't fall when the cables broke. Elisha's son, in my line, was named James, after the orator, and he was born in 1841."

"Any more famous ancestors?" asked Ed, thrilled because they had identified such a well-documented candidate.

"Not a one," said Joan. "Next was John, 1866, David, 1885, and Solomon, in 1910. Next came my grandpa, Paul, in 1939, then my mother, Ruth, in 1960."

"That's amazing, Joan," said George. "How could you remember all those dates?"

"Numbers." answered Joan. "I've got a thing for numbers, as you know, George."

"That's ten generations," said Ed. "Terrific! Now, what do you know about them?"

"I know a lot about James, the orator, and Elisha, the inventor. They're in the history books. My great grandpa, Sol, died just 10 years ago, so I know some things about him. My grandpa and mother are still living. They will remember, or maybe I should say, 'they will be able to recall' something about David, and maybe John."

"Sounds good, Joan," said Ed. "We're going to ask you to do some more research on the events in your ancestors' lives, and even what was happening in the news during their time."

"Fine, no problem."

"Can we have it on Monday?" asked Anna.

"You've got it," Joan responded, clearly enthusiastic about her new role.

"Are you allergic to anything in particular?" asked Anna.

The question caused Joan to pause. The reality of what she had just volunteered for came forward in her mind. "Nope, not a thing, Anna."

"Do you plan to test on Monday, Anna?" asked George.

"Tuesday. We will want to spend a day with Joan and her report to select the memories she will recall and to study them."

A chill went through Joan, but everything still sounded exciting to her. Sort of like the time she had volunteered to be one of the first to ride the new Eagle roller coaster at the theme park. Then the question came to her. *"Why do they want my history to go back so far?"* she thought. *"Up till now Anna re-experienced only her grandmother's memories. Could they be planning to take me back further. I'll bet they are!"* The chill returned.

On Monday morning Anna greeted Joan as she entered the Link test lab. "Good morning, Joan."

"Good morning, Anna. Are we going to meet here?"

"Yes. We thought it would be best to get you to talk about your history here, so that when you concentrate on a single memory the different surrounding won't distract you. Look, we've added a little sitting area."

Joan turned in the direction that Anna had pointed and saw a comfortable-looking settee, a basic love seat, two chairs and a coffee table. There was a thermos of coffee there with a plate of Anna's favorite pecan sandies.

"Nice," Joan said and moved toward the settee with Anna. After they were comfortable, they had a cup of coffee and talked about Anna's grandmother's wedding dress. The dress was still in its box on the main conference table, along with a printout of Anna's percept, for everyone to see. Ed walked in and quietly joined them. He poured himself a cup of coffee and stirred in a heaping teaspoon of sugar.

Anna changed the conversation to the subject at hand. "Well, Joan, did you bring your report in with you?"

"Yes."

"Can we go over it?"

"Sure."

"Why not just talk it through informally in your own words," said Ed.

Joan agreed and pulled a few violet index cards from the pocket of her slacks. "This will sound like American history. I'm proud of that fact," she said.

Joan thought a moment and began. "James Otis was born in West Barnstable, Massachusetts, became a lawyer, statesman and orator. He's best known for arguing against the Writs of Assistance in the Massachusetts Assembly in 1761. He had turned 36 by then, a year before his son Jacob was born. Prior to that he was leader of the Boston Bar and advocate general when the revenue officers demanded his assistance in obtaining, from the superior court general, search warrants allowing them to enter any man's house in a search for smuggled goods. He refused, of course, setting the stage for his discourse for which he became known."

"Interesting. And what memory would he have passed on to you which you would like to try to recall?" asked Ed.

"I knew it!" said Joan. "You expect me to go back further than Anna did with her tests."

"Does this change your mind about being our next volunteer?" Ed asked. "It's up to you, you know."

"No, it doesn't," answered Joan. "I'm prepared, as you'll see." She immediately went on with what she had planned to say about James Otis. "James had strong feelings about the rights of the colonies. He gave an impassioned speech before the chief justice of the Massachusetts Assembly in 1761. The moment was certainly etched in his mind and passed on through generational memories. I want to concentrate on that scenario."

"Good," said Anna.

"Great!" added Ed.

Joan continued. "Jacob, born in 1762, also lived out his life in Boston. He was 14 in 1776. He might just have witnessed the British evacuating Boston. Perhaps, I envision, from a narrow second-story balcony, he saw the troops and heard the shouts and footsteps. I want to concentrate on that possible scenario in his life."

"You have prepared well. Please continue," Anna said.

She did. "Joshua, born in 1780, was married in 1805 and moved with his young wife to Vermont, where Elisha Otis was born in 1811. Joshua was nine when George Washington became president, but political leaders did not impress me when I was nine, so I won't try to recall that. He was 13 when Washington was re-elected. Same answer. Though he couldn't vote, I'm going to take the chance that Joshua remembered the election of John Adams with Thomas Jefferson as vice president. He was 17. I imagine that Adams and Jefferson traveled to Vermont prior to their election, and I picture my ancestor with his father, Jacob, watching Adams speak in the town square on a platform, stage or gazebo."

"You're incredible," said Anna. "I think this is going to go very well."

Joan smiled and continued. "James II was born to Elisha in 1841, when Elisha was 30. Since he was old enough to own the factory in which he invented the safety device for elevators, I assume James was already conceived. However, elevators no doubt needed rubber boots and bumpers of some kind, so Joshua probably was keenly interested in Goodyear's invention of vulcanized rubber, patented in 1839. Before that, industrial rubber products had a very poor life, and being interested in safety, Elisha certainly discussed the advancement with his engineers, perhaps over a workbench or something. I'll concentrate on Elisha and Goodyear's invention."

"Next?" Anna was now taking notes.

"James II lived from 1841 to 1921. His son John, in my line, was born in 1866. So I researched the years 1861 to 1865. What would James have witnessed?" Joan paused and looked at Ed.

"Ah, my mind's a blank," answered Ed. Joan and Anna laughed.

"Abraham Lincoln!" Anna said to Ed.

"That's right!" Joan said. "He was elected in 1861 and re-elected in 1864, when on April 14, 1865, he was shot to death by John Wilkes Booth. My grandpa often tells me how the death of President Kennedy affected everyone in America, so I'm certain there was a moment when James first heard of Lincoln's assassination, a moment which was etched in his memory. That's not technically correct, is it?" she asked, referring to her words, "etched in his memory."

"Guess not," said Ed.

"Doesn't matter," said Anna. "What's next?"

"Well, the Brooklyn Bridge was opened when John was 17, and the great floods in the Ohio Valley occurred in 1884, when he was 18, but I'm betting that sensitized him to really be tuned in to the Johnstown flood in 1889, when he was 23. John was also married when he was 18, and David was born in 1885. Even though he was only 15, I'm betting David was very impressed by the turn of the century. He was probably allowed to stay up for the New Year's Eve party. Pop-Pop, my great-grandfather, was born in 1910. He was very affected by the Great Depression in 1931, and he moved his family to Wisconsin the following year, looking for work. He was a lineman for the power company in

Milwaukee County. Sol was always a cautious man, and I think it was the Depression which he remembered best."

"Got it," said Anna, writing and calculating furiously.

"My grandpa, Paul, was born in 1939, and was only two when World War II broke out. He says he doesn't remember any of it, but clearly remembers listening to the atomic bomb tests on the island of Bikini in 1946. His family listened to a live report on the radio, he said. He also remembers, as if it were yesterday, when he bought his first car--a 1954 Ford-- but I think I'll try to recall the bomb test."

"Why?" asked Anna.

"I've pictured the scene. Pop-Pop and Mom-Mom and Grandpa Paul, as a seven year-old boy, sitting around their old Philco, or whatever, listening to such an event together. Yes, I think that will be a recallable memory."

"I agree," said Ed.

"That leaves my mom, Ruth. If I'm going to be a volunteer, I want to experience something no one else has ever experienced."

"And what is that?" asked Anna.

"I want to be present at the birth of my older sister, Pam."

Ed began to say something, but stopped to think again about Joan's request.

"Why not?" said Anna with a smile.

"My dad died when I was two," Joan went on to explain. "He was present at Pam's birth, in 1979, and mine in '81. I'd rather recall my mother's memory of my birth, but that wouldn't be stored in my particle. Seeing Pam the moment my mother first saw her with my father looking on might tell me more about what he was really like. Mom says he was always very supportive."

"Ok," said Ed, rather business-like. "Let's go over the list Anna has made. Then we'll talk about each recall at length, break for lunch and pick up on it again this afternoon. What do you have Anna?"

Anna had prepared the following detailed list:

James I	1761		249	1.000
Massachusetts Assembly				MA
Jacob	1776	15	234	.940
British evacuation		Balcony		MA
Joshua	1797	21	213	.855
Adams's speech		Town square		VT
Elisha	1839	42	171	.687
Goodyear invention		Lab bench		VT
James II	1865	26	145	.582
Lincoln's death		First heard?		VT
John	1889	24	121	.486
Johnstown flood		Newspaper?		VT
David	1900	11	110	.442
Turn of the century		Party		VT
Solomon	1931	31	79	.317
Great depression		Radio/paper?		VT
Paul	1946	15	64	.257
Atomic bomb - Radio with family				WI
Ruth	1979	33	31	.124
Birth of Pam		Hospital		WI

Anna turned the list so Ed and Joan could see it.

"Hmm. I see you have listed the dates of the events, followed by the number of years since the last event, followed by the number of years which have elapsed since the event from today, but what is the decimal figure which follows that?" asked Joan.

"You're quick," said Anna. "The decimal value is the factor we will use to calculate the strength of the special chemical we plan to administer to you. Ed will explain."

"Joan," began Ed, "we plan to start the test by having you concentrate on . . ." he checked the list again, ". . . your ancestor John Otis and the Johnstown flood."

"Halfway back?"

"That's right," answered Anna.

"We've developed a means to have you inhale a newly discovered neurotransmitter which Anna's husband has named Promaxonin. It is in a form which very quickly passes the blood-brain barrier, and it naturally dissipates or breaks down after it is in your brain for only a few seconds. There is no build-up of the neurotransmitter in the brain at all. Therefore, we can let you inhale it continuously and very accurately adjust its concentration in your brain by adjusting the concentration going into your lungs."

"What's the purpose of my inhaling Promaxonin?" Joan asked Anna.

"It will make your cortical neuro-networks function much faster by an order of magnitude."

"For how long?"

"Everything will return to normal in seconds after we stop the atomized flow," said Ed.

"How will I feel when I'm on it?"

"It'll give you a wonderful, clear-headed feeling. I tried it yesterday after we met with you," said Anna.

"A rush?" Joan asked Anna.

"I have nothing to compare it with," said Anna.

"And how will you adjust the concentration to start?"

"We have a good idea of where to begin, based on Anna's experience, but we plan to adjust it by trying to get you to recall an event which occurred halfway through the ten generations with good clarity. Then we will decrease the dosage and come forward in time. After that we will be able to calibrate the concentration with greater accuracy for you in particular."

"And after that?"

"We can start with James II and gradually go back to memories stored by James I," Anna answered. Her eyes lit up as she spoke.

Joan thought for a moment, and Ed immediately asked, "Are you certain you want to go through with this?"

"Absolutely," she answered without hesitation.

Chapter 23

July 4th

"I am honored and pleased to stand before you this day," began the senator, standing on the steps of the Capital and in front of the largest recorded gathering of the Women's Right to Choose League. With a large warm smile she continued, "It is the day on which we celebrate our freedom--freedom from tyranny. We celebrate the self-evident truth that all men and women are created equal, and that no one has the right over the body of another, and that even a young woman, caught in an unwanted pregnancy, has the right to life, liberty, and the pursuit of happiness.

The roar of applause echoed amongst the wings and steps of the stone building. The senator's face darkened as she looked down at her notes.

"To secure these rights," she said, "governments, deriving their just powers from the desire of the governed, learned today through electronic polls, institute laws to prohibit those who desire to force their beliefs on others. And, when any ruling body--township, city, county or state-- becomes destructive of these basic rights, including the right to choose, it is the right and even obligation of the people to take matters in their own hands in such a way that shall seem most likely to effect the safety and happiness of all women and all men.

"Prudence indeed demands that laws, such as those resulting from the case of *Roe v. Wade*, long established and supported by the majority, should not be changed because of the pressures from the few, out of touch with the will of the many. But when a long train of abuses evidences a design to take away the right to choose, now supported by the laws, it is time to take drastic action to see that our rights are not usurped in any way.

"Yes!" the crowd shouted, and applause followed.

"If demonstrations prevent your loved ones from receiving the medical care they need, you have a right to stop the demonstrators from doing so. If your loved ones are made to feel guilty, for terminating the continued growth of conception products taking place within their bodies, and thereby destroying their happiness, then you have the right to stop those spreading lies about the reproductive process and to keep them away from all who are already in torment for having found themselves in need of a legal and safe abortion.

"Let us stand up and declare our independence from the intolerant."

The crowd began to cheer and applaud.

"Let us stand up and declare our independence from the extreme religious right. Let us stand up and face them eye to eye, those who desire to take from your loved ones the right to control what happens within their own bodies. Then we can truly celebrate our independence--independence from tyranny. Thank you, and God bless America."

The cheering and applause became thunderous. The senator smiled broadly, raised her fist, and turned from left to right, scanning the crowd.

Chapter 24

Family Snapshots

Joan arrived at the Link test lab at 9:00 on Tuesday morning and found Allen, Anna and Ed preparing for the test.

"Good morning," she called out as she entered the room.

Ed and Anna looked up and smiled. "Good morning, Joan," said Allen.

"Joan, Allen is going to explain the entire process to you," said Ed, "but first I want to know again whether or not you still want to go through with this test?"

"Yes, Ed," she said with some insistence. "Give me the lowdown, Allen," she said to get the process moving forward.

"We'll start the test at . . ." Allen checked his watch, "10:05, which gives you 5 minutes to down the Link milkshake." At her quizzical look, he elaborated. "You need to drink it an hour before the test begins."

Joan took it from his hand, looked down into the container, and put it to her lips to start drinking. "It has a funny odor," she said.

"It's the nicotine," said Allen. "It doesn't taste bad. Besides real vanilla ice cream, the shake contains an ingestible nicotine, glutamic acid, and Anna's special sedative."

"Sedative?"

"You won't get drowsy. It'll just relax you," said Anna.

Joan began drinking the concoction. "What else, Allen?"

"We add a special paste which contains caffeine, citric acid, and glucose to the donut-shaped Link." Allen picked up the Link cuff assembly and pointed to the smear of paste on the shiny Link surface. "This we attach to you like so," and he wrapped the cuff around Joan's biceps.

"It's cold."

"Sorry. Next I ask you to sit down while we complete preparations."

Joan walked over to the "dentist's chair" and slid onto it and got comfortable.

"Now I attach this small coaxial cable to the cuff, and if you turn your head around, you'll be able to see I'm already recording your heart rate. It's 85. Not too bad."

Joan turned, looked and turned back.

"Next we attach this grounding strap to your left wrist. Did I understand that your ancestor, James Otis, was electrocuted?"

"Allen!" Anna said loudly.

"Just a joke, Joan, just a joke. You won't get a shock. I guarantee."

"I'm ok, Anna," said Joan.

"Last of all I am going to slip this oxygen set, called a nasal canula, over your head and position the tubes just inside your nostrils . . . maybe if you push your hair behind your ears this will lie more comfortably."

"Ok, Joan," said Anna. "We just want you to relax now. We'll start the test in about 45 minutes or so. Ed and I will be working around you, but just try to ignore us and relax."

"I have earphones and music for you, if you'd like," said Allen.

"No thanks," Joan replied. "I'll just sit quiet."

For Joan it was like waiting in the reception area for the dentist's assistant to call her into the little cubical where all the work is done, or lying in a hospital bed waiting for the orderly to take her into the operating room. She knew the theory behind the Link process, but this wasn't theory that she was about to experience. She thought of Scott Dennison's reaction after the accident, and she remembered seeing Anna lying on the floor with Clyde Hart hovering over her. *"Why did I volunteer?"* she asked herself.

"Are you ready?" Anna asked Joan in almost a whisper.

Joan looked up and into Anna's eyes. *"Could such a sweet person put me in any danger?"* she asked herself. "I'm ready, Anna," she said in a confident voice. "Is George Evans going to observe the test?"

"No, he felt you would relax better without him here," said Ed.

"The opposite is true," said Joan.

"We'll meet with him and the rest of your BioChip team tomorrow," said Anna. "Ed and I have been talking," she continued, "and what we would like to do first is give you a very . . . easy, simple experience. We're going to ask you to concentrate on the day you graduated, the day you received your bachelor's degree in math. I'm sure your mother was there."

"And my grandpa."

145

Anna nodded. "And I suppose you walked up on stage, received the rolled diploma . . ."

". . . Blank parchment," Joan smiled.

"And shook hands with the dean . . ."

". . . President of the school," she corrected.

"Ok, now, is it all clear in your mind?"

"I can almost picture it."

"*You will*," thought Allen.

"Keep concentrating on the moment. Just think about the instant you were handed your diploma."

Joan nodded, then Anna glanced quickly at Allen. He manually triggered a 10-volt pulse to the Link on Joan's arm.

"Oh!' exclaimed Joan. "That was more than just a memory. For a brief second I was there!"

"You've just experienced the phenomenon," said Anna smiling.

"It's wonderful."

"I know."

"Heart rate's up by only a couple of beats," said Allen.

Ed turned the solution atomizer setting to .100 and pressed a momentary toggle switch on a panel. A red indicator light came on, then changed to orange after five seconds, then went out. Ed nodded to Anna. She asked Joan, "How do you feel?"

"Just fine," she answered and smiled. "Exhilarated!"

"Ok, now begin to concentrate on your ancestor, John. How old was he when the Johnstown flood occurred?"

"Twenty-three," Joan answered. "Six years younger than I am now."

"Think of yourself as 23, think of yourself as John, hearing or reading about the disaster."

"Just keep concentrating," Ed said. "Don't wait for something to happen. Keep concentrating." He increased the digital setting to .200 and tripped the timer again, as he would with each increase.

"I will," she said. "I imagine he looked something like my Pop-Pop. It was 1889. Benjamin Harrison was president."

Ed increased the setting to .350. Anna, Ed and Allen remained very still.

"North and South Dakota, Washington, and Montana became states later that year."

Anna mouthed a "Wow," impressed by Joan's knowledge of history.

"Unbelievable!" said Joan suddenly. "That huge steam engine must have been tossed about like a toy. 'Twenty-two thousand people dead,' the headline says."

"Are you ok, Joan?" asked Anna.

"Oh, Anna, that was different from the first. John's eyes! I read the paper through John's eyes!"

"121 years ago!" said Ed. "Can you believe it?" He laughed out loud.

"And it was all in my mind, my soul, just like our research revealed."

"Did you notice anything else in the paper?" asked Allen.

"I was . . . John was clearly focused on the photograph of that huge engine. The rest was not that clear, but I remember a small headline to the left of the main story. 'Revolution,' the large print said."

"I'll be able to see more on the video disk," Allen said as he thumbed through the old history reference he had brought with him that day from his home. "And we can enhance the images," he added.

"Anna, it was so clear, so very clear. It was happening to me at that moment, and it wasn't me. It was John. I feel strangely close to him, a man I know as my ancestor, one who died almost 100 years ago. I felt what he felt, saw what he saw. I can't believe it!"

"Believe it," said Allen, pointing to the page he found. "That 'Revolution' was in Rio de Janeiro, in 1889, just like you saw in the paper."

"Wow!" Joan said.

"Can we continue?" asked Ed. "Are you feeling ok? What's her heart rate, Allen?"

"Pulse, heart rate, blood-oxygen, all normal, just slightly elevated. Less than we would have expected," he answered.

"I'm fine," answered Joan.

"Ok, Joan," Anna said, reading from her list. "Now let's think about the turn of the century."

"My great-great grandpa David," said Joan.

"How old was he again?" asked Allen.

"Fifteen."

"And it was a midnight to remember?" asked Anna.

Ed punched at his calculator. Joan had reached the 1889 event with an atomizer setting of only .350. *"Three-fifty times four forty-two divided by four eighty-six equals three eighteen,"* he said to himself, and reduced the atomizer setting to .318. He then again triggered the timer and watched Joan.

"What a time!" she called out. "What a party! All those adults, acting silly. Kissin' and stuff." Joan gathered her composure and said, "Anna, Ed, what a difference there was looking through the eyes of a 15-year-old--just eight years younger than John."

"How are you going to verify this one, Allen?" Ed asked.

"Don't think I can. We'll have to look at the disk. Perhaps some piece of furniture which dates back to before the turn of the century. Maybe a dress which was only popular that year."

"Let's move on," Anna said, looking at the instruments recording Joan's vitals.

"My wonderful Pop-Pop is next," said Joan.

"Your great grandfather was born in 1910," said Anna. "You're going to concentrate on the Great Depression of 1931."

"*Three-fifty times three-seventeen divided by four-eighty-six equals two-twenty-eight,*" Ed thought to himself. He adjusted the atomizer to .228, and hit the timer toggle.

"My mother called him Pop-Pop Solomon--Oh, excuse me," Joan said. "Let me do that again, Ed," and she thought hard about the Depression and her ancestor.

Ed hit the timer again. Five seconds later there was still no reaction from Joan.

"Let's skip the Great Depression, Joan," said Ed. "Focus on the next scenario. Maybe we'll have better luck."

"Too bad," said Joan. She had seen some disconnected events, but she knew she wasn't concentrating properly on a specific event. "Now I'm listening to my parent's old radio," she said, thinking hard about the announcement of the atom bomb tests at Bikini. "I'd probably be lying on the floor . . ."

Ed reduced the setting to .185 and triggered the timer while Joan was speaking.

". . . maybe with my dog, if I had a dog. That is, if Grandpa Paul had a dog when he was a boy."

Allen counted down to himself, "1005, 1004, 1003, 1002 1001." Then to Joan he said, "Watch for the brand name on the radio."

"Zenith!" Joan almost shouted.

"Circa 1946," said Allen quietly. "I will be able to verify the make and model from the video image you just generated."

"And next to it," Joan continued, "a wooden box, unfinished, about nine inches square, with old, old looking earphones plugged into it and a black knob and dial on top."

"Hey, a crystal set!" exclaimed Ed. "My dad had one from his childhood." Ed was adjusting the dosage to a level of .090 as he spoke. "What can you do with that percept, Allen?"

"Now your mom, Joan," said Anna. "Let's take our time with this one. It promises to be so special for you."

"Yes," Joan said, closing her eyes. "This is going to be special."

Ed hit the timer. Five seconds later the 10-volt pulse passed through Joan. She breathed in deeply. Her eyes filled with tears. She began to sob, but there was a huge smile on her face. No one spoke. They gave her time to recover from the experience.

"My dad was there," she said softly. "He stood to my left, supporting my lower back with his hand. My back and bottom were all wet, but I didn't care, because in front of me the doctor was holding this beautiful baby girl . . . my sister Pam. I couldn't see my dad's face--Ed, can we do it again? Let me concentrate on my dad's face. He's to my left, and if I think about lifting my head . . ."

Ed didn't answer. He had triggered the timer as soon as Joan had asked to do it again.

"Oh, thank you, Ed," and Joan began to sob again. "He was beautiful, and crying like I am now. He looked so happy--so loving. Thank you, Ed. Thank all of you."

Joan closed her eyes and rocked her head from side to side as the tears streamed down her smiling face.

"Ok, Joan?" Anna asked. Allen nodded his head, pointing to the instrumentation.

150

"Anna, we must move on," said Ed. "I don't know if we have enough Promaxonin, and it's the last of it."

"Joan," Anna called, "We must go back now. Are you ready?"

"Yes, Anna, whatever you say."

"James II--Lincoln's death."

"Oh, yes. 1865. April 14. Who told me? What did I read?"

The atomizer had already been set to .420 and five seconds elapsed.

"'Let the thing be pressed!' Lincoln's last military order!" Joan said with surprising seriousness.

"What?" asked Allen.

"The paper I was holding--the article I was staring at was not the main headline. James was so taken by a column on the side. 'Let the thing be pressed.' What does it mean?" asked Joan.

Allen paged to the back of his thick red *History of the American People.*

"Lincoln, Abraham, death of," he read from the index. "Page 584. Here it is. Not much here, surprisingly. 'The spring of 1865 saw the hopes of the South fade . . . Grant trapped the remnants of Lee's ragged army . . . and sent a telegram to Lincoln stating, "If the thing is pressed I think that Lee will surrender.'" Allen's voice grew louder, and he almost shouted, "The president replied characteristically, 'Let the thing be pressed!'"

"Hey!" exclaimed Joan.

"You found it, Allen! Great!" said Ed. "But we have to move on quickly."

"Elisha," said Anna.

"Ah, the one I was waiting for," said Allen.

Ed adjusted the atomizer to .494 and hit the toggle.

151

"Goodyear," said Joan, "1839. Elisha's laboratory. Safety issues. Vulcanized rubber . . ."

Ed shook his head as he watched the Promaxonin solution drop further in its flask.

"Oh, my!" cried out Joan "I saw the lab, but it wasn't rubber which was on my mind. I just received a copy of my patent for the safety device. A gold seal was in the corner. I saw it in my hand, but something is wrong. The abstract says the invention provides a means to prevent an elevator from falling if all of the cables are cut, but I know that isn't true. I don't understand."

"I do," said Allen. "My dad told me that if the main cables from the motor are cut, the car will begin to fall, and a safety cable looped through a pulley on the top of the car will cause a governor to pick up speed and at some point engage a gear, causing a set of shoes to be pushed out against the rails, stopping the car. But if all of the cables are cut, including the safety cable, the car will still fall like a rock."

"I still don't understand," said Joan. "Do you, Anna?"

"Nope. Let's move on to Joshua and candidate Adams' speech."

"We'd better skip that one, Anna," said Ed, shaking his head.

Anna understood, and said, "Okay, Joan, we best go on to--"

"James I," said Ed. "This will be our last. At this flow rate the Promaxonin will run out at any second." He turned the control on the atomizer to .720 and hit the toggle switch, hoping Joan would catch up by the time the Promaxonin concentration in her brain reached the maximum level they would try that day.

"I've pictured this scenario the most. I am so adamant about the rights of the colonists, and I am speaking in the hall to the chief justices . . ."

Joan's right arm shot up in the air, pulling the coax attached to the cuff from the tape Allen used to secure it to the floor. Her finger shook to make a point. "Instruments of slavery!" she shouted.

"Gone," said Ed, referring to the Promaxonin in the flask.

Joan's arm gradually came down. She had a strange look on her face. She looked suddenly at Anna, without smiling. "I wasn't prepared for that," she said. "My mind was so clear, so sharp. I was in control. It was a thrilling feeling. I was captivating the chief justice. He was staring at me--my ancestor--totally enthralled with the logic I--he-- had thrown at him. 'I would do this for nothing,' I--he had said to himself."

"He was hired by the merchants," Allen said, reading from his history book. "What else did you see?" he asked Joan.

"A throne-like chair on which the chief justice was seated."

"Describe it."

"Pointed at the top like the roof of a house. It had huge arms on which only his hands were showing through his flowing robe."

"Really?" asked Allen.

"I'll never forget the scene," said Joan.

"You never did," laughed Allen. "Look."

Allen showed the black-and-white print of an artist's rendering of what the artist had seen in the court that day to Joan, Anna and then Ed. The roof-peaked chair, a glaring chief justice and massive chair arms were all there, depicted by the artist in 1761, and recalled by Joan from an ancestral memory which had been stored by James Otis 249 years ago!

"Success!" exclaimed Ed. "A total success! You were amazing, Joan! You did a wonderful job!"

Joan was still recovering.

"I think the sedative has reached its half-life," said Anna, touching Joan's cheek to look into her eyes.

"I need a rest," said Joan. "Maybe some food."

"Let's all just take a couple hours for lunch," said Ed. "We can talk about the test at the Black Eagle. They make a great chicken soup, which I bet will help you get your energy back."

"I'm all right, really."

"That's what I said just before I passed out," laughed Anna.

"She's not going to pass out," said Allen. "Look at her vitals. This is a very strong lady."

Joan's smile came back. "Thank you," she said politely. "Chicken soup it is."

As they left for the Black Eagle Joan said to Anna, "What a family I have!"

"I'll have the snapshots ready for you in the morning," Allen laughed. "Family snapshots," he added.

Chapter 25

The Formula

"Well, Ed, Joan, Anna, Allen," George said, calling the meeting to order, "we're all anxious to hear the marvelous results you obtained yesterday."

"Joan did a fantastic job," said Anna. "She was strong, calm and very helpful."

"You guys made it easy," Joan said.

"It all depended on you, Joan," said Ed, "and you came through for us." Turning toward Allen, Ed said, "Tell us how you were able to verify almost 90 percent of Joan's recorded percepts."

Allen enthusiastically told the gathering how he had found, at Madison's library on microfiche, the precise news photo captured on video disk from Joan's recall of the huge steam engine lying on its side in the mud of the channel carved by the water from the broken dam. He told how the sub-headline Joan saw related to a revolution which was occurring in Rio de Janeiro at the time of the flood. In Montpelier, Vermont, the curator of a museum there found a party horn distributed throughout the state for the "Turn of the Century" celebrations which matched one held by a guest at David Otis' home as recalled by Joan and recorded on video disk. Just as he expected, Zenith supplied Ed with the graphics file of a Zenith radio, the very make and model

Joan had produced from her memory. The dial on the radio, as visible on the videodisk, was set to 620, the frequency of Milwaukee's principal station, WTMJ.

Anna interrupted Allen. "Joan, why don't you tell us your favorite experience?"

"I saw my daddy," Joan began, "at the birth of my older sister."

LaShauna's mouth opened, Clyde's eyes opened wide, and Gary looked up from his notes, smiling at Joan. She saw his smile and returned it.

Joan couldn't help but laugh and cry during her story. "My daddy died when I was two," she explained, "and seeing his face at such a moment was very special for me."

Allen continued to tell how he found the meaning of Lincoln's last military order, "Let the thing be pressed." He embellished the story about Elisha Otis and his elevator safety device by reminding everyone that in 1945 a bomber had crashed into the Empire State Building, cutting all of the cables on one of the elevators, sending the car crashing to the basement. Finally he told how he had found in his own history book, one his mother had given him, a black-and-white photo of an oil painting depicting the very courtroom scene Joan had re-experienced in color, showing the very chair on which was seated the chief justice, who was staring at James Otis, in awe of his masterful presentation.

"Though James Otis was eventually electrocuted by lightning," Allen finished, "Joan came through the test with only the shock of seeing American history through the eyes of her ancestors."

"How dramatic," said Charlie, who had entered the room in the middle of Allen's report.

George Evans spoke next. "I wanted all of you to hear the report of Joan's excursion into the past. There is no doubt in my mind that we have investigated, hypothesized, theorized, tested and confirmed what may be the greatest discovery of all time. Proof of the existence of the human soul--proof that the spiritual side of creation is as real as the temporal side. Now, what are we going to do with it? Shall we stop here, announce our discovery and go on to develop a new toaster? Or should we continue our research--looking for what?"

"George," began LaShauna, "I know that you have your reservations about the Link project research. We all know that. Everyone on the BioChip team, including Father Christopher, believes we should continue. And what are we looking for? Let's all answer that question individually."

Gary began. "I'm no longer an agnostic. I know now there is a spiritual existence. I don't believe everything you Christians apparently do, but I know, at least intellectually, that there is a God--a Creator. I would like to see the work go forward to gather more evidence--not for me, but for others like me who thought the spiritual was all nonsense."

Joan was beaming, obviously pleased with what Gary had said and how he had said it.

Clyde Hart was next. "George, the hypothesis which continues to develop--Gary's in charge of writing a formal version--will completely change the way we think about the human cell. Mitosis, for example, i.e., cell division, and how healing and growth take place. We will truly understand the role of DNA, what it is and what it isn't. Birth defects will take on a whole new meaning. The research must continue."

"I am in awe once again of my Creator," said Father Christopher. "I believe the fear of God will return to the next generation who hear the truth about Him instead of the liberal nonsense they're taught now. I see Christians resolving their differences that have been founded on misunderstanding God's creation. Unity may become possible."

"You really think so?" asked Charlie with a touch of sarcasm.

157

"I really think so," Father Christopher responded. "My God, some Christians today don't even believe in a spiritual soul!"

LaShauna spoke next. "Such answers have always resided in the understanding of the human mind. It's why I majored in biophysics. I wanted to understand the total function of the brain. Now I learn what every believer should have known, that the soul is involved in every act, every thought, every decision and every memory. And what more has God placed in the particle for us to discover? We must go on. Can we learn more about brain injuries or injuries to the spinal cord as a result of the new path the hypothesis puts us on, and which our tests have been confirming?"

Joan spoke last. "I can no longer think about the phenomenon purely as a scientist, yet it is a scientific question I ask. How far back in man's ancestral memory can we go? I want to know."

"It sounds a lot like you've all been talking to Anna," said George. He turned toward her and smiled.

She said, "George, all disease is a disease of the cell. Instructions for every function of the cell come from the particle, which we're investigating. The more we learn, the more we'll know about every disease that plagues mankind. We're on the leading edge of all medical research. We can't stop now."

"And Ed?" George asked.

"I'm just an old chemist, George, albeit a believer and now a better one. For me, as I know you've said, this is the best and may be the last project in my career. I'm prepared to help see it to the end."

"No need to take this to a vote. Mine would be the only 'nay.' Ok, then, where do we go from here? I seem to be just going along for the ride."

"George," said Ed, "you know we are out of Promaxonin. You know what it costs, and how long it took to acquire. It was also a depressing process, knowing how those people died."

"Ghastly," said Charlie.

"Since Mike Pierson and I began our work together," Ed continued, "I've been developing a formula for a synthetic version of Promaxonin. Call it, Promax-2. I recently had this unbelievable breakthrough. I couldn't repeat it in a million years. I think Promax-2 is ready for a trial. I plan to try it first, so that I can experience the effect and confirm its potency. No one else could do that without first-hand knowledge of the formula."

"With all due respect," said George, "I think the phenomenon is an experience for the younger generation."

"I don't plan to do anything dramatic like we did with Joan or Anna," explained Ed. "I just plan to see how Promax-2 enhances my thought process and short-term memory. We're planning to use a computer test called Think Fast, developed by Cognitive Science. It's available free on the Internet. I'll be ok, I promise you."

"I want to be there," said George.

"Fine," Ed answered. "No problem."

"When?"

"This afternoon."

"Okay," said George. "Allen, what do you make of all of this."

"A one-word response, George. Wow!"

"Charlie?"

"I think you're all nuts - but this is exciting," he said with his usual toothy grin. "Lunch anyone?"

That afternoon Anna walked into the Link lab.

"Well, Anna," said Ed, "you always say, 'Wait till you try this.' Now here I am."

Ed was in the dentist's chair and completely prepared for the test. The atomizer had been filled with Ed's Promax-2, and the control had been moved to a cart so that Ed could reach it with his left hand. He would make the adjustments as he experienced the results, just as he had planned. Ed would not be going back to ancestral memories as Anna and Joan had. It would be necessary to test the effectiveness of Promax-2 and compare it to the natural neurotransmitter. He was planning to concentrate on events in his recent past--a few weeks, a few months ago. If the synthetic neurotransmitter was as effective as he thought, the memories of the events would sharpen in his mind, and of course, the Link would record the recalled percept. First, however, as he said to George, Ed planned to run the "Think Fast" program to test his responses prior to and immediately after his first dose of Promax-2.

George Evans entered the lab.

"It serves you right," joked George. "You've abused Anna for so long, now she's going to throw the switch."

Allen stood in front of the impressive control panel against the wall behind the dentist chair. He would be observing the vital signs as he had for Joan.

"Let's get started," said Ed.

"You know what to do," said Anna.

"I'm concentrating now. I'll be thinking about my Friday night meeting with George at the Black Eagle. I'll be looking at you, George,"

George smiled. Ed set the control to its lowest setting, .001, and nodded to Anna. Five seconds passed.

"MY LIFE!" Ed screamed. He stiffened in the chair. His left arm clutched at his chest.

"What is it, Ed?" Anna cried.

"Anna, his heart rate! It's flat!" Allen shouted.

Ed's eyes were staring at the ceiling.

"Ed!" George shouted.

"Let's get him out of the chair and onto the floor," cried Anna. "Hurry!"

George and Anna pulled Ed off the chair, almost dumping him to the floor. Allen stayed by the instruments, hoping to report some life signs.

Anna dropped to the floor alongside Ed and touched his neck.

"No pulse," she confirmed. "Allen, call 911 and call Clyde, too. Tell him to bring the Code Blue kit."

Allen grabbed the wall phone and punched in the numbers. Anna began CPR immediately. "George, breath for Ed every four compressions," she said.

"Ed, my God!" said George and followed Anna's instructions.

Clyde Hart came in with the Code Blue kit. He had the stethoscope out and began unwrapping the defibrillator cables as he hit the floor next to Anna.

"Still no pulse," Allen called.

"He's not fibrillating," Clyde said, listening with the stethoscope to Ed's chest. "No heart beat at all."

Anna tore Ed's shirt open and lifted his T-shirt. Clyde positioned the defibrillator pads and Anna leaned back. Ed's body jerked. No pulse. "Again," she called. His body jerked less this time. "Nothing," Allen said.

"Allen, call my husband," Anna shouted. "Tell him we need to get Ed to the hospital immediately."

Allen grabbed the phone again.

"Mike will get us the hospital's emergency helicopter," she said to Clyde and George. "In the meantime we've got to keep breathing and pumping for him."

The helicopter arrived on the front lawn. Two emergency medical technicians ran in with a helicopter stretcher while the pilot kept the aircraft ready for the return trip. Clyde and Anna came out of the building with Ed in the stretcher, carried by the two EMTs. George got in the helicopter on the opposite side as they loaded Ed into the helicopter. Ed had received the fastest and best treatment from the moment of his attack to his arrival at the hospital, but on arrival he was pronounced dead.

When Rachel arrived at the hospital emergency room she found George sitting alongside Ed's body, with Anna and Clyde standing at his side, comforting her sobbing husband.

Chapter 26

Scott Dennison

Dave Kasten was sitting at his desk in his office when he heard his high-frequency scanner squawk. The hospital's emergency helicopter had been summoned to Search. Kasten jumped from his chair and went jogging down the hall to the newspaper's entrance. *Now what?* he wondered. He drove directly to the hospital, knowing he could not reach Search before the helicopter would be on its way back. When he arrived he looked for a spot to observe the helicopter's landing without being seen. The cafeteria on the second floor looked over the heli-pad. From there, in a few minutes, he watched the EMTs unload an unconscious man in his late forties, nearly Kasten's age. He saw a man and a woman step out and join the EMTs with the stretcher. Both were wearing white lab coats, and the man had a stethoscope around his neck. Then George Evans appeared, rushing to keep up with the others.

"It must be Ed Lukin they're carrying," Kasten said to himself. He had only met Ed once, at the Black Eagle, the Friday night George talked with him about God and the Link project. As George passed out of sight through the entrance below, Kasten pulled his cell phone from his pocket and dialed the hospital. Quietly he asked for the emergency room. He knew an orderly on duty, and he asked to speak to him. "It's urgent," he told the nurse who answered the phone. Despite his "urgent" statement, he was kept on hold for seven or eight minutes.

"Dave?" a voice asked.

"Yes," Kasten said in little more than a whisper. "Who was taken off the helicopter?"

"The man's name is Lukin, Edward Lukin," the voice said quietly. "He's dead. There was nothing we could do for him."

"What was the cause of death?"

"Cardiopulmonary arrest."

"Heart fibrillation?"

"Not according to the doctors that were with him. His heart just suddenly stopped."

"Diseased?"

"Can't say, but I doubt it. Dave, I've got to go."

"Thanks," Kasten said and terminated the call. He stood there for a moment and then reached in his pocket for his organizer. "Scott Dennison," he said and he saw the engineer's name and number show up on the display. Kasten punched the number into his phone.

"Hello?" a young female voice answered.

"Hi, this is Dave Kasten of the *Madison Journal*. Is Scott at home?"

"No, he isn't. He's at work."

"Do you have his work number handy?

"Yes, of course," she answered.

"May I have it? It's important that I talk with him."

Kasten entered Dennison's work number into his organizer with his thumb. He dialed the number he had been given. It was Scott Dennison's direct line.

"Dennison," Scott answered.

"Scott, I'm Dave Kasten of the *Madison Journal*."

"Yeah?"

"I'm at the hospital, and I just learned that Ed Lukin of Search International has died."

"Lukin!"

"Right. I understand his heart stopped, and he could not be revived."

"No kidding? Ed Lukin?"

"Yes, Scott, and I couldn't help thinking about your accident at Search."

"How'd you hear about that?"

"Through the grapevine," Kasten answered, not wanting to disclose that he had actually discussed Dennison with Search's management.

"Yeah, well, I'm not interested in talking about the accident."

"Then I won't ask," said Kasten, "because what I'd really like to know is whether or not you think Lukin's death was related in any way to what you experienced."

"Who knows?" answered Dennison. "They damn near killed me."

"Are the tests they're conducting, relating to the Link research, dangerous?"

Dennison paused. "Could be," he finally answered.

"You said they nearly killed you," said Kasten. "Who nearly killed you?"

"Evans," Scott answered without hesitation.

"What else can you tell me? How was he responsible for your accident?"

"Evans thinks he knows everything," answered Dennison. "He says he's a specialist at doin' things he's never done before. Well, I'll tell you, it wasn't him sitting in my chair doin' the test that hadn't been done before. He wasn't takin' the risk. He never even told me the experiment

165

was dangerous. He's going to kill someone someday. Maybe he did."

"Lukin?"

"Maybe," answered Dennison. "Lukin always looked healthy to me. He used to jog every day. I saw him. Lukin was the chief chemist at Search. Evans probably had him involved in the Link project. Maybe they tried to reproduce what I experienced, and it killed the guy. Evans is going to get his, one of these days, the arrogant bastard. Him and his son-in-law."

"Martinez?"

"Yeah, Carlos. He had the nerve to call me after I left the company and ask me not to talk about the 'accident,' he called it. I said I wouldn't, but what the hell. Why should I be loyal to them? They never even paid me a severance!"

"I understand you picked up your check and walked out. Did you expect severance?"

"How do you know that? Whose side are you on?"

"I see you're working for someone new. What's the name of the company?"

"My business," Dennison answered and hung up the phone abruptly.

Kasten's finger hit the pound sign and the zero. "I was just talking to a party, and we were cut off," he said to the cell phone operator.

"I have the number," she said. "Should I reconnect you?"

"No, he's probably trying to reach me on my office line. Just give me the billing address, and I'll head over there."

"I can tell you the number has a Delavan prefix; the name on the line is Med-Diagnostics."

"Thanks, Operator," said Kasten. "I'll take it from there."

Chapter 27

Committed to Memory

At the start of the week following the memorial service at Ed's church, George Evans called Search's personnel together in his office. Some sat around the octagon work surface, while others stood behind them. The room was nearly filled. George sat at his desk.

"It's not for Ed that we mourn. He's with God," George told his people. "But Ed was such a good, loyal man, he will be terribly missed by his wife and teenage children, by his family in Pennsylvania, by all of you, and by me, until we see him again."

Later that morning George called Anna and LaShauna back to his office. He closed the door as they entered. They sat down at George's round work surface. He offered them coffee. They both refused. George held the mug he had poured earlier in both of his hands, which rested on the table. The lighting was low and warm.

"I'm not going to get over this," he began. "I don't really care to continue here at Search. Our work was always light and fun, but now . . . it killed my best friend. I want the Link research stopped. I want the Link lab taken apart, and I want the remaining Promax-2 destroyed, along with Ed's formula and the sequential procedure to produce the chemical. I want to end it all, NOW."

George sat quiet, staring at his favorite mug, turning it in his hands.

"I feel so bad for you, George," Anna said "I can't imagine how you feel, losing a friend you have worked with for twelve years."

"Anna and I may be too young," LaShauna began, "to fully understand the loyalty you and Ed felt toward each other, even though we saw it every day since we joined the firm. But we're not too young to know that the Link research promises to keep many people from losing their loved ones, in their prime, victims of many diseases."

"You heard all of the personnel involved in the Link project say, just a week ago, how each one felt about continuing our work," said Anna, "but LaShauna and I have shared even more. We both are convinced that the Link research will lead to a much, much better understanding of life, growth, healing and death."

"Death?" George asked. "Death?"

"Yes, George," said LaShauna. "I never liked to talk about death before, but the discussions the BioChip team has been having changed my mind--changed my life! Father Christopher, believe me, is also a newly enlightened man. He has tied our work to our beliefs so beautifully that we're beginning to consider the hypothesis a 'unified theory.' It ties everything together--answers so many questions asked by both scientists and laymen about God, His creation, and His love for us."

"Tell me what you've learned about death," George said. "What was it that my dear friend experienced? And Anna, why did Ed shout, 'My life' when he had the heart attack?"

"I thought immediately that Ed was trying to tell us that something had gone terribly wrong," Anna said. "His words didn't leave my mind from that awful moment. Yesterday I went over his notes and formula. I saw his careful comparisons between Promaxonin and Promax-2. It was critically important to match the effectiveness of the two neurotransmitters. He developed a K factor. I saw where he had written, P sub x equals P times 2 times K. The value of K, he determined, was 995, meaning that Promaxonin was 995 times more potent than Promax-2. George, it was an error. The ratio should have read, P times two equals P sub x times K. The synthetic neurotransmitter was 995 times more potent."

"So when he set the atomizer at .001 . . ." George began.

"He received a dose of .995," Anna continued, "just .005 short of full-strength Promaxonin as taken from cadavers, and with no preparation. His heart--"

"He expected to see my face, and saw . . . he saw his life flash before his eyes," George said. The edges of his eyes began to redden.

"Yes, George," Anna said.

"And, what did he experience as he died, LaShauna?" George asked.

"It was a transition, George." she answered. "He found himself, body and soul, in the sequential state. Perhaps that's what an out-of-body experience is all about."

"He may have seen us working over him--knew of your concern and love," added Anna.

"I will see him again, and he will recognize me?" George asked LaShauna.

"You both look forward to the meeting, but Ed will not have to wait. Time for him is no longer a factor. The Lord has taken him to the place He has prepared for Ed, and he has found you there."

Anna spoke next. "It was an accident which brought us into the Link research, and it was an accident which shortened Ed's temporal life. LaShauna and I had both talked to Ed about the importance of the research we've been doing. He too would encourage you to continue the work. Perhaps he is, through us."

George sat back and remained quiet for several minutes.

"I'm going to meet Carlos in Ed's lab at 1:00 o'clock," he finally said. "Carlos and I were going to destroy the Promax-2 and all of Ed's notes and formula. We have both been worried that if Ed's formula got into the wrong hands, much more evil than good could result. What if our military intelligence got a hold of the process, or a foreign power? I'll talk with him at 1:00 and let you know my decision in the morning."

George and Carlos met LaShauna in the hallway the next day. "Come with us," George said, and the three walked quickly into Anna's office. Anna was taking off her jacket to put on her shop coat when they arrived. Carlos closed the door behind them. LaShauna and Anna looked at each other and then at George.

"Only the two of you will know what we are about to say," George began. "You must never reveal this to anyone. I don't want you to even discuss it with one another, ever. Do you understand?"

Anna and LaShauna both nodded. "We promise," said Anna.

"What's left of Promax-2, almost a liter, is in a container in the company's trade-secret safe. You probably don't know this, but if that safe is opened by anyone except Carlos or me, without following a special procedure, everything inside will be destroyed by a contained, sodium-fed fire. We've already disposed of all of Ed's notes and written formula, just as I told you and others we planned to do. However, Carlos . . . has committed the actual details of the formula to memory."

"There are ten steps in the process of producing Promax-2," Carlos told them, "and I applied a memorization trick I learned at a memory-enhancement seminar the company sent me to, which I've often used to recall up to ten items or steps. It's foolproof."

"I did not look at the formula," George added, "except to identify it for Carlos. He says he has the formula down exactly. He is now the only one who knows how to produce Promax-2."

"You saved a liter of Promax-2?" asked Anna. "That means you'll permit the tests to continue?"

"Yes, Anna, but when it's gone, it's gone—unless, of course, some overwhelming need surfaces, and then we'll have to rely on Carlos' memory."

"What we've done," said Carlos, "is to make fairly certain that no one outside of this building is going to be able to produce the depth of recall we did with Joan. The most that others will be able to do is produce a percept or two from someone who is very willing to concentrate on what they need to recall. We all saw what could be done with a little suggestion and Promaxonin. Promax-2 is almost 1,000 times more powerful. It must never get into the hands of those who would use it to extract information from others."

"We understand the risks, and we agree with your precautions," said LaShauna, looking at Anna. "You won't be sorry for letting us continue."

"In my gut," said George, "I'm very fearful, and I'm already sorry. Be careful. Be extremely careful. Had I not heard how benign the process had become from Joan, I would not have gone along with your wishes. We lost Ed. . . ." George stopped, shook his head, turned, and left the room.

"He's been devastated by Ed's death," Carlos said. "I don't know what you told him to convince him to let the testing continue, but I share George's fear of the future."

LaShauna and Anna wondered what was in store.

171

Chapter 28

The Reporter Returns

"Talk about deja vu . . . ," Carlos said with a smile. "George Evans, here is Dave Kasten, the science editor of the *Madison Journal*."

Carlos ushered Dave Kasten into George's office.

"George, how are you?" he asked.

"I'm fine, Dave. What brings you to Search?"

"I read about Edward Lukin's death here at Search. The article said he had a heart attack and was taken to Madison General, where he died."

"He was my best friend, Dave."

"I'm very sorry, George. Did you know each other a long time?"

"Twelve years," Carlos answered for George. "I can get you a bio on Ed, if that's what you came for?"

"Now, George, Carlos, you know I'm going to show up asking questions when anything that sounds significant happens here."

"And?" Carlos asked, with a slightly unfriendly tone.

Kasten was flustered. He could read through the sorrow on George's face better than he could his usual smile. There was something wrong, yet here was Carlos, playing cat and mouse.

"Was Ed involved in the ongoing Link research project?" Kasten asked, punching every word.

"Yes," Carlos said.

"Was his death in any way connected with his work on the project?"

"His heart stopped," answered Carlos, "and our medical personnel did everything for him they were trained to do. He could not be resuscitated."

"Did he have the same experience Scott Dennison had?" asked Kasten.

Carlos knew that George would stop him if he put a confusing spin on the truth in answer to Kasten's last question. He looked to George to answer.

"No, Dave, not really," George answered. "But to leave you thinking the two experiences were not in any way connected would not be honest."

"Connected how?"

"We've come a long way in understanding what happened to Scott Dennison. If he had had the character to remain with us as we searched for the answer, it would not have taken us as long as it did."

"What have you found? Can you explain it to me?" asked Kasten.

"Dave," said George, "you know not what you ask."

"George, I'm a reporter . . ."

"What if I told you that stored in your soul are the memories of your ancestors from as far back as hundreds of years, and we can enable you to recall them so completely that you can literally re-experience what your ancestor did?"

Kasten's expression did not change. He continued to look into George's eyes. "The Link research has a 'spiritual' aspect," he remembered George telling him at the Black

173

Eagle tavern. "We have a bioethetist involved," he had said. "If God understands the spiritual, would He have been limited to the physical when He gave us a 'mind?'" George had asked. Kasten stared on in silence.

"Dave, you're a reporter," George said, teasing his friend. "Ask questions."

"Hundreds of years?"

"That's your question?"

Kasten nodded.

"Actually, Dave, we've already gone back 249 years and confirmed the experience with historical fact. How far back we can go, we don't really know."

"George, this sounds like science fiction."

"Shall we astound you with a demonstration?" asked George.

"What do you have in mind?" asked Carlos, his head jerking toward George.

"I'm going to ask this reasonable gentleman to hold back his investigation until we complete our next phase of research. In return, I'm going to let him witness the first test of the bio-synchronizer. Will you do it, Dave? Will you stop with the questions and file no report until the demonstration? If you do, I will see to it that you're the only reporter here."

"You intrigued me with your questions about my kindergarten experiences, and the memories I was able to recall from 46 years in the past. Neuroscientists have pretty poor explanations as to how it's possible for me to recall such detail from so long ago in an instant. I'm going to bet that you have better answers, and I want to see the demonstration. I'll file no report until then."

"Good," George said.

"When?" Kasten asked.

"If my empirical research team can be ready, three weeks."

Kasten rose to leave. Carlos Martinez blocked his path.

"Mr. Kasten," Carlos said. "It is critically important that you say nothing about this meeting until you see the demonstration George has in mind for you."

"He's good," Dave said to George. "I'll do my best," he said to Carlos.

"You know the way out." Carlos said, "Thanks for comin' in."

"Good day, gentlemen," Kasten said as he left through George's office door.

"Demonstration?" asked Carlos at little more than a whisper. "Bio-synchronizer? What are you talking about, George?"

"Carlos, it's going to come out sooner or later--what we've done here, that is, what happened to Scott and Ed. I want the world to know the positive side--like what Anna and Joan have experienced. I want the world to hear the spiritual side, and I want them to listen to what God has been saying through this research. I want to turn the heads of atheistic scientists with some evidence they can't dismiss. I want those who've lost loved ones, like me, to stop thinking that dead is dead and that they'll never see them again. I want the medical research community to recognize that they stopped too short when they declared that DNA was the final frontier in cellular research. Like Anna said, I want us all to have a much better understanding of life, growth, healing and death."

Carlos was dumfounded. This was the first time he heard George talk like this.

"If we're going to go ahead with this research," George continued, "leading the biologists, neurologists and psychologists by the nose onto the true path, then I want to do it right. I want to finish my career with a bang heard all over the world--one which results in more good than the evil the idiots on this planet are going to produce by the misuse of this technology."

"And what in the world do you have in mind?"

"One. I've been developing, conceptually, a means to allow the recall of not just one percept at a time, but a series, allowing a subject to experience--"

"--a full memory of an event, not just a single percept," Carlos interjected.

"Exactly," George said.

Carlos' eyes squinted as if to see into George's more clearly.

"Two," George continued. "With that capability I want to take people back through the memories of their ancestors--with historical evidence," he emphasized, "to prove that man is not just a bunch of neurons like Dr. Francis Crick believes, that man is a body-soul unity, not a body with an ethereal soul floating around somewhere, that man's soul is truly involved in every thought, every decision, every action and every memory. Anna already believes the same thing."

"How will taking people back to ancestral memories convince the world of these things?"

"Carlos, the particle, the soul, is a biological singularity, just like the BioChip team said. The cosmic singularity brought astronomers and physicists to the intellectual point-of-no-return. They either had to say the singularity, a perfectly symmetrical sphere of no volume and infinite mass, came from 'perfect nothingness,' or admit there was a God. The biological singularity will do the same thing. It'll bring the scientist again to the point-of-no-return. We'll be able to show there is no limit to the memory-storage capability of the particle, and its infinite nature will become apparent. We'll be able to prove that the particle, the soul, of every human being is in fact the united particles, or souls, of their parents--how else could the memories be retained from generation to generation, when a human begins as a one-cell zygote?"

"And how will the world hear about all of this?"

"Starting with that man that walked out of my office just a few minutes ago."

"But I thought you were convinced we had to keep the process a secret from the military establishment, from the CIAs and FBIs of the world, so they couldn't use it to torture military secrets out of some poor souls?"

"Carlos, you have to separate keeping the process from the world and keeping the scientific discovery of the human soul from the world. We've destroyed Ed's notes on how to extract and reduce Promaxonin. We've destroyed Ed's formula for Promax-2. Without either they'll be able to get nothing from an uncooperative witness. On the other hand, what we're discovering using Promax-2, we can share for the benefit of mankind."

"The dark side may try to get what's left of Promax-2, then reverse engineer it," Carlos said.

"At this moment, they don't know about it. When we start the series of tests which Dave Kasten will report on, we'll move quickly to finish what we want to accomplish. After that, no more Promax-2. We'll let it be known that it's gone and the formula is lost."

"Then our main risk will be to get the series of tests done before they, whoever that might be, decide to acquire it."

"You're right, Carlos. The answer is to be totally prepared--prepared to run all of the tests in rapid succession, and--"

"--be prepared to destroy the Promax-2 remaining on a moment's notice."

"I thought you'd see the total picture," George said, smiling.

"Now what about this concept you have to--"

"--recall full memories?"

"Yes," Carlos said.

"Give me a few days to get the device down on paper. Maybe I'll build one."

"Build one? How will it work?"

"Never mind, Carlos. You've got the formula in your particle. I'll keep the device in mine."

George's phone rang. It was Kasten.

"George, I don't feel right about not telling you what I learned before coming over today."

"What is that, Dave?"

"When I first heard the news about Ed Lukin, I actually contacted Scott Dennison to see if I could learn anything at all about the hazards of the Link project."

"And what did you learn?" asked George.

"He's pretty angry with you. Angry enough to get back at you."

"About what is he angry?" asked George.

"Well, he went into this lengthy story about his uncle, whom he idolized, and his father, with whom he had a poor relationship. His uncle was an engineer, the main reason Scott became one. His father had always said that he gave his brother, Scott's uncle, a gold watch to finance his education, and that he never paid him back. His uncle denied ever receiving a watch from Scott's father. Apparently, what Scott experienced, through his father's eyes, was the very event his uncle had always denied."

"And he's angry with me for this?"

"Yes, George, for some convoluted reason. Had you not assigned him to such a 'dangerous' project, he never would have had such an emotional experience. You destroyed his idol."

"Strange fellow," said George.

"I thought I should tell you," said Kasten. "Oh, and by the way, Scott is working for a Delavan company called Med-Diagnostics."

"I've heard of them. They're owned by a Swedish company. Thanks, Dave."

George hung up the phone and said to Carlos, "Let's keep an eye out for Scott."

Chapter 29

The Technique

Both teams, empirical and theoretical, met with George Evans in the Link lab. He had something to show them.

"LaShauna," George said, "you gave me the idea for this device."

"I did?"

"Well, Clyde also gave me a clue.

"How?" Clyde asked.

"You, LaShauna, said that data arriving at the base of the brain is probably controlled by the locus ceruleus, a region of the brain stem in which the neurons can have an enormous number of synapses, often extending over a large region of the cerebral cortex."

"I remember. You said you were intimidated when you heard it," said LaShauna. "Sounds like you understood and remembered what I said."

"I was, and I did."

"And what did I say that helped?" asked Clyde.

"You told us that the locus ceruleus is basically inactive when you're asleep."

"How did that help?" he asked.

"It told me that if you want to synchronize an activity with the frequency of the brain, you would want to monitor the locus ceruleus, which is somewhat in control of the activity of the cortex."

"And your device does that?" asked Allen.

"It applies a new 'technique' to the process. We know that to transfer a percept from the particle in a cell on the surface of the hand or arm, or anywhere, we have to cause a differential to appear across the cell, not unlike the action potential which fires a neuron."

"That's right," said Gary.

"But it's the cortex of the brain which communicates the 'focus' of the mind to the particle," said George, "and it's the locus ceruleus which controls the activity of the cortex."

"Correct," Clyde affirmed.

"You also said, LaShauna, that the locus ceruleus passes on the data arriving at the base of the brain to the cortex every .5 to 1.0 milliseconds."

"Yes, George," said LaShauna.

"Well, what if we fire our triggering pulse at a frequency synchronized with the locus ceruleus?" asked George.

George pulled from a large anti-static bag what looked like a white plastic horseshoe, with a fine coil of wire exposed, wrapped about its midsection. "I propose that we place this device around the neck of the subject with the coil positioned toward the back. It uses, essentially, the electronics of a Link to pick up the frequency of the pulses from the locus ceruleus, so that it can be synchronized with the triggering pulse we apply between the Link on the arm and the grounding strap on the opposite wrist."

"George," asked LaShauna, "what does your device do-- in simple language?"

"Okay, in simple language, instead of one percept each time we trigger a cell, or a series of percepts in stroboscopic fashion when we trigger a pulse every so many seconds--"

"--we'll experience a full memory in perfect synchronization with the brain," finished Anna. "Wow," she added.

"It sounds simple," said Gary. "How do you know your device works?"

"I tried it on Mike Young Friday night. Scared the wits out of him," said George.

"You put Mike through the process?" Anna asked.

"No, no, no. I just monitored his locus ceruleus in the main lab. I picked up a strong signal which varied directly with his fright," George laughed. "It is simple, Gary, and it introduces no new risk for the subject."

"Let me try it," said Anna suddenly. "I'll be the first to use it in the process."

George's knees nearly buckled. Others noticed him stagger slightly. Ed's death during the testing of Promax-2 flashed through his mind. He didn't want to ever witness such a terrifying moment again in his lifetime, and here dear Anna wanted to try the process again, this time with a device he had personally developed. George looked around the room. "I don't want any of you to be first to try this," he said. "Let me do it."

"No, George," Anna said firmly. "That may be the brave thing for you to do, but it doesn't make any sense. You have no experience with the phenomenon. You can't compare the effect first-hand. I've gone through the process many times. I'm used to it, and . . ." she said, thinking for a moment, "I have just the memory to test it on."

"What's that?" George asked.

"I've already looked down the aisle of the church at my grandmother's wedding, through her eyes. Now I'll walk down that aisle on the arm of my great grandfather, her

182

father, to meet my husband--that is my grandfather. It's perfect. I know what to concentrate on, and I know what to expect. I've been there before. I'll be okay."

George stood there for a long moment, wondering again if the risks were worth continuing with this research. He enjoyed designing and building the prototype device, but now one of his close associates--and of all people, Anna--was asking to be the first to test it and experience something no human had ever experienced before.

"Are you insisting, Anna?" he asked with a frown uncommon to him.

"Absolutely," she answered.

George's shoulders slumped, and he felt very old and weak. "*Perhaps*," he thought, "*my judgment is slipping away, and I'm losing control of my people.*"

"She's right, George," said LaShauna.

He looked at LaShauna, but just stared through her.

After a long moment he answered. "All right," George said. "One test."

The Ministry of Business Development

"There is a call for you, sir," a voice on the intercom said, "a conference call from a Swedish firm and its American subsidiary."

"Let's take it in the board room on the speaker phone," the Minister of Business Development responded. He waved to his assistant, and both crossed the hall quickly. The lights came on as they walked into the large conference room. A long, wide mahogany table was perfectly centered between the four walls, and the table was surrounded by eighteen black leather chairs. There was a speaker phone at one end. The Minister hit the "connect" button.

"We're ready for the call," he said.

"Hello?" a distant voice said.

"Hello," responded the Minister.

"Hello . . . I think we are all connected, but I am afraid the delay is a little confusing."

"One at a time," the Minister said, quite familiar with international telephone protocol.

"Minister, I'm president of Med-Diagnostics in Stockholm, Sweden, and I have on the line the president of our subsidiary in Delavan, Wisconsin, in the United States."

"How do you do, gentlemen?" the Minister responded.

The three men exchanged names and confirmed the spelling of each.

"Thank you for the call, gentlemen," said the Minister, "now what can I do for you?"

"There is a Jerusalem company that is heavily involved in cybernetic medicine," said the Swede. "We are hoping that you can locate it for us."

"Forgive me," said the Minister, "but I am not familiar with the field of cybernetic medicine."

The Swede responded, "It is the science of the principles underlying the common elements between the functioning of computers and the human brain."

"Oh, yes," said the Minister, "and what is your interest in this field?"

"We manufacture diagnostic equipment," said the American, "and we are embarking on a major development program to produce a computer that will provide physicians with an early detection means for Alzheimer's disease."

"And how do you think the Jerusalem company can help you?" the Minister asked.

"We need a sensor that can directly communicate with the brain, to test for short-term and long-term memory problems," the Swede said.

"We have an engineer," said the American, "that is aware of a presentation the Jerusalem firm made in November 1996 in the city of Atlanta."

"That's fourteen years ago!" the Minister laughed.

"We know, but we felt it would be worthwhile to see if we could contact them," said the Swede.

"What else can you tell me that would help?" asked the Minister.

"Our engineer says he was told the device we are interested in was little more than a band--wrapped around one finger--which was attached to a personal computer," answered the American. "The user could then control graphic objects on a display."

"I think I know this firm," said the Minister, "but they are no longer in Jerusalem, due to the unrest. They are located here in Tel Aviv. The company is primarily interested in stress control."

"That sounds right," said the American.

"Why are you looking to Israel for the solution to your problem?" asked the Minister. "Don't you have the technology in the United States?"

"Frankly, Minister," said the American, "we are concerned that a competitive firm here in the States, not far from our facility, has technology very similar to that of the Israeli firm--"

"--and so," said the Swede, "we find ourselves behind the eight ball. We need to play catch-up, and do it soon. We intend to be the leader in Alzheimer diagnostics."

"So you wish an alliance with our Israeli company?" asked the Minister.

"Exactly," said the Swede.

"What is the name of the competing firm you are concerned about, and where is it located?" asked the Minister.

"Search International," answered the American. "Madison, Wisconsin."

"I'll see what I can do and get back to you," said the minister.

"We will be very appreciative," said the Swede.

"Good day, gentlemen," said the Minister. He slowly, thoughtfully placed the handset back on the telephone cradle. "We must pay a visit to Dr. Matthias ben Charash," he said to his assistant.

Chapter 31

Virtual Movies through Grandma

Anna prepared the Promax-2 solution with Allen at her right hand and LaShauna at her left, checking every step. During the actual test, Allen would be controlling the atomizer and, as usual, the power and triggering pulses. Promax-2, though not needed in Anna's past experiences, would be used to enhance the recall process for continuous percepts. Clyde would be monitoring the vital-signs instrumentation. Gary would be standing at the video-disk recording-system console. Allen and Gary had modified its software so as to rapidly compress the typical string of data which was received. A compressed and complete percept would now be available seconds after it was re-experienced. They had replaced the computer monitor in front of the dentist chair with a huge, flat display hung on the wall, so that everyone in the room could see the results. A substantial sound system was also added to the facility. George had told them to be prepared to receive a continuous series of percepts for as long as sixty seconds. They were prepared for that, but there was something George hadn't told them.

"Anna, LaShauna, Allen, Clyde, Gary, I'd like you to meet Dave Kasten of the *Madison Journal*," George said as he walked in the door of the Link lab with a stranger and

Carlos Martinez. Everyone looked up, but no one spoke or made a move.

"I can see by your reaction," said Carlos, "that George didn't tell you about Mr. Kasten being an observer when you all last met."

"No," LaShauna said, lighting up with her usual smile. She stepped forward and reached out her hand to Kasten. "It's nice to meet you, sir."

"Forgive me for not getting up," said Anna, already in the dentist chair, wired to the control panel against the wall behind her.

"There goes Anna's pulse," Allen joked, pointing Clyde to the instruments.

"No change," Clyde remarked dryly.

"George believes it's time," Carlos continued, "for this gentleman to begin to observe what we're doing today and on future days. I'm sure he'll give you his reasoning as he did for me."

"Yes, I will," George said. "I didn't want to do so until this test was completed, and I'll then explain my timing and plans for a series of tests to come."

Anna and LaShauna looked at each other and back to George. Clyde and Allen did the same.

"Ok, now," said George, "go on with your work, and show Mr. Kasten just how exciting and important our research has been."

Not knowing what Kasten knew, there was little they could say. They continued to prepare for the "VMTG test," they called it, or "virtual movies through grandma."

"Allen," called Anna, "would you come over here a moment?"

Allen responded quickly.

"Would you check everything one more time--all these connections? Since we expect the experience to last for

189

several seconds, I think I'll be more likely to move during it. I don't want to pull anything loose and lose important data. LaShauna, would you stand beside me? Be prepared for anything."

Kasten looked at George and back to Anna. She seemed so fragile and vulnerable sitting in the dentist chair. *"What is George subjecting this little lady to?"* he asked himself.

"Everything's fine, Anna," Allen said and stepped back to his post.

"Then I'm ready," announced Anna in a strong voice. "Clyde?" she called.

"I'm ready. All of your signs look great."

"Allen?"

"I'm prepared to set the Promax-2 atomizer to .200."

George jumped in. "That sounds like a setting for Promaxonin!"

"The solution was diluted 1000 to 1, George," LaShauna responded.

"What's the difference between Promax-2 and Promaxonin, and what are they?" asked Kasten quietly of George.

"Ask your questions after the test," George whispered back.

"Gary?" Anna continued with her query.

"Ready to start the video-disk recording. I'm reading your locus ceruleus, Anna."

"Ok, team," said Anna, again in a strong voice. "Let's begin."

"Power on," said Allen. "Promax-2 flowing. Trigger pulses starting . . . now."

"Disk running," said Gary.

Everyone remained silent from that point on. Kasten began to whisper something to George, but George touched his shoulder quickly, and he stopped. Anna concentrated on her grandmother's wedding and the specific scene she had experienced before, looking down the aisle at her husband-to-be. Her eyes were closed. Suddenly, her right arm raised up lightly off the chair.

"She's grasping her father's arm," George thought.

Seconds later a picture appeared on the monitor. The team saw the same church they had seen before—the same people, the same aisle and altar, but this time there was action! Although some sort of synchronization problem caused the scenes to blink in stroboscopic fashion, it appeared as though Anna's grandmother was walking down the aisle with a video camera strapped to her head. Music was heard, but the "sync" problem added a repeating noise, which spoiled the effect. Anna's grandmother was walking slowly toward the altar, turning her head back and forth looking at the smiling attendees. When she turned to the right one could see more of Anna's great grandfather. After about 45 seconds the picture broke up, then cleared up for a few more seconds. At that moment Anna said, "Cut," as though she were directing a movie. The team broke out in laughter and then cheered.

Kasten spoke first. "I have absolutely no idea as to what I just witnessed, but there are chills going up and down my spine."

"Well, there should be," George said. "Gary," he continued, "what was the stroboscopic phenomenon, and why the momentary loss of the picture just before the end?"

"I've got an answer for the strobe effect," said Gary. "I think what we should do is tap into the signal from the locus and use it to actually sync the video. Then there won't be the gaps when our recorder is looking for the next percept. I can't explain the loss of video near the end, though."

"I can," said Anna softly, still very much affected by the experience.

191

It was then Kasten noticed that her face was wet with tears, and LaShauna's brown face was also.

"The experience is, of course, overwhelming," Anna continued. "If anyone doubts that, please come sit down in this chair."

George motioned to Kasten with his eyebrows raised suggesting the question, "Would you like to try?"

"Where was the clock when that happened?" Anna asked Allen.

"Forty-three," he replied.

"At that point I just started to think about what was happening through me. I opened my eyes for a second and saw the image on the display. The two or three second delay threw me. I closed my eyes and tried to concentrate again, but after that much of a re-experience of something that happened 69 years ago, it's hard to do, I'll tell ya."

"Understandable, Anna," said George. "Gary, go ahead with your idea. Sounds like it'll work."

Gary nodded.

Everyone in the room was smiling, except Kasten.

"I'm the only confused person in this room. That's for sure," he said.

"We'll explain," consoled George. "What you've just witnessed may be the most exciting moment in our careers."

"It is in mine," said Gary, uncharacteristically. Joan nodded repeatedly, as she and Gary exchanged looks.

"Dave, before we discuss what you've seen here, I have a video disk we call 'Family Snapshots' set up in the conference room for you," George continued. "Allen has dubbed in his 'historical proofs,' and then you'll be more inclined to believe that you have just watched Anna recall a memory of her grandmother's wedding, as seen through her grandmother's eyes."

"That's impossible!" exclaimed Kasten. "How can that be?"

"That question," said George, "has taken us from the accident which occurred to Scott Dennison to what you have just witnessed, and, now that we know we can retrieve complete memories, we are moving on."

Chapter 32

The Hypothesis

"So it's my understanding," said George, "that the theoretical team is going to give us their final report, which amounts to a briefly presented hypothesis, as it now stands."

"That's right," said LaShauna. "Mr. Kasten, welcome to our proceedings. We have allowed time for your questions, so fire away at will. Gary will present the hypothesis."

They were all gathered in the large conference room once again. Kasten had seen Joan Kenny's "Family Snapshots" recording of re-experienced percepts of events as far back as 1761. He was still very skeptical, of course, and wanted some scientific detail to support what they claimed was happening. Gary, on the other hand, still did not understand why George was permitting a newspaper reporter, albeit a science editor, to receive information on their secret research. He also did not believe that Kasten would understand enough of what was being presented to ask intelligent questions and to report the work accurately or fairly. A computer slide projector was turned on, and Gary began. On the screen were the words, "The Astonishing Hypothesis by Dr. Francis H. C. Crick," and underneath were the words, "The Truly Astonishing Hypothesis by the Search BioChip Team."

"According to Francis Crick in his book entitled *The Astonishing Hypothesis*, and I quote," Gary said, "'You, your joys and sorrows, your memories and your ambitions, your sense of personal identity and free will, are in fact no more than the behavior of a vast assembly of nerve cells and their associated molecules.' I used to believe that, too," continued Gary, "after all, I'm a microelectronics engineer, and sooner or later, I thought, we would understand that the brain was just a bunch of electronic neuro-networks, functioning in parallel, with an electro-chemical means of storing huge amounts of data." He paused. "But the work we've done has turned this agnostic," pointing a thumb to himself, "into an entry-level believer. Joan's experience alone," he said, smiling at her, "demonstrates the gap between my earlier belief and reality, for there is no capacity in the brain to store data in great detail for 250 years nor the ability to recall it instantly! The reason Crick was convinced that the physical brain cell, the neuron, and its counterparts had to be the mind, was that he believed--or wanted to--or had to--that DNA was the last frontier, that it stored the blueprint of man--which is a laugh when you think about it--and therefore the cell in which it resided had to be the ultimate component of the network responsible for man's thoughts, decisions, emotions, memories, ideas and actions. He and his partner, James D. Watson, discovered the structure of DNA, and Crick just could not believe that there was a whole world of discovery beyond theirs."

"What better place to look beyond than through the mind of one who saw to that point but no further," George said.

"Profound," Kasten said under his breath, and began to type away on the small keyboard on his lap without looking down.

"In Francis Crick's book," Gary continued, pointing to the title on the screen, "he pretended to be searching for the human soul. We found it. He could not answer the 'binding problem,' as he called it. How an object can be seen, heard,

195

smelled and felt at the same time across many parts of the brain. We have answered it. Crick can't explain how or why, and I quote again from the book, 'memory appears to be stored in the very same locations which carry out current operations.' We've explained this. Let's face it, by denying the existence of the atemporal state, he denies the rest of the story. Now I will quote from Dr. Clyde Hart, one of the BioChip team members, Mr. Kasten," Gary said pointing to Clyde, "and you can type this into your laptop. 'It is not the purpose of the brain to remember anything! The brain is the temporal component of the control process. One of its highest-level roles is to facilitate focus, allowing humans to concentrate on the most important parallata returned by the particle.'"

"Parallata?" asked Kasten.

"I'll get to that," said Gary.

Kasten nodded.

"So, I have been calling our hypothesis The Truly Astonishing Hypothesis, because ours turned into an honest search for the soul, and we found it!"

The next slide displayed only hypothetical statement number 1, and Gary began delivering the hypothesis. "There are three states of existence:" Gary read, "temporal, sequential and concurrent. In the temporal state events are spaced by time. The limiting factor is mass. In the sequential state events occur sequentially, but are not spaced by time. Mass is not a factor. In the concurrent state all events are concurrent."

"Question," said Kasten.

"Yes?"

"What's the difference between events happening sequentially with no time in between and events happening concurrently?"

"In the sequential state," Gary answered, "the limiting factor is sequence. A cause cannot follow its effect, even though there is no time between a cause and its effect. By definition, they follow each other. In the concurrent state all events *are* concurrent. They don't *happen* concurrently. There is no sequential limitation."

"Who or what exists in the concurrent state?" asked Kasten.

"Only the Creator of the first two states." answered Gary. "In fact, the Temporal State and Sequential State make up Creation."

"This is tough to grok," said Kasten, using an old English term.

"The concurrent state is impossible for us to . . . understand," said Gary, "but these first statements--at least the temporal state and sequential state--have to be accepted in order to understand the rest of the hypothesis."

"Let me play devil's advocate," said Joan to Gary.

"Shoot," said Gary, but he was thinking how little Joan looked like a devil at the moment.

"Mr. Kasten may have heard that, depending on the relative motion of the observer, events can in fact be observed to have occurred in a different order than logic tells us they must have. A string of firecrackers, for example, may fire in a particular sequence because each firecracker is designed to ignite a subsequent one when it explodes, yet move by the action at an enormous speed, and you may observe the last firecracker as firing first and so on."

"Thank you, Joan," laughed Kasten. "That very question crossed my mind." He smiled at George.

"Remove time from the equation," answered Gary, "and the firecrackers will all fire at the same instant, but sequentially. Never out of order, regardless of your observation."

Kasten's smile left, he nodded and typed away.

"This next slide may help," said Gary.

The slide contained three figures. Figure 1 presented five photographic plates, each having recorded an instantaneous event of a disk moving from the top left corner of plate 1 to the bottom left corner of plate 5. The plates were spaced, representing the time between events.

"Figure 1 illustrates the temporal state-- ," Gary said.

In figure 2 the same plates were stacked, with no space between.

"Figure 2 illustrates the sequential state-- ,"

Figure 3 presented only one plate on which all five events were recorded.

"And figure 3 illustrates the concurrent state."

Gary went on to the next slide. Each of the following slides presented three hypothetical statements. Gary read each slide, and then paused for questions.

"Hypothetical statement 2. At the functional center of every living cell is an atemporal particle of zero temporal mass existing in the sequential state.

"3. The same Particle is a component of every cell in the organism.

"4. A state-bridging field (defines our use of the word 'field') enables communications between the sequential-state particle and the temporal-state, or physical, component of the cell."

"A particle," interrupted Kasten, "is a minute piece of something. Your particle is a minute piece of nothing."

"Nothing in the temporal sense, yes, but in atomic physics they also argue whether or not some particles have mass," Gary answered.

"And," continued Kasten, "how can the same particle be a component of every cell?"

"Having no mass, no dimension and therefore no true location," answered Gary, "the same particle can be at the functional center of every cell."

"So that's how every cell in the body is connected, which is what puzzled Crick?" asked Kasten.

"Yes, but only every neuron is capable of two-way communications with the particle, as I will explain in a moment."

"What is the field in number 4?" Kasten asked.

"I don't have a good answer for that question, except to say it is probably an extremely high frequency electromagnetic field."

"Are you talking about the morphogenetic field," asked Kasten with a smile.

"Close, but there is nothing morphogenetic about the morphogenetic field," replied Gary.

"Please explain," said Kasten, now frowning.

Gary look around the room. Anna and LaShauna were smiling, but everyone else was clearly looking puzzled.

"Some scientists," he began, "who were looking for an explanation of everything, and especially how so much information could exist in a single cell at conception, have considered that the information necessary to develop the form of a new individual must come from a field that is surrounding the primary cell--a field that somehow has all of the information necessary, specific to the individual. They call it the morphogenetic field. They also believe it pervades all space, interacts with all matter and energy, and is even the basis of the Unifying Field Einstein was searching for.

"Fascinating," said Charlie, with his head in his hands.

"Some even suggested," Gary continued, "that the morphogenetic field interfaces with the electromagnetic field of the brain and is involved in how we can recall memories."

"And the difference between the morphogenetic field and your field?" Kasten asked.

"The field I am proposing merely transfers information from the atemporal particle to the temporal cell."

"I see," said Kasten. "Let's not get off track here. Please proceed."

The next slide appeared. Gary continued to read.

"5. All cells are capable of receiving information from the particle.

"6. All neurons are capable of transferring data to the particle.

"7. Temporal-state data communicated to the particle is stored as sequential-state data, defining 'parallata.'"

"So you see," said Gary, "all cells including neurons can receive data from the particle, but only neurons are structured to transmit data to the particle."

"What do you mean, 'stored as sequential-state data?'" asked Kasten.

"The data is stacked in the particle with no time in between," answered Gary.

"So its storage capacity is . . . unlimited," surmised Kasten.

"That's right," said Gary, surprised by Kasten's logical conclusion. "That's what the very next slide begins with," and he went on to the next slide.

"8. The information-storage capacity of the particle is infinite.

"9. Parallata transferred to the particle are instantly returned, that is, reflected, to the temporal-state nuclei of the source neurons.

"10. The transfer of data between temporal-state nuclei and the sequential-state particle, enabled by the field, converts random data to comprehensible data."

"Neurons," said Gary, "receive and transmit data to the particle in random, analog fashion. It comes back comprehensible, because it is returned to the neurons in a synchronous fashion."

"That does answer a question that came to my mind," said Kasten. He was beginning to believe that these people might actually know what they're talking about.

Gary advanced to the next slide.

"11. Sight is a joint process of the temporal and sequential components of visual cortex neurons.

Allen repeated his favorite line: "The eyes are truly the windows to the soul."

"How so?" asked Kasten.

"The neurons of the optic nerves have direct access to the particle," answered Gary.

"No further questions," said Kasten, rubbing his forehead.

"12. Memories are a series of parallata stored permanently in the particle.

"13. The particle is able to recall memories instantly."

The next slide appeared.

"14. When a memory is recalled, it is returned to the same neuron-group which transferred the parallata, where it is 're-experienced.'

"15. If the neuron-group which transferred the stored data to the particle has been damaged or destroyed, and not replaced, the memory cannot, under normal conditions, be recalled, completely, accurately or at all.

"16. The particle contains the source of all necessary information relating to the cell, including an encoded, perfect likeness (defines our use of the term, 'likeness') of the living organism to which the cell belongs."

"Regarding 14," Kasten began, "is this why memories seem to be stored in the brain at the brain location which produced them?"

"You mean, if you hear a particular sound, and later recall it, frequency, tonal qualities, etc., that Statement 14 explains why scientists see an increase in blood flow in the aural part of the brain?"

"Yes," Kasten answered, not totally understanding Gary's question.

"Then the answer to your question is also yes," Gary said.

"I *think* I'm getting the hang of this," Kasten said, looking at George Evans.

George smiled. It was crucial for Kasten to understand the hypothesis. If he could not, George's plan to use him to incrementally inform the media of their work would turn into a circus.

"Well, then," said Kasten, feeling more courageous, "Number 15. Does it explain why brain damage can cause a loss of memory even though the memory is still stored in the particle?"

"Right again," said Gary. "So therefore we should not talk about a loss of memory, but a loss of the ability to recall."

"Explaining why some memories come back when the brain heals?" Kasten asked.

"Exactly," said Gary. "Neurologists don't understand how a memory can be recalled from neurons which replaced those which were damaged. We can."

Kasten's mouth dropped open as he finally read statement number 16. He hadn't been listening when Gary read it because he was formulating his question regarding number 14.

George said, "I see you got to 16?"

"Statement 16," Gary said, "just suggests that it takes much more than DNA to 'encode' a human being. We believe that the source of this huge amount of data is stored in the particle. Don't confuse the likeness with the 'homunculus.'"

"I won't," said Kasten, looking at George and shrugging his shoulders.

Gary went on to the next slide. "Here are some tough ones," he said.

Kasten shifted in his chair. George took the cue. "Gary," he said, "I think Dave has heard enough for the moment. I know you can show how the hypothesis suggests plausible explanations to much more regarding the role of DNA," and turning to Kasten he added, "Gary's going to put the whole thing into a white paper."

"I'd like to see a copy of that," Kasten said somewhat relieved that his mind would not be stressed further.

"Yes," said Gary. "The building blocks of DNA from both male and female that fuse into the chromosomes of a new and unique cell, a zygote, are controlled by the new particle that's created."

"I look forward to reading your white paper," said Kasten. He began to recall his conversation with Senator Sneed. She too had used the term zygote, but to mean the first "product of conception." These people were telling him it was much more.

"Now this I would like to talk about for hours," said Kasten. "I believe they may hold answers to many questions I've had most of my life." To George he said, "This is certainly not just a scientific project."

George replied, "We believe every scientist should consider the atemporal aspect of his scientific endeavor. It's absurd to believe that the cosmos came from nothing or that life began by accident."

Gary turned off the projector and sat down, saying, "It's all yours, George."

Chapter 33

The Assignments

The meeting continued, but George Evans' portion on the agenda was entitled "Assignments." No one, except perhaps Carlos Martinez, knew what George had in mind.

George began immediately, addressing his first remarks to Kasten. "Dave," he said, "I trust you. I brought you into our confidence because I knew that what we've discovered must be released to the public, and must be released in a proper fashion and with a specific timing. The impact of our discoveries will be molded by your structured release. I'll want to discuss this with you more later."

Kasten nodded.

George continued, still directing his words at the reporter. "You've seen the video disk entitled 'Family Snapshots,' produced by Joan Kenny during a Link experiment. You've seen Anna's virtual movies, demonstrating our new technique, and you've heard the full hypothesis developed by the BioChip team, having had the opportunity to ask questions."

George paused, and Kasten nodded.

"Now I expect you to release a carefully prepared piece which will not panic, confuse, offend, or cause the general public to come knock down our doors. The piece should be based on what you've learned thus far, not on what I plan to say next, nor on speculation. There are going to be more releases of ever-increasing amazement . . . "

George paused again and looked around the room. Everyone's attention was riveted on him. He continued, now addressing everyone in the room. "And, as Dave Kasten said, this is no longer just a scientific research project. Let me say it again. This is no longer just a scientific project. How could it be? We've discovered the human soul. The impact on the scientific community and public at large could have enormous consequences--eternal consequences."

George stopped again and paced for a moment.

"The primary goal of this project from this moment forward is to demonstrate the existence and purpose of the human soul. That's the general assignment I have for every one of you. Demonstrate man's true body-soul nature."

Everyone relaxed somewhat, believing that George's exhortation would end there, but he continued.

"Here are the specific assignments I have for you. Gary: a body-soul being, made in the image and likeness of God, could not have evolved 'through natural selection over many, many generations of animals' as Dr. Crick says. How did it happen? Prove it!"

Gary looked up, bewildered. He didn't even see the connection between his assignment and the Link research. Joan's glance gave him no help.

"LaShauna: Christ supposedly emptied Himself of His divinity and was a man like us in every way during His temporal life. If that's not true, if He instead knew He was God through His own knowledge, then who could follow Him? So prove it! Prove He was a man like us."

LaShauna's eyes were wide, but she felt her head nodding in approval, not just acceptance.

"Joan." Joan jumped an inch off her chair. "Jesus Christ was born 2,010 years ago, yet He said before Abraham came to be He IS. You're the numbers person. Prove He was right!"

Joan began to scribble notes rapidly, nervously clicking her pen tip in time with Kasten's keyboard. Gary reached over and touched her forearm.

"Father Christopher," George continued.

Fr. Christopher began to explain that he was just an outside consultant, but never got it out.

"God walked with man in the garden of Eden and with others at times," George said. "Some say it was Christ. Prove it!"

"Anna." George noticed Anna was smiling, and he began a slight smile also. "The life of a child begins at conception. Focus on proving, beyond a doubt, when a baby is, in fact, a baby."

Anna was pleased with her assignment, but had absolutely no idea how to do what was asked of her.

"Clyde," George continued. "Reincarnation makes no sense in God's creation. Prove it's nonsense."

Clyde didn't look up or move.

"Those, my dear people, are your assignments. Charlie has been told to take the lid off the expense accounts."

Charlie made an unintelligible mumbling sound.

"Do whatever it takes to accomplish your tasks," George continued. "You have six months to complete the six assignments I've given you. Dave, be prepared to witness a test and write a report about once per month."

A few quiet conversations began in the room. No one at that moment had any idea as to how to accomplish his assignment.

"I'm not finished," said George - the smile caused by Anna was gone. "The reason I appear to be in a hurry is that I believe in about six months we'll be stopped by outside forces. I don't know what they'll be, but Anna, Allen and

LaShauna, I want our supply of Promax-2 to be gone before they get here. I intend to destroy every chemical, every instrument and every device we have and will have relating to the Link project, six months from today."

"What do you think might happen, George?" asked Anna.

"The work we're doing," George answered, "has great potential for good and great potential for evil. I'm not going to let the other side place a hand on any of the tools we've used."

Heads turned back and forth, but no one spoke.

"Father Christopher," George said, "what do you think of all this now?"

"I thank God for permitting my involvement, and I just now asked the Holy Spirit for guidance in the awesome assignment you've given me," he answered.

"Let me add," said Dave Kasten, "I am thanking God for the very same reason. Never in my wildest dreams did I imagine I would be reporting on the scientific discovery of the human soul and what it will mean to the beliefs of billions of human beings."

Chapter 34

Article One

"The Hypothesis of Search International."

"Could it be," Dave Kasten wrote, "that most scientists have it all wrong? Could it be that they have missed, ignored or simply denied a truth that could change our understanding of just about everything? I met recently with a talented group of scientists, engineers and physicians that believe most scientists have done and are doing just that. The scientists, engineers and physicians I met with are all employees of Search International, a product research firm in my own hometown of Madison, Wisconsin. They have shaken the very foundation of my science education.

"There are three states of existence, they say, not just one: the temporal, sequential and concurrent state. God alone exists in the concurrent state, they've told me, and they never ignore the Creator in their research. There's much more. At the functional center of every living cell, there is a biological singularity which is the repository of all memory, including all ancestral memory. Hold onto your hats. The same singularity (particle, they call it) is at the functional center of every cell in an organism, for the particle is atemporal and has no dimension or mass and, therefore, no physical location. I hope you are sitting down, because it may startle you further to learn that these scientist, engineers and physicians are actively studying the purpose and function of the human soul!

"What follows in this article is a quasi-layman's presentation of a twenty-eight-statement hypothesis that Search International has developed and is presently testing. George Evans, chairman and CEO of Search International, has told me to be prepared to write five subsequent articles, 'about one per month,' he said, reporting on the results of a series of assignments he has given his creative scientific staff. I am not permitted to tell you what the assignments involve, not until I personally witness the test each professional plans to conduct tests which George Evans says will demonstrate the existence and capabilities of the soul!

"But before I begin my presentation of 'The Hypothesis of Search International,' let me tell you a few things that may cause you to read on with greater interest. In a conference room at Search, I viewed a video disk containing 'snapshots' of the ancestral memories of a young scientist, Joan Kenny, that went back in American history to 1761! The most recent snapshots were taken through the eyes of her mother moments after the birth of her older sister! I personally watched 'virtual movies' produced from the mind of physician Anna Pierson. They were of her grandmother's wedding, which happened 41 years before the physician's birth! The following hypothesis explains how and where ancestral memories are stored and how they can, under certain circumstances, be recalled.

"It all began with an accident that occurred in Search International's test lab. An engineer named Scott Dennison was testing a new device, called a 'Link,' being developed by Search that actually allowed the user to control a computer directly with the mind! Two teams of scientists, engineers and physicians have concurrently studied the phenomenon experienced by Scott Dennison during the accident. One team was instructed to study the phenomenon empirically, and they have reproduced it under scientifically controlled conditions. The second team was instructed to study the phenomenon theoretically, and it is their hypothesis I now present to you.

"It may be impossible for you to accept the first hypothetical statement, since you and I are immersed in time, but if you can, the logic that follows may . . ."

The full text of Dave Kasten's first article appeared in several science news magazines. Excerpts appeared in two business-news weeklies and in Kasten's own syndicated newspaper column entitled, "The Exponential Curve." The reaction to his first article was milder than he had expected. He was invited to speak at Madison's largest service organization's luncheon, and 52 letters arrived at his office from irritated readers, amateur scientists and would-be scientists. Most seemed to have their own "unified theory" regarding God and Creation. One Southern Baptist pastor, searching for science articles that supported Scripture, wrote and said, "You might be onto something." A few of Dave's friends and associates suggested Dave was "tipsy" when he wrote the article. George Evans turned down two local news interviews and a science fair speaking engagement. Several callers to Search International inquiring of Scott Dennison were told he was no longer with the company. Neither Dave Kasten or George Evans realized the extent of the quiet stir the article had caused in the professional scientific community.

Chapter 35

On a Clear Day

"George," called Clyde, seeing him nearing his office down the long hallway from the reception area. George stopped and looked at Clyde walking quickly toward him with a lady at his side.

"George, I'd like you to meet Barbara Shaw. Barbara, this is George Evans, the chairman of the company."

"It's a pleasure to meet you, Barbara. What brings you to see us on this beautiful day?"

"George," Clyde answered for her, "I used to go to high school with Barbara. I hadn't seen her in years, but I did hear where she had gone, and why, from the mutual friends I've kept in touch with."

"And where did you go?" asked George, trying to let Ms. Shaw do some of the talking.

"I was drawn to the Lancaster-York area," she answered.

"Pennsylvania or England?"

"Initially Pennsylvania."

"And what drew you there?" George asked with slightly less sincerity than usual.

"The names, I'm afraid."

The three entered George's office, and he pointed to chairs around his favorite work table. As they all sat down George turned to Clyde and raised his eyebrows.

"My assignment," Clyde explained.

"Please," said George, "from the beginning."

Clyde told George that he had been searching for an individual who believed very strongly that he or she had been reincarnated--lived a past life. He read biographical sketches on many women and a few men who made such claims when he remembered what he had heard about his former classmate, Barbara Shaw. She had been hypnotized at a high school prom by an entertainer, and when it was over she told everyone she had these strange thoughts about living in the 15th century. Thinking it was a suggestion left over from the hypnotist the night of the prom, she eventually went to a psychologist who was a trained clinical hypnotist with the idea that she might wipe away the post-hypnotic suggestion. The psychologist put her into a trance and attempted to do just that, but when Barbara woke up the memories were stronger than ever--as though she had just re-experienced them. The psychologist was baffled and signed off on her case.

"Did anyone ever suggest to you that you had actually lived before?" asked George.

"No," she answered. "I never believed in reincarnation, until, that is, the memories began to be strengthened even when I slept very soundly after a hard day's work or play. Then I read in the news about a series of murders which occurred in York and Lancaster, Pennsylvania. I was strangely attracted by the names of the towns. Subsequent dreams seemed to focus on 14th century people speaking the names 'Lancaster' and 'York.' I went to Pennsylvania and lived there for a while, which is when Clyde lost track of me, but I found no relief from the recurring memories. It was at the Lancaster library that I researched the names, Lancaster and York, and came to recognize that they were also names of two of the ruling houses of England."

"The House of York and the House of Lancaster?" George asked.

"Yes," she continued, "and through my continuing dreams I came to believe I had lived during the time the House of Lancaster ended with the end of the reign of Henry VI, and the House of York began, with the reign of Edward IV, both of which occurred in 1461. I studied British history, circa 1461, and my dreams seemed to be faithfully representing what had gone on during that time frame. How else would I know these things, I concluded, if I hadn't been there to live them?"

"A question, my dear lady, which may have an answer even more shocking than your theory," said George.

As George came into the Link test lab, Barbara Shaw was just sliding into the dentist chair. She had had the usual Link cocktail an hour earlier. George walked directly to her side.

"Good afternoon, Barbara," he said.

"Hello," she said, somewhat startled.

"You should be relaxed," George said. "Anna and Joan have done this many times."

"Oh, I'm not worried about the process, as Clyde calls it. I'm just a bit nervous about what I'm going to learn. Excited, actually."

"That's ok," encouraged George, "but I'm here to be sure that you want to go forward."

"Oh, yes," Barbara said. "By all means. I signed all the documents you required."

"I wasn't asking about the documents, I just wanted to hear from you."

"Thank you," she responded.

George nodded and stepped behind the chair. Carlos walked in with Dave Kasten, and the three sat together to watch the large monitor. George turned to Kasten and said, "Month one." Kasten thought he knew what George meant and nodded. Anna and Gary were both at their posts. Clyde stepped in front of Barbara to tell her about the protocol the team intended to follow. George turned to Kasten again and whispered, "Listen closely to this."

"Barbara," Clyde began, "forgive me for being very objective about all of this, but for us this is a scientific experiment which has a very specific objective." Barbara nodded. Clyde continued. "You've said you believe that you lived before--in the 1400s."

"Yes," she said.

"Your reason for believing this is that you appear to have information in your mind about the 1400s which you could not have gained through any contemporary means."

"That's right," she said. "I would have had to have lived at that point in time."

"Okay," Clyde continued. "We're going to start with a simple exercise. We're going to ask you to remember talking with me in the classroom hallway at the high school when we were both just 18."

"Well, I know that we did, but I don't remember any occasion specifically."

"That's ok. We're going to enhance your ability to recall past events, as I explained this morning. All I want you to do is close your eyes and concentrate on the likelihood of such an event." Clyde paused, but Barbara kept looking at him. "I need you to start right now," he added.

Barbara closed her eyes and seemed to relax. Clyde looked at Allen, and a low dose of Promax-2 was added to the oxygen she was breathing. Five seconds later Allen flipped a toggle switch which began the synchronized pulses which would trigger the experience. The screen flickered and an action image appeared. Allen smiled when he saw how young Clyde looked. The room filled with the sound of high school students changing classrooms. As suddenly as it began, the scene ended. Barbara's eyes opened wide. Much wider than usual.

"Wow! You'd be amazed how clearly I just remembered you standing outside my homeroom. I was talking about the upcoming prom. I could hear all of the kids."

"I know," said Clyde with a smile.

"But if you only saw what I saw--"

"We did," said Clyde.

"For a moment I was not in this room. I was there," said Barbara, mentally denying that it could possibly have been a shared experience.

"Let me ask you, Barbara, was what you experienced a previous life, or was it your life?"

"My life, of course--just better remembered."

"Recalled," corrected Clyde.

"Yes, recalled," Barbara confirmed.

"Let's move on now," said Clyde. "We want you to concentrate on a time when you were a very little girl--just some memory you recall only vaguely now."

"Walking along the river in Esterbrook Park with my daddy."

"Sounds fine," said Clyde. "Concentrate on some detail like the color of the river or the high weeds along the bank."

"All right."

"Start now," Clyde said. Barbara closed her eyes, and Clyde nodded to Allen.

The sound of the river, the birds and little Barbara's chatter caused grins all around. The scene was . . .

"--Beautiful!" Barbara exclaimed. "What a time we had. My dad looked so young."

"So did you," said Clyde.

"You saw and heard what I did?"

"Yes, we all did," said Clyde, nodding his head. "Now tell me, Barbara, was that an experience of another life? Or was it your life you were recalling?"

"Mine," she said with pleasure.

"Barbara, we're going to take one more step before letting you go back further."

"Ok."

"Where did your mother go to school, that is, before she was married?"

"The University of Wisconsin-Eau Claire campus."

"Have you ever seen it?"

"No. I was never north of Tomah."

"I've been to the Eau Claire campus," said Clyde. "There are beautiful tree-lined walks between buildings on the main grounds. Your mother probably walked with friends between classes along those paths. Concentrate on that. The first day of spring, perhaps."

Barbara did as she was told. She closed her eyes and relaxed.

An image flashed on the monitor and campus sounds rose up, but they lasted little more than three seconds. Barbara sat up suddenly, and her eyes expressed her disbelief. "I recognized the girl walking toward my mother. It was Elaine Crawford. She died just last year. They were best friends all their lives. I didn't even know she went to that school."

"We can confirm that," said Clyde.

"Confirm what?" asked Barbara.

"That Elaine Crawford went to the University of Wisconsin in Eau Claire that year. Now tell me, Barbara, how were you able to recall the scene of Elaine walking toward your mother?"

"Clyde! For a moment I <u>was</u> my mother. I was seeing Elaine through her eyes."

"That's more accurate. One thing is for certain. You could not have been your mother in an earlier life. You were not yet born, but you were able to recall a 'memory' of your mother's in great detail. It was short, but we saw it, too."

Barbara shook her head. Her eyes remained wide. Clyde became concerned. He looked up at Anna, manning the vital signs instrumentation. "Barbara's fine," Anna said.

"It's important for you to accept what you've experienced and to relax," Clyde continued. "Stretch a moment. Push back in the chair. Think of this next experience as you did the others. You're going to recall things you didn't know you could, but you're still going to be sitting in this chair, in this room, with me, your long-lost friend, in front of you. There is nothing to worry about. Enjoy the experience." He paused, then began again in a quieter voice. "It's 1461. The Houses of York and Lancaster clashed in a war called the War of the Roses with the House of York in victory." Clyde paused again. "Are you ready, Barbara?"

Allen gradually increased the Promax-2 setting to 1.600.

"Yes," Barbara said.

"Try not to let the vision startle you. Just relax and experience it for as long as you can."

Barbara nodded. So did Clyde to Allen.

"Ohhhhh," came from Barbara. She was smiling, which was reassuring to Clyde.

Sounds of horses, carriages and crowds began to rise up. The image scanned back and forth up and down the square. It was a coronation procession, viewed from a first floor

217

window of a gray stone house, based on what could be seen of the window masonry. Barbara's ancestor, a girl, had a perfect view, and she had the unaided perfect vision of a child. She turned her head into the room, capturing the elegance of a wealthy home and a loving mother. The memory ended.

"I was so happy," Barbara said smiling. "Not a care in the world."

Clyde smiled back. "You said, 'I was so happy.'"

"I mean my ancestor, who ever she was. The experience of looking through her eyes was just like looking through the eyes of my mother on the campus. Somehow both memories are a part of me, but I did not live them before, Clyde. It's hard to let go of the concept that it was a previous life, having believed it for so long, yet the evidence of the experience is overwhelming. Will you explain how it's possible, how I can have these ancestral memories?"

"Yes," Clyde said. "I'd be happy to spend the rest of the day with you. I've got the time. I just completed a major assignment," he said with a smile.

Kasten sat through Barbara's experience with his hands folded, prayer style, in front of his face. As Clyde began to help Barbara out of the chair, after un-attaching the Link device from her arm, Kasten turned to George and said one word: "Incredible." His first story had just hit the national news, and now he had his follow-up story. "Incredible," he repeated.

As Allen, Anna and Gary began to shut down the instrumentation and controls with which they had monitored the process, Allen began to sing an appropriate theme song. "On a clear day, you can see forever . . ."

Chapter 36

Article Two

"Reincarnation Disproved"

"'On a clear day,' sang the engineer who had helped monitor the test, 'you can see forever.'

"Barbara Shaw, the test subject, claimed to have lived a past life. She had good reason to believe so, since she had once been hypnotized, by an entertainer and subsequently by a trained psychologist, and she had awaken with strong memories of having lived in the 15th century, during the time of the transition between the House of Lancaster and the House of York in England. With a device called a Link attached to her arm--which allowed the video recording of the memories she was recalling--Search International's Dr. Clyde Hart took Barbara back to her high school days, and then to her early childhood. To this reporter's shock and amazement, Dr. Hart took Barbara back to memories only her mother could have experienced! She walked along a tree-lined path on an Eau Claire, Wisconsin, college campus and watched, through her mother's eyes, a woman approaching who Barbara was able to identify. Barbara experienced for the first time the recall of her ancestral memories!

"But it didn't end there. 'Ohhhh,' cried Barbara, and the Search staff and I saw on the home-theater-sized monitor what Barbara, with eyes closed, saw in her mind! There were horses pulling carriages through throngs of people shouting and cheering with excitement. Then a gold carriage passed by. We were observing the coronation of Edward IV in 1461 through the mind of Barbara Shaw! Barbara was looking through the eyes of a little girl, her ancestor, viewing a memory recorded 549 years ago!

"I sat with George Evans, the chairman and CEO of Search International, directly behind Barbara. She sat in a revised dentist's chair. Here is what I saw and heard . . ."

Dave Kasten's second article created quite an uproar among the New Agers, several Hindu groups and the friends of one well-known American Hollywood actress. Kasten was interviewed on the leading network's "The Morning Show." It was a popular discussion subject for weeks on several national radio and television talk shows.

Chapter 37

King of the Jews

Dave Kasten arrived early. George had asked him to. "You did a nice job on your first two articles. They, in fact, are helping us to help you write the third. Month two," he added.

"I received plenty of negative letters from the first article," Kasten said. "Mostly from intellectuals who didn't understand what I was talking about."

"That was your intention?" George asked.

"Hell, I didn't know what I was talking about," he laughed. "But the second article is really causing a commotion. Even Hollywood's involved."

"Well, your title, 'Reincarnation Disproved!' was not exactly subtle."

"Just following your lead, George. Now, what's this one going to be about? Which of your geniuses is ready?"

"The three who received assignments relating to Christ have teamed up," said George.

"And they're ready?"

"They say they are. They've spent a small fortune, and they're ready to pick up their candidate at noon."

"You told me there was a spiritual aspect to this project, and I've been uncomfortable ever since."

"Wait till you hear what the team has in mind."

As if on cue, LaShauna, Joan and Fr. Christopher walked into George's office. They greeted Kasten with new respect, knowing that their work would also soon receive national syndication.

"LaShauna, you're heading things up as usual?" asked George.

"I was democratically elected," she answered.

"We picked straws," Joan laughed.

"Give Dave a brief report," said George.

"Your articles have helped us a lot, Mr. Kasten," said LaShauna.. "The first one got our prospects' attention, and the second--though it just came out--moved them to action."

"I'm lost."

"As a team we have three assignments," said LaShauna.

"I know," Kasten said. "Prove that Christ, though God, was just a man like us during His temporal life, prove He existed before Abraham--without being reincarnated--and prove Christ walked and talked with Biblical characters long before He was born in Bethlehem."

"You've got it," said LaShauna. "Father Christopher helped us see our three assignments as one. I'm sure he would be glad to explain." She nodded to Father Christopher.

"The truth we believed George was looking to prove with Link experiments seemed to crystallize for us into one concept--God is timeless, and Christ is God," said Father Christopher, "but George made it clear that although Christ is God, from His birth to His death He was like us in every way--otherwise, how could we as humans be expected to follow Him?"

"Sounds like contradictory concepts," said Kasten.

"Not at all, but I understand why you say that," said Father Christopher. "God explained to Moses His true nature. He referred to Himself as 'I AM.' For God, everything is in the present. There is no past or future. It is all NOW."

"Concurrent?" Kasten said.

"Yes," Father Christopher responded. "He exists outside of His Creation in a state we call concurrent. He is not limited by time and not even by the sequence of events. Therefore, for God, the instant Christ was incarnated--became man--and the instant He died on the cross was, for Him, in our understanding, the same instant. Christ was always God, but because He chose to become one of us through the Incarnation, He--in temporal terms--'began' as a single cell, just like us, grew in His mother's womb, just like us, and had to learn to walk and talk, just like us."

"But He must have known all along He was God," said Kasten.

"On the contrary," said Father Christopher. "His decision to become one of us in the manner He did precluded Him from even being aware, on His own, of His divine relationship with His Father."

"He couldn't recall He was the Son of God?"

"Exactly. As His brain developed, He could recall only the memories stored in His particle which His neurons had recorded there."

Kasten flipped through his notes. "Hypothetical statements 14 and 15," he mumbled to himself. "Then who told Him?" he asked out loud. "Who told Him He was God?"

"Probably Mary."

"Why would God do such a thing?"

"So that a true human would show us the way back to the Father," answered Father Christopher.

"But what about the miracles?"

"If you believe, that is, trust in God, you can do greater things than Jesus. That's what He said."

"And He always knew what to say," Kasten argued.

"They were the words of His Father, He told us."

"Then He was able to talk directly with God, His Father?"

"No different than you or me."

"God was invisible to Him as He is to us?"

"Hidden from Him as He is from us."

"Then, during His ministry, how did He know what He knew?" asked Kasten.

"He was indwelled by the Holy Spirit, just as all believers. Keep in mind that it took 30 years for Him to prepare Himself for His ministry through prayer and the study of Scripture."

"How have you combined the three related assignments?" asked George.

"Prove that Jesus Christ--God--was a man in every way for a temporal segment, and you've proved His timelessness," said LaShauna.

"And how do you plan to do this?" asked Kasten.

"We have found," began Joan, "an individual whose ancestors were almost certainly living in the vicinity of Nazareth during Christ's time. His name is Matthias ben Charash--pronounced 'khaw-rawsh.' His last name means 'carpenter.' His father is a cabinet maker, a trade he says goes back 'ad infinitum' in his family. Matthias is a doctor at an Israeli research hospital. We had a good number of candidates from Israel respond to our inquiries, but he's our choice for the test because he, like Clyde's subject, has had recurring dreams of past and ancient lives. He's extremely interested in the process, George. He's studying the cellular nature of all diseases, especially how cancer cells lose their source of control and information."

"Is there any suggestion he's connected in any way with Israeli military intelligence?" asked George.

"We couldn't come right out and ask him," answered LaShauna, "but it seems unlikely, due to his research interests."

"Let's be extra careful," said George. "Go on describing your plan, LaShauna."

"We're first going to ask the subject, Dr. ben Charash, to concentrate on the dreams or visions he has had. We'll then try to determine their timeframe and adjust the Promax-2 mist accordingly to get the subject to go to the year 10-- sounds weird to even say what I'm saying, but we--"

"--but we're hoping," broke in Joan, "just hoping that, if Dr. ben Charash's ancestor was a carpenter in Nazareth, that he knew Joseph and his family, including the 12- or 13-year-old Jesus--assuming, of course, that Christ was born in 5 to 6 B.C."

"George, I don't know what to think," said Kasten. "These kinds of discussions are so foreign to me, and present-day science--"

"I understand, Dave," said George, "but you had better prepare yourself for more. Gary has started to build a test which will certainly blow what's left of your mind away, and we've yet to hear from Anna."

Gary looked over at Joan, again with a bewildered look on his face. Joan winked.

"I'm just saying," continued Kasten, "I don't know if I can do justice--"

"Oh, Dave, you've done a great job so far. The words will come to you when you need them," said George.

"Rely on the Holy Spirit," added Father Christopher. "He will tell you what to say."

Kasten laughed. "I guess I'd better," he said.

The plane carrying Matthias ben Charash was due within minutes. George drove his travel vehicle to the airport with Kasten, Father Christopher, LaShauna and Joan on board. Carlos served as "copilot." He had made arrangements with the airport authority, and George was cleared to drive up to the private jet when ben Charash arrived. "Let's treat him right," said George. "He's come a long way."

George remained seated in the driver's chair of his 23-foot, converted GMC motor home, but rotated his chair toward the door. Kasten stood to his right. Carlos waited outside, prepared to meet the visitor as he exited the plane, and to usher him into the vehicle. LaShauna and Joan were seated in the "Lounge," a U-shaped, cushioned seat positioned around a Plexiglas coffee table. Father Christopher stood in the middle of the vehicle near a computer work station. There was a kitchenette behind him with beverages and snacks on display. The Search staff were all a bit nervous, and it showed.

Carlos began talking to someone on his pocket phone. He snapped it shut, dropped it in his suit coat pocket and stuck his head in the door. "That's the plane on the horizon," he spoke toward the interior of the vehicle.

"How did you want to be introduced?" George asked Kasten.

"It's up to you, George," he answered.

"Science editor for the *Madison Journal*?" George suggested.

"Fine."

"LaShauna, who talked with ben Charash last?"

"I did, George," she answered.

"Then you step forward as Carlos ushers him in. Introduce yourself and us. Direct him to the swivel chair over by Father Christopher, and I'll take off. You carry the conversation on our way back."

"Yes, George."

Wisps of smoke appeared from the landing gear tires as the sleek jet touched down. It came to a stop and paused as the pilot was receiving instructions to taxi over to the waiting vehicle. The pilot saw Carlos standing by the vehicle and the words "Welcome to Search International" on the open door. He stopped at a safe distance and turned off the seatbelt light. Moments later the jet's door opened, and the short stairway was lowered by a crew member. Two men in suits disembarked.

"There's two," Carlos said out of the side of his mouth. He wasn't pleased, because he hadn't been told. Carlos walked over to the plane, greeted the men and pointed to the travel vehicle.

George jumped out of the driver's seat, waved LaShauna aside and stepped down to the tarmac.

Carlos saw the expression on George's face and let him do the talking.

"Dr. ben Charash, I presume," said George to the first man, who looked to be about forty.

"No, my name's Wittstein, Abraham Wittstein. I've accompanied Matthias," and he turned to the graying man behind him.

"I'm ben Charash," the second man said.

George reached out his hand to ben Charash. "Welcome," he said. His actions stopped the four at the door of the vehicle. George reached over and closed the door.

"Is there a problem?" asked Wittstein.

"Yes, there is," said George. His eyes looked friendly, but he wasn't smiling. "There are two of you," George said.

"I told you," said Wittstein, "I accompanied Matthias. He asked me to come along with him."

"We weren't told," Carlos said. "Ms. Jackson and I spoke to you, Dr. ben Charash, about the need for strict security."

"Your work is being published internationally!" Wittstein said.

George knew he could not here and now explain the incremental release of information, which Kasten was publishing. He also knew he was about to introduce Kasten, a writer permitted to meet ben Charash.

"Matthias," said George. "Can you vouch for Mr. Wittstein?"

"Absolutely," he answered. "I've known him for many years. He works in administration at the very hospital which employs me."

There followed a very uncomfortable pause in the conversation. Carlos and George looked at each other intently.

"Forgive us," George finally said. "We're just trying to be careful. The technology can easily be misunderstood."

George opened the door and ushered the men in. Dr. ben Charash stepped up first, followed by Wittstein and George. Carlos pulled the door shut behind him and took his place in the copilot's chair. LaShauna proceeded with introductions--a little confused as to what had transpired-- and they all took their seats, Matthias and Father Christopher in the swivel chairs, LaShauna, Joan and Wittstein on the U-shaped seat. LaShauna smiled at Matthias as George drove off the tarmac and onto the access road. As soon as they reached the freeway Joan stood up and served the refreshments. Small talk about the Wisconsin countryside kept them busy until they arrived at Search's drive and the front of the building. George stopped the vehicle, and Carlos jumped up to open the door.

"Ladies and gentlemen," George said, pointing to the door. "LaShauna, we'll meet in the conference room, and then they have lunch ready for us."

"Yes, George," she said and led the way into the building.

After everyone except George, Kasten and Carlos had entered the facility, George said to Carlos, "You as nervous about Wittstein as I am?"

"Yes," Carlos said.

Kasten looked back and forth between George and Carlos, but said nothing. The three entered the building, greeted the receptionist, and walked toward the conference room.

"Carlos," George said turning his head toward him, "let's keep a close eye on them both."

Carlos nodded.

In the conference room the BioChip team presented pretty much what Kasten had reported in his first article. There were a few questions from Matthias, but none from Wittstein.

Lunch was more relaxed. The staff put on a great spread from the Black Eagle hotel. An Outdoor Action Simulator had been placed in one corner of the lunchroom (the very same machine which Mike Young had borrowed), and both visitors were coaxed into trying a ride--less strenuous than Mike had attempted. George walked the men along the "Achievement Wall," which incorporated photos, active LCD displays and some functional models of products Search had developed over the years. They were sincerely impressed, but George thought that Wittstein had his mind on something else. George's distrust showed too clearly.

"Mr. Evans," Wittstein finally said, "I am not a spy, not an agent, not a crook, not even a scientist. I am just Matthias' friend. I had the time, he asked me to come, and I came along with him."

"Ok, Abraham," said George. "You'll see why we're being so careful, but ok, I'm all right."

The two shook hands, patted each other on the back, and followed LaShauna and Matthias to the Link test lab. Carlos and Kasten followed.

In the lab LaShauna introduced Anna and Allen. "They will be monitoring the process," LaShauna said. Gary would not be introduced until the tests were about to begin in the morning. "This is the chair you'll sit in, and there is the screen we expect to be riveted to during your experience. Both Anna and Joan have been through the process many times, and it's very safe. Tonight we would like you to get a good night's rest, so we plan to take you to your hotel now, and let you relax after your long trip. George will pick you up again in the morning with his travel vehicle. His wife Rachel will serve you breakfast en route, a favorite treat George enjoys applying to visitors." The men laughed. "I'll be there too," she added.

Matthias and Abraham looked well rested when they were picked up in the morning. During the breakfast ride they were downright jovial. LaShauna went right along with the mood. Rachel enjoyed the laughter, but said little. She was busy, of course, serving the "meal on wheels," as LaShauna called it. When they all arrived at Search, the visitors met first with George, Carlos and Rachel in George's office while LaShauna, Joan and Father Christopher finalized the test protocol. George's phone chimed, and a moment after he answered he said, "They're ready for us in the Link test lab." The group rose and quietly followed George out of the office and down the hall. Rachel slipped away and left for home.

Everyone said good morning, and Gary was introduced. LaShauna motioned to Matthias to take his seat in the dentist chair, and Allen stepped over to attach the Link, synchronizing yoke and ground strap to Matthias. Anna attached the nasal canula to his head. Abraham sat down with George as Kasten entered the room. He joined them without a word.

LaShauna stood in front of Matthias to his right. "Try your best to relax," she said to him. The milkshake I gave you after breakfast, as you know, contained a mild sedative. It should be taking effect now."

"It is," Matthias noted.

"Joan was taken back 249 years," LaShauna continued, "recalling the memories of an orator-ancestor delivering a speech in 1761. Mrs. Shaw went back 300 years further to 1461, almost 550 years ago, and she recalled the memories of her child-ancestor observing the coronation procession of King Edward IV. We're able to control the depth of recall quite precisely. You and I have talked about the dreams--"

"--visions," Matthias corrected.

"Yes, visions," LaShauna agreed. "You told me you had seen the Temple in Jerusalem during these experiences."

"Yes, I did."

"I asked you if you had seen the Wailing Wall, in real life, and you said you had. You also told me that upon seeing it you had a strong feeling of deja vu."

"Yes, very strong--eerie."

"How old did you appear to be in your visions?'

"When I saw the Temple? Perhaps 10 or 12."

"Let's start by concentrating on that timeframe, when you saw the Temple as a . . . boy?"

"Yes, a boy," Charash agreed.

"--of 10 or 12," continued LaShauna. "Think of the Temple, the sun shining against its walls, the huge stone blocks which formed them, the noise of the people around the temple and in the inner courtyard. Those sorts of things. Try to reproduce that particular vision. Closing your eyes is best, Anna tells me."

231

"Aren't I supposed to look at the monitor screen?"

"No," answered LaShauna. "We've learned that doesn't help. The memory you'll re-experience will surface in your mind, in greater detail, I'm sure, than you've experienced before. Are you ready, Doctor?"

"Yes, I believe I am."

"Ok, then, Allen?" LaShauna inquired, looking up at Allen's station.

"We're ready," said Allen. "I plan to begin, as we agreed, with a setting of 1.600, which would equal Barbara's dose, that took her back 549 years. Christ was born in 5 or 6 BC, 2,015 or 16 years ago. He was ten, which therefore, was about 2,006 years ago. I'll be prepared to gradually increase the dose to 5.800 over a period of ten minutes, or until Matthias indicates he has repeated his vision."

"Okay, Allen," said LaShauna. "Gary?"

"We're ready to record and compress up to thirty minutes of video data," said Gary.

"Anna?"

"Doctor ben Charash is doing very well, and our vital-data monitoring system is getting very clear data," said Anna.

"Then let's proceed," said LaShauna. "Relax, now, Matthias. You've been there before. Just let your mind take control. If you can, at the moment you feel a vision is beginning to crystallize, raise your left hand, but continue to concentrate."

"I will do as you say, LaShauna," ben Charash said.

The minutes passed slowly. LaShauna kept her eyes on the doctor, glancing occasionally at the clock above Allen's head on the wall, now and then at George Evans. *"Will this work?"* she thought. *"We put all of our eggs into the ben Charash basket."*

Seven minutes passed. Dr. ben Charash's hand did not move, but his head began to sway back and forth as though to keep in time with some music. None was heard by the others. Nine minutes passed. Mathias's head stopped moving. He seemed to stiffen his body. George's eyes widened, and he turned his head abruptly toward Anna. Anna nodded. Mathias was all right.

"Hey!" Mathias hollered, causing everyone to jerk to attention. Then the noise began. Crowds, people close and far, speaking Aramaic and Hebrew. Children laughing. A baby crying. The monitor became alive, and Gary began to try to bring into sync the image which was forming.

"LaShauna," Gary called quietly. "Tighten the yoke slightly. It's fallen away from the doctor's neck."

LaShauna did, Matthias's eyes remained closed, and the image cleared into a spectacular picture. Mathias's left hand raised up off the arm of the chair.

Mathias's ancestor was looking down from a second-story rooftop to the main street below. He was focused on two Roman legionaries walking away from two others, who were still watching a money changer and a customer at the corner of an alley across the main street. The soldiers were walking toward the house atop which Mathias's ancestor was standing. They wore shiny armor which covered their torsos and shoulders over red-maroon tunics. Huge short swords were sheathed at their waists. Metal helmets covered their heads and wrapped around the sides of their cheekbones to their chins. The helmets had bright red crests. The soldier on the left looked up at Mathias's ancestor for a moment. They were in no hurry, and Mathias later said that he--his ancestor--was not afraid of them, though they represented unforgiving authority.

Next to the money changer's corner, and to the left, were clothing shops in a row of two story buildings. Behind that row of buildings many others on other streets could be seen. There were people resting on top of some of those

233

buildings, too, and on the edge of a two-story building directly across the street a man sat watching eight men carry a stretcher-like conveyance covered with a wood frame with a domed roof and curtains on all four sides. A trim, bearded young man walked alone alongside the conveyance down the main street. He had striped, full-length clothing and carried a shepherd's walking stick. On both sides of the street people were milling around talking with vendors of textiles, copper, pottery and baskets.

Mathias's ancestor (whose eyes recorded the event) was apparently standing on the short wall that surrounded the roof. A dark-haired woman spinning wool with crude tools stood in the south corner of the roof near the short wall. There was a child on the floor playing near her with a tiny lamb. The woman turned to Mathias's ancestor and shouted something to him in Hebrew. Above her one could see two more two-story houses. On the roof of the nearest house a woman was watering some red flowers. Her building and most on the main street had various striped awnings, held up with wooden poles jammed against the walls of the buildings.

But the most spectacular view loomed over the top of the houses to the south. There a monumental fortress of Roman design occupied a full quarter of the view, blocking much of the horizon with its height. Yet above the garrison appeared the white stone Temple of Jerusalem against the blue, cloud-broken sky. Mathias had in fact produced the Temple, recalled from ancestral memories, just as LaShauna, Joan and Father Christopher had hoped.

Dr, ben Charash's body relaxed. The crowd noise stopped, and the image faded to video static. "158 over 84," Anna called out. "Heart rate, 99. He did just fine."

"An understatement if I ever heard one," LaShauna said, and applause broke out as Matthias, eyes still closed, broke into a broad smile. His face was wet with tears.

"Wonderful, Matthias," LaShauna said to him. "Just wonderful."

Mathias's eyes opened and, continuing to smile, he looked up at LaShauna and said, "It was a bit frightening at first--the images and sounds and smells--all so real. But it felt comfortable, too, as though I had been there before. No wonder some are fooled into believing in reincarnation."

Anna came over to ben Charash and wiped his face with the tissues she had learned were a necessary part of the lab's outfitting. Allen disconnected the Link, synchronizing yoke and grounding strap from Mathias. Anna removed the nasal canula. George and Wittstein walked over and shook ben Charash's hand, then helped him from the chair. He was a bit unstable on his feet at first. Kasten sat still in his chair, his head in his hands. How would he tell the world what he had seen? How would he make them believe how it happened? And this afternoon the next test was scheduled, promising to unveil--perhaps--Christ Himself. This was beyond news. It was "revelation."

A quiet, private lunch in George's office was attended by Matthias ben Charash, Abraham Wittstein, George Evans and Carlos Martinez. The "proof of Christ team" met over lunch separately to revise the protocol for the afternoon's test. At about 12:30 LaShauna, Joan, Father Christopher and Allen arrived at George's office.

"If you're finished with lunch," said LaShauna, "we'd like to speak to Matthias for a few minutes. We have some questions which need to be answered before we complete our preparations for this afternoon's test."

"Sure, LaShauna, come on in," said George. "The first question you should ask Matthias is, does he want to continue?"

"Nothing but a heart attack could stop me," Charash said. George didn't smile with the others.

235

The team and Allen filed in and sat down around George's work surface.

"Allen has reviewed the video disk with all of us, and since it is his job to verify the historical accuracy of the experience, as well as to calculate the Promax-2 dosage to be used, we've asked him to come with us to interview you," LaShauna said to ben Charash.

"Fine," he answered.

"We need to pinpoint the time frame of the Experience you had this morning within a couple of years," said Allen. "We know that the memory was definitely stored sometime before 70 A.D."

"Is that incredible or what?" George asked.

Allen continued. "Jerusalem was destroyed by the Romans at that time. The huge fortress you saw, blocking the view of the outer walls of the Temple area, was the Fortress of Antonia, built by Herod in about 28 B.C. That's a total span of about 100 years, far from our goal. However, the presence and actions of Roman legionaries--not just ordinary soldiers--in the street below your ancestor suggests two things: first, there's a major, imminent problem in Jerusalem--Jewish insurgents were planning their move to drive the Romans out of Jerusalem, which they did in 66 A.D., and second, since they were still there, it hadn't happened yet. I believe we were looking at a memory which was stored in 65 A.D. Also, the doctor experienced the recall at a Promax-2 setting of 5.63. Right on the money for 1,945 years."

"Very good, Allen," said George.

"Now we have a question for you, Dr. ben Charash," continued Allen.

"Yes, sir," he answered.

"What did the woman on the roof with your ancestor say to him?"

"Ah . . . it's funny, but I wasn't paying attention--I mean, my ancestor wasn't paying attention."

"We have it on disk, it should be easy to understand, but she is speaking in Hebrew or Aramaic, and we don't have anyone here who does," said Allen.

"I'm sure if I heard the recording--," began Charash."

"I know what she said," interjected Wittstein.

"Good," said Allen.

"She was speaking in Hebrew, and she told the boy, 'Akim!'--the boy's name--'Get down from there. You'll fall to your death. Wait till your father comes back to take you to Nazareth.'"

The room grew silent. Everyone except Wittstein and ben Charash seemed to recognize the significance of what the woman had said. They looked around at each other. Dave Kasten came to George's door, and George waved him in.

"Well, I'll be," George said, breaking the silence. "We have a man named Charash--'carpenter'--coming to take, probably, a 10- or 12-year-old son back home to Nazareth in the year 65."

"In April, I would guess," said Allen.

"Why April?" asked Joan.

"Jewish families who lived in Nazareth traveled each year to Jerusalem for the Passover."

"Didn't they travel to Jerusalem more often than once a year?"

"Not too likely," answered Allen. "It's a 65-mile trip. No cars, planes or trains, you know."

"Let's talk a minute about the ages of the principals we're interested in," said Joan. "Let's say the boy, Akim, is 11. His father was probably married when he was 18. There's no way for us to be sure, but let's say the boy was his firstborn, and so the boy may have been born a year after

237

the marriage. Sixty-six, minus eleven, minus one, minus eighteen, equals thirty-five. Perhaps Akim's father was born in 35 A.D., five years after Christ's death and resurrection. Now, if Akim's grandfather was married when he was 18 and Akim's father was born a year later, that would mean your ancestor's grandfather was born in--thirty-five, minus one, minus eighteen, equals sixteen--the year 16 A.D. If we're looking for someone in Dr. ben Charash's ancestry who saw Christ during his ministry, we're looking for an 11- to 14-year-old."

"And where would this 11- to 14-year-old have seen Christ?" asked George.

"I would guess within walking distance of Nazareth, unless he was in Jerusalem for one of the three Passovers which occurred during Christ's ministry," said Allen. Opening the last pages of a Bible he was holding and consulting a map, Allen said, "That would mean somewhere between Nain and Capernaum."

"Does Cana fall in there somewhere?" asked George.

"That's just nine miles north of Nazareth," said Allen. "Why?"

"If he were the son of a carpenter, living in Nazareth late in 26 A.D., his family certainly knew Joseph, Mary and Jesus," began George, "and it is reasonable to speculate that Matthias's ancestral family was invited to the same wedding celebration which Mary, Jesus and His friends were invited to."

"They may have witnessed Jesus' first miracle!" said Joan.

"A long shot, Allen?" asked George.

"Sure," Allen answered, "but we've been hitting long shots from the beginning of this project. It almost seems as though we're destined to discover these things."

"*Revelation*," repeated Kasten to himself.

"I think we all agree," said LaShauna, "that we should focus this afternoon's test on the Fall of the year 26 A.D., through the eyes of an 11- to 14-year-old carpenter's son, to see what we can see."

"Agreed," said George.

Dr. ben Charash nodded and shook his head almost simultaneously. *"Will I remain an orthodox Jew,"* he was thinking, *"after I see Jesus Christ?"*

The group's discussion ended, and Matthias ben Charash was soon back in the Link lab and seated in the dentist chair.

"Your blood pressure and pulse are where they were when you ended the last test," said Anna. "Are you sure you're all right?"

"Yes, Doctor, I am fine. I am just excited about the prospects of the unknown."

"Are you certain you want to proceed?" asked George.

"By all means."

"We were able to deal with the translation problem we had this morning," George explained to Matthias. "Allen contacted a professor at the University of Wisconsin who specializes in the languages of the writers of the New and Old Testaments. He's fluent in Hebrew and Aramaic. Gary and Allen have him in an adjacent room, where he'll be able to hear everything picked up by the Link through earphones. He'll translate whatever he hears into English, which is what we'll hear from the system in this room."

Matthias nodded.

"Ok," said LaShauna. "And what does the monitoring team say?"

"I'm ready for 26 A.D.," said Allen.

"Ready to record," said Gary. "The sync yoke looks good from here."

"Matthias is excited, but healthy," said Anna.

"Then let's begin," said LaShauna. "Matthias, this time we don't have a specific vision to concentrate on. Perhaps that's what you meant by 'the prospects of the unknown."

"It was."

"I suggest you concentrate on the images the following words bring to mind: Cana, wedding, Jesus Christ, carpenter, miracle, wine."

"Like a keyword computer search?"

"I guess that would be a good analogy," LaShauna responded. "We don't know if this will work, but it seems that the more related information one can concentrate on the better chance there is of recalling what one is looking for."

Dr. ben Charash's eyes closed, and the room became still. "Cana, wedding, Jesus Christ, carpenter, miracle, wine," he repeated aloud.

LaShauna nodded to Allen, who began the flow of Promax-2 and, as usual, after five seconds the flow of synchronized electrical pulses. After about thirty seconds the sound system bellowed a statement from an unknown voice. "I was there!" the interpreter said, and an image of the individual he was speaking for appeared and disappeared from the monitor screen.

"I'm sorry," said ben Charash. "I feel strongly that I can recall the scene again, but whoever it was startled me, and the delay between what I am experiencing and what you hear was overwhelmingly disturbing."

"Ask Mike Young to bring up a pair of ear protectors," called George to Allen. Allen picked up the wall phone nearby, and Mike appeared with the ear protectors in just a minute or two. His eyes were wide with curiosity.

"Thank you, Mike," said George with a wave that convinced Mike he had better not stay.

"But then ben Charash won't hear what's going on," said Kasten quietly to George.

"You've forgotten," reminded George, "that the test subjects hear and see everything in their minds."

Mathias put on the ear protectors, and Anna adjusted the nasal canula so that the ear protectors did not interfere with the oxygen flow or his comfort.

"Thank, you, Doctor," Charash said too loud. "Please let's start again," he said to LaShauna.

Charash closed his eyes, and the room became quite again. LaShauna delayed a full minute before nodding to Allen.

Moments later, "Did you hear what happened at the wedding?" came from the interpreter. Everyone in the room thought it was ben Charash speaking, but LaShauna shook her head when George pointed at him, signaling his question. The image which appeared next explained what was happening. A man to the right of Charash's ancestor had asked the question of a man they were approaching. "I was there!" he said. "I'll never forget it."

"Tell us what happened," the voice said again.

"Probably the boy's father," George whispered to Kasten.

"Jesus the carpenter and his friends were sitting together," the man continued. [Electricity filled the room with the mention of Jesus' name.] "They were laughing and talking when Jesus' mother came over to Him," he continued. "She told Him the wedding host had run out of wine. 'My dear lady,' Jesus said to her, 'this is not the time or place.' He knew what she was asking. She said nothing more to Him, but turned to the servers and told them to 'do whatever He tells you.'

"Jesus looked at his friends, and He wasn't smiling. Mary had left him no alternative, and He almost seemed embarrassed, but He turned back to Mary, and an impish sort of smile came to His face. He began to speak to the servers while still looking directly at his mother. 'Take those six stone jars and fill them with water.' Mary's hand covered her mouth, and her eyes opened wide. The jars would represent enough wine for ten such weddings.

"The servers looked at each other, then at Mary. She nodded, and they left to fill the jars. They had to call others to help, because the jars held about 25 gallons each and would be very heavy once filled. They returned after a quarter of an hour and began to bring the jars to the stand where they had found them, against the outer wall near the door.

"'Draw some out and take it to the head waiter,' Jesus said to them. One server began to fill a small pitcher with a ladle, and all were shocked to see that the water had become purple in color. The server who was filling the pitcher raised the ladle to his nose, and he exclaimed, 'Wine!' Jesus pointed again to the headwaiter, and all of the servers who saw what had happened went to the headwaiter with the pitcher.

"The headwaiter tasted the liquid. His eyebrows went up, and he called over to the bridegroom. We could hear him say, over the noise of the celebration, 'Everyone serves the good wine first, then the lesser quality. You have kept the good wine until now.' The bridegroom nodded, but clearly did not know what the man was talking about.

"The servers were shocked by all of this and talked excitedly among themselves. Jesus' friends were watching with wide eyes. When they heard what the headwaiter said they turned to Jesus. He put his finger to his lips and waived them off. Several got up and walked over to Jesus' mother, who was smiling broadly. I moved closer to hear, because I knew they would be speaking quietly.

"'Mary, how did your Son do this?' they asked. 'Give the glory to God,' she answered. 'But you knew,' one of them said, 'that He could help when you asked. How did you know?' 'I know my Son,' she answered, 'and He has done this before.' 'Tell us,' they pleaded. She paused and then said, 'You must not speak of this.' They nodded. 'Jesus and I visited a friend whose husband had died. She had no food or wine for her family. We had little to give her. Jesus told her that the Father provides for all of the needs of His children, that it is important to trust Him. The widow answered, ''We trust in God, and know He is ever faithful.'' Jesus and I prayed with her and asked God to bless her. When we left and were walking toward our home my friend came running after us. Her cupboard, which had been empty, was found to contain seven loaves of fresh bread. Her wine jar was filled to the brim. There was oil and dried fish where there had been none. She was so grateful. 'Give the glory to the Father,' Jesus said. 'These things were done for you by your faith and the power of the Holy Spirit.'"

The memory ended abruptly. Mathias had maintained the experience for almost five minutes. "Astonishing," he said.

"Truly," Gary added.

"What did all of this mean?" asked Charash.

"Have you not heard the New Testament story of the wedding feast of Cana?" LaShauna asked him.

"No," he answered. "I never heard any story which related to what I just experienced."

"Matthias, you just gave us an accurate account right out of Christian Scripture," George said.

"Astonishing," ben Charash repeated.

"Truly," Gary added again.

"*But I did not see the Christ*," ben Charash thought to himself.

The next morning ben Charash, Wittstein, George Evans and Anna had breakfast together at the Black Eagle Hotel.

Dr. ben Charash did most of the talking, describing the amazing detail that he had seen when he recalled his ancestor's experience in the year 24 A.D.

"It was the Promax-2," Anna said, her face flushing at the mistake she had just made.

"Just what is Promax-2?" asked Wittstein.

"Sorry, Abraham," George answered, "we shouldn't even be talking about the action of the chemical."

"I didn't mean to pry," said Wittstein. "Mr. Nolte also mentioned it yesterday."

"I know," said George, "and we don't mean to be overly secretive, but we must not talk about Promax-2. That is our decision, and we are determined to uphold it."

"What is on the test schedule for today?" asked ben Charash, changing the subject.

"Our team is finalizing that this morning, but I know we're still looking for an encounter with Jesus Christ," George answered.

"LaShauna is determined to show that Christ grew up as a normal human," said Anna. "The hypothesis you read in Dave Kasten's report suggests that although Jesus was the Son of God, the process with which He entered His temporal life made it quite impossible for Him to have any knowledge of His divine nature. He wasn't able to recall His relationship with the Father, and He suffered the same faulty genes all men have since the Fall of Adam and Eve."

"I hope we're not offending you by speaking of a Christ you do not believe in," George said.

"Oh, we believe Jesus lived and did marvelous things," answered Wittstein. "We have read about Him in the works of Josephus. But, we do not believe He was the Messiah, nor that He was God or the Son of God."

"I'll have to ask you to speak for yourself," ben Charash said. "The Sanhedrin clearly condemned and executed an innocent man. After the experience I had yesterday, I admit I am beginning to wonder whether or not He was the Messiah after all."

Wittstein looked a bit shocked. "Really, Matthias?" he asked.

Matthias stared at his coffee and then finished the cup.

"We'd better be on our way," said Anna.

The Link team was ready, and so was ben Charash. Kasten, George and Carlos observed the test. The interpreter was in position in the adjacent room.

"You have the blood pressure of a twenty-five-year-old," Anna told ben Charash. He smiled.

"Matthias," said LaShauna, "concentrate this time on these key words and phrases: carpenter, Joseph, the boy Jesus, father--"

"Abba," said ben Charash.

"Yes," confirmed LaShauna. "Jesus would have called His father 'Abba' or 'daddy.' Concentrate also on the image of you--that is, your ancestor--and Jesus as children, with their fathers, both carpenters. It seems logical to us, therefore possible, that Joseph, Jesus' stepfather, would have on occasion required the help of another carpenter--your ancestor. Think about that possibility."

Charash placed the ear protectors over his head, and Anna rushed over to adjust the nasal canula. Mathias's eyes closed, and Allen started the correct flow of Promax-2. Less than a minute elapsed.

"I can smell fresh cut wood," ben Charash said softly.

"What's your name?" the interpreter said for a small, plain-looking boy of about ten who appeared on the monitor.

"Daniel," answered ben Charash's ancestor, through whose eyes the scene appeared. "My father is a carpenter."

"I know," the boy answered. "He is helping My daddy put the beams up. He is making a new roof for the widow who lives here in Sepphoris."

"And what is Your name?" Daniel asked.

"Jesus," He answered.

A change came over everyone in the room that was hard to describe. No one moved, except for Allen, who shook his head as if to clear a dizziness which had come over him. He needed to constantly observe the Promax-2 outflow, and he struggled to concentrate on the task. George's head began to move back and forth, and his eyes filled with tears as the boys continued their conversation.

"My daddy's name is Joseph," Jesus continued. "Do you want to play?"

"I'm hungry," said Daniel. "Let us go to the booths where they sell fruit."

"I have no denarii," said Jesus.

"Neither do I," said Daniel, "but perhaps we will find a kind shopkeeper."

The two ran off together along the rows of shops, with Jesus out front, staying close to the buildings, apparently to stay in the shade of the stores' awnings. The tongues of a cart protruded from the corner of the next building. Mathias flinched and called out, but Jesus tripped on the first tongue and crashed His shoulder into the second. He lay there and began to cry.

"Are you hurt?" Daniel said, running ahead to his new friend.

Jesus whined and nodded His head.

"Should I get your daddy?" Daniel asked.

Jesus nodded again and sobbed quietly. Daniel ran back to where his father and Joseph were working.

LaShauna and those seated behind ben Charash saw the street as Daniel turned and ran. They saw, through Daniel's eyes, the house he was focused on and the door he was running to.

Daniel stopped at the door and looked inside. One man was standing on a heavy table at one end of the one-room house, and the other on a crude ladder leaning against the far wall. There was no roof above them. One of the men was striking the beam, with which they were struggling, with a large mallet, presumably to force it into proper position.

"Joseph," Daniel called out.

The man with the mallet stopped and looked at the boy.

"Jesus fell and is hurt," Daniel said.

Joseph got down off the ladder and tossed the mallet to the floor. Daniel pointed the way, and Joseph walked quickly ahead. When Jesus saw him coming He started to get up and reach out to His father, starting to cry even harder.

"You took a bad fall?" Joseph asked.

"Yes, Daddy," Jesus said.

"What did I tell you about running near the buildings where there are so many things to trip on?"

"I forgot, Daddy," Jesus said. "I'm sorry."

Joseph scooped Jesus up, looking Him over as he did so. He lifted the sleeve of Jesus' right arm, which was soiled by the fall. His shoulder had a bad scrape, but was not bleeding.

"Your mother will scold us both," Joseph said.

The experience ended. It left ben Charash breathing deeply. "What can one say?" he sighed.

And no one said a word. The Link cuff was removed from ben Charash, and the equipment shut down. Everyone filed out of the lab as though they were leaving a sacred place. George instinctively headed for his office, almost forgetting about the others. Kasten, ben Charash and Wittstein followed him. LaShauna stopped outside the lab and gathered Anna, Allen and Gary into a huddle. They put

247

their arms around each other in silent congratulations. Allen left to give the interpreter a break. He remained at Search the rest of the day.

As George entered his office, still followed by the other men, Kasten said to his back, "I don't know if I can take more tests like that."

George stopped and spun around. "There'll be more. There'll be more," he said. "You'll find the words," he added, knowing that this concern was causing Kasten's frown.

The two Israelis stopped behind them, confused by their conversation.

George turned to ben Charash. "Was it Jesus Christ?" he asked.

"How could I be sure? He looked so ordinary. Nothing remarkable that would one day cause a billion people to follow Him."

"Abraham?" George said, turning to Wittstein. "What do you think?"

"A boy named Jesus in Sepphoris, four miles northeast of Nazareth, with a father named Joseph who is a carpenter . . .? In that timeframe the odds would be very much in favor of it being Him." Wittstein answered.

"But He looked so ordinary," repeated ben Charash. "And He ran and tripped and fell, just like an ordinary boy of nine or ten."

"Jesus was a man like us in every way," George said. "Yet He did not sin."

"Didn't He disobey his father?" asked Wittstein.

"He said He forgot," George answered.

"But you believe He was the Son of God! The Son of God forgot to follow His father's instructions?" asked Wittstein.

"Abraham," George answered, "Jesus emptied Himself of all His divine knowledge and power by becoming one of us through the natural process of conception, prenatal development, and birth."

"You believe this?" asked Wittstein.

"Yes, I most certainly do," answered George. "And I just had a thought which put goose bumps back on my arms."

"What is that?" Kasten asked.

"Matthias, could you take us back to the same timeframe?"

"Yes, I am confident," said ben Charash, "but with what purpose?"

"Add one key phrase to your focus points--'Son of God.'"

"What do you think we might learn?"

"If your ancestor as a young boy is again with Jesus, and this time the phrase 'Son of God' is used in their conversation, it will be Jesus speaking about what He knows of His divine Father."

"I am willing," said ben Charash. "At the moment I am weak for food."

"After lunch, then," said George.

To himself Kasten thought, "*How can I even think of food having experienced such a thrilling morning and anticipating an even more thrilling afternoon?*"

"Coming?" George said to Kasten as he followed the two Israelis out of his office.

Kasten gave a start and nodded.

By 2:00 in the afternoon ben Charash and the team were ready for another trip back in time through the memories of the Israeli doctor's ancestors, stored in his soul. Matthias had his instructions from George, so LaShauna sat in a chair she had positioned near his side. Allen had been instructed to back off on the Promax-2 setting by an equivalent year, enhancing ben Charash's ability to recall events a year later than he had that morning. LaShauna nodded to Allen after she saw ben Charash, with his eyes closed, relaxing into the dentist chair.

This time again less than a minute passed when an image appeared on the monitor, and the interpreter voiced the words of ben Charash's ancestor, Daniel.

"What is wrong? Why are you so quiet?" he asked the boy walking at his right. It appeared to be Jesus, the carpenter's son, but it was difficult to tell until the two stopped and faced each other.

"We are good friends," Jesus answered, "and I wish to answer your question, but you must not ever tell anyone what you hear. Do you promise?"

"Yes, Jesus," answered Daniel, "we are good friends, and I will honor our friendship by never telling anyone what You will say."

Jesus was silent, and they began to walk along again. Daniel waited patiently without repeating his question about what was bothering Jesus.

After several dozen paces Jesus said, "My mother told me I am the Son of God."

The boys stopped again and faced each other.

"But, Jesus, we are all children of God. Why does this disturb You?"

"She said I am the Son of the Most High!"

"The Son of the Most High?" Daniel questioned.

"Yes," said Jesus, "the One foretold by the Prophets."

"The Messiah!"

"The Messiah," Jesus repeated.

"But where are your armies; where is your sword?" Daniel laughed. "'To him he delivers the nations and subdues the kings; With his sword he reduces them to dust, with his bow, to driven straw,'" he said, quoting Scripture.

"He is quoting Isaiah," LaShauna interjected quietly.

"No, Daniel," Jesus continued. "My mother says the Messiah will be like a lamb, and He will give His life as an offering for sin."

"I will never tell others You have told me this because we are friends, but also because they will never believe that the Messiah will be like a lamb."

"I know," said Jesus.

"Where are Your powers, if You are the Son of the Most High?"

"I have no powers, Daniel. I am like you, a boy. But My Father is powerful, and I must learn more about Him."

"Joseph is Your father. You know him well."

"I must believe My mother, Daniel. I must put My trust in God. He has spoken through Scripture. I will learn more of Him there, and I will learn what the Prophets say about the Messiah."

"Shall we walk to the fruit market?" asked Daniel.

"Yes, this time we shall walk," answered Jesus, smiling. The two boys walked along together, then looked at each other and began to run.

The image faded, and ben Charash pulled the ear protectors from his head. They tangled with the nasal canula, and Anna came over to help. LaShauna stood up and looked around the room. There was hardly a dry face to be found.

"Thank you, Jesus," George said. To the research team he said, "Two down and four to go."

Charash and Wittstein were due to leave the following afternoon. George had breakfast with the two men at the Black Eagle and told them he would be happy to take them to several local scenic spots for relaxation. Dr. ben Charash appeared very tired, and he declined; however, he had a request of George.

"Last night," he said, "I had a dream, a very vivid dream--perhaps another vision. Would it at all be possible to experience the process one more time to recall . . . to re-experience the vision?"

George was hesitant.

"I dreamt I saw the Christ during His ministry as an adult. I must see Him again with the enhancement of the process," Matthias insisted.

"All right," said George, "but are you up to it? You look exhausted."

"Yes," said ben Charash, "I feel fine. I was awake much of the night after the vision."

George touched a communications device on his belt and placed a small receiver to his ear. "LaShauna, please," he said. There was a brief pause. "LaShauna, Matthias would like one more Link experience. He had a dream last night and wants to recall it with the process . . . .Ok, ten o'clock. See you then."

"LaShauna will be ready for us at ten. That will give me time to show you a little of Madison anyhow."

The three men talked of their homes and children as George drove them around Madison's scenic areas in his travel vehicle. They arrived at Search just before ten o'clock. The team was waiting for them in the Link laboratory.

As George, Wittstein and ben Charash entered the lab, ben Charash turned to George and said, "George, the vision, though very short, was a very personal experience for me. I would prefer that the monitor not be used. I will describe the experience to all of you when it is over."

"I trust you, Matthias," answered George, "but aren't you asking a bit much?"

"Please, George," ben Charash responded. "It will be a very short experience, of that I'm sure."

George stopped, looked at ben Charash, and thought, "*What is this?*" Since he knew the recording system would remain on, he agreed to ben Charash's request.

"Ok, Matthias," said George. "Team, hook him up."

"What timeframe?" asked Allen.

"25 A.D.," answered ben Charash without hesitation.

"No problem," answered Allen.

The experience was, as ben Charash had predicted, very short. It seemed as though it ended moments after he climbed into the dentist chair. But ben Charash's countenance had changed significantly. His face was white at first, then became flush. Tears filled the corners of his eyes. He sat silent for a full five minutes, then began speaking from the chair, still too emotionally affected to stand and face the group. Everyone gathered around him. Only Kasten was missing, since this test was not part of the schedule he had been given.

"Jesus was in the Temple area," ben Charash began, "on the Portico of Solomon. Many Jews were gathered around Him, questioning Him. 'How long are You going to keep us in suspense?' they asked. 'If You are the Messiah, tell us plainly.'

"Jesus said to them, 'I have told you, and you do not believe Me. The works I do in My Father's name testify for Me.' He said to them plainly, 'The Father and I are one.'

"They picked up rocks to kill Him. He said, 'I have shown you many good works from My Father. For which of these are you trying to stone Me?'

"They shouted, 'We are not stoning You for a good work, but for blasphemy. You, a man, are claiming to be God.' Jesus continued to try to make them understand, but they would not.

"Then . . . Jesus . . . turned to me . . . and said, 'If you do not believe me, then believe on the evidence of the miracles.'"

Charash broke down and began to sob.

Anna said to him, "Jesus was looking at your ancestor, Matthias. Not at you."

"Oh, no," he responded. "I could see in His eyes He was aware that I too was watching Him through the eyes of my ancestor. He was speaking to me!"

"He loves you," said George.

"I am a Jew," said ben Charash. "I have my loyalties. I must remain an Orthodox Jew."

"But, Matthias," responded George, "You can remain a Jew and believe in Jesus."

Dr. ben Charash shook his bowed head.

The chartered jet landed as George pulled onto the tarmac. George thanked Matthias profusely for traveling the great distance. Matthias just shook his head. Kasten walked over from the gate and also said good-bye to ben Charash and Wittstein. Carlos had called him and suggested that he drive over to the airport on his own. LaShauna hugged ben Charash. Allen waved. Anna smiled. Matthias saluted from the door of the plane, and he was gone.

"What an experience," Allen said. "What could top it?"

Allen drove the travel vehicle for George on the way back. "Suddenly, I feel a bit tired myself," George had said. He sat with Anna and LaShauna on the cushioned seat with his left hand on the Plexiglas coffee table and his right arm resting behind Anna. "Perhaps," he said, "Christ was speaking to us through ben Charash telling us to present the evidence of the miracles of Creation to the world. The hypothesis and the video evidence we're collecting will make a good start."

Anna and LaShauna smiled and nodded. There was not much they could add.

Chapter 38

Before Abraham

Fr. Christopher read from the open Bible in his hand, "'For Christ also suffered for sins once, the righteous for the sake of the unrighteous, that he might lead you to God. Put to death in the flesh, he was brought to life in the spirit. In it he also went to preach to the spirits in prison, who had once been disobedient while God patiently waited in the days of Noah during the building of the ark, in which a few persons, eight in all, were saved.' That passage is from the first book of Peter, Chapter 3, verses 18 through 20."

Both research teams, George Evans, Dave Kasten and Carlos were gathered in the main conference room to hear Fr. Christopher and Joan discuss the status of their assignments.

"Our assignments," Joan began, "are to prove that Christ existed before Abraham, and to show that Christ Himself walked and talked with man long before He was born 2,016 years ago. Father Christopher and I are working together, and we found the passage from 1 Peter that he just read to you."

"Noah existed around 4,500 years ago," said Allen. "Are you suggesting . . !!"

"Let them talk, Allen," said George.

"Let's not get ahead of ourselves here," said Joan. "First we want to look at the controversy which still surrounds Peter's statement. Some believe that in His preincarnate state, Christ went and preached through Noah to the godless people of his time. Others believe that between His death and resurrection Christ went to the prison where fallen angels are incarcerated and there preached to the angels. Still others believe that between His death and resurrection Christ went to the place of the dead and preached to the souls of Noah's wicked contemporaries."

"All seem to ignore God's timeless existence," said George.

"The concurrent state of God," added Gary, looking at Joan.

"Peter must have had a revelation," Joan continued, "to have known this. And I'll quote again: 'He (Christ) also went to preach to the spirits in prison, who had once been disobedient while God patiently waited in the days of Noah.' If Peter had an understanding of the concurrent state of God," Joan said pointing to and smiling at Gary, "he may have said it this way: 'Christ also delivered the gospel to those who died as a result of the Flood, because so many were killed by this act of God, an act God promised never to repeat.'"

"But that would still mean they were given an opportunity to accept God and the salvation He offered them after they had died as a result of their sins," said George.

"We thought the same thing," said Fr. Christopher. "It doesn't seem to fit with the concept of Creation as we understand it."

"What then does the hypothesis suggest happened?" asked Allen.

Fr. Christopher paused before he answered. "Because God was about to wipe out all of mankind except for the eight people of Noah's family, Christ brought the message of salvation, personally, to each and every adult and child before they were lost in the Flood."

"Then why wasn't this recorded in Scripture? Why didn't Moses include it in Genesis?" asked Allen.

"Our first answer to that question," said Joan, "was because everyone who experienced Christ in this manner died in the flood. But, we asked ourselves, then how did Peter know what happened--believing that all of history is stored in souls of later generations?"

"Peter recalled the event through the will of God," said Fr. Christopher.

"Therefore, if you buy into our hypothesis so far, someone passed on at least the fact that Christ Himself preached to the wicked of Noah's days."

"Now that sounds more like what God would do," said Anna. "I often wondered how it was fair to kill off so many when there was only Noah and his family preaching repentance. You are saying that Christ gave them the same opportunity we have, to listen and hear or to ignore the Word of God."

"Ok, but why wasn't Christ mentioned in Genesis?" asked Allen again.

"He wasn't called Christ," said Fr. Christopher. "He was the only God the people knew. Who walked with Adam and Eve in the garden? Who walked with Enoch, an ancestor of Noah, and with Noah himself? A spirit?"

"It was the Son of God," said Joan.

"And John 1:1 says," added Anna, "'In the beginning was the Word, and the Word was with God, and the Word was God.' Jesus is the Word. He was there at the beginning of time."

Everyone paused to take in the thoughts presented by Joan, Fr. Christopher and Anna.

Fr. Christopher spoke again, slowly. "Until the Holy Spirit indwelled believers from Pentecost on, mankind has really known only one Person of the Trinity, Jesus Christ. 'Before Abraham came to be,' Christ said, 'I AM.'"

"It was, in fact, common for a God-like man to appear to men throughout the Old Testament," said LaShauna. "There was the Stranger who visited Abraham, foretold the birth of Isaac and destroyed Sodom and Gomorrah."

"And the fourth man in Nebuchadnezzar's furnace," added Joan.

"Now to your proof of it," said George.

Joan responded. "Father Christopher and I have found a man--"

"Oh, boy!" said Allen.

"Relax, Allen," said Gary.

"--an American Indian, who is a Christian," Joan continued. "His tribe calls him--you guessed it--Noah. The reason is that in recent years he has had visions of the earth being covered with water, and he preaches repentance. He does not say that the world-covering floods are coming again, but his visions definitely are driving the urgency of his message. He predicts a great disaster in the Midwest relating to the Mississippi."

"He's not the only one," said LaShauna. "There are several prophets today that say the same thing."

"We know it's another long shot, Allen, but we'd like to test him," said Joan.

"But why an American Indian?" asked Gary. "Don't you want to look for a descendent of . . . whoops. We're all descendants of some of Noah's family." He looked a little embarrassed.

"That's right, of course," said Joan. "We're considering the Indian because of his visions and message. He may be recalling the Great Flood and God's warning from his ancestral memories."

"Let's fly him in," said George. "You've convinced me."

Thomas Grey Fox, a.k.a., Noah, was 88 years old, but had the energy of a man thirty years younger. He thoroughly enjoyed the short flight to Madison in the company's twin-engine Cessna. Gary piloted the plane with George serving as copilot. Joan and LaShauna kept Tom comfortable in the back. "He preached to us all the way," said LaShauna later, "and good, powerful stuff too!"

At Search, Tom insisted upon being introduced (as Tom Grey Fox) to everyone he saw. "Do you know Christ?" he would often ask them. The process was explained to him, and, when asked if he had any concerns, he said, "God brought me here, not you. God will do with me what He will. I fear nothing, for even my death would result in seeing Jesus face to face." George did not ask his usual question, "Are you sure you want to proceed with this?"

Allen prepared a series of twenty steps for the introduction of Promax-2, that would, in theory, take a person back through his or her ancestral memories 250 years at a time. Anna was getting excellent vital signs for a man of Tom's age, and Gary seemed to have an unexplainable grin on his face during the entire setup procedure. Fr. Christopher was overly respectful toward Tom until Tom asked him if he had offended him in any way. "Not at all," answered the ex-priest, and he and Tom were fast friends from that moment on. LaShauna and Joan had fallen in love with Tom on the flight, and he loved every measure of their affection.

"I'm ready," Tom said suddenly. "Let's get started."

"Ok," said Joan, "we're ready, too. Now all we want you to do is close your eyes and think hard about the visions you've had about the flood."

"Yes," said Tom, "you want me to concentrate on the visions of the flood."

"You have it," said Joan, laughing. "Just close your eyes, concentrate, and be patient. It will take a few minutes at least."

Tom Grey Fox closed his eyes. When he seemed to be relaxed, Joan looked over at LaShauna, sitting with George and Dave Kasten. LaShauna nodded her head, which Allen observed. He started the flow of Promax-2, and after five seconds he also began the low-voltage pulses synchronized with Tom's locus ceruleum. "Better increase the signal amplification," said Gary. Allen did and everything looked normal at all stations.

No one expected the images which appeared on the monitor. They heard the sound of a terrible storm, a deafening roar from the rain hitting the roof above. Tom's ancestor must have been onboard an old wooden vessel being battered by a hurricane-force wind or aboard the Ark itself. As the ship swayed, rose, and fell with the waves, the water outside the square opening he or she was looking out of seemed to fall and rise through fifty feet at least. Occasionally in the water was an uprooted tree, a wall of a destroyed dwelling, or the naked body of a human, drowned in the torrent. Tom cried out, "The vision!" and the image and sound disappeared.

Anna and LaShauna rushed to join Joan at Tom's side. He opened his eyes, looked up at them and smiled. "What's the matter?" he asked. "You all look worried."

"Are you ok?" asked Anna.

"You're the doctor," Tom answered.

"Anna?" George asked.

"He's fine," she said.

"Tom," called George. "What did we see and hear?"

"You saw the vision?" he asked.

"Oh, yes," answered Joan. "I explained that to you."

"It was the Flood," answered Tom. "It was the Great Flood."

"Tom, have you had a vision of the days just before the flood began?" asked Fr. Christopher.

"Yes, I have," answered Tom. "They are very sad times. There was much evil in the world."

"Would you please try to recall this vision also?"

"Yes, if you wish," Tom answered.

"Tom," Joan said, "concentrate then on the time just before the Flood. Scripture tells us Noah walked with God. Think about the times that God visited the people who lived near the construction site of the Ark."

"I will," said Tom, and he closed his eyes. Allen began the flow of Promax-2 immediately.

The echo was disturbing when Tom began to repeat everything he heard aloud. The interpreter was speaking English, but Tom's repetition in the original language caused everyone to reach for earphones.

"Yahweh-among-us is telling all to repent, to turn from their evil ways, but they do not!"

The man speaking, who appeared on the monitor, was sitting on a plank supported by bamboo scaffolding next to a huge wooden wall presumed to be the Ark. He was applying a black material with a crude wooden trowel to the cracks between the rough, horizontal boards. Tom's ancestor was apparently doing the same thing, to the right of the speaker.

"He enters their locked rooms of sin, but they pay no attention, so corrupt are their hearts. He says they will die in their sins unless they turn back to their Creator. He heals those who become ill by abusing their bodies, but they are not grateful and return to their evil ways. Yahweh-among-us warns them that their depraved lives will not go unpunished and tells them a great flood is coming. Some have told us

He weeps when He speaks of their destruction. They try to kill Him, but He vanishes from their presence. Noah has often walked and talked with Yahweh-among-us."

The vision ended. Tom opened his eyes and smiled, none the worse for wear.

"Yahweh-among-us?" asked George.

"That is apparently the interpreter's way of saying what he heard," said Joan.

"God-among-us," said Anna. "In Hebrew, Immanuel!"

"Jesus Christ!" exclaimed LaShauna.

"You did it, Joan!" said Gary. "You did it!"

"Four down and two to go," George said to Kasten.

Chapter 39

The Leak

Carlos Martinez met George Evans in the lobby of Search as George walked in the door.

"There's a call holding for you from Israel," Carlos said.

George nodded, and the two walked down the long hall to George's office. When they arrived at his desk both picked up a phone handset simultaneously.

"George Evans," George said.

"George," the distant caller said, "I'm glad I was able to reach you. I felt I must tell you that there has been a breach of the secrecy you expected of us. The Israeli Army Intelligence Service has been completely briefed on our trip and on the process you successfully demonstrated. I learned on the flight back to Tel Aviv that my dear friend Dr. ben Charash is chief of psychological services for the IAIS, though employed also by the Tel Aviv Medical Research Hospital where I work. I want you to know that although he is my friend, I never knew of his association with the military agency. He told me only because of my commitment to you and the experiences he had while at Search."

"Abraham," George said. "Are you in any danger?"

"Not if you're careful with what I'm telling you. I could be detained, if the military finds out I called you."

"Detained?"

"Arrested without charge."

"We will not let on that we know of the leak," assured George. "We'll put in place the normal additional security measures which we have planned all along."

"Thank you," said Wittstein.

"Thank you, Abraham. If there is anything we can do for you, please contact me."

"I will, George. I had better get off now."

"Yes, Abraham, and be careful."

"Good-bye."

"Good-bye, Abraham."

"Well, you heard it," said George to Carlos. "Let's initiate the security measures we considered for this event when the ladies convinced me to continue with the project."

"Aren't you shocked it was Dr. ben Charash?" asked Carlos.

"I thought they were both agents," answered George. "I thought there was a possibility that Abraham was the head agent and Matthias the reluctant cooperative. But why would the IAIS send someone to just observe the process being experienced by a non-agent? Look how much more they got by having an agent go through the process. They know now exactly what we can do, and they're going to want to do it. My surprise was that Abraham was the honest, innocent Israeli visitor."

"But was he?"

"You know, I don't know," said George. "Maybe by calling us and telling us what he did they're in better control. They have some assurance we won't report the incident to keep Abraham from getting into trouble."

"Intrigue," Carlos said.

"Intrigue," George agreed. "Get started and keep everything we just said to yourself."

A guard replaced the receptionist. A computer with photos of every authorized employee was used to screen everyone who entered. Photo-badges were already in use. Guests were now electronically searched for wireless devices, recorders and cameras, and they had to remain in authorized areas. Guards were stationed at every exit 24 hours a day, since Search never shut down except for holidays.

When George first saw the guards he said to himself, "Not much longer."

Chapter 40

Article Three

"Changed for Life"

Dave Kasten's third article was written in a much more personal style.

"I will never again think of Jesus Christ as a mystical figure in the Bible. He really existed. He was really God, and He was really one of us. I saw Jesus as a child in Nazareth, playing with a friend named Daniel. I saw Him on a display monitor that was recording the images and sounds produced from the mind of one of Daniel's descendants, Dr. Matthias ben Charash, a doctor on the staff of an Israeli research hospital. Dr. ben Charash came to Search International, in Madison, Wisconsin, because he had had visions of ancient Jerusalem and was therefore chosen as an ideal test subject by Search's LaShauna Jackson. LaShauna heads the theoretical Link research team at Search.

"Then there was the wedding feast of Cana. I heard and saw it described by an eyewitness from the mind of Dr. ben Charash and through the eyes of his ancestor, who stored it in his memory in the year 24 A.D.! The witness heard Mary, Christ's mother, tell others that she knew Jesus would help her friends when she asked, because Jesus had done it before!

"All of these incredible experiences which have changed my life forever occurred at Search during a test of the Link recall-enhancement process. I told George Evans, chairman of Search, that I felt I could not report the results of this latest test with words worthy of the experience. Here is my attempt.

"I was there when Dr. ben Charash arrived at Madison's airport. The Search staff had told me that my two earlier articles helped in attracting Dr. ben Charash and in convincing him to volunteer. When we arrived at Search. . . ."

Kasten's third article produced a groundswell of reaction from many segments of the population. Some denominational religious groups took exception to his report, while others, including many nondenominational Christian churches, where obviously thrilled by it. Network news-show producers followed up with Kasten from that point on, hoping to scoop others with the announcement and coverage of his next release. All three articles were republished internationally, translated into many languages. George Evans held a news conference with Dave Kasten, and George said that neither he nor any member of his staff would be available for interviews until the entire series of tests were completed. He directed all questions to Kasten.

Chapter 41

Islands of Genius

"George, I'd like you to meet Willy," Gary said with a nervous break in his voice. Gary stood in the doorway of George's office. In front of him was a curious, friendly looking, small man with a balding head and a full beard. He wore a colored T-shirt with the words "Genius at work" printed across the chest in brilliant magenta on black. His pants were slightly too large, held in place by a braided leather belt.

Gary's assignment had been the most 'distant' of all, in terms of time-frame. "A body-soul being, made in the image and likeness of God," George had said to him, "could not have evolved 'through natural selection over many, many generations of animals' as Dr. Crick says. Prove it," George directed. Perhaps for the first time in his adult life, Gary had proceeded strictly on his intuition, as if guided by a knowledge beyond himself.

"Hi," said Willy.

"How do you do?" said George.

"I don't know," said Willy. "It's amazing what I can do."

George looked up at Gary. Behind Gary stood a thin man in his early fifties.

"And George," continued Gary, "this is Mr. Steve Thomas. He is Willy's guardian."

"Yes, sir," George said, getting out of his chair and walking toward the trio. "I'm pleased to meet you."

George guided them to his work surface and lowered the ceiling light.

"Wow," said Willy. "That's amazing."

"Thank you, Willy," said George with a big smile. "Can I get you all something to drink?"

"Soda pop," said Willy.

"An iced tea," said Gary, knowing that George kept a private brew in his under-the-desk refrigerator.

"Sounds good," said Mr. Thomas.

"Amazing," said Willy when he saw George reach under his desk and pull out a ginger ale.

When everyone had been served George sat down and looked at Gary.

"Willy is a savant," Gary said.

"That means I know things," said Willy. "It's amazing what I know."

"More than that," Gary continued. "Willy can play eleven different musical instruments, and he is able to draw beautiful pictures of things he has only seen for a few seconds. He can walk through a complex building and draw an accurate sketch of the floor plan."

"Where did you learn to do all of that?" asked George.

"I don't know," repeated Willy. "It's amazing what I can do."

"What's more," said Gary, "if you give Willy a date up to 40,000 years ago, he'll tell you the day of the week it fell on, assuming the current calendar system of course."

"Really?"

"When were you born?" Willy asked George.

"March 21, 1937," answered George.

"Palm Sunday," said Willy without hesitation.

"Remarkable," exclaimed George.

"Amazing," said Willy.

"Willy," continued Gary, "has been tested by many psychologists to see how he does the calendar calculations so fast. They've concluded that he doesn't use eidetic imagery."

"Eidetic imagery?"

"An ability to remember an image of something to the extreme. They wondered if Willy could picture a perpetual calendar and simply look up the answer."

"I just know the answer," said Willy, grinning.

"They concluded also that he did not use any mathematical principles, and that since he did many things so well--his music, for example--he did not seem to be using his skill as a compensation for normal learning. They hypothesized that Willy had extraordinary powers of concentration."

"Bingo," said George.

"Bingo," repeated Willy, enjoying the new word.

"Willy also has a phenomenal ability to recall memories, at will," said Mr. Thomas.

"Most savants exhibit phenomenal memories," said Gary.

"I just know the answer," said Willy.

"Is it your plan to test Willy?" asked George.

"Yes, it is," answered Gary.

"Is this ok with you?" George asked Willy.

"I like to be tested," said Willy. "It's amazing what I do."

"And what about you, Mr. Thomas?"

271

"Willy and I have discussed the test with Mr. Richardson, and he has told us that the research your company is doing may lead to new knowledge in the field of genetics."

"That's true," said George.

"So we have decided to go forward with your test of Willy's memory."

"It's more than that," said George. "You must understand that we believe the true repository for all memory is the soul. We will be recording images and sounds recalled from Willy's ancestral memories."

"Will it not show that Willy is just like the rest of us?" asked Mr. Thomas.

"We all come from the same two ancestors," answered George.

"Adam and Eve," said Willy, "in the Bible."

"Do you know about that, too?" asked George.

"God made them and put them in the Garden of Eden," said Willy.

"Be careful," said Mr. Thomas. "Willy will recite the entire Book of Genesis, if you pursue that line of questioning. I read it to him once, mind you."

"He may know that God created man, but can he grasp the real meaning of that concept?" asked George.

Willy answered, "God made me, and He loves me, and that's all I need to know."

"That's about it," George said to Willy. "Ok, Gary, you and Willy are authorized to proceed."

"Amazing," said Willy.

The setup routine was as usual, except that Anna and LaShauna made a bigger fuss over the test subject than normal. Willy took it all in. Allen used the same 250-year-

step procedure, but increased the rate of flow-rate changes. Anna held a wireless button in her hand so that if she saw any sign of trouble from any point of view she could stop the test in an instant. Dave Kasten, Carlos and George sat in their usual places.

"Willy," said Gary, feeling somewhat awkward standing in front of a test subject this time, "I want you to concentrate on the Book of Genesis. Think of nothing else but what God did for all of us. Think about how He created all things and how He created Adam and Eve."

"Ok," said Willy, a bit nervously.

"Just relax, Willy," said Mr. Thomas.

"Ok, Mr. Thomas," said Willy.

"Close your eyes now," Gary said. "Think of nothing else but what God did for all of us."

"Ok," Willy repeated, and closed his eyes very peacefully.

Gary nodded to Allen, and Allen began the flow of Promax-2. Five seconds later he turned on the trigger pulses, synchronized with the locus ceruleous in Willy's brain stem.

Immediately a terribly loud rushing noise came from the sound system, and the monitor burst into a rainbow of colors which converged to a brilliant white screen. Nearly all of them jumped from their seats. Allen jerked and knocked the flask of Promax-2 to the floor. It did not break.

As fast as it had started, it all ended, and Willy's eyes opened wide as his face broke into a broad grin. "Amazing," he said.

Anna had instinctively hit the "trouble button," and Allen had killed the test, but Willy was fine.

"What, Willy?" asked Gary. "What was amazing?"

"I know how He did it!" exclaimed Willy.

"What did you experience, Willy?" asked George, thinking the test was a failure.

273

"We have nothing recorded," said Joan, who had been manning the video disk recording system for Gary.

As soon as Willy began to relate what he had experienced mouths began to drop open and eyes widened. Chairs were pulled around Willy, and Dave Kasten typed everything he heard. Joan left the recording system on and took a chair behind Kasten and George Evans. Willy spoke using words he could not have known or fully understood, and he delivered them as would a highly educated speaker. It seemed as though he had memorized a complete story told in the first person. But no one in the room had ever heard it before, nor was it the Genesis read to Willy by Mr. Thomas. It was Genesis, all right, Chapter 1 and part of 2, but reported as though it came through the mind of a modern-day scientist.

"I asked God to permit me to see the process of creation," began Willy, "so that I could share the knowledge with others that they might come to believe Scripture to truly be the Word of God. He agreed, and told me that I would experience the process, as did the author of Genesis, from the point of where I stood here on earth. He said it would be an exhausting experience, because I would be privileged to see everything, sequentially, as fast as my temporal mind could accept it.

"In the beginning, when God created the universe and the earth, there was nothing but a dimensionless form of infinite mass in utter darkness surrounded by tremendous energy. Space and time did not exist.

"Then God said, 'Let there be light,' and with those words alone there came a brilliant flash of light followed by a gigantic explosion of immense proportions. The infinite mass expanded at great speed into the darkness. I watched billions of galaxies unfold, and when evening came, God smiled at me, and I slept till morning–the first day.

"When I awoke I experienced being engulfed in water as I stood. Then God said, 'Let there be a dome in the middle of the waters, to separate one body of water from the other.' And so it happened: I was able to watch a primordial earth go through its primitive stages and saw its atmosphere develop with explosive energy, leaving a thick, dark cloud cover over a flooded earth. Evening came again, and soon it was morning–the second day.

"Then God said, 'Let the water under the sky be gathered into a single basin, so that the dry land may appear.' And so it happened: the water drained from the continents, and the dry land appeared. When I saw the earth again below me and the sea within its boundaries, I smiled, and God smiled back. He was clearly enjoying my experiences.

"Then God said, 'Let the earth bring forth vegetation: every kind of plant that bears seed and every kind of fruit tree on earth that bears fruit with its seed in it.' And so it happened: In what seemed to be seconds, I watched millions of different kinds of plants and trees develop, all according to His plan. The earth became--in a single day!--a beautiful green, brown and blue planet, just like the pictures I've seen from outer space. God smiled again. Evening came, and morning followed–the third day.

"Then God said: 'Let there be lights in the dome of the sky, to separate day from night. Let them mark the fixed times, the days and the years, and serve as luminaries in the dome of the sky, to shed light upon the earth.' And so it happened: The cloud cover began to dissipate, and I could feel the warm sun again on my face. As evening came I saw the moon and the stars for the first time during this experience, and I realized how perfectly and timely God's plan was developing before me. God nodded. Soon it was morning–the fourth day.

"Then God said, 'Let the waters teem with an abundance of living creatures, and on the earth let the birds fly beneath the dome of the sky.' And so it happened: I watched single cell amoeba develop into one kind of sea creature after another, all according to His plan. As each species adapted, there came a sudden and noticeable change, clearly indicating God's hand in the process. Millions and millions of species were created by Him as I watched. Birds next appeared above me. The species was so different from anything that came before it that God was clearly, personally involved in its creation. He appeared to be particularly pleased that I noticed. All of the species of sea creatures and birds multiplied as He instructed and as He provided in their design. I was overwhelmed as evening came. Morning followed–the fifth day.

"Then God said, 'Let the earth bring forth all kinds of living creatures; cattle, creeping things, and wild animals of all kinds.' And so it happened: Animals of every kind imaginable developed before my eyes, and as before, the changes which indicated new species had been created happened so suddenly it was as though they appeared from nowhere. There was an apparent design connection between species, but no gradual evolution from one to the other. The hand of God was obvious in the process, with which God was pleased. I was already exhausted from watching the sequential work of God's creation of all animal life as it flashed through my mind, but then God said, 'Let us make man in our image, after our likeness. Let them have dominion over the fish of the sea, the birds of the air, and the cattle, and over all the wild animals and all the creatures that crawl on the ground.' Immediately I saw what I knew to be the person of Jesus Christ. I watched Jesus reach down and carefully, lovingly form a man from the clay of the ground– in His own likeness. He breathed into the man's nostrils. The mud-gray color left the likeness, and man looked into the eyes of his Creator.

God created man in His image;

In the divine image He created him;

Male and female He created them.

"Then I knew--man was not the end result of billions of years of evolution; he was the purpose of Creation. Man was not the last step in an evolutionary process; he was the focus of the entire work of Creation. This is why we find biological similarity between man and animals of various kinds, not the other way around. And so it happened. God looked at everything He had made, and He found it very good. Evening came, and morning followed–the sixth day.

"On the seventh day I rested with God. Now I understood; now I knew. Yet even though I had just seen the entire creation process as it occurred, I still had to ask the question of Him, 'Did what I experienced over the last six days really take only six days in the beginning?'

"God said, 'It happened as you saw and as recorded in Scripture.'

"'But, Father,' I said, 'what I saw happened sequentially, but with almost no time between events, time which was seemingly placed there only so that my mind could process the information. The process appears to have taken billions of years in real time!'

"'Son,' God said, 'I am who AM.'

"So God blessed the seventh day and made it holy, because on it He rested from all the work He had done in Creation.

"Such is the story of the heavens and the earth at their creation," Willy concluded.

Everyone in the room was stunned. They sat or stood in absolute silence. Gary leaned against the wall in front of Willy, mouth still open. Willy looked around, hoping for some sign of approval. George finally broke the silence. "Willy, where did you hear all of this?"

"I told you," said Willy. "It's amazing I can do this."

"It wasn't the Promax-2," said Allen. "He barely received a setting for 250 years, and it was over."

The room was quiet again. Willy looked back and forth at the faces of those looking at him.

"Is it possible," asked Anna thoughtfully, "that Willy was the one experiencing Genesis just like he said; that this is his story?"

"Dr. Pierson," said Mr. Thomas to Anna, "Willy can neither read nor write. He has a vocabulary of about 250 words and an IQ of not much more than 50."

"That may be true for Willy in his temporal state," said Anna, "but in the sequential state Willy will have full access to all of his ancestral memories and knowledge. He will have a perfect mind and a perfect body."

Mr. Thomas looked confused.

"God, Himself," George said in a strong voice, "may have just paid us a visit . . . through Willy."

"Amazing," said Willy.

Joan walked over to Willy and gave him a hug. Then she hugged Gary.

"Five down, and one to go," George said to Kasten.

Chapter 42

Opportunities

"Anna," said George, "I expected Gary to be last with his assignment. Where are you with yours?"

"Life of a child begins at conception," George had said to Anna when giving out the assignments that would change the lives of so many. "Focus on proving, beyond a doubt, when a baby is, in fact, a baby," he had directed.

"I need another two months," Anna replied.

The Link staff was assembled to see what could be done to help Anna with her assignment. George had given the staff six months to complete the assignments, and eight and one half months had already elapsed. He was clearly getting nervous. He wanted to destroy the synchronizer and the balance of Promax-2 before they fell into the wrong hands. The Israelis already had similar technology, and it was being used by their military to interrogate suspects, and their biochemists, involved in cloning technology, had surmised successfully (though not entirely correctly) that a small electrical current would facilitate the transfer of data from the brain. It was rumored that the Israelis were also currently conducting experiments, in some cases causing severe mental and physical injury to their subjects, but in others obtaining the results they hoped for: single percepts recalled from the subject's past.

"I see great opportunities for evil with this new technology of ours," George said. "What can you tell me that will stop me from destroying the remainder of Promax-2 and the BioSync device now? I'm convinced the Israelis-- and perhaps our own government--will soon be after the details and formulas of the advanced technique. Carlos and I hold the keys to the process, and I am even concerned about the safety of our families."

"We understand your concern, George," LaShauna began. "But when you hear what we have to tell you, we hope you will focus your creative mind on how to control the use of the technology, not how to destroy it. Ultimately we see that the technology will point to the finger of God in Creation, so clearly that scientists the world over will agree there is a Creator. It may even bring unity to the many Christian sects of the world, so clear and singular will be the related interpretation of the Bible. As we said before, we see possibilities for a 'healthy' treatment for cancer, a better understanding of and therapy for brain and spinal cord injuries, and a more thorough understanding of gene-related illnesses."

"In just two months we'll run our first test," Anna added, "which will, hopefully, make it so clear that a human fetus is a human child, that laws and hearts will finally be changed."

"What's the hold-up, Anna? Why do you need another two months? How do you know it will just be another two months? We don't have much time," said George.

"When I received the assignment, LaShauna and I searched for a woman who was six weeks pregnant and willing to subject herself and her unborn child to the process. We found one right in Madison, and under strict scientific protocol we had her learn and sing a lullaby to her baby."

"You subjected her to the process without my knowledge?"

"No, no, George," answered Anna. "All we did was have the woman sing the new lullaby into a microphone attached to an audio transducer--a special speaker--placed on her abdomen."

"Why a 'new' lullaby?" he asked.

"Joan wrote it for us," said Anna.

"The words of the song," Joan explained, "actually contain a digital code. In order to interpret the code correctly the same number of words has to be repeated in exactly the same order."

"The baby girl was born a month ago today," Anna continued, "and in just two months we plan to use the process to see if the baby remembers the lullaby completely and exactly. As a further control, only one of the three verses was actually heard by the baby. The woman wore earphones and was not aware we did this, so there is no way she could affect the results."

"That does sound exciting," said George.

Fr. Christopher broke in. "What I've learned is that Christ was truly a human and truly God at the same time, just as I have always believed. But now I know **how** He set aside His divinity. Through His incarnation as a human ovum, He literally caused Himself to forget He was God! He could not access His divinity. He lived a life just like us, except for sin, and when He called us to follow Him, He was calling us as a Man Who trusted in our Father and Who cured the sick just as He said we could through the power of the Holy Spirit, not because He was God, but because He was an obedient Child of God, which we are called to be, and--"

"Father Christopher," George responded, "slow down. Those are reasons to distribute the BioChip team's findings both to the scientific community and to the faithful, but not reasons which will stop me from destroying the technique and Promax-2."

"George, you must wait a while longer," said LaShauna. "We have to prove that our science is good. We need the technique for our first tests in the reversal--not remission--of the growth of metastasized melanoma cells in the brain, the most common cause of brain tumor deaths."

"Really?" George said.

"Yes, yes," LaShauna said.

"All right, team," said George. "I'll reconsider. Anna, you've got your two months."

"George," said Allen, "there's very little Promax-2 left, enough for Anna's experiment, but no more. Are you going to formulate another batch?"

"Carlos and I will talk about it," George answered. "Father Christopher, you're going to be excommunicated, tarred and feathered at some point. You know that, don't you?"

"I'm already preparing a lengthy letter to my bishop."

"Well, I hope your bishop is open-minded," George said with a smile. "Oh, yes, team," he continued, "part of my reason for calling this meeting is to tell you that Rachel and I had planned to get away for a few weeks immediately after you either completed your assignments or gave up. Either way, I expected to destroy the process and make myself unavailable before the news of what I did--through Dave Kasten--hit the media. While we're waiting for our volunteer's baby to be born, I'm going to go ahead with my plans to get out of the office for three weeks. Don't look for Carlos and Jennifer either, they're going to do the same thing. They've had reservations somewhere for months."

"I hope that when you return," said Anna, "LaShauna and I can demonstrate that a 42-day-old fetus, whose neurons have just started firing, can hear, remember and recall her mother's song to her when she's three months old."

"I hope all goes well for the mother, the baby girl and your assignment," said George. "Meeting adjourned. See you all in three weeks."

Chapter 43

Articles Four and Five

"Despite the Warning"

Kasten's fourth article reported the recorded visions of the full-blooded Indian named Thomas Grey Fox, also known as "Noah" to his people.

"Back we went this time through the ancestral memories of an 88-year-old American Indian, often called Noah because of his visions of the Great Flood. Search International staff member Joan Kenny and bioethicist consultant Christopher Braun, an ex-Jesuit priest, organized and arranged the test that left this observer speechless. Through the eyes of Grey Fox's ancestor, I looked through a crude porthole in a huge and ancient ship and saw the raging 'Flood of the Ages' creating worldwide death and destruction. I heard Grey Fox's ancestor talk of 'God-among-us' who had preached Christ's message of Salvation to each and every adult on earth before the rains began. They heard, but did not listen.

"'Noah' was flown in on Search International's corporate jet. I joined George Evans just as the test began..."

Kasten's fourth article initially seemed to cause the mainstream news media to take a step backward. It was all too difficult to believe. However, the tabloids jumped on the story immediately, as Kasten had expected. But he was prepared. He gave the tabloid reporters a few carefully worded comments and reactions, which they published promptly. This brought out the television tabloids, and, finally, national mainstream news reporters got full interviews from Kasten, which in some cases refuted the errors published by the tabloids. Kasten and his syndicated column, "The Exponential Curve," were again the subject of national talk shows.

Then Kasten's fifth article appeared.

"Genesis from a Genius."

"Even if you have been following this series of articles I have been writing, reporting the results of an incredible research project called Link, still in process at Search International, you may nevertheless be shocked to hear me, a scientific investigative reporter, say that God Himself spoke through a test subject this time, and I was there as a witness. To add to this unbelievable statement, I must also tell you that the test subject was none other than an idiot savant named Willy.

"God did not need Search International's high-tech Link device or their other secret recall-enhancement means. He spoke directly and personally to Willy, and this friendly little man, with 'an IQ of around 50 and a vocabulary of no more than 250 words,' according to his guardian, recited to us a brilliantly composed and delivered message, the message of Genesis.

"Though Search's recall-enhancement process was not involved, they did record Willy's delivery, and they intend to make it available on video disk in a few months. I have been given the privilege-of-a-lifetime of reporting by George Evans. He gave me a copy of the audio recording and asked me to quote Willy to you, word for word, in this, my fifth article. Here it is:

"'I imagined asking God to permit me to see the process of Creation. . . .'"

Beyond belief was Kasten's article, and beyond belief was the response. More than 10,000 letters arrived at Kasten's office, from all over the world, in the first few days after the article was published. Evolutionists and anti-evolutionists (both suggested by Willy's "revelation" to be in error) came out in droves. Church officials from many denominations both praised and condemned his article, sometimes in the same letter or news interview. Some Christian astronomers said the equivalent of, "I told you so." Christian biologists remained silent, as they had been all along. Genesis and Willy became hot national topics. Willy's whereabouts were kept secret at that time.

Chapter 44

Judas

No one at Search noticed that over a short period of time all three night-shift security guards were replaced by the security company.

"Have you got your people in place?" asked the Swedish executive on the phone.

"Yes, we have," answered the American president of Med-Diagnostics. "Scott Dennison also has an inside contact that has been of great help. Search not only has the diagnostic interface we want, the device they call a Link, but they also use a bio-synchronizer in the recall-enhancement process. He claims it was tested on him."

"What's it for?" asked the Swede.

"We can only guess," answered the American, "but it seems to be an important component, because now they can obtain full memories of an event, not just a instantaneous moment. Have you read all of the articles the Madison reporter has written?"

"Every one," answered the Swede. "If only a tenth of what he says is true, and I certainly don't buy the spiritual stuff, there's no doubt in my mind they have the diagnostic tools we're looking for."

"I agree," answered the American.

"Can you reverse engineer the Link and bio-synchronizer if you get your hands on them?"

"No doubt in my mind."

"Let's plan to move forward with that idea."

The American paused, and then asked, "What do you suggest?"

"I'll hire an individual here in Sweden to go to the States and enter Search's facilities at night. He'll bring the devices here, and then I'll ship them to you. They'll never trace our steps."

"Sounds good," said the American. "Getting through our security guards is one thing, but Search personnel are also onsite twenty-four hours a day. Your man will need a security badge to move around in the building looking for the Link and bio-synchronizer."

"Not if he knows exactly where to look."

"Where will this information come from?" asked the American.

"Which official at Search is responsible for security?" asked the Swede. "He'll know where our man should look."

"His name is Carlos Martinez."

"Sounds Mexican. Are you sure?"

"Very. Dennison tells me Martinez is George Evans's son-in-law," answered the American.

"Have you seen Martinez?"

"No," answered the American, "but Dennison knows where he lives and what he drives. He can point him out to your man when he gets here."

Chapter 45

Forbidden Fruit

George had known Darrell Johnson since the start of Search. It had always been a part professional, part personal relationship. They trusted each other and often shared personal history and current events. They seldom wrote to each other and almost never called, but when they would meet again, they could pick up a conversation that their separation had interrupted years earlier. This time George dropped into Darrell's small office, lab and workshop at Pepperdine University in southern California on the last leg of their trip, without notice.

"What the--? What are you doing here?' asked Darrell as he opened the door to his lab. The two men shook hands and embraced.

"You know, Darrell, I think the main reason we chose to come to California was to see you."

"That's nice of you to say. Where's Rachel? She usually comes along."

"She said she was going to Sea World in San Diego."

"Didn't she go there last time you visited?

"Yes, she's an animal lover. Your zoo is next."

"What did bring you out here, George? I know there's always a business reason."

"This time, Darrell, it's just the opposite."

"The opposite?"

"Yes, I came to get away from the business."

"Hard to believe those words are coming from you."

"I'm getting old."

"Nonsense. That'll never change your desire for the creative thrill."

The two walked through the office to the lab, where both were always much more comfortable.

"No, it won't," said George. "It's not so much the business I needed to get away from. It's the fear of the future which I face every time I go into the office these days."

"Again, strange words."

"Have you read about the hypothesis Search has developed? There's been international attention."

"I can't say that I have, George. You know how I am when I get on a project. I'm developing a new knee for an athlete who lost his in an accident, and I haven't turned on the TV or read a newspaper in six months."

"That would do it. And if that knee has to interface with a neural circuit, I'd get in touch with my Anna Pierson, if I were you."

"She knows about those things?"

"And then there's LaShauna. She can talk circles around both of us in that area. The two have headed up the most remarkable research I've ever been involved with."

"Sounds terribly exciting. Why the gloom?"

"Darrell, I feel like the chief physicist on the Manhattan project--thrilled with the technology and the good which can come from understanding the positive side, but sick over the evil it can release on the negative side."

"Wow, you needed this vacation, and we need to talk. What's this about, George?"

Darrell pointed to a stool next to a work bench.

"You've known me a long time, Darrell," George said as he sat down on the stool, "and you know I deal strictly with the facts--no blue smoke. You're a bioengineer, so you have the background necessary to understand what we've been doing. Nonetheless, you won't believe what Search has been up to, and what I've bought into, hook, line, and sinker."

"You have my undivided attention."

"We have discovered . . . the human soul."

"This is news? You weren't sure humans had souls before this revelation?"

"You used the right word, 'revelation,' but you have the wrong idea. Let me put it clearly. We can tap it."

"Tap what?"

"The soul, my soul, your soul."

"And your meaning of the word 'tap,' would be?"

"Let me put part of our discovery in the words of Dr. Clyde Hart, one of our research physicians. 'It is not the purpose of the brain to remember anything.'"

"You're confusing me. Then what is its purpose?"

"Control and focus are primary, but in unity with the soul all functions of the mind are made possible."

"Combined with the soul?"

"It is the soul that stores all memory."

"I knew it!"

"You did?"

"How else? No, seriously, how could the brain store what it does--perhaps everything we've ever perceived--and recall it instantly?"

"Darrell, you never told me you had such thoughts."

"I had no answer to the question. It sounds like you do."

"We do."

"Then what is it you're trying to escape from? I would want to be doing the research day and night, and normally so would you."

"We have the technology to help an individual recall a memory and to record what he or she recalls on video disk," George said.

"Oh, boy!"

"That's not all, Darrell. We can play back the memory with all details--video and sound. I think it will even be possible for us to tell you what the individual was smelling at the time the memory was stored."

"Don't tell the CIA about that . . . or even the local fire marshal. 'There you are, judge,'" Darrell mimicked, "'We've placed the perpetrator at the scene--it's in his memory--and we can smell the gasoline.'"

"You've got part of my problem, but the scope will even be beyond your fertile imagination."

"Tell me."

"If John Wilkes Booth fathered a child after he assassinated Lincoln, and we found a descendant alive today, we could place Booth at the scene and perhaps smell the gunpowder."

"Ancestral memories?"

"As far back as you want."

"Did you read *The Heart Code* by Paul Pearsall?" Darrell asked. "I heard him speak about it in Santa Monica."

"I didn't read the book, but one of our Link research team members did."

"Link?"

"That's the device which literally taps the soul. Gary, our microelectronics specialist, calls it 'Jacob's Ladder.'

Pearsall had a glimpse of the truth, but he didn't have the faith to carry it to its logical conclusion."

"How does your hypothesis differ?"

"The soul--we refer to it as the particle--is at the functional center of every cell of the organism."

"We have billions of souls?" questioned Darrell.

"Just one. The particle is atemporal and has no mass, therefore, it has no dimension or location."

"Spiritual."

"Yes, and the hypothesis really redefines that term also."

"This technology will have great application in my industry. I mean, if I can tap into the skill memory, I can make people walk again."

"My staff has a long list of benefits possible from the technology. I'm developing a long list of the evil which it can be used for."

"Why? What frightens you the most?"

"We've already had a spy from Israeli Military Intelligence in our lab experiencing the process. That was four months ago, and they're now conducting similar experiments."

"Do they have the technology?"

"They can get a cooperative test subject to recall a single percept--like a single snapshot--but our test subjects produce virtual movies. The Israelis have no knowledge of where we got the neuro-transmitter which enhances one's ability to recall even ancestral memories, and even when they do, they won't be able to reproduce our synthetic version, which is 1,000 times more potent."

"What if they break into your place and steal the formula?"

"Carlos and I destroyed all written and computer-disk copies, and when I get back Anna Pierson is going to conduct one last experiment, after which I believe I am going to destroy the apparatus which makes it possible and what's left of the synthetic neuro-transmitter."

"The evil outweighs the good?"

"In my judgment."

"Then what's the hold-up?"

"My staff. They have their hands on the discovery of a lifetime, and I should snuff out the light?"

"Watch for something--perhaps from the Holy Spirit--which will swing you one way or the other," said Darrell.

"Why do you say that?"

"I don't know, George. Perhaps it's my intuition."

"Let me ask you this," said George.

"Shoot."

"You're a quasi-biologist. What kind of fruit grew on the tree of the knowledge of good and evil?"

"You're joking?"

"Not really. What kind of fruit? What chemicals were dissolved in its juices?"

"I have no idea. Wasn't it an apple?"

"No. All I know is it was the fruit of a tree that grew in the middle of the garden. I also know it looked like good food and was pleasing to the eye."

"Why is this on your mind? What does the tree of the knowledge of good and evil have to do with the research that Search is doing?"

"'Cause I think we have its juices in our lab, and I'm scared to death."

"The juices of the forbidden fruit?"

"That's what I've been thinking. And what about the fruit of the tree of life?"

"You've got me."

"That tree has a cherubim stationed near it with a fiery sword. The hypothesis suggests an answer to why we grow old. Have we stepped too close to that tree also?"

"You're really taken up with this research, aren't you?"

"My staff says all these wonderful things could come from our work. I should ask them, 'What's next?' 'Where is it all going to lead?' Surely Anna and LaShauna are going to conclude, 'If the particle has infinite storage capacity for information, containing even all that is necessary to control the growth, life and healing of every cell in the body, then isn't it capable of containing even more?'"

"A logical scientific question."

"But, Darrell, don't you see? We're opening doors God has closed. Does He want this? Then why would He station a sword-bearing angel to guard the tree of life? What is contained in its juices, another neuro-transmitter?"

"George, it's a beautiful day. Why don't you put these things out of your mind and come with me to look out over the hills of Malibu. Let's let the wind blow through our ears and clear out the evil cobwebs you've been spinning. Let's look at God's Creation as it really is. He saw that it was good, and He was pleased."

"Maybe we ought to."

"It'll do us both good."

"Take your digital with us. Rachel is sure to call here soon," said George.

"Got it," Darrell answered.

Darrell threw his free arm over George's shoulder. "Wait till you see the sunset from up there."

As they approached the front door a four-door sedan pulled up to the curb. Darrell was busy securing his suite, but George watched four men in suits get out of the car simultaneously.

"Mister Evans? George Evans?" the driver called as he came around the front of the car.

Darrell spun around and one of the men placed the back of his hand against Darrell's shoulder to stop any further movement.

"Who are you, and what do you want?" George asked.

"We're with the FBI," the driver said, showing his identification, "and we need to talk with you in private."

"Speak your piece here. I'm not going anywhere, and neither is my friend."

"Mister Evans, this is serious government business."

"I'm listening."

The driver paused, then explained. "The U.S. Government has just been contacted by the Israeli prime minister. Most of his cabinet members have been assassinated during a cabinet meeting. The assassins missed him, and his security people caught one of the perpetrators." He paused again, seeming to expect George to understand the rest.

"I'm not going to help you with this," said George.

"Let me explain further."

"You don't have to explain further. I'm not going to use our technology to help the Israelis interrogate their man. They're working on the same technology. Let them use theirs."

"The perpetrator obviously won't cooperate," said the driver.

"Neither will I," said George, "and that's final."

The driver looked at the agent standing close to Darrell who still held his hand against Darrell's shoulder, and then he looked back at George. "What reason do you have not to cooperate?" he asked.

"I don't have to give you a reason."

The driver glared at George.

"Step aside," said George. "We're going to look at the sunset, and it's getting late."

The driver turned and moved toward the car. The other men followed. As the car drove away George said to Darrell, "I wonder how they found me? Who cares," he said, answering his own question. "I've got to call Carlos."

"Here you go," said Darrell, handing George the digital phone. "Say hello for me."

Still standing at the door to Darrell's suite, George punched in the number Carlos had given him. Carlos and Jennifer were staying with friends in Florida.

"Hello?"

"Jennifer, is that you?"

"Yes, Daddy. What's up?"

"Where's Carlos?"

"He's at the front door with our friends. Some men just arrived."

"Put him on, and don't take no for an answer," George said in a strong voice.

George nervously ran his hand over the back of his neck. Darrell put his hand on George's shoulder.

"Yes, George?"

"Carlos. I was just approached by four FBI agents."

"There were three at our front door," said Carlos.

"You are not to go with them. You are not to tell them anything. You are not to cooperate. Do you understand?"

"George, you didn't have to say anything. I know what's going on, and I held my ground. I sent them on their way. Are you ok, George?"

"I knew I could count on you, Carlos. I'm a bit upset, but yes, I'm ok."

"And Rachel?"

"She should be calling in at any moment. They were after you and me. I doubt they had any plans regarding Rachel. I think they were confident we would want to use our technology for the government's purposes. They didn't seem to know what to do when I refused."

"Same here," Carlos said. "What do we do now?"

"Alert Anna, LaShauna, Clyde, Gary and Allen. Put Allen in charge of security until we get back."

"What about Charlie and Father Christopher?"

"Yes, of course. Maybe it would be wise to get them all to stay inside Search until we get there."

"Done," said Carlos.

"See you tonight," George concluded. "Thanks, Carlos."

"We'll leave immediately," said Carlos.

Darrell and George looked at each other, and George terminated the call. George shook his head.

"You'll see this through," said Darrell.

Just then the digital phone rang. George punched a button and answered.

"Rachel?'

"Yes, George," she responded. "I've been followed, but whoever it was has left. What's going on?"

"Come pick me up," George said. "Leave immediately. Everyone's ok. I'll tell you more while we drive to the airport."

"We're leaving California then?"

"On the first plane out," answered George, and to Darrell he said with anger, "Forbidden fruit."

Chapter **46**

The Israeli Demand

The men were comfortable, but they waited until Air Force One leveled off and the pilot reduced the thrust of its engines before they began to discuss the urgent issue at hand.

"Just what did your people say to the man?" asked the Israeli official.

"Our agents did not expect him to refuse to cooperate," answered the vice president.

"So they did nothing?"

"What did you want us to do?"

"Detain him or his son-in-law. Apply some pressure."

"There's been a series of articles published and reported by national U.S. news media about Search International and its chairman, Evans. If we were to pick up either him or Martinez, it would be nationally known immediately."

"Sometimes I don't think you understand," said the Israeli. "Our cabinet has been butchered, and your technology can help us find the perpetrators and planners of this heinous crime."

"It's not our technology. Search International is a private firm."

"Owned by Evans?"

"By Evans," answered the vice president. "Have you been able to learn anything from the perpetrator you caught?"

The Israeli official glared at the vice president. "*Fool,*" he thought. "We used our memory-recall technology and almost killed him. He will not cooperate," he said with his voice rising in pitch. "Your technology can extract from him what we want even if he is in a coma," he shouted.

"What do you suggest we do?" asked the vice president, trying to calm the man.

"We demand that Search International's technology be made available to us immediately," he responded, still at a high pitch.

"We can't just walk in and take it. What alternative do you propose?"

"Get us the formula for Promax-2."

"And if we do, what good will it do you without the Link technology?"

"*Fool,*" again thought the Israeli. "We have similar technology," he said to the vice president in a much calmer tone. "We invented it first. All we really need is the formula for Promax-2. Go and get it for us, or we'll get it ourselves."

Chapter 47

When a Baby Is a Baby

"It's nice to meet you, Mary," said George with a warm smile. "I hope all this security doesn't disturb you. What we've been doing here lately is highly confidential, and we need to be vigilant. Say, that's one beautiful little baby girl."

When George and Carlos had returned to Search six weeks earlier, the entire Link research team was waiting for them in the lunch room. Pizza had been ordered and enjoyed by all. Anna and LaShauna hugged George and asked if he was ok. Carlos got lots of smiles and back-pats. They looked like returning heroes, but George felt quite the opposite. "*What have I done to my people and my company,*" he thought when he walked by the guard at the front door. "People I don't even recognize are guarding our offices," he had said to Carlos.

Five weeks later Anna was ready to test the baby through the process. George's mood had improved somewhat, due to the prospects of proving that a 42-day-old fetus is a baby, a person, a human being. Anna had told him that at around 42 days a baby's brain has developed to the point that the firing of its neurons can be detected. Gary was already receiving a strong signal from the three-month-old child's locus ceruleus, despite the padding which was added to the bio-synchronizer to protect her tiny neck. Allen had been working on a mini-Link interface for the past two weeks, and it too seemed to be functioning well, sending vital signals to the medical console which LaShauna watched diligently. Dave Kasten sat with George, as usual. Joan stood by the mother, who was seated in the dentist chair. The baby, lying on her back, rested on her mother's abdomen.

"Are you sure you want your baby to experience this?" George asked Mary, whose last name was being kept confidential.

"Oh, yes," Mary answered strongly. Anna had gone over the details of the procedure with her. "Think of all the babies' lives this experiment may save," Mary said.

"I have, Mary," said George. "Ok, team," he added, "proceed."

Anna stepped forward and said, "As we rehearsed, Mary, I want you to sing the first six words of the lullaby you learned from Joan and sang to your baby when you were here last; just the first six words. Allen will tell you when to begin."

"Ok, Doctor. I'll start when Allen tells me to," Mary said with remarkable calmness.

A few moments of silence passed. The baby was alert, turning her head back and forth, smiling when she caught the eye of someone. Joan was grinning so much Anna thought it might distract the baby.

"Ok, Mary," Allen said, and Mary began to sing.

"I love you, my dear child."

The baby continued to look around, totally enjoying her surroundings. "Again," Anna said.

"I love you, my dear child," Mary sang again.

"She's only three months old," said George in a whisper to Kasten. "Have you ever seen a more active, happy baby?"

Kasten shook his head, and Anna put her finger to her mouth to stop George from continuing. "Again," she said to Mary.

"I love you, my dear child," Mary sang, this time with a laugh as she did when she had first sung it to the baby in her womb.

The baby seemed to pay a bit more attention this time. "Again," Anna said.

"I love you, my dear child." Tears were beginning to stream down Mary's face, not for her concern for the experiment, as felt by others, but for the love she felt so strongly for the baby on her abdomen.

"Please, again," Anna said.

"I love you, my dear child," Mary sang with a slight sob in her voice.

"Anna," George called quietly, "turn off the lights."

LaShauna, closest to the door, immediately reached over and turned of all four light switches.

"I love you, my dear child," Mary sang without a prompt from Anna. "I love you my dear child," she repeated.

And then they all heard the beautiful lullaby coming from the sound system. The words were muffled, but recognizable as those of the baby's mother, Mary.

"I love you, my dear child,

My baby, oh, so small,

You're growing day by day.

Do you hear your mother call?"

It would be impossible to describe the emotions experienced by everyone in the room. Gentle "Oh's" and "God love her" were heard. Allen and Gary looked as though they were going to cry. LaShauna and George were. Kasten put his head in his hands as usual.

The baby girl wasn't done. Again and again she recalled her mother's song,

"I love you, my dear child,

My baby, oh, so small,

You're growing day by day.

Do you hear your mother call?"

"You heard me," Mary sobbed. "You heard me, honey."

"She sure did, Mary," said Anna with one of her tearful smiles. "Mr. Kasten," she called.

Kasten's head popped up, exposing his wet face.

"Will you confirm that the song was not coming from the baby's mother?"

"I . . I can confirm that," he stuttered.

"Joan," called Anna again, "can you confirm that the phrase we are hearing is the only phrase that the baby heard?"

Mary looked up, surprised. She had sung three phrases to the baby in her womb.

"I can confirm that," said Joan, "and our recording during Mary's first session with us will also."

Joan's and Gary's eyes and smiles met.

"And Gary," Anna called one last time, "was the computer able to analyze the words of the song, and has it given you the sum of the digital codes embedded by Joan in those words?"

"It has," Gary answered with a breaking voice, "and the sum is 777."

The number matched exactly the digital code that Joan had embedded in the song.

"Praise God," LaShauna cried.

"Wow," Joan laughed.

With tears still streaming down his cheeks, George leaned over to talk quietly to Kasten. "The whole issue of abortion is based on the controversy, 'when is a baby a baby?' At least we've moved the time a baby is a baby back to 42 days, and we have proof!"

"I can write this story," said Kasten, "and it will be read around the world."

"How many unborn babies have they killed so far?" George asked him.

"More than 50 million," he answered.

Mary began to sing with joy, "I love you, my dear child, my baby, oh, so small . . . You heard your mother's call!"

"How can I stop this research now?" George asked Carlos as they left the Link lab. "What harm can come from this?"

Chapter 48

Article Six

"Proof - A Fetus Is a Baby!"

Kasten's sixth and last article in the series was the most controversial of all.

"I can't get the words out of my head:

'I love you, my dear child,

My baby, oh, so small,

You're growing day by day.

Do you hear your mother call?'

"It was a simple but beautiful melody created by Joan Kenny, a mathematician at Search International. She also wrote the words, but it wasn't her singing them that I heard. It wasn't the research physician, Anna Pierson, who was heading up the test, that I heard. It wasn't the mother of the three-month-old baby I saw, lying on her mother's abdomen. No, the song in perfect pitch and tempo was coming from the mind of the baby! From the baby's soul! And when did she hear it, you might ask? Not since she was born, I would answer, to your astonishment. She heard it only once when she was a 42-day-old fetus!

"The mother's name and that of her baby are being kept confidential, for obvious reasons. The mother's first name, though, is Mary. Appropriate, I think. The story I am about to report to you was, as in all previous articles, experienced firsthand by yours truly. Nothing has ever affected me emotionally as did my observation of this test. 'How many unborn babies have they killed so far,' George Evans, chairman of Search International, asked me after the test ended. I answered with a lump in my throat and a pain in my heart. . . ."

A rock came through Kasten's office window, and pro-choice advocates picketed his newspaper as well as his home. Carlos added perimeter guards when the crowd in Search's parking lot grew to a dangerous size. Both Pro-choice and Pro-life rallies caused police to go on double shifts in many cities in the U.S. The "proof" was ridiculed by many liberal scientists. Conservative syndicated writers all took up the defense.

Slowly and gradually, after carefully reviewing the polls and learning that a small trend against late-term abortions was developing once again, a few conservative Congressmen began to discuss, in secret meetings, the new case against the *Roe vs. Wade* Supreme Court decision. "Will it take a change in the Constitution to overturn it?" they cautiously considered.

Chapter 49

The Senator's Problem

The shouting could be heard through the senator's suite of offices. Her shrill voice echoed off the glass doors. "Have you read it? Have you heard it on the news? Do you know what this means? Decades of work rapidly going down the drain. Scientists and physicians are joining the damn bandwagon. People are starting to think . . . to think we've been killing babies all these years. Well, of course, we have, but it's a woman's choice. If it weren't for the majority not wanting to think about it, we would never have gotten this far. The partial birth abortion ban was all but forgotten, till now, that is. You can choose to have your doctor stab your fully developed fetus in the neck and suck out its brains without an outcry from the public!"

The senator paused and began to pace.

"We've got to stop these research people," she continued in a lower tone. "They're planning to put that stupid singing baby on *The Morning Show*. They say that in nine months they're going to do it again on live TV. We've got to stop these demonstrations and stop them now!"

She glared at the three men sitting in her office. They shifted in their chairs. None of them said a word.

"What?" she asked. "What are we going to do? Say something," and she kicked at the leg of one of the chairs, missed, and hit the man in the shins. He didn't wince, didn't move.

"All right, you bunch of idiots, I can see I'm scaring you to death. Let's talk about this. I won't jump down your throat. I need to hear from you. Tell me what we should do?"

As she finished she seemed to calm down. A toothy smile began to develop on her wide mouth. Her eyes squinted to feign friendliness, which she had done so many times before.

"Come on, guys, talk to me," she said, now in a full grin.

The only gray-haired man in the room put up his hands as if to surrender.

"Here's the problem," he began. "To stop them you're going to have to do something pretty drastic."

"Drastic times, drastic measures," the senator said.

"Based on what we learned from the IAIS," the gray-haired man continued, "we will need to get into their facility and destroy the Link interface and monitoring system, but those can be rebuilt."

"What's a Link?" she snapped.

"It's a gadget they strap to your arm which picks up memories right from the cells on your skin."

The senator just stared at him, so he continued.

"There's some chemicals involved. Some in a paste form they put on the Link, but the chemical Promax-2 is the key. You breath it in through your nostrils. The chemicals can be destroyed. A fire would take care of that, but chemicals can be reformulated."

"Do it," she said.

The gray-haired man looked at the others and continued as though the senator hadn't said what she did.

"You can, at the same time, destroy all of the documentation, but the formula for Promax-2 is probably known by someone. How can you destroy that?"

The Senator belched a laugh.

One of the other two men felt he should be contributing.

"There's a report that the company's chief chemist died at work not long ago. Maybe they're still using the Promax-2 he formulated. Makes sense," he said, complimenting himself. "If that's the case, perhaps no one else in the company has gone through the formulation process, and destroying the Link interface," he started to count on his fingers, "the recording system, the chemicals on hand and the documentation will do the trick."

The senator looked at the younger man with disgust and turned back to the gray-haired man.

"What about security?"

"Security?" he asked.

"Their security, stupid," she screamed.

"It's light, if we go in heavy, but good if we try to get in surreptitiously," he answered.

"What about at night?"

"The place is active 24 hours a day."

"Who's responsible for their security?" she asked.

"The owner's son-in-law."

"Names, I want names," she demanded.

"The chairman's name is George Evans. His son-in-law's name is Carlos Martinez."

"He's our man," she said with what sounded like a snarl.

They all looked up from their chairs at the tall senator hovering over them.

"A son-in-law in charge of security? Evans trusts him. Trusts him with all of the information we need. He will know who could recreate the formula."

Chapter 50

Dr. ben Charash

"But you must!"

"I won't," said Dr. Matthias ben Charash.

The men were speaking in a small room at the Tel Aviv headquarters of the IAIS.

"Are you telling me," the official asked, "that if we obtain the Promax-2 formula, you will not use your knowledge to replicate Search International's recall-enhancement process?"

"That's what I'm telling you."

"Why not?"

"I cannot."

"What do you mean, you cannot?"

"I have given much thought to this. I know the very stability of our government is at stake. We must find who was behind the mass assassination, but if the Search International process is in our hands, in the hands of any government, it will lead to greater evils."

"But you helped us spy on the Americans!"

"Yes, I did."

"You actually experienced the process, and you are the only one of us that did so."

"That's correct," said ben Charash.

"And now . . .?"

"What I experienced at Search prohibits me from giving the process to our government."

"What!!? What did you experience that would cause you to turn your back on your country in this time of crisis?" asked the official.

Dr. ben Charash's face reddened, and his jaw muscles tightened. He paused, and the official waited.

"I saw the Messiah, and He saw me."

Chapter 51

The Face of Evil

Carlos was on his way to work when two men got into his car at a downtown Madison stoplight. They told him where to drive. He was taken into a relatively new and unused single-story stucco building in an industrial park. They walked him toward the back of the building and into a small room probably intended to be used to store office supplies. There were three new folding chairs in the room. A microphone lay on the floor in plain sight, and the cord was draped up one wall, passing through a lifted ceiling tile. The larger man quietly closed the door.

Carlos assumed that he was going to be questioned regarding his refusal to cooperate with the government when the agents came to his friend's house. He sat in the center chair as directed to do.

"What's your name?" the smaller man asked.

"You get in my car and make me drive here, and you don't know my name?" asked Carlos.

The larger of the two men got up, with a blank expression on his face, reached back and then punched Carlos in the stomach. They waited as Carlos recovered from the painful blow.

"Now, what's your name?"

"Martinez."

"Martinez what?"

"Carlos Martinez."

"Where do you live?"

"In a new development on the west side."

"I want an address."

"150 Brookfield Lane."

"Where do you work?"

"Search International."

"What do you do there?"

"I'm the facilities manager."

"Is that it?"

"Pretty much."

"What does Search International do?"

"Product research."

"What kind of products does it research?"

"Most anything you can think of. Hard goods."

"Industrial stuff?'

"No, mostly consumer products. Some medical."

"What kind of medical products?"

"Health monitors. That sort of thing."

"What do they monitor?"

"Blood pressure, pulse, you know, health monitors."

"Would you like me to explain again how serious this questioning is?" the larger man said.

"I'm trying to do my best," Carlos said. "I don't know what you're after."

Carlos distinctly heard a guttural sound from the next room.

"So, Search International does medical research?"

"Some."

The large man got up and walked behind Carlos. Through the space between the seat of Carlos' chair and the backrest he kicked Carlos in his kidney area. The blow knocked Carlos forward off the chair. The other man caught him by the shoulders and pushed him back down onto the seat.

"Why don't you just tell me what you want," Carlos choked.

"What kind of medical research?"

Carlos knew that his usual answer, "That's confidential," would just result in further abuse.

"I'm sure you read about the work we're doing regarding human memory."

"What are you referring to?" the smaller man asked.

"The Link project," Carlos answered, wondering what question the disclosure would bring.

"Tell us about it. What is a Link?"

"With the Link we can help individuals recall distant memories," Carlos said, trying to remember just what they allowed Kasten to include in his articles.

"How does the Link help individuals recall memories?"

"The Link just records the recalled memories, it's the chemicals we administer that do the memory-recall enhancement."

"Where is the Link secured at Search International?"

"In a special safe."

"Where is the safe?"

Carlos looked back at the large man. "In the administration office."

"Where in the building is the administration office?"

"In the front far-left corner."

"What kinds of chemicals are used to do the memory-recall enhancement?"

"Just known memory enhancers like glucose, caffeine, that sort of thing."

"There must be some other not-so-well-known memory-enhancing chemical used to get results good enough to have articles written about your experiments."

"There are some."

"What are they called?"

"I'm not at liberty to say," Carlos answered.

The big man still standing behind Carlos grabbed Carlos' chair and threw it and Carlos across the room against the wall. The smaller man walked over, picked up Carlos' chair and put it back in its place. He pointed to it as Carlos staggered to his feet.

Why are they being so violent? Carlos asked himself.

As Carlos slumped down on the chair. The smaller man asked again, "What are the other chemicals called?"

"Glutamic acid, nicotine, and then there's one called Promax-2."

"What is Promax-2?"

"A synthetic neuro-transmitter," Carlos answered, knowing his interrogators would not stop until he told them what they wanted to hear.

"Is Promax-2 something you buy on the outside?" the smaller man continued.

"No, we make it up in our lab," answered Carlos.

"Your chemist makes it up for you?'

"He did."

"What do you mean 'he did'?"

The big man moved toward Carlos, but the smaller man raised his hand to stop him.

315

"He's dead," Carlos said. "He made up the only Promax-2 we have left."

"So, why don't you make up some more?" the smaller man asked.

"The formulas and documentation have been destroyed," Carlos answered.

The big man raised his arm to strike Carlos in the head, but the smaller man stopped him again.

"How did that happen?" he asked, clearly surprised.

"My father-in-law and I destroyed it."

"Why?"

"My father-in-law is concerned the formula would get into the wrong hands."

"Like your government's hands?" the man asked.

Carlos did not answer.

"Who's your father-in-law?"

"George Evans."

"What's his job there?"

"He's the chairman."

"He owns the company?"

"Most of it," Carlos answered.

"So, you and your father-in-law destroyed the documentation of the formula?"

"Yes."

"Who else was there at the time?"

"No one."

"Is your father-in-law a chemist?"

"No."

"Are you?"

"No, I'm an industrial engineering graduate."

"What happens when you run out of Promax-2?"

"We almost have."

"Then you won't be able to continue your memory research?"

"That's right."

The smaller man motioned to the big man, who hit Carlos with a sharp blow in the face, breaking his nose. Carlos moaned in pain, holding his face in his hands, blood streaming between his fingers.

"Do you expect me to believe," the smaller man sneered, "that Search came up with this great invention, the Link, and to use it for memory research Search International needs Promax-2, but your father-in-law, who owns the company, and therefore the invention, was so worried Promax-2 would get into the wrong hands he destroyed all means to produce more of the chemical for all time, making the invention worthless?"

"He may have changed his mind," Carlos said weakly, trying to get the man off the line of reasoning that led him to his angry response.

"What do you mean?"

"He may not stop the research after all. The last memory experiment involving a baby may have changed his mind."

"But it's too late," said the smaller man. "You're almost out of formula, no more Promax-2, no more experiments, no more demonstrations."

Demonstrations? wondered Carlos to himself. *Who mentioned demonstrations?*

"Well, isn't it?" the man asked.

"Isn't it what?" Carlos asked, growing faint.

"Isn't it too late? The formula documentation was destroyed, and no one can make more Promax-2. Isn't that right?""

Carlos felt trapped. Answering "yes" would surely result in more violence. Answering "no" would require an explanation that would focus even more attention on him. Any other answer might place George in danger. He couldn't risk that.

"The documentation was destroyed, but I committed the formula to memory," Carlos answered.

"You did? You're not a chemist."

"I used a memorization trick. I don't know the chemistry, but I know the formula. I'm the only one."

"You're the only one?"

"Yes."

"My father-in-law wanted it that way. He knows the bio-synchronizer, and I know the formula. Neither of us knows both."

Suddenly the door to the room slammed open and against the adjacent wall. In the doorway stood a tall woman in a red skirt and blazer. She glared at Carlos with an evil, toothy smile. The men looked shocked that the senator would expose herself this way.

"*A face of evil if I ever saw one,*" thought Carlos to himself, and a shiver went through his body.

She continued the questioning. "So if you can't remember the formula, Search International can't go on demonstrating its worthless technology?"

She didn't wait for an answer, and Carlos didn't give her one.

"So if you can't remember the formula, Search can't go on demonstrating that a six-week-old piece of useless tissue is a baby?"

She stood closer to Carlos and looked directly into his eyes.

"So if you can't remember the formula, Search can't convict me in front of my constituents of being a baby killer?"

She got louder and louder as she spoke, and Carlos became terrified.

"So if you can't remember the formula, Search can't destroy decades of success we achieved for the right of women to choose?"

Her face began to contort, and her mouth opened wider than Carlos thought possible when she screamed, "So if you can't remember the formula, Search can't help my enemies overturn *Roe versus Wade*?"

Suddenly her voice was quiet, and she looked almost normal, except for her eyes, which squinted in a feigned smile.

"So if you can't remember the formula, my problems are over!"

Carlos' burned-out car was found smashed against a bridge abutment along a country road. His blackened body was unrecognizable. An autopsy confirmed he had overdosed on cocaine. The police report called it a DUI accident, but there were doubts in the minds of several police officers on the scene.

Chapter **52**

Conception of the Next in Line

A month passed following Carlos' funeral. George Evans had not yet gone back to work. He wondered if he ever could. George and Rachel were visiting Jennifer, as they had almost every day since Carlos died. That morning they were sitting in Jennifer's family room listening to *The Morning Show* on TV.

"There has been a new development in the death of a man named Carlos Martinez," they heard the anchor say.

George got up and increased the volume.

"He was the facilities manager for the research firm now known for its development of memory-recall enhancement technology, as reported by Dave Kasten in his series of controversial articles. We have, this morning, Sergeant Jerry Reynolds at the Madison, Wisconsin, state police headquarters, and Mr. Kasten in his home near the state capitol. Good morning, gentlemen. Thank you for joining us so early this morning."

"Yes, good morning," the sergeant said. Kasten nodded.

"Mr. Kasten, you know about the research firm, Search International, better than either of us. What role did Carlos Martinez play there?"

"Well," said Kasten, "as you said, he was the facilities manager, and I'm sure a good one. But he was also responsible for security."

"In what way?"

"He was the one you had to see if you wanted to talk with George Evans or--toward the end there--if you wanted to get in the front door."

"Why the step-up in security?"

"Both George and Carlos were worried that the process, as they called it, would get into the wrong hands--"

"--and be used for what?"

"Interrogation of prisoners, for one thing," Kasten answered. "Their technology could allow you to recall an entire book you read when you were a child, word for word, just like some of those with the savant syndrome can do."

"Didn't Search also get into experimenting with reincarnation?" the anchorman asked.

"They demonstrated to me," Kasten responded, "as I wrote in my series, that our souls store all memory, including ancestral memories, and that reincarnation is baloney."

"So my child has in his memory all of my memories and those of our ancestors?"

"That's right, your memories which were stored prior to his conception, and with Search's technology those memories can be recalled."

"You wrote about a test Search conducted with an idiot savant. The savant's experience was pretty unbelievable."

"Believe it," responded Kasten. "I'll never forget it."

"Sergeant, did Carlos Martinez's relationship with Search International prompt you to study this accident more thoroughly than others?" the anchorman asked.

"No, I didn't even know of his connection to Search. I know where they're located, I've been past there many times, but I didn't know Martinez worked there."

"Tell us now, what did you discover regarding the accident?" asked the anchor.

"Well, first of all it was a terrible wreck. The car must have been going about 45 miles an hour--66 feet per second--when it hit the solid concrete bridge abutment."

"Were there any skid marks?"

"Not just before the impact, but there were skid marks 22 feet long about 100 yards up the highway leading to the crash."

"How can you be sure they were from Martinez' car?"

"We can't be, but they were fresh--little rubber had blown away--and a trooper who had passed the area earlier said he remembered no skid marks being there."

"So Martinez hit the brakes 100 yards from impact, and then perhaps passed out and hit the abutment?"

"No," said the sergeant, "further examination of the skid marks showed that the rubber was on the wrong side of the pits in the concrete to be caused by braking. They were caused by accelerating."

"Are you suggesting that Martinez committed suicide in a drugged state of mind?"

"Some suggested that, until we studied the autopsy report in greater detail."

"And what did you find?" asked the anchorman.

"An unusual combination of things. First of all, Martinez's nose was broken."

"Not unusual, I'm sure, in such an accident," said the anchorman.

"No, but Martinez was wearing his seatbelt, which had a shoulder strap, and it was clear his head did not hit the steering wheel or dashboard."

"Wasn't the seatbelt destroyed in the fire?"

"Sure," said the sergeant with a slight irritation in his voice at the step-by-step re-analysis by the TV anchorman, "but the steel latch was in its receptacle. Second," he went on without waiting for the anchorman to ask, "Martinez's right kidney was bruised."

"Again, that doesn't sound unusual for an automobile crash victim," said the anchorman.

"That's true," answered the sergeant, "but we couldn't see how that happened when we looked again at the wrecked car, and bruising of that sort doesn't occur after death. Third," he went on, "Martinez' right shoulder joint was damaged. The pathologist told us it appears to have happened before the crash, based on the coagulated blood found in the shoulder socket."

"Where are you going with this?" asked the anchor.

"Fourth," the sergeant continued, ignoring the anchorman's question, "the cocaine he had in his system was a lethal dose."

"We know that," said the anchorman, trying to recover. "He overdosed."

"Our pathologist says he thinks the cocaine killed Martinez before the crash."

"What are you saying?" asked the anchorman.

"I'm suggesting that Martinez was beaten and killed before his car hit that bridge abutment," said the sergeant.

"Killed? How could he have driven into the abutment if he was dead?" the anchorman asked.

"The car could easily have been rigged to run into the abutment, and the rigging removed before the car was set on fire."

"So you think the fire was set? Wouldn't your investigation have discovered an accelerant in the car?"

"Not after the gas tank exploded," said the sergeant.

"Have you charged anyone?"

"No."

"Do you have any suspects?"

"No."

"Mr. Kasten, how well did you know Carlos Martinez?" the anchorman asked.

"Quite well, I talked with him and met with him over a period of about a year," Kasten answered. "He was a very nice young man, and totally loyal to his father-in-law."

"Do you also know his father-in-law well?" asked the anchor.

"Yes," said Kasten, "he and I have gotten to know each other very well."

"What did he say when he was told his son-in-law was reported to have overdosed?"

"I'm sure he said it was absurd," answered Kasten.

"Isn't it true, Mr. Kasten, there's a great deal of controversy surrounding Search because of your internationally syndicated science articles?"

"I suppose so," Kasten answered, wondering where he was going with this line of questioning.

"Isn't it also true that you're an anti-abortion activist, and that the purpose of your entire article series was to support your position and discredit that of the pro-choice proponents?"

"No, the purpose of my article series was to inform," he answered.

"Then why was your final article so strongly worded against abortion?" the anchor asked.

"I reported what happened. What happened proved, to me, that abortionists have been killing human babies for decades. It proved that a 42-day-old fetus can hear and remember its mother's voice."

"This all took place in Search's lab, did it not?"

"Yes, the Link laboratory," Kasten answered.

"And couldn't they have easily faked the entire experiment?" the anchorman asked.

"They didn't," Kasten answered. "Did you hear the recording of the mother's song?"

"Sergeant," the anchorman continued, "are there any other developments in the case?"

"A few sketchy details. A commercial real estate agent showed a Madison business park property and building the day after Mr. Martinez died. She found blood on the floor of one room and dents in an adjacent wall. The blood matched Carlos'."

"Is that it?" asked the anchorman.

"A tall women in a red skirt and jacket was seen leaving the site in a luxury vehicle with black tinted windows approximately two and a half hours before the estimated time of the accident.

"Any lead on who that was?" asked the anchor.

"No, none," answered the sergeant.

"Gentlemen," concluded the anchorman, "thank you for your time. We'll be right back after this short commercial break."

George Evans turned off the TV. It was devastating news. They had experienced Carlos' death all over again, but now they had learned that he had probably been beaten and . . .

"Murdered!" Jennifer cried. "He was murdered! Why? Why would anyone want to murder Carlos?"

George felt such a great pressure on his chest and shoulders that he thought he might be having a heart attack. Suddenly, he believed that Carlos' death was now clearly his fault. His daughter was without her husband and his grandchildren without a father because of decisions he had made.

325

"Jennifer," George began, "honey, Carlos was the only one who knew the formula for Promax-2, the synthetic neurotransmitter which made it possible to recall ancestral memories."

"Are you saying someone may have killed him because he knew a formula they wanted?"

"If a government agency wanted the formula," said George, "they would have gotten it from him and turned him loose. The episode would have been the government's word against Carlos'. Killing him would have made no sense."

"Then who? Why?" Jennifer asked.

"Someone must have found out that Carlos was the only one who knew the formula, and that no more Promax-2 could be produced if he was killed."

"Who wanted the experiments stopped? I thought everyone would benefit from the technology," asked Rachel. "I know there were those who wanted to steal the technology, but I didn't know anyone wanted to destroy it at all costs."

"It never occurred to me that Carlos' life was in serious danger, even though it should have," said George. "Perhaps…"

"Daddy!" cried Jennifer before he had a chance to completely answer Rachel. "Oh, Daddy!"

Jennifer's face showed that she was terribly frightened.

"What is it? What is it?" asked George.

"Oh, God, no," she continued. "Please, God, no."

"Jennifer, what are you thinking?" asked George.

"They killed Carlos to destroy his memory of the formula," she said, "but they didn't, and they're going to realize they didn't, and they're going to try to kill my baby."

"What are you saying?" asked George.

"You've proven that children have the memories of their parents, and they know Search's technology can get the children to recall them."

George began to understand.

"Jennifer, Jennifer," he said gripping her by her shoulders so that she looked into his eyes, "both of your children were conceived and born before Carlos ever knew the formula. Neither have it in their memory."

"But, Daddy," Jennifer sobbed. "I missed my last period. I may be five weeks pregnant!"

Epilogue

George Evans went to Search that very day, after calling his friend Dave Kasten to observe what he was about to do. Without an explanation to his staff, he methodically, systematically and thoroughly destroyed the Link, the bio-synchronizer, and all of the sophisticated recording equipment. He confirmed that no Promax-2 remained. George also destroyed the stock of other memory-enhancing drugs and the formulas for their compounding. He then called a news conference and, with Dave Kasten, announced what he had done before the national media.

Dave Kasten has continued to write about his experiences with Search, and he has written an investigative report entitled "What Really Happened to Carlos Martinez?" which was aired on national television. The report was the subject of talk and Sunday TV news shows. He openly implicated the senator, who lost her seat in the Senate the following November. She filed a lawsuit against him.

George retired as chairman of Search and later sold the company to its employees. He and Rachel have been traveling about the country in George's favorite "travel vehicle," giving talks to Christian communities and colleges. Rachel has developed a healing ministry, based in part on the hypothesis. Jennifer changed her family's name and moved to southern California with her four children. She later purchased Darrell Johnson's home when he moved to Madison, Wisconsin, to join Search.

Gary Richardson finished his scientific paper entitled, "The Truly Astonishing Hypothesis," which was published in an obscure scientific journal after being turned down by those publishers and journals that wanted to remain "politically correct." The paper got the attention it deserved, however, when Dave Kasten put the entire story of "Search and the Link Project" on the Internet, with George's approval, including his conclusions regarding the death of Carlos.

Gary and Joan married, and they began flying around the country on speaking engagements. What listeners have heard from Gary sounds more like a revival sermon than a scientific paper presentation.

Charlie Shuster also retired and is living with his wife of 40 years in Kenosha, Wisconsin. He has talked to anyone who was interested in his Search experiences.

Anna Pierson, the new president and CEO of Search, changed the company's strategic direction, and Search International is now dedicated to medical research, based on the hypothesis. The company's work is substantially funded by an alliance of Christian denominations brought about by the publication of "The Truly Astonishing Hypothesis" and Dave Kasten's articles. LaShauna Jackson, now vice president of research, has been given the assignment of discovering what other information the particle might contain, since its capacity is infinite. She will try to develop a hypothesis which suggests explanations for ESP and the foreknowledge of future events. She is also working now with identical twins adopted by different families and separated since birth.

Allen Nolte remained as head engineer at Search and has become very active in his church. Mike Young earned an engineering degree and works with Scott Dennison for Med-

Diagnostics. Clyde Hart became a missionary physician to Tom Grey Fox's people in northern Wisconsin.

Barbara Shaw has made it her personal mission to undo the damage done by certain Hollywood stars who have promoted the nonsense of reincarnation. Willy and Steve Thomas have a new ministry of their own. Willy has recited "his" version of Genesis before astronomers and school children alike, all over the world. "It's amazing what he can do!"

Father Christopher Braun wrote a 13-page letter to his former bishop. He hasn't heard anything from him, but friends of his, still in the clergy, say it has caused quite a stir in the Vatican.

Letter to Bishop Monsonto

Christopher Braun
12224 Walnut Street
Hales Corners, Wisconsin

January 18, 2011

Bishop Anthony Monsanto
Diocese of Madison
Diocesan Offices
Capital Square
Madison, Wisconsin

Subject: **"The Truly Astonishing Hypothesis"**

Dear Bishop Monsanto:

I have had the most wonderful experience of participating with a team of research engineers, scientists and physicians at a company called Search. I am sure you have heard of Search, the work they have been doing relating to human memory, their claim to the scientific discovery of the human soul, the recent murder of the company's facilities manager, and most importantly their demonstration that a six-week-old fetus is definitely a full-human baby. I am writing to you today regarding a scientific paper just published by Gary Richardson, a member of the team I worked with. A copy of his "Truly Astonishing Hypothesis" is enclosed.

A hypothesis "suggests." It does not "prove." But this hypothesis suggests that Scripture is true, literally true, fundamentally true, scientifically true. It suggests that those who believe that Scripture is full of error are wrong. It even suggests that most scientists are wrong about "life" and that billions of Christians are right. But *how* right? For it suggests that we Christians, too, have a lot of wrong ideas. And how many of these wrong ideas separate the brothers and sisters of the Body of Christ! How many of these wrong ideas are used to build walls between them!

I have observed that many, many Scripture verses support the ideas expressed in the hypothesis, both in the New and Old Testament. If any ideas incorporated in the hypothesis are in conflict with Scripture's teaching, then that part of the hypothesis is wrong. We should attribute the error to man. The Bible is the Word of God, and it cannot be in error. It is not the mythical document the secular world and many Christians have made it out to be.

You will find, I believe, that the Hypothesis also suggests explanations for some of the truths in Scripture we call "mysteries of our Faith." I believe it is important today that we search for explanations to these mysteries, to give Christians a better response to those coming from the secular world. God's perfect plan is also perfectly complete and, I'm sure you will agree, He does not need mysteries or magic to demonstrate His omnipotence or omniscience. That would suggest He omitted to provide for some event in human history. Today it would seem that Jesus is saying, "If you do not believe Me, then believe on the evidence of the miracles of Creation." We learn more every day.

Christians today should be prepared to discuss (not argue) the incredible beauty and "complex-simplicity" of God's Creation with non-believers, but not by ignoring the atemporal nature of our Creator. Theologians have for years argued the pre-existence of Christ, when it is clear from Scripture that the answer to the question, "Did Jesus Christ, born of Mary, exist before Abraham?" is yes. "Did God create the cosmos in six days?" Yes. "Did the process appear to take billions of years?" Yes. How small we try to make our God!

A Catholic pastor friend of mine recently told me I should not use Christ's words, "Many are called, but few are chosen," in a literal sense, because theologians throughout the centuries have concluded that Jesus could not have meant them to be taken to mean that God calls many, but chooses few. "It seems," the pastor suggested, "unjust for God to call many and then choose only few."

"But, Jesus repeats the fact," I said, "that only few find the narrow gate while many are on the broad road to destruction."

"Those words," the pastor continued, "also must not be taken to mean that most of mankind are headed for destruction, since God wills that all be saved." The same pastor explained Jesus' statement, "Before Abraham came to be, I AM," to mean that the Son of God as Christ existed before Abraham, but that as "Jesus" was born much later, just 2,010 years ago. Jesus Christ, who is God, must, therefore, have changed.

The hypothesis, as you will see (if you have not already read it), suggests that Jesus meant what He said, and that Scripture "is meant to be taken literally unless the context clearly indicates otherwise." It suggests that Jesus Christ existed when time began and that He was born to Mary two thousand years ago, for to God the two events were concurrent. It suggests that God calls all men and chooses few simultaneously, the few that truly choose Him. There is, therefore, no contradiction in God. He is three Persons in one God. He is all merciful and, concurrently, all just.

God is not a supernatural being. He exists neither in nature nor in super nature. He simply and perfectly IS. He created both the natural and the supernatural, and is not a part of His Creation. God is everywhere, unlimited by time. His Creation is perfectly complete, and we will always remain a part of it, unless He wills differently. He is the only Being that can create from nothing and destroy into nothing. Yet it is clear from Scripture (and the hypothesis suggests) that He loves us like a perfect parent would love His child with an unconditional love.

If (or when) you exist in the sequential state and are given a spoon with which to move a mountain, which exists in the temporal state, you will do it in no time at all, since there will be, for you, no time between events (i.e., each spoonful moved). This will be true even though you move the mountain one spoonful at a time. Imagine now (we can't) the awesomeness of God in the concurrent state. The mountain will move at a moment in time, in accordance with His will, having willed it before time began and therefore before the mountain existed. We cannot consider the process of Creation without considering the timelessness of God (please read, if you have not already, the "Genesis from a Genius" report written by Dave Kasten, scientific editor of the *Madison Journal*).

Christians believe the Son of God became man. But who is this Savior whom man was called to follow to the Father and life everlasting? He is the Lord of all, the Son of God, as you know and profess. All events in His Creation occur, therefore, concurrently for Him. Who was Christ when He called men to follow Him? This question requires a different, temporal answer. Through the power of the Holy Spirit, Christ united His divine Spirit with the particle at the functional center of an ovum in Mary's reproductive system, thereby creating a new, unique Soul* and a perfect Likeness* of Christ's body. [* Capitalized because of Christ's divine nature.]

Concurrently, the building blocks of DNA present in Mary's ovum formed the chromosomes of a new and unique cell in accordance with the perfect Likeness contained in the particle of Christ's Soul--the identical Likeness of the male, Adam. It is the Likeness stored in the soul that sets and corrects the chromosomes, using the building blocks of DNA present.

Because of His divine nature, before Adam was, Christ is. Christ was truly the second Adam, since Adam was made in His Image (soul) and Likeness (body). Also, the hypothesis suggests that the instant of Christ's Incarnation and the instant of Christ's death are events that occurred together for God, existing in the concurrent state. Jesus never ceased being God.

Though Catholics believe she carried no stain of Original Sin, Mary nonetheless suffered the consequences with all mankind. Her DNA was imperfect, and, therefore, the communications between Christ's atemporal particle and body were also imperfect. He was like us in every way, except He did not sin. His earthly appearance was unremarkable. Further, since His brain developed and functioned like ours, He had to learn all things gradually like we do. Because He could recall readily only those experiences His neurons delivered to His Particle, He was unaware He was the Son of God until Mary told Him, when He was a child, what she knew. Even then, He had to trust her words, and those of His stepfather, words of quite ordinary people. Mary's role in Christ's ministry appears to be defined by her role at the wedding feast of Cana.

In the manner described above, Christ, the Son of God, truly emptied Himself of His divine knowledge and power. Simply, He caused Himself to be unable to recall He was God. As He grew, He thirsted for knowledge of the God whose Son Mary said He was. He prayed, read Scripture and learned about the promise of a Messiah. Mary told Him about John the Baptist, and what Elizabeth had said. Elizabeth told John about Jesus. Both Jesus and John had to rely on their belief and trust in God. Both knew, and grew up with, the people of their time, and they recognized the risk of delivering the message of a prophet.

Through frequent prayer to the Father, Christ received the level of faith (i.e., belief and trust) He said we too could have, and by this faith, and through the power of the Holy Spirit, He taught the Good News and healed the sick and the lame--just as He said we could and should do. Jesus was obedient to the Father, even unto a death He did not want to experience. When He returned His spirit to the Father on the cross, He was restored to life, just as He said He would be, demonstrating the restoration to eternal life all true followers of His can expect at the time of their temporal death. From

His birth to His death He was a Man, just like us, except He did not sin. A Man we can and must follow.

Christ said, "Follow me," to His disciples, and "I will teach you to be the fishers of men." Then He immediately went about teaching the Gospel and healing those who came or were brought to Him, demonstrating what He said His followers can and should do. If God said we can heal the sick and the lame just as Jesus did, then He must have provided a mechanism in His Creation to permit us to do so. That mechanism may be the "laying on of hands." It may be possible to share one's spirit, the Breath of God, with one another--not unlike the sharing of the spirit by parents during the process of procreation. In most recorded healings, Christ attributed the miraculous results to the faith (belief and trust) of the recipients, or at least to the person requesting the healing. Man is the link in this healing mechanism and therefore must believe in it. Concentration (focus) may play a role. It enhances the memory process, improving the communications between one's brain and soul. Perhaps trust permits an even deeper level of concentration.

The hypothesis suggests that the mechanism God created for healing one another through prayer is available to us today. It is the same mechanism used by Christ, by His faith in the Father and through the power of the Holy Spirit, to heal the sick and the lame.

Christ said that the Father would send the Advocate, the Holy Spirit, to all those who love Him and keep His commandments. He is the Spirit of truth, the divine Source of all knowledge. For this to be possible, God must have provided a mechanism in His Creation. It is envisioned that the atemporal particle--the soul--has a functional, though spiritual, form. It may be that of a perfect, multi-layered sphere, with each layer representing a range of memory (i.e., short-term, long term, ancestral, etc.) and other functions. At the "center" of the particle is a cavity (defining the "medius," meaning "midmost" point). When it is not "filled" through a relationship with God, it may well represent the emptiness we all feel when estranged from Him.

Being pure spirit, the Holy Spirit can communicate with and literally reside within the human soul without undermining the human's free will. There He can have a direct effect on man's subconscious thinking, causing the mind to consider better alternatives as it searches for comparisons. In this way, God is with Christ's followers, as Christ promised, to teach them everything and remind them of all He told them. "Do not worry beforehand about what you are to say. But say whatever will be given to you at that hour. For it will not be you who are speaking but the Holy Spirit," Christ said.

Are the knowledge and power of the Holy Spirit available to true believers today? The hypothesis suggests they most definitely are. Does the Holy Spirit, the third Person of our Triune God, speak to us as individuals? Most definitely. Question: Can we cause material changes to occur through our sequential-state component (the soul) and the power of the Holy Spirit as Christ apparently did (changing water to wine and feeding thousands with a few loaves and fishes)? He said we would do greater things than these!

Christ said He, personally, would also always be with His disciples. He then proceeded to introduce the most controversial concept in the history of religions. He said they must eat His flesh and drink His blood to have life everlasting. Why would He introduce such a divisive concept if it was not to become a necessary mechanism for Him, as a resurrected God/Man, existing outside of man's temporal State, to be with His followers as He promised?

Catholics and Episcopalians believe that to "nourish" (be with) man, body and soul, Christ changes the substance of bread and wine into His Body and Blood, just as He explained at the Last Supper. While Christ's Body and Blood progress to the very cells of a man's body as true

337

nutrients, Christ's Soul enters the functional center of every cell, permitting Christ to be with man, in every sense of the word, as a divine Body-Soul being. [Christ's indwelling may be temporary, requiring frequent reception by the believer.] His words, "Do this in remembrance of me," should probably be interpreted to mean, "Do this to personally re-experience my presence with you."

God is the God of the living, not the God of the dead. The hypothesis states that we do not die but transition to sequential-state existence. Christ demonstrated the process with His physical death on the cross and resurrection on the third day. "Touch me and see, because a ghost does not have flesh and bones as you can see I have. Have you anything here to eat?" He said. He was alive, solid to the touch, but He had just entered the room through a locked door. He came to the apostles in the sequential state, "controlling" the time between events.

Many Christians believe that after our physical death we continue to exist in the spiritual state. That is true. The hypothesis suggests the "spiritual state" is actually the same as the sequential. But, we are body-soul beings. At death we transition to fully sequential-state beings with a body and a soul. We are never without a body. Christ said, "And do not be afraid of those who kill the body but cannot kill the soul; rather, be afraid of the one who can destroy both body and soul in Gehenna." If we have no body after death, what body was He talking about? (Not our earthly "resurrected" body, for only the righteous will be resurrected.)

One of the basic, underlying reasons for division between Christian communities and denominations is the "mystery of life after death." Most Christians have their own belief of what "life after death" means. There is no unified concept, even though Christ demonstrated the process so clearly. The hypothesis suggests that our transition to the sequential state will be very natural, with nothing to fear. Ask yourself the following questions:

If we were absolutely certain that at the moment of death that we would be restored to life, body and soul, how then would we live our present lives?

If we were absolutely certain that life after death was not mysterious and could be far better understood by us than it is now, would we view the "hereafter" differently, more realistically?

If we learned how the Holy Spirit indwells us as Christians, and how He is able to be our Helper and Counselor from within our souls, would we learn to listen and accept His counsel?

If we were told convincingly how we could cure the sick and heal the lame, and how the entire process takes place, would we step forward and do greater things than Christ did, as He said we could?

The hypothesis suggests that we could learn much more about death, the indwelling of the Spirit, healing and more, if we seriously consider that we are, as God has said, body and soul beings; we could learn much more if we stopped thinking that everything about the spiritual is mysterious, and realized that both the physical and the spiritual are just two component parts of God's Creation.

The following are other issues which have been used as barriers between Christians and between denominations:

Prayers to or for the dead. There is no clear conclusion one can draw from the hypothesis regarding prayers to the dead. God alone knows our every thought through the field which He has provided. Therefore, the mechanism for communications with the Father, Son and Holy Spirit is clearly suggested by the hypothesis. What would prevent God from sharing our prayers with those He chooses in the sequential state? (I can imagine God saying to a mother in heaven, "I have a message for you from your children. They love you very much." Can't you imagine that?) And further, since God, exclusively, is in the concurrent state, the hypothesis suggests that prayers for those alive or dead are equally effective. That is, we can ask God for the spiritual well-being of any person because our God is the great I AM.

Intentional Abortion. The hypothesis leaves little doubt that from the true moment of conception (i.e., when the particle of the female unites with the particle of the male), a new being exists, is alive and growing. There is no point in the process of development when the fetus becomes more human. The intentional termination of the life of a human zygote, or later a fetus, is murder no matter where it is, in the women's uterus or in a laboratory dish.

Homosexuality. The hypothesis suggests it is possible, in some cases, probably as rare as an unusual birth defect, that the likeness of the body of a human is in fact opposite in gender to that of the temporal body. The hypothesis in no way suggests that overt homosexuality (the homosexual lifestyle) is excusable. Scripture says it is always wrong. Nor does the hypothesis suggest that homosexuality is any more common than birth defects, certainly not as common as homosexual activists claim. Those with the defect must carry their cross until their transition to the sequential state when their body will be a perfect reflection of their likeness. All should be treated with respect and love.

Medical intervention. Nothing in the hypothesis suggests that it is wrong to utilize the services of medical professionals or the medicines they prescribe. It does suggest, on the other hand, that the natural process of cellular regeneration and healing through the power of the Holy Spirit is underutilized and sometimes ignored because of a lack of understanding of human nature (i.e., we are body-soul beings). It also suggests that the present methods of treating cancer (i.e., radiation, chemotherapy and surgery), are absolutely contrary to the health and well-being of the human. It also suggests that a better understanding of the body-soul system will lead to new answers regarding severed extremities and injuries to the central nervous system.

Predestination. The hypothesis suggests that because of the concurrent nature of God, predestination has no purpose. God knew (knows is more accurate) from the beginning of time the course of all history and how your temporal life begins and ends. He knows where you will spend eternity and why. He can, therefore, before time began, have chosen those who will choose Him with their own free will during their lifetime. "Many are called; few are chosen" means exactly that. God calls all to Him, but chooses the few who accept His call.

Reincarnation. Those who believe they have lived a life before their present life, because they have recalled under hypnosis or in dreams events which happened before their time, may actually be re-experiencing memories from their ancestors as stored in their soul (particle). The hypothesis suggests this logical explanation which also applies to "deja vu" experiences of having been places we have never been before. Our God, existing in the concurrent state, would have no purpose in re-incarnating His created beings.

It is time Christians stop talking in mythical, magical and mysterious terms about their very real God and Savior. The majority of men are on the broad road to destruction, because they do not take the time to think in real terms about their God, Creation, life, and death. Christ said that those who believe will never die. He meant what He said in real terms. Intellectual belief in Him is insufficient for salvation. Man must believe so as to trust, with his heart. Furthermore, man can be certain that the evidence of his faith will be used to judge him when his temporal life ends, because Christ said this will be the case. Being baptized and confirmed, attending church services every Sunday, does not save him. Knowing Christ and following Christ will.

I propose that Christian theologians and scientists meet and prayerfully consider the hypothesis to see where it leads, having unity in the Body of Christ as their goal.

Respectfully,

Christopher Braun

The *Truly* Astonishing Hypothesis

By Gary Richardson

The Nobel laureate Dr. Francis H. C. Crick, who collaborated with James D. Watson in the discovery of the molecular structure of DNA, says in his book, *The Astonishing Hypothesis - The Scientific Search for the Soul,* that, "You, your joys and sorrows, your memories and your ambitions, your sense of personal identity and free will, are in fact no more than the behavior of a vast assembly of nerve cells and their associated molecules." This is the "Astonishing Hypothesis" he offers up to the scientific community and the world to prove true with scientific facts.

In his book he goes on to say, "Most religions hold that some kind of spirit exists that persists after one's bodily death and, to some degree, embodies the essence of that human being. Without its spirit a body cannot function normally, if at all."

"As Lewis Carroll's Alice might have phrased it: 'You're nothing but a pack of neurons,'" says Dr. Crick.

Dr. Crick concludes, "If the scientific facts [gathered by the scientific community as prompted by his hypothesis] are sufficiently striking and well established, and if they support the Astonishing Hypothesis, then it will be possible to argue that the idea that man has a disembodied soul is as unnecessary as the age old idea that there was a Life Force. This," he arrogantly says, "is in head-on contradiction to the religious beliefs of billions of human beings alive today."

On the back cover a reviewer says, "In his new book, *The Astonishing Hypothesis,* Nobel laureate Francis Crick boldly straddles the line between science and spirituality by examining the soul from the standpoint of a modern scientist, basing the soul's existence and function on an in-depth examination of how the human brain 'sees.'" Yet the reader will find that Dr. Crick himself concludes, "By the standards

343

of exact science, we do not yet know, even in outline, how our brains produce the vivid visual awareness that we take so much for granted."

"What better place to look beyond than through the mind of one who saw to that point but no further." - George Evans.

Dr. Crick only feigned his "scientific search for the soul." I propose that the scientific community search for the soul in earnest, because therein will lie the answers to visual awareness, consciousness and man's search for meaning. Theoretical physicist Stephen William Hawking has said, "We pretty well know how the cosmos came into being, but we still don't know why." Scientists must return to considering the "why" in their search for the "how"; and the scientific discovery of the soul, its purpose and function will lead to unprecedented advances in all biological fields.

So, I too now offer for consideration by the scientific community and the world:

The *Truly* Astonishing Hypothesis

Preface

Dr. Francis Crick is an avowed atheist. It can be assumed, therefore, that he accepts as fact that the cosmos came into existence from nothing and that man evolved from a lucky protein through natural selection over billions of years. These absurd ideas look like truth in comparison to the statement that the blueprint and biological orders for a complete, living, functioning, thinking human being are stored in the 750 megabytes of DNA code contained in the zygote (a fertilized ovum). Nothing, however, is more off the mark than Dr. Crick's "Astonishing Hypothesis." It seems scientists today must mutter such absurdities while they hide in their Darwinian caves, hoping the rocks will fall on their heads rather than face God.

I too doubted the existence of God, until I came out of my intellectual hiding place to view Creation with an open mind. Once I accepted His existence, He provided a means for us to communicate. I had many questions and received many answers. The ideas that follow did not come from my mind, but did pass through it. Therefore, I want to be certain that any truth found in The *Truly* Astonishing Hypothesis (hereinafter referred to as the "Hypothesis") is credited to the Creator and any error to me.

The Hypothesis was not originally developed as an answer to Dr. Crick's book or to answer the scientific or theological questions it appears to address. It developed from logical answers to the following questions posed to the Search International research team I was a part of just one year ago. 1. How can the single human cell, at conception (the zygote), possibly contain all of the information necessary to develop into a unique, living, thinking being? (Scientists presently reply with an absurdly incomplete answer to this question, i.e., "DNA coding.") 2. If a single human cell contains all of the information to "produce" a complete human being, isn't it probably capable of containing more?

The Truly Astonishing Hypothesis was developed from the answers to two intriguing questions posed to Search International.

Gradually God opened our eyes to the logical answers that follow. It was only then that we began to realize how the answers applied to the Creator, creation, life, death, reproduction, healing and more that you, too, may uncover as you review this document.

The Hypothesis

All of the hypothetical statements of the Hypothesis are in italics. Those which follow some of the statements are my interpretations, explanations, references and opinions.

The first hypothetical statement may pose an insurmountable barrier to the reader. It is central to the Hypothesis, yet, in part, impossible to rationalize, because man is immersed in the temporal state. The figures that follow may help.

1. *There are three states of existence: Temporal, Sequential and Concurrent. In the Temporal State, events are spaced by time. In the Sequential State, events happen sequentially, but are not* (necessarily[1]) *spaced by time. In the Concurrent State, all events happen concurrently.*

Figure 1 is a drawing of five photographic plates that have recorded the movement of a disk from the top-left corner of the plate to the bottom-right corner. Each plate has recorded the disk at a given position as an instantaneous event. The top plate has recorded Event 1 (E1), and so forth. In between each event, represented by the space between the plates, is time (the measurement of which depends on the relative motion of the observer). This drawing represents the Temporal State.

The next drawing, Figure 2, represents the Sequential State. The same series of events is recorded, but there is no time between events.

The last drawing, Figure 3, represents the Concurrent State. The same series of events is recorded, but all have occurred concurrently. God alone exists in the Concurrent State ("I am that AM." Exodus 3).

2. *At the functional center of every living cell is an atemporal particle of zero temporal mass existing in the Sequential State (defining "Particle" - a biological singularity).*

3. *The same Particle is a component of every cell in the organism.*[2] The Particle is the "fabric of the soul."

---

[1] I will leave my reason for adding "(necessarily)" to the discovery of the reader.
[2] i.e., there is only one Particle in each organism and it is at the functional center of each cell.

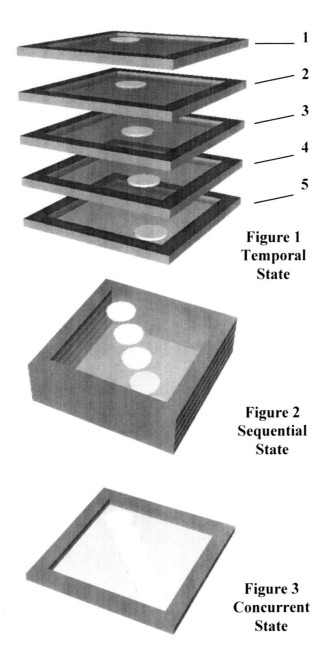

1
2
3
4
5

Figure 1
Temporal
State

Figure 2
Sequential
State

Figure 3
Concurrent
State

The "Binding Problem," which obsessed Dr. Francis Crick, is defined by him as the problem of how (a set of) neurons temporarily become active as a unit. He says, "As an object seen is often also heard, smelled or felt, this binding must also occur across sensory modalities. Our experience of perceptual unity suggests that the brain in some way binds together, in a mutually coherent way, all those neurons actively responding to different aspects of a perceived object." Dr. Crick's brilliant mind is blinded to the truth because of his choice to ignore God. All neurons (all cells) are "linked" by the Particle.

4. *A state-bridging field ("Field") enables communications between the Sequential State Particle and the Temporal-State (physical) component of the cell.*

If the Field is withdrawn, the cell and the organism will die. Every living organism, therefore, is a trichotomy of its a) Temporal-State components, b) Sequential-State Particle, and c) Field. The Field may be the "Breath of God," and in the human, the body, soul and spirit define the trichotomy. God sustains all life.

5. *All cells are capable of receiving information from the Particle.* Neurons (the basic structural and functional units of the nervous system) are capable of receiving a different level of information from the Sequential-State Particle and transferring it to other neurons.

6. *All neurons are capable of transferring data to the Particle.* Further, neurons are capable of accepting information from other neurons and transferring the information to the Particle.

The following reference is an excerpt from an article in the September 1992 issue of *Scientific American* entitled, "How Neurons Communicate," by Gerald D. Fischbach.

> A neuron that has been excited conveys information to other neurons by generating impulses known as 'action potentials.' These signals propagate like waves down the

length of the cell's single axon, and are converted to chemical signals at synapses, the contact points between neurons (i.e., contact points on dendrites leading to other neurons).

When a neuron is at rest, its external membrane maintains an electrical potential of about minus 70 millivolts (the inner surface is negative relative to the outer surface). At rest, the membrane is more permeable to potassium ions than to sodium ions. When the (neuron) is stimulated, the permeability to sodium increases, leading to an inrush of positive charges. This inrush triggers an impulse--a momentary reversal of the membrane potential (known as an action potential). The impulse is initiated at the junction of the cell body and axon, and is conducted away from the cell body.

When the impulse reaches the axon terminals (synapses) it induces the release of neurotransmitter molecules. Transmitters diffuse across a narrow cleft (in the synapse) and bind to receptors in the postsynaptic membrane. Such binding leads to the opening of ion channels and often, in turn, to the generation of action potentials in the postsynaptic neuron.

"(Action potentials) have also been traced by fine-tipped micro-electrodes positioned close enough to a (neuron) or an axon to detect the small currents generated as an action potential passes by." Gerald D. Fischbach.

The following is proposed by the Truly Astonishing Hypothesis: In all neurons the physical structure of DNA plays a key role in addition to the storing of coded genetic traits. In all cells[3] two turns of the double helix DNA are wrapped around bead-like nucleosomes (containing histones). DNA is negatively charged, and the nucleosomes are positively charged. The assembly is twisted tightly, further coiled, folded and packed into a chromosome.

When a neuron of the brain fires, after receiving an action potential from another neuron, the pulse is coupled to its nucleus and to the DNA contained therein. The electrical characteristics of the string-like DNA wrapped around the nucleosomes produce a "disturbance" in the Field, which propagates the signal to the Particle where it is stored and instantly returned (see Statement 9) in the fashion of that described above.

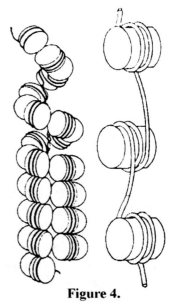

The DNA/ nucleosome assembly, coiled as shown in Figure 4, appears to be an extremely high frequency electronic (electromagnetic) device.

The signal from the Particle causes a disturbance in the Field, which is propagated to the Temporal-State nucleus of the cell. There it may be translated into cellular instructions or, in the neuron, cause the neuron to fire, resulting in the transfer of

Figure 4.

the information to other neurons as described in Gerald Fischbach's article.

The Field signal originating from the functional center of the nucleus of a cell envelops the cell and overlaps nearby cells. In non-neural cells, it does not matter if the Field enveloping each cell overlaps adjacent cells, since the communications are generally one way. Regarding neurons,

---

[3] i.e., all cells containing DNA

however, an overlap of sufficient signal strength could be problematic, if a disturbance in the Field enveloping one neuron is sufficient to trigger an action potential in an adjacent neuron that may not be in the proper signal path. This is one reason why neurons are separated as they are by axons leading to synapses connected to dendrites leading to other neurons, etc.

What if, however, in the developing brain of a young child, the Field signal is strong enough or the neurons are close enough that a disturbance in the Field enveloping one neuron, under certain conditions, causes an adjacent neuron to fire, which causes another adjacent neuron to fire and so on. A signal "flashover" would occur in a part of the brain, stopped only by a break in the chain-reaction by a lesser Field signal or greater separation between neurons. This condition is called "benign childhood epilepsy." It is termed "childhood" because the child "grows out of it." The Hypothesis suggests both the cause for the condition and the reason it does not last into adulthood, both of which are presently not known.

7. *Temporal-State data communicated to the Particle is stored as Sequential-State data (defining "Parallata," pl. of Parallatum).* Neurons of the brain receive pulsed, analog, incomprehensible information, in parallel fashion, directly or indirectly, from every nerve cell in the body and neurons in other parts of the brain.

8. *The information-storage capacity of the Particle is infinite.*

9. *Parallata transferred to the Particle are instantly returned (reflected) to the Temporal-State nuclei of the source neurons.*

10. *The transfer of data between Temporal-State nuclei and the Sequential-State Particle, enabled by the Field, converts random data to comprehensible data.*

This Statement appears to address the question that so puzzles Dr. Crick. All sensory analog data arriving at

351

different parts of the brain causing neurons to fire at various rates left him with a few unsatisfactory answers as to how all of this activity is tied into coherent, conscious thought.

The eyes, in truth, are "the windows of the soul," for the soul is linked directly to every one of man's senses.

11. *Sight is a joint process of the Temporal and Sequential components of visual cortex neurons.* The sensor neurons of the retina receive analog information coming through the lens of the eye. Neurons of the brain receive and transfer this analog information to the Particle, and it is returned to the brain in a synchronous, comprehensible manner. It is, therefore, the communication of information between the Temporal and Sequential components of the neurons of the brain, enabled as always by the Field, that makes vision possible.

The eyes, in truth, are the "windows of the soul." The soul (Particle), in fact, is involved in every movement man makes, every sight he sees, every smell, every sound and every touch. Man is a living being only if body and soul are communicating. Together, the source of information stored by the Particle and the neurological system of the brain form the "mind" of man, an intellectual tool controlled and focused, when man is conscious, by the soul-body unity sometimes called the "heart" of man.

12. *Memories are a series of Parallata stored permanently in the Particle.*

13. *The Particle is able to recall memories instantly.*

14. *When a memory is recalled, it is returned to the same neuron-group that transferred the Parallata where it is "re-experienced."*

How often have you heard a memory recalled with, "I can almost feel the sun on my face and smell the spring air"?

Not only must the same neural network be in place to receive memories through the field, but the DNA contained in a chromosome acts as a filter[4] so that only uniquely matched information can be received.[5]

15. *If the neuron-group that transferred the stored data to the Particle has been damaged or destroyed, and not replaced, the memory cannot, under normal conditions, be recalled* (completely, accurately or at all).

It is the transfer of information through the Field that permits the "stacking" of Sequential data in the Particle, and it is the Field that introduces time between the synchronous Parallata returned to the neurons of the brain. If it were not for the cooperative process of the body-soul unity, consciousness would be impossible.

It is the infinite speed of the Particle that permits the amazing ability in man to recall events almost instantly from his past, in great detail (limited only by the relatively slow speed of the physical brain). It is, therefore, the Particle that makes possible the thought process and the instant comparisons necessary for simple activities like extemporaneous speech.

It is not the purpose of the brain to remember anything. The brain is the temporal component of the control process. One of its highest-level roles is to facilitate "focus," allowing the being to concentrate on the most important Parallata returned by the Particle. "Memory" is not stored in the brain by any neuron, neural circuit or neural network. Not even skills are stored in the physical brain. Nor are spinal reflexes the result of direct "wiring" between sensor and motor neurons. The Particle is involved in all memory-related activities. It takes six hours for the brain to "encode" a new skill, we are told. What is actually taking place is the construction of a neural skill circuit to by-pass the "focus function," so that the being can concentrate on other

---

[4] both in receiving traits and field-borne information.
[5] God knows who we are and how to communicate with us.

activities or on the fine points of the skilled activity in process. Spinal reflexes are produced by pre-wired focus-control bypasses, but the neurons involved in any reflex action also receive related, synchronous information from the Particle. (Note: when the spinal cord above the sensor/motor neuron set is damaged, the brain cannot "modulate" the resulting action and gross reflex actions sometimes occur.)

16. *The Particle contains the source of all necessary information relating to the cell including an encoded, perfect likeness ("Likeness") of the living organism to which the cell belongs.*

Do not confuse the encoded Likeness with the imaginary "homunculus" Dr. Crick refers to. Biochemists today suggest that the genome is the encoded "blueprint" of a human being. The Hypothesis is just suggesting it takes much, much more than DNA to "encode" a human being.

17. *Information from the Particle regarding the Likeness is filtered, figuratively, through the hereditary traits encoded by the structure of DNA in the nucleus of the cell.* Temporal factors, such as the physical health of the cell and other environmental factors, can affect the communications between the Particle and Temporal component.

Although the Particle is indivisible, it can be united with another Particle to form a new and unique Particle.

18. *At the true moment of conception, the Particles of both male and female unite, creating a new, unique Particle incorporating a perfect Likeness of a new and unique body.*

19. *Concurrently at conception, the building blocks of DNA from both male and female fuse into the chromosomes of a new and unique cell (zygote) as controlled by the new Particle.*

20. *The shared Field gives life to the new cell and cell division begins, as guided by the organism's Particle* (Items 18, 19 and 20 define procreation - "with the help of God." Genesis 4).

The Hypothesis leaves little doubt that from the true moment of conception a new being is alive and growing.

21. *Growth and healing are the same process and are similarly directed by the Particle.*

Excerpts from:

"Stem Cells: A Primer"

Human development begins when a sperm fertilizes an egg and creates a single cell that has the potential to form an entire organism. This fertilized egg is **totipotent**, meaning that its potential is total. In the first hours after fertilization, this cell divides into identical totipotent cells. This means that either one of these cells, if placed into a woman's uterus, has the potential to develop into a fetus. In fact, identical twins develop when two totipotent cells separate and develop into two individual, genetically identical human beings. Approximately four days after fertilization and after several cycles of cell division, these totipotent cells begin to specialize, forming a hollow sphere of cells, called a blastocyst. The blastocyst has an outer layer of cells and inside the hollow sphere, there is a cluster of cells called the inner cell mass.

The outer layer of cells will go on to form the placenta and other supporting tissues needed for fetal development in the uterus. The inner cell mass cells will go on to form virtually all of the tissues of the human body. Although the inner cell mass cells can form virtually every type of cell found in the human body, they cannot form an organism because they are unable to give rise to the placenta and supporting tissues necessary for development in the human uterus.

Cells are **pluripotent** - they can give rise to many types of cells but not all types of cells necessary for fetal development. Because their potential is not total, they are not totipotent and they are not embryos. In fact, if an inner cell mass cell were placed into a woman's uterus, it would not develop into a fetus.

The pluripotent stem cells undergo further specialization into stem cells that are committed to give rise to cells that have a particular function. Examples of this include blood stem cells which give rise to red blood cells, white blood cells and platelets; and skin stem cells that give rise to the various types of skin cells. These more specialized stem cells are called **multipotent**.

A primary goal of (stem cell research) would be the identification of the factors involved in the cellular decision-making process that results in cell specialization. We know that turning genes on and off is central to this process, but we do not know much about these "decision-making" genes or what turns them on or off. Some of our most serious medical conditions, such as cancer and birth defects, are due to abnormal cell specialization and cell division. A better understanding of normal cell processes will allow us to further delineate the fundamental errors that cause these often deadly illnesses.

Source: NATIONAL INSTITUTES OF HEALTH - May 2000

22. When an organism is injured or diseased, and cells are damaged or destroyed, it is the Particle that provides the correct code (Likeness) with which to direct the physical regeneration process when possible.

Each living cell receives specific instructions from the Particle, including instructions to divide, when necessary, for the growth or healing of the organism. If a cell is missing, diseased or sufficiently damaged, it cannot receive these instructions, nor can it in any way report its condition. Instructions to divide for the growth or healing of the organism must be given to a healthy cell adjacent to or in line with (heretofore defines "Corresponding") the position of a missing, diseased or damaged cell.

The Field, carrying the instructions from the Particle to the cell, radiates from the cell, reaching the nuclei of Corresponding cells. There the cell-specific information is forwarded (reflected) by the Corresponding-cell nuclei (i.e., the structure of the chromosomes and DNA) to the Particle. Non-reporting cell positions are identified in this manner. When the need for cell division is recognized, and a divide instruction is sent, other Corresponding cells are inhibited from dividing by the cell-specific instructions radiating from the dividing cell. In this way the growth or healing process is controlled.

When a cell receives instructions from the Particle, and existing, even healthy, Corresponding cells do not, for any reason, forward the cell-specific instructions carried by the Field, the originating cell may be instructed to divide even though there is no need for division. Since a cancer cell does not recognize proper instructions regarding shape, purpose, color, structure, location or division limits, it can be assumed it may also be incapable of being a source for correct cell-specific instructions to Corresponding cells. Thus no

Corresponding cells are recognized by the Particle, and the cancer cell continues to receive instructions to divide.[6]

Although the DNA code of a cancer cell remains identical to a healthy cell, the physical structure of some of the cell's DNA (or perhaps nuclear pore complexes) may have been altered or damaged in some way. Many cancers are associated with a chromosome defect in which part of one chromosome appears to have broken off and joined with another chromosome. This improper assembly of a chromosome could clearly occur during the cell-division process (mitosis). Interference in the Field during mitosis may cause the dividing cell to misinterpret critical instructions from the Particle.

Regarding skin cancers, squamous cells comprise most of the upper layers of skin. Squamous cell carcinoma is the second most common skin cancer after basal cell carcinoma. Melanoma is a malignant tumor that originates in melanocytes, the cells which produce the pigment melanin that colors our skin. Both of these cancer cell types do not recognize proper instructions regarding shape, purpose, color, structure, location or division limits and, therefore, can metastasize. Basal cells, which are at the bottom of the epidermis, when cancerous, do not appear to metastasize, suggesting that the structure of their chromosomes and DNA are not as easily damaged by exposure to sunlight radiation due to their deeper location in the skin.

---

[6] It can also be assumed that cancer cells Corresponding to healthy cells are incapable of receiving and reflecting to the Particle cell-specific information from the healthy cells, and are thereby identified by the Particle as non-reporting cell locations, causing even the healthy cells to divide. This could multiply the rate of unwarranted growth.

Mitosis   During mitosis it appears to be the centrosome that is receiving cell division instructions from the Particle, since the structure of DNA is disassembled during the process.

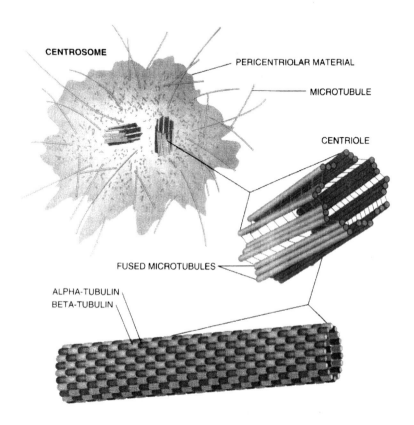

"The centrosome consists of two structures called centrioles set at right angles to each other and are surrounded by a cloud of pericentriolar material. Seen in cross section, a centriole reveals a pinwheel structure made of structural elements called microtubules.

(Scientific American, June 1993 – David M. Glover)."

"In recent years one of the intriguing discoveries has been that while one part of the DNA polymerase molecule functions as a polymerase, attaching nucleotides, another portion of the same molecule acts as an "exonuclease" (nucleotide - cutting - out enzyme) and performs a "proofreading" function. It is estimated that about one time in 10,000 to 100,000 the wrong base is added to a growing DNA strand. *Somehow* the exonuclease portion of the DNA polymerase molecule recognizes nearly all such mistakes and removes each erroneous base as fast as it is added so that another attempt to add the correct one can be made. The result is that there is an estimated error rate of only one in one billion base pairs copied (during mitosis)."

The above paragraph was taken from the *Biology Coloring Book* by Robert D. Griffin. The "*somehow*" is explained by the Hypothesis. If the communications between the Particle and the cell were perfect, no errors would result (or remain). Gross mistakes causing the displacement of part of a chromosome could also result in repeating errors in reception of information from the Particle through the Field Such flaws would also affect the ability of cells to "reflect" cell-specific information back to the Particle as described in later paragraphs.[7]

Cell division is normally inhibited if nutrient levels are below certain limits. Cancer cells (and possibly healthy adjacent cells), on the other hand, will divide even when nutrient levels are one tenth of this limit. The reason may be that the Particle recognizes the non-reporting cell positions as an injury to the organism, not just normal cell replacement as in the case of surface skin cells.

Though the strength of the Field signal may drop in direct proportion to the square of the distance from the functional center of the nucleus from which it is originating,

---

[7] Do some wavelengths of Electromagnetic Radiation interfere with the Field? Probably.

the Field reaches more than just the Corresponding cells or even cells of the same type. In this manner the Particle receives an encoded "picture" of the entire organism. So it is with the epithelial cells of the skin. The Particle receives a precise thickness measurement when it sends cell-specific information to a germinating layer cell through the Field, which radiates to (and probably beyond) the unattached surface layer cells.

If a missing, diseased or damaged cell is beyond the physical range of the Field radiating from a healthy cell, it is not recognized as a non-reporting cell location because no cell is expected within the range covered. Through action potentials, neurons are capable of transferring information from other neurons to the Particle by means of the Field and from the Particle to other neurons. In part, neurons are spaced to avoid causing an action potential in an adjacent neuron when its neighboring neuron generates a data-carrying disturbance in the Field, which also overlaps the adjacent neuron. This requirement makes the strength of the radiating Field more critical with regard to neurons, especially in adults, when it comes to the process of recognizing adjacent, damaged, diseased or missing neurons.

The tree-like structure of cells forming the central nervous system, versus the layered structure of epithelial cells, further complicates cell replacement, and the healing of large gaps in the structure from injury, disease or other causes of cell death would seem to require a different process, guided by the Particle. However, when new neurons are surgically deposited in these gaps the cell replacement process described above would be facilitated.

[Note: Perhaps the body needs sleep because the thought process (consciousness) occupies the temporal/atemporal "link" during waking hours to the extent that non-REM sleep periods are required for communications involving cell functions and healing. Perhaps, also, in between these regeneration communications the "system" releases the mind temporarily, which begins to dream.]

23. *Man is a body-soul-spirit being during his temporal life.*

Without his soul man does not exist, and without a body he does not exist. At the same time, without the spirit (Field)--God's gift of temporal life--he would not know he exists, and his body would die, because his atemporal soul (Particle), in the Sequential State, could not communicate with his body in the Temporal State.

24. *At the moment of the death of his Temporal body, man's spirit (Field) returns to God, and, as a human, he transitions from a temporal/atemporal being to an atemporal being in the Sequential State (defining "Transition").*

25. *A physical, but Sequential-State, body is generated in accordance with the perfect Likeness stored in the soul.* Man is, thereby, "restored to life."

26. *With Transition, all faculties are also restored, including full access to all personal and ancestral memories.* Man will have access to all of the memories of his ancestors[8], from his parents back to Adam, the first man. He will also have access to all of the knowledge that God has chosen to share with him.

27. *Restored to life with an atemporal body, man will experience perfect, unaided communications between his soul and body, since both soul and body will exist in the Sequential State.*

28. *Man's Temporal body was designed to live forever. It is the imperfect communications between the Particle and cells that gradually bring aging to the organism.*

"Aging occurs on the cellular level in a number of ways. The strands of DNA that guide a cell's physiological process [through instructions from the Particle] can be damaged during the normal function of generating RNA, the cell's messengers. The presence of repair mechanisms [the

---

[8] This refers only to events that occurred prior to the conception of the next in line.

polymerase molecule directed by the Particle] substantiates this notion, because if the DNA was not properly repaired, it would impair cellular functions. Thus, it is thought that by either wear and tear or through improper repair over time the DNA could be destroyed and the cellular reproduction function impaired." (Grolier Multimedia Encyclopedia)

In an article by astronomer Dr. Hugh Ross, he says, "Medical experts agree that cosmic radiation plays a significant role in limiting human life spans. Astronomers agree that the vast majority of this life-limiting radiation comes from supernovae, cataclysmic explosions of super giant stars." The article goes on to say that astronomers Erlykin and Wolfendale confirmed that the Vela supernova is indeed the prime contributor.

The Hypothesis confirms much of what is known about wellness and long life. Adequate sleep is necessary. During non-REM sleep communications between the Particle and cells are uninterrupted by conscious thought which may fully occupy the "system" during waking hours. Eating healthy foods maintains healthy cells and provides the chemical components for cell reproduction. Undernourished cells, including neurons, may not be as able to receive, decipher and carry out instructions from the Particle relative to the Likeness. Neurons may not be able to produce disturbances or respond as quickly (or fully) to disturbances in the Field produced by the Particle, therefore cognitive powers and memory-recall will be affected.

Avoiding radiation takes on a whole new meaning when the Field is taken into consideration. We know that ultraviolet radiation damages the DNA structure of cells. Instructions from the Particle will be either not received, will be misinterpreted or not acted upon. Dr. Michael Reacholi, manager of the WHO's Electromagnetic Fields Project, told a news conference that, "There are key issues that still need to be resolved because there have been suggestions that electromagnetic fields may produce cancers or memory loss or other neuro-degenerative diseases." Using a cellular phone with its antenna close to the brain is probably not a good thing to do. Living near low-level electromagnetic radiation (EMR) from power lines over a long period of time may not be safe. The Hypothesis suggests that EMR could disrupt communications through the Field. However, there will be no direct cause/effect found until the existence of the Field is recognized.

Conclusion regarding Dr. Francis Crick's "Astonishing Hypothesis"

In some parts of Dr. Crick's book, *The Astonishing Hypothesis*, he seems to express his amazement about the construction of the brain when compared to that of a digital computer. He also recognizes the relative difference in operating speed (many millions of operations per second for computers compared to "in the region of only 100 spikes per second" for a neuron) and the problem this presents to how man sees, thinks and recalls memories.

Dr. Crick says, "A brain does not look even a little bit like a general purpose computer. Different parts of the brain, even different parts of the neocortex, specialize, at least to some extent, in handling different sorts of information. Most memory appears to be stored in the very same locations that carry out current operations."

The *Truly* Astonishing Hypothesis explains the apparent speed of the brain (millions of times faster than the digital computer), and suggests how the specialized parts of the brain are all interconnected (through the atemporal Particle), and also why most memory appears to be stored in the very same locations that carry out current operations (memories are efficiently stored in the Particle and are returned to the same neuron-group that transferred them).

"The sensual and spiritual are linked together by a mysterious bond, sensed by our emotions, though hidden from our eyes."

- Karl Wilhelm Von Humboldt (1767-1835)

Dr. Crick's explanation for the unusual structure of the brain is as follows: "While a computer has been deliberately designed by engineers, the brain has evolved by natural selection over many, many generations of animals. This tends to produce a radically different style of design."

I am an electronics design engineer, not a physicist and biochemist as Dr. Crick is. Here I can speak with greater authority. If the brain functions in a far, far superior manner than a computer, as we know it does, it is only logical to believe its design is superior, not just radically different. I attribute the superior design to a superior Designer, having reviewed the designs of many engineers for more than 35 years. Dr. Crick attributes the "radically different style of design" to "natural selection over many, many generations of animals." He says this, but cannot explain the evolution of the smallest component of the brain, the neuron.

Dr. Crick calls on the scientific community to prove his hypothesis. So do I call on the scientific community to test my Hypothesis. And, borrowing his words, "If the scientific facts (gathered by the scientific community) are sufficiently striking and well established, and if they support the *Truly* Astonishing Hypothesis, then" man will have proven the existence of the human soul, a discovery that will surpass in importance the discovery of the structure of DNA. At the same time, it will reinforce "the beliefs of billions of human beings alive today."

Final Comment

To the scientist who believes in God, His Son, and the Holy Spirit: I have read some of your books defending your belief in a Creator. I have attended some of the conferences in which you called Darwin's theory of natural selection preposterous, when it comes to the evolution of the cell. I listened to some of your talks about the "fingerprints of God" on the creation of the human cell, but when I asked about the human soul you answered, "I don't know how the soul figures into all of this." Did God forget to tell you, or did you forget to ask? The world needs to hear from you.

Gary Richardson

CPSIA information can be obtained at www.ICGtesting.com
Printed in the USA
BVOW05s1000020315

389917BV00031B/501/P